The Whistler

The Whistler

John Grisham

W F HOWES LTD

This large print edition published in 2017 by
W F Howes Ltd
Unit 5, St George's House, Rearsby Business Park,
Gaddesby Lane, Rearsby, Leicester LE7 4YH

1 3 5 7 9 10 8 6 4 2

First published in the United Kingdom in 2016
by Hodder & Stoughton

The right of John Grisham to be identified as
the author of this work has been asserted by him
in accordance with the Copyright, Designs and
Patents Act, 1988.

A CIP catalogue record for this book is available
from the British Library

ISBN 978 1 51006 257 3

Typeset by Palimpsest Book Production Limited,
Falkirk, Stirlingshire

Printed and bound by
T J International in the UK
Printford   herlands

CHAPTER 1

The satellite radio was playing soft jazz, a compromise. Lacy, the owner of the Prius and thus the radio, loathed rap almost as much as Hugo, her passenger, loathed contemporary country. They had failed to agree on sports talk, public radio, golden oldies, adult comedy, and the BBC, without getting near bluegrass, CNN, opera, or a hundred other stations. Out of frustration on her part and fatigue on his, they both threw in the towel early and settled on soft jazz. Soft, so Hugo's deep and lengthy nap would not be disturbed. Soft, because Lacy didn't care much for jazz either. It was another give-and-take of sorts, one of many that had sustained their teamwork over the years. He slept and she drove and both were content.

Before the Great Recession, the Board on Judicial Conduct had access to a small pool of state-owned Hondas, all with four doors and white paint and low mileage. With budget cuts, though, those disappeared. Lacy, Hugo, and countless other public employees in Florida were now expected to use their own vehicles for the state's work,

1

reimbursed at fifty cents a mile. Hugo, with four kids and a hefty mortgage, drove an ancient Bronco that could barely make it to the office, let alone a road trip. And so he slept.

Lacy enjoyed the quiet. She handled most of her cases alone, as did her colleagues. Deeper cuts had decimated the office, and the BJC was down to its last six investigators. Seven, in a state of twenty million people, with a thousand judges sitting in six hundred courtrooms and processing a half a million cases a year. Lacy was forever grateful that almost all judges were honest, hardworking people committed to justice and equality. Otherwise, she would have left long ago. The small number of bad apples kept her busy fifty hours a week.

She gently touched the signal switch and slowed on the exit ramp. When the car rolled to a stop, Hugo lurched forward as if wide awake and ready for the day. 'Where are we?' he asked.

'Almost there. Twenty minutes. Time for you to roll to your right and snore at the window.'

'Sorry. Was I snoring?'

'You always snore, at least according to your wife.'

'Well, in my defense, I was walking the floor at three this morning with her latest child. I think it's a girl. What's her name?'

'Wife or daughter?'

'Ha-ha.'

The lovely and ever-pregnant Verna kept few secrets when it came to her husband. It was her calling to keep his ego in check and it was no small task. In another life, Hugo had been a football star in high school, then the top-rated signee in his class at Florida State, and the first freshman to crack the starting lineup. He'd been a tailback, both bruising and dazzling, for three and a half games anyway, until they carried him off on a stretcher with a jammed vertebra in his upper spine. He vowed to make a comeback. His mother said no. He graduated with honors and went to law school. His glory days were fading fast, but he would always carry some of the swagger possessed by all-Americans. He couldn't help it.

'Twenty minutes, huh?' he grunted.

'Sure, or not. If you like, I'll just leave you in the car with the motor running and you can sleep all day.'

He rolled to his right, closed his eyes, and said, 'I want a new partner.'

'That's an idea, but the problem is nobody else will have you.'

'And one with a bigger car.'

'It gets fifty miles a gallon.'

He grunted again, grew still, then twitched, jerked, mumbled, and sat straight up. He rubbed his eyes and said, 'What are we listening to?'

'We had this conversation a long time ago, when we left Tallahassee, just as you were beginning to hibernate.'

'I offered to drive, as I recall.'

'Yes, with one eye open. It meant so much. How's Pippin?'

'She cries a lot. Usually, and I say this from vast experience, when a newborn cries it's for a reason. Food, water, diaper, momma – whatever. Not this one. She squawks for the hell of it. You don't know what you're missing.'

'If you'll recall, I've actually walked the floors with Pippin on two occasions.'

'Yes, and God bless you. Can you come over tonight?'

'Anytime. She's number four. You guys thought about birth control?'

'We are beginning to have that conversation. And now that we're on the subject, how's *your* sex life?'

'Sorry. My mistake.' At thirty-six Lacy was single and attractive, and her sex life was a rich source of whispered curiosity around the office.

They were going east toward the Atlantic Ocean. St Augustine was eight miles ahead. Lacy finally turned off the radio when Hugo asked, 'And you've been here before?'

'Yes, a few years back. Then boyfriend and I spent a week on the beach in a friend's condo.'

'A lot of sex?'

'Here we go again. Is your mind always in the gutter?'

'Well, come to think of it, the answer has to be yes. Plus, you need to understand that Pippin is now a month old, which means that Verna and I have not had normal relations in at least three months. I still maintain, at least to myself, that she cut me off three weeks too early, but it's sort

4

of a moot point. Can't really go back and catch up, you know? So things are fairly ramped up in my corner; not sure she feels the same way. Three rug rats and a newborn do serious damage to that intimacy thing.'

'I'll never know.'

He tried to focus on the highway for a mile or two, then his eyelids grew heavy and he began to nod. She glanced at him and smiled. In her nine years with the Board, she and Hugo had worked a dozen cases together. They made a nice team and trusted each other, and both knew that any bad behavior by him, and there had been none to date, would immediately be reported to Verna. Lacy worked with Hugo, but she gossiped and shopped with Verna.

St Augustine was billed as the oldest city in America, the very spot where Ponce de León landed and began exploring. Long on history and heavy on tourism, it was a lovely town with historic buildings and thick Spanish moss dripping from ancient oaks. As they entered its outskirts, the traffic slowed and tour buses stopped. To the right and in the distance, an old cathedral towered above the town. Lacy remembered it all very well. The week with the old boyfriend had been a disaster, but she had fond memories of St Augustine.

One of many disasters.

'And who is this mysterious deep throat we are supposed to meet?' Hugo asked, rubbing his eyes once again, now determined to stay awake.

'Don't know yet, but his code name is Randy.'

'Okay, and please remind me why we are tag teaming a secret meeting with a man using an alias who has yet to file a formal complaint against one of our esteemed judges.'

'I can't explain. But I've talked to him three times on the phone and he sounds, uh, rather earnest.'

'Great. When was the last time you talked to a complaining party who didn't sound, uh, rather earnest?'

'Stick with me, okay? Michael said go, and we're here.' Michael was the director, their boss.

'Of course. No clue as to the alleged unethical conduct?'

'Oh yes. Randy said it was big.'

'Gee, never heard that before.'

They turned onto King Street and poked along with the downtown traffic. It was mid-July, still the high season in north Florida, and tourists in shorts and sandals drifted along the sidewalks, apparently going nowhere. Lacy parked on a side street and they joined the tourists. They found a coffee shop and killed half an hour flipping through glossy real estate brochures. At noon, as instructed, they walked into Luca's Grill and got a table for three. They ordered iced tea and waited. Thirty minutes passed with no sign of Randy, so they ordered sandwiches. Fries on the side for Hugo, fruit for Lacy. Eating as slowly as possible, they kept an eye on the door and waited.

As lawyers, they valued their time. As investigators, they had learned patience. The two roles were often in conflict.

At 2:00 p.m., they gave up and returned to the car, as smothering as a sauna. As Lacy turned the key, her cell phone rattled. Caller unknown. She grabbed it and said, 'Yes.'

A male voice said, 'I asked you to come alone.' It was Randy.

'I suppose you have the right to ask. We were supposed to meet at noon, for lunch.'

A pause, then, 'I'm at the Municipal Marina, at the end of King Street, three blocks away. Tell your buddy to get lost and we'll talk.'

'Look, Randy, I'm not a cop and I don't do cloak-and-dagger very well. I'll meet you, say hello and all that, but if I don't have your real name within sixty seconds then I'm leaving.'

'Fair enough.'

She canceled the call and mumbled, 'Fair enough.'

The marina was busy with pleasure craft and a few fishing boats coming and going. A long pontoon was unloading a gaggle of noisy tourists. A restaurant with a patio at the water's edge was still doing a brisk business. Crews on charter boats were spraying decks and sprucing things up for tomorrow's charters.

Lacy walked along the central pier, looking for the face of a man she'd never met. Ahead, standing

7

next to a fuel pump, an aging beach bum gave a slight, awkward wave and nodded. She returned the nod and kept walking. He was about sixty, with too much gray hair flowing from under a Panama hat. Shorts, sandals, a gaudy floral-print shirt, the typical bronze, leathery skin of someone who spent far too much time in the sun. His eyes were covered by aviator shades. With a smile he stepped forward and said, 'You must be Lacy Stoltz.'

She took his hand and said, 'Yes, and you are?'

'Name's Ramsey Mix. A pleasure to meet you.'

'A pleasure. We were supposed to meet at noon.'

'My apologies. Had a bit of boat trouble.' He nodded down the pier to a large powerboat moored at the end of the dock. It wasn't the longest boat in the harbor at that moment, but it was close. 'Can we talk there?' he asked.

'On the boat?'

'Sure. It's much more private.'

Crawling onto a boat with a complete stranger struck her as a bad idea and she hesitated. Before she could answer, Mix asked, 'Who's the black guy?' He was looking in the direction of King Street. Lacy turned and saw Hugo casually following a pack of tourists nearing the marina.

'He's my colleague,' she said.

'Sort of a bodyguard?'

'I don't need a bodyguard, Mr Mix. We're not armed, but my friend there could pitch you into the water in about two seconds.'

8

'Let's hope that won't be necessary. I come in peace.'

'That's good to hear. I'll get on the boat only if it stays where it is. If the engines start, then our meeting is over.'

'Fair enough.'

She followed him along the pier, past a row of sailboats that looked as though they had not seen the open sea in months, and to his boat, cleverly named *Conspirator*. He stepped on board and offered a hand to help her. On the deck, under a canvas awning, there was a small wooden table with four folding chairs. He waved at it and said, 'Welcome aboard. Have a seat.'

Lacy took quick stock of her surroundings. Without sitting, she said, 'Are we alone?'

'Well, not entirely. I have a friend who enjoys boating with me. Name is Carlita. Would you like to meet her?'

'Only if she's important to your story.'

'She is not.' Mix was looking at the marina, where Hugo was leaning on a rail. Hugo waved, as if to say, 'I'm watching everything.' Mix waved back and said, 'Can I ask you something?'

'Sure,' Lacy said.

'Is it safe to assume that whatever I'm about to tell you will be rehashed with Mr Hatch in short order?'

'He's my colleague. We work together on some cases, maybe this one. How do you know his name?'

'I happen to own a computer. Checked out the website. BJC really should update it.'

'I know. Budget cuts.'

'His name vaguely rings a bell.'

'He had a brief career as a football player at Florida State.'

'Maybe that's it. I'm a Gator fan myself.'

Lacy refused to respond to this. It was so typical of the South, where folks attached themselves to college football teams with a fanaticism she'd always found irksome.

Mix said, 'So he'll know everything?'

'Yes.'

'Call him over. I'll get us something to drink.'

CHAPTER 2

Carlita served drinks from a wooden tray – diet sodas for Lacy and Hugo, a bottle of beer for Mix. She was a pretty Hispanic lady, at least twenty years his junior, and she seemed pleased to have guests, especially another woman.

Lacy made a note on her legal pad and said, 'A quick question. The phone you used fifteen minutes ago had a different number than the phone you used last week.'

'Is that a question?' Mix replied.

'It's close enough.'

'Okay. I use a lot of prepaid phones. And I move around all the time. I'm assuming the number I have for you is a cell phone issued by your employer, correct?'

'That's right. We don't use personal phones for state business, so my number is not likely to change.'

'That'll make it simpler, I guess. My phones change by the month, sometimes by the week.'

So far, in their first five minutes together, everything Mix said had only opened the door for more questions. Lacy was still miffed at being stood up for lunch, and she didn't like the first impression he made. She said, 'Okay, Mr Mix, at this point Hugo and I go silent. You start talking. Tell us your story, and if it has huge gaps that require us to fish around and stumble in the dark, then we'll get bored and go home. You were coy enough on the phone to lure me here. Start talking.'

Mix looked at Hugo with a smile and asked, 'She always this blunt?'

Hugo, unsmiling, nodded yes. He folded his hands on the table and waited. Lacy put down her pen.

Mix swallowed a mouthful of beer and began: 'I practiced law for thirty years in Pensacola. Small firm – we usually had five or six lawyers. Back in the day we did well and life was good. One of my early clients was a developer, a real high roller who built condos, subdivisions, hotels, strip malls, the typical Florida stuff that goes up overnight. I never trusted the guy but he was making so much money I finally took the bait. He got me in some deals, small slices here and there, and for a while it all worked. I started dreaming of getting rich, which, in Florida anyway, can lead to serious trouble. My friend was cooking the books and taking on way too much debt, stuff I didn't know about. Turns out there were some bogus loans, bogus everything, really, and the FBI came in with one of its patented RICO cluster bombs and indicted half

12

of Pensacola, me included. A lot of folks got burned – developers, bankers, realtors, lawyers, and other shysters. You probably didn't hear about it because you investigate judges, not lawyers. Anyway, I flipped, sang like a choirboy, got a deal, pled to one count of mail fraud, and spent sixteen months in a federal camp. Lost my license and made a lot of enemies. Now I lie low. I applied for reinstatement and got my license back. I have one client these days, and he's the guy we'll talk about from now on. Questions?' From the empty chair, he retrieved an unmarked file and handed it to Lacy. 'Here's the scoop on me. Newspaper articles, my plea agreement, all the stuff you might need. I'm legit, or as legit an any ex-con can be, and every word I'm saying is true.'

'What's your address now?' Hugo asked.

'I have a brother up in Myrtle Beach and I use his address for legal purposes. Carlita has a place in Tampa and I get some mail there. Basically, though, I live on this boat. I have phones, fax, Wi-Fi, a small shower, cold beer, and a nice lady. I'm a happy guy. We bounce around Florida, the Keys, the Bahamas. Not a bad retirement, thanks to Uncle Sam.'

'Why do you have a client?' Lacy asked, ignoring the file.

'He's the friend of an old friend who knows my shady past and figures I'll roll the dice for a fat fee. He's right. My friend looked me up, then

13

convinced me to take his case. Don't ask for the client's name, because I don't have it. My friend is the intermediary.'

'You don't know the name of your client?' Lacy asked.

'No, nor do I want to.'

'Are we supposed to ask why or just accept this?' Hugo asked.

'Gap number one, Mr Mix,' Lacy said. 'And we don't do gaps. You tell us everything or we'll leave and take nothing with us.'

'Just relax, okay?' Mix said as he chugged some beer. 'This is a long story that will take some time to unfold. It involves a ton of money, corruption that is astonishing, and some really nasty guys who wouldn't think twice about putting a bullet or two between my eyes, yours, my client's, anyone who asks too many questions.'

There was a long pause as Lacy and Hugo allowed this to sink in. Finally, she asked, 'Then why are you in the game?'

'Money. My client wants to pursue a claim under the Florida Whistleblower Statute. He dreams of collecting millions. Me, I'll take a nice cut, and if all goes well, I'll never need clients.'

'Then he must be a state employee,' Lacy said.

'I know the law, Ms Stoltz. You have a demanding job, I don't. I have plenty of time to pore over the code sections and case law. Yes, my client is employed by the State of Florida. No, his identity cannot be revealed; not now, anyway. Perhaps, way

14

down the road, if money is on the table, then maybe we can convince a judge to maintain a closed file. But, to kick things off, my client is far too frightened to sign a formal complaint with Judicial Conduct.'

'We cannot proceed without a signed, formal complaint,' Lacy said. 'The statute, as you know, is very clear.'

'Indeed I do. I'll sign the complaint.'

'Under oath?' Hugo asked.

'Yes, as required. I believe my client is telling the truth and I'm willing to sign my name.'

'And you're not afraid?'

'I've lived with fear for a long time. I guess I'm accustomed to it, though things could get worse.' Mix reached for another file and withdrew some papers, which he placed on the table. He continued, 'Six months ago, I went to court up in Myrtle Beach and changed my name. I'm now Greg Myers, the name I'll use on the complaint.'

Lacy read the court order from South Carolina and, for the first time, doubted the wisdom of traveling to St Augustine to meet this guy. A state employee too frightened to come forward. A reformed lawyer so spooked that he went to court in another state and changed his name. An ex-con with no real address.

Hugo read the court order and, for the first time in years, wished he could carry a gun. He asked, 'Do you consider yourself to be in hiding at this moment?'

15

'Let's say I'm just real cautious, Mr Hatch. I'm an experienced boat captain who knows the water, the seas, the currents and cays and keys and remote beaches and hideaways far better than anyone looking for me, if, in fact, anyone is back there.'

Lacy said, 'Well, it certainly sounds like you're hiding.'

Myers just nodded as though he agreed. All three took a sip. A breeze finally arrived and broke some of the humidity. Lacy flipped through the thin file and said, 'A question. Were your legal troubles in any way connected to the judicial misconduct you want to discuss?'

The nodding stopped as he weighed the question. 'No.'

Hugo said, 'Back to this mysterious client. Do you have any direct contact with him?'

'None whatsoever. He refuses to use e-mail, snail mail, fax, or any type of traceable phone. He talks to the intermediary, the intermediary either visits me face-to-face or calls me on a burner, one of those disposable phones. It's awkward and time-consuming, but quite safe. No trail, no records, nothing left behind.'

'And if you needed him right now, how would you find him?'

'That's never happened. I suppose I would call the middleman and wait an hour or so.'

'Where does this client live?'

'I'm not sure. Somewhere along the Florida Panhandle.'

Lacy took a deep breath and exchanged glances with Hugo. She said, 'Okay, what's the story?'

Myers gazed into the distance, across the water, beyond the boats. A drawbridge was opening and he seemed mesmerized by it. Finally, he said, 'There are many chapters to the story, some still being written. The purpose of this little meeting is to tell you enough to make you curious, but also to frighten you enough to back off if you want. That's the real question right now: Do you want to get involved?'

'Is there judicial misconduct?' Lacy asked.

'The word "misconduct" would be a massive understatement. What I know involves corruption at a level never before known in this country. You see, Ms Stoltz and Mr Hatch, my sixteen months in prison were not completely wasted. They put me in charge of the law library and I kept my nose in the books. I've studied every single case of judicial corruption that's ever been prosecuted, in all fifty states. I have the research, the files, notes, everything. I'm quite the resource, just in case you ever need a know-it-all. And the story I can tell you involves more dirty cash than all the others combined. It also involves bribery, extortion, intimidation, rigged trials, at least two murders, and one wrongful conviction. There's a man rotting away on death row an hour from here who was framed. The man responsible for the crime is probably sitting on his boat right now, a boat much nicer than mine.'

He paused, took a drink from his bottle, and gave them a smug look, satisfied that he had their complete attention. 'The question is, do you want to get involved? It could be dangerous.'

'Why call us?' Hugo asked. 'Why not go to the FBI?'

'I've dealt with the FBI, Mr Hatch, and things went badly. I don't trust them or anyone with a badge, especially in this state.'

Lacy said, 'Again, Mr Myers, we are not armed. We're not criminal investigators. It sounds like you need several branches of the federal government.'

'But you have subpoena power,' Myers said. 'You have statutes that give you the right to obtain subpoenas. You can require any judge in this state to produce every record maintained in his or her office. You have considerable power, Ms Stoltz. So in many ways you do investigate criminal activity.'

Hugo said, 'True, but we're not equipped to deal with gangsters. If your story is true, it sounds like the bad guys are well organized.'

'Ever hear of the Catfish Mafia?' Myers asked after another long pull on the bottle.

'No,' Hugo replied. Lacy shook her head.

'Well, it's another long story. Yes, Mr Hatch, it's a gang that's well organized. They have a long history of committing crimes that are none of your concern because they do not involve members of the judiciary. But, there is one enterprise in which they've purchased a judge. And that does concern you.'

The *Conspirator* rocked in the wake of an old shrimp boat and for a moment all three were quiet. Lacy asked, 'What if we decline to get involved? What happens to your story?'

'If I file a formal complaint, aren't you required to get involved?'

'In theory, yes. As I'm sure you know, we have forty-five days to do an assessment to determine if the complaint has some merit. We then notify the target, the judge, and ruin his day. But we can also be very adept at ignoring complaints.'

Hugo said with a smile, 'Oh yes. We're bureaucrats. We can duck and delay with the best of them.'

'You can't duck this one,' Myers said. 'It's too big.'

'If it's so big, why hasn't it been discovered before now?' Lacy asked.

'Because it's still unfolding. Because the time hasn't been right. Because of a lot of reasons, Ms Stoltz, the most important being the fact that no one with the knowledge has been willing to step forward until now. I'm stepping forward. The question is simply this: Does the Board on Judicial Conduct want to investigate the most corrupt judge in the history of American jurisprudence?'

'One of our very own?' Lacy asked.

'You got it.'

'When do we get his name?' Hugo asked.

'You're assuming it's a male.'
'We're not assuming anything.'
'That's a good way to start.'

The tepid breeze finally gave up, and the oscillating fan rattling above them did little more than shove around the sticky air. Myers seemed to be the last of the three to realize their shirts were sticking to their skin and, as host of the little gathering, finally made a move. 'Let's take a stroll over to the restaurant there and have a drink,' he said. 'They have a bar inside with plenty of AC.' He clutched an olive-colored leather courier bag, well used and seemingly attached to his body. Lacy wondered what was inside. A small pistol? Cash, a fake passport? Perhaps another file?

As they walked along the pier, Lacy asked, 'Is this one of your hangouts?'

'Why would I answer that?' Myers retorted, and Lacy wished she'd said nothing. She was dealing with an invisible man, one who lived as if his neck was always near the block, and not some casual sailor who bounced from port to port. Hugo shook his head. Lacy kicked herself in the rump.

The restaurant was empty now, and they took a table inside, overlooking the harbor. After roasting in the heat for the past hour, they found the air almost too frigid. Iced tea for the investigators, coffee for Mr Myers. They were alone; no one could possibly hear them.

'What if we're not too enthused about this case?' Hugo asked.

'Then I suppose I'll eventually go to Plan B, but I don't really want to. Plan B involves the press, a couple of reporters I know, neither of whom is completely reliable. One is in Mobile, the other in Miami. Frankly, I think they'll spook easily.'

'What makes you so sure we won't spook easily, Mr Myers?' Lacy asked. 'As we've said, we're not accustomed to dealing with gangsters. We have a full caseload anyway.'

'I'm sure you do. No shortage of bad judges.'

'Actually, there aren't many. Just a few bad apples, but there are enough disgruntled litigants to keep us busy. Lots of complaints, most of which have little merit.'

'Right.' Myers slowly removed his aviator shades and placed them on the table. His eyes were puffy and red, like a drinker's, and they were encircled by pale skin, a contrast that gave him the resemblance to an inverted raccoon. It was obvious he rarely took the glasses off. He glanced around once more, as if to make sure those after him were not in the restaurant, and he seemed to relax.

Hugo said, 'About this Catfish Mafia.'

Myers grunted with a smile, as if he couldn't wait to spin a yarn. 'You want the story, huh?'

'You brought it up.'

'I did.' The waitress placed their drinks on the table and disappeared. Myers took a sip and began: 'It goes back fifty years or so. Kind of a loose gang of bad boys who misbehaved in various parts of Arkansas, Mississippi, and Louisiana, anywhere they could bribe a sheriff. Mainly bootleg booze, prostitution, gambling, sort of the old-fashioned sins, I guess, but with a lot of muscle and no shortage of dead bodies. They would pick a wet county near a Baptist desert, preferably on a state line, and set up their operations. Invariably, the locals would get fed up, elect a new sheriff, and the thugs would leave town. Over time, they settled along the Mississippi coast, around Biloxi and Gulfport. The ones who didn't get shot were indicted and sent to prison. Almost all of the original gangsters were gone by the early 1980s, but there were a few leftovers from a younger generation. When gambling was legalized in Biloxi, it really knocked a hole in their business. They moved to Florida and discovered the allure of bogus land deals, along with the astonishing margins in cocaine trafficking. They made a lot of money, reorganized, and morphed into an outfit known as the Coast Mafia.'

Hugo was shaking his head. 'I grew up in north Florida, went to college here, and law school, lived here my whole life, and for the past ten years I've investigated judicial corruption, and I've never heard of the Coast Mafia.'

'They don't advertise, and their names are never in the papers. I doubt if a member has been arrested in the past ten years. It's a small network, very tight and disciplined. I suspect most members are blood kin. It probably would have been infil-trated, busted, and everyone sent to prison but for the rise of a guy I'll call Omar for the moment. A bad dude but a very smart man. In the mid-1980s, Omar led the gang to south Florida, which at the time was ground zero for cocaine trafficking. They had a few good years, then things went to hell when they crossed up some Colombians. Omar got shot. His brother got shot too, except he didn't survive and his body was never found. They fled Miami but not Florida. Omar has a brilliant criminal mind, and about twenty years ago he became infatuated with the idea of casinos on Indian land.'

'Why am I not surprised?' Lacy mumbled.

'You got it. As you probably know, there are now nine Indian casinos in Florida, seven of which are owned by the Seminoles, which is by far the largest tribe, and one of only three recognized by the federal government. As a whole, the Seminole casinos are grossing four billion a year. Omar and his boys found the opportunity irresistible.'

Lacy said, 'So, your story involves organized criminals, Indians who own casinos, and a crooked judge, all in bed together?'

'That's a fair summary.'

'But the FBI has jurisdiction over Indian matters,' Hugo said.

'Yes, and the FBI has never shown much enthusiasm for going after Indians for any type of wrongdoing. Plus, Mr Hatch, and please listen as I repeat myself, I'm not dealing with the FBI. They don't have the facts. I do, and I'm talking to you.'

'When do we get the whole story?' Lacy asked.

'As soon as your boss, Mr Geismar, gives the green light. You talk to him, relay what I've said, make sure he understands the dangers involved, and when he tells me, on the phone, that the Board on Judicial Conduct will take my formal complaint seriously and investigate it fully, then I'll fill in as many blanks as possible.'

Hugo tapped his knuckles on the table and thought about his family. Lacy watched another shrimp boat inch through the harbor and wondered how Geismar would react. Myers watched them and almost felt sorry for them.

CHAPTER 3

The Board on Judicial Conduct's home was one-half of the third floor in a four-story state office building in downtown Tallahassee, two blocks from the Capitol. Every aspect of its 'suite' – from the worn, fraying carpet, to the narrow, prisonlike windows that somehow managed to deflect most sunlight, to the paneled ceiling squares still stained by decades of cigarette smoke, to the walls covered by cheap shelving that swayed and bent under the weight of thick briefs and forgotten memorandums – all of it reeked of straining and declining budgets, not to mention the obvious fact that the agency's work was not exactly a pressing priority with the Governor and the legislature. Each January, Michael Geismar, BJC's longtime director, was forced to walk over to the Capitol, hat in hand, and watch as the house and senate committees split the revenue pie. Groveling was required. He always asked for a few more bucks, and he always received a few less. Such was the life of the director of an agency that most lawmakers did not even know existed.

The Board was comprised of five political

appointees, usually retired judges and lawyers who found favor with the Governor. They met six times a year to review complaints, conduct hearings that resembled trials, and get updates from Geismar and his staff. He needed more staff but there was no money. His six investigators – four in Tallahassee and two in Fort Lauderdale – were working an average of fifty hours a week, and almost all were secretly looking for other jobs.

From Geismar's corner office, he had the view, if he chose to take it, which he rarely did, of another bunker-type edifice even taller than his, and beyond that a hodgepodge of government office buildings. His office was large because he'd knocked out walls and added a long table, the only one in the maze of cubbyholes and cubicles BJC called home. When the Board met for official business, it borrowed a conference room in the Florida Supreme Court building.

Today, four people gathered around the table: Geismar, Lacy, Hugo, and BJC's secret weapon, an ancient paralegal named Sadelle, who, even pushing the age of seventy, was still able not only to research vast amounts of material but to remember it all as well. Thirty years earlier, Sadelle had finished law school but failed the bar exam, on three occasions, and was thus relegated to the role of permanent paralegal. Once a heavy smoker – a good portion of the smoke-stained windows and ceilings could be blamed on her – she had been battling lung cancer for the past three years but had yet to miss a full week of work.

The table was covered with paperwork, with many of the sheets unstapled and highlighted in yellow or edited in red. Hugo was saying, 'The guy checks out. We've talked to contacts in Pensacola, people who knew him when he was a lawyer. Nice reputation and all, at least until he got indicted. He is who he says he is, albeit with a new name.'

Lacy added, 'His prison record is spotless. Served sixteen months and four days in a federal prison in Texas and for most of that time he ran the prison law library. Quite the jailhouse lawyer, he helped several of his buddies with their appeals, even sprang two on early release because their lawyers had screwed up the sentencing.'

'And his conviction?' Geismar asked.

Hugo replied, 'I dug deep enough to verify what Myers said. The Feds were after a real estate swinger named Kubiak, a transplant from California who spent twenty years spreading sprawl around Destin and Panama City. They got him. He's serving thirty years for a long list of crimes, mainly bank fraud, tax fraud, and money laundering. As he flamed out, he hurt a lot of folks, including one Ramsey Mix, who was quick to roll over and cut a deal. He squealed on everybody else in the indictment, especially Kubiak, and did some major damage. Probably a good thing that he's hiding on the high seas with a different name. He got only sixteen months. Everybody else got at least five years, with Kubiak taking the grand prize.'

'Personal?' Geismar asked.

Lacy replied, 'Two divorces, single now. Wife number two left him when he went to prison. One son from the first marriage, guy lives in California and owns a restaurant. When Myers pled guilty he paid a fine of a hundred thousand. At his sentencing, he testified that his legal fees were about the same. That plus the fine wiped him out. He filed for bankruptcy the week before he went to prison.'

Hugo tossed around some enlarged photos and said, 'Which makes this somewhat intriguing. I snapped a picture of his boat when we met him. It's a fifty-two-foot Sea Breeze powerboat, a very nice little rig, range of two hundred miles and sleeps four comfortably. It's registered to a Bahamian shell company so I couldn't get its number, but a good guess on the value is at least half a mil. He was released from prison six years ago, and, according to the Florida Bar, his license was reinstated three months ago. He doesn't have an office and says he lives on his boat, which I guess he could be renting. Regardless, it appears to be an expensive lifestyle. So the obvious question is, how does he afford it?'

Lacy took the handoff. 'There's a good chance he buried some of the loot offshore when the FBI came in. It was a big RICO case with a lot of casualties. I chatted with a source, a former prosecutor, and he says that there were always suspicions that Mix-now-Myers hid some money. He says a lot of the defendants were trying to hide cash. But, we'll probably never know. If the FBI couldn't find it seven years ago, it's safe to assume we won't find it now.'

Geismar mumbled, 'As if we have the time to look.'

'Exactly.'

'So this guy's a crook?' Geismar asked.

Hugo said, 'He's certainly a convicted felon, but he's served his time, paid his dues, and is now an upstanding member of our bar, same as the three of us.' He glanced at Sadelle and offered a quick smile, one that was not returned.

Geismar said, 'Maybe saying he's a crook is a bit too strong, so let's just say he's shady. I'm not sure I buy the theory of hidden money. If he stashed it offshore and lied to a bankruptcy judge, then he's still on the hook for fraud. Would the guy run that risk?'

Hugo replied, 'I don't know. He seems pretty careful. And, keep in mind, he's been out of prison for six years. You gotta wait five years in Florida before you can reapply for admission to the bar. While he was waiting, perhaps he was making a buck here and there. He seems pretty resourceful.'

Lacy asked, 'Why does it really matter? Are we investigating him or a corrupt judge?'

'Good point,' Geismar said. 'And he implied the judge is a woman?'

'Sort of,' Lacy replied. 'He wasn't real clear.'

Geismar looked at Sadelle and said, 'And I'm assuming we have our politically correct number of female judges in Florida.'

She inhaled with effort and spoke with the usual raspy voice, one ravaged by nicotine. 'Depends. There are dozens of girls handling traffic court and such, but this sounds like a bad actor at the circuit court level. There, out of six hundred judges, about a third are female. With nine casinos scattered over the state, it's a waste of time to start guessing.'

'And this so-called mafia?'

She sucked in as much as her lungs could hold and said, 'Who knows? There was once a Dixie Mafia, a Redneck Mafia, a Texas Mafia, all similar gangs of thugs. It looks like most of them were long on legend and short on criminal efficiency. Just a bunch of Bubbas who liked to sell whiskey and break legs. Not one word anywhere of a so-called Catfish Mafia, or a Coast Mafia. Not to say it doesn't exist, but I found nothing.' Her voice collapsed as she gasped for breath.

'Not so fast,' Lacy said. 'I ran across an article in the Little Rock newspaper from almost forty years ago. It tells the rather colorful story of a man named Larry Wayne Farrell who owned several catfish restaurants in the Arkansas delta. Seems he sold catfish out the front and bootleg liquor out the back. At some point, he and his cousins got ambitious and expanded into gambling, prostitution, and stolen cars. Just like Myers said, they

30

moved through the Deep South, always looking for a sheriff to bribe so they could reorganize. They eventually settled around Biloxi. It's a long article and not worth the details, but these guys left behind an astonishing number of dead bodies.'

Sadelle announced, 'Well, I stand corrected. Thanks for the enlightenment.'

'No problem.'

Hugo asked, 'May I ask the obvious question? If he files the complaint, and we serve it on the judge, and we begin our investigation, and things do indeed become dangerous, why can't we simply go to the FBI? Myers can't stop us at that point, right?'

'Of course not,' Geismar said. 'And that's exactly what will happen. He does not control the investigation, we do. And if we need help, we'll certainly get it.'

'So we're going to do it?' Hugo asked.

'Damned right we're doing it, Hugo. We really have no choice. If he files his complaint and accuses a judge of misconduct or corruption, under our statutes we have no choice but to do the assessment. It's quite simple. Are you nervous?'

'No.'

'Lacy, any hesitation?'

'Of course not.'

'Very well. Notify Mr Myers. If he wants to hear my voice, then get him on the phone.'

It took two days to get him on the phone, and when Lacy finally made contact Myers showed

31

little interest in talking to her or Geismar. He said he was 'tied up' with business matters and would call back later. The connection was weak and scratchy, as if he was somewhere far from land. The next day, he called Lacy on a different phone and asked to speak to Geismar, who assured him the complaint would be given priority and investigated immediately. An hour later, Myers called Lacy again and asked for a meeting. He said he wanted to see her and Hugo again and discuss the case. There was a lot of background material he could never put in writing, crucial information that would be essential to their investigation. He would refuse to sign and file the complaint unless they met with him.

Geismar said go, and they waited for Myers to pick his spot. He waited for a week, said he and Carlita were 'puttering around Abaco' in the Bahamas, and would head back to Florida in a few days.

Late on a Saturday afternoon, with the temperature hovering around a hundred degrees, Lacy drove into a subdivision, one with gates that never seemed to close, and weaved through a series of man-made ponds, all with cheap fountains spewing hot water into the air. She passed a crowded golf course, passed rows and rows of identical houses, all designed to showcase their two-car garages, and finally parked near a large open park with a series of connecting swimming pools. Hundreds of kids splashed and played in the water as their mothers sat under large umbrellas and sipped beverages.

The Meadows had survived the Great Recession and been remarketed as a multiracial community for young families. Hugo and Verna Hatch had bought there five years earlier, after child number two. Now that they had four, their 2,200-square-foot bungalow was crowded. Moving up, though, was not an option. Hugo's salary was $60,000 a year, same as Lacy's, and while she was single and able to save a little, the Hatches lived from paycheck to paycheck.

They liked to party, though, and on almost every Saturday afternoon in the summer Hugo was at the grill by a pool, cold beer in hand, cooking burgers and talking football with his pals as the kids splashed in the pool and the women hid in the shade. Lacy joined the ladies, and after the usual greetings made her way to a pool house where Verna was holding the baby and keeping her cool. Pippin was a month old and so far had been an extremely cranky child. Lacy occasionally babysat the Hatch kids so their parents could have a break. Babysitters were usually not hard to find. Both grandmothers lived within thirty miles. Both Hugo and Verna came from large, sprawling families with countless aunts, uncles, cousins, and no shortage of drama and conflict. Lacy often envied the security that came with such a clan, but she also felt thankful she didn't have to bother with so many people and their problems. Occasionally,

Verna and Hugo needed a hand with the kids but wanted to avoid the relatives.

She took Pippin as Verna went to fetch drinks. As she rocked the child she surveyed the crowd on the patio: a mix of blacks, whites, Hispanics, and Asians, all young couples with small children. There were two lawyers from the Attorney General's Office, friends of Hugo's from law school, and another one who worked for the state senate. There were no other singles present, no prospects, though Lacy had not anticipated any. She seldom dated because there were so few eligible men, or so few who appealed to her. She had one bad breakup in her past, an awful split that, after almost eight years, was still baggage.

Verna returned with two beers and sat across from her. She whispered, 'Why does she always get quiet when *you* hold her?'

Lacy smiled and shrugged. At thirty-six, she wondered every day if she would ever hold a child of her own. She didn't have the answer, but as the clock ticked she worried that her chances were getting slimmer. Verna looked tired, as did Hugo. They wanted a large family of their own, but, seriously, weren't four kids enough? Lacy wouldn't dare start that conversation, but to her the answer was obvious. The two had been lucky to go to college, the first in their families to do so, and they dreamed of their children having the same opportunity. But how can you possibly expect to afford tuition for four kids?

In a quiet voice, Verna said, 'Hugo says Geismar has given the two of you a big case.'

Lacy was surprised because Hugo was a firm believer in leaving his work at the office. That, plus the BJC stressed confidentiality for obvious reasons. Occasionally, after a few beers late at night, the three of them would laugh at the outrageous behavior of some judge they were investigating, but they never used a real name.

Lacy said, 'It could be big, or it could turn into nothing.'

'He hasn't told me much, he never does, but he seems to be a little worried. What's odd is that I've never considered your jobs to be dangerous.'

'Neither do we. We're not cops with guns. We're lawyers with subpoenas.'

'He said he wished he could carry a gun. That really bothers me, Lacy. You gotta promise me you guys are not getting into something dangerous.'

'Verna, I'll make you a promise. If I ever feel the need to carry a gun, I'll quit and find another job. I've never fired a gun in my life.'

'Well, in my world, our world, there are too many guns and too many bad things happen because of them.'

Pippin, asleep for all of fifteen minutes, suddenly erupted with a screech. Verna reached for her and said, 'That child, that child.' Lacy handed her over and went to check on the burgers.

CHAPTER 4

When Myers finally made contact, he told Lacy to meet him at the same marina in St Augustine. Everything was the same – same sweltering heat and humidity, same slip at the end of the dock; Myers even wore the same floral-print shirt. As they sat at the same wooden table under the shade on his boat, he drank the same brand of beer from a bottle and began talking.

His Omar character was in real life a man named Vonn Dubose, the descendant of one of the original gangsters who did indeed begin their mischief in the rear room of a catfish restaurant near Forrest City, Arkansas. His maternal grand-father owned the restaurant, and years later died in a police ambush. His father hanged himself in prison, or at least the official report said they found him hanging. Numerous and various uncles and cousins met similar fates, and the gang had pretty much thinned out until Vonn discovered the allure of cocaine trafficking in south Florida. A few good years there provided the means to resolidify his little syndicate. He was now approaching the age of seventy, lived somewhere along the coast, and did not maintain a legitimate address, bank account, driver's license, Social Security number, or passport. Once Vonn struck gold with the casino, he whittled his gang down to just a handful of cousins so there would be fewer hands in the till. He operated with complete anonymity and hid behind a wall of offshore companies, all of which were overseen by a certain law firm in Biloxi. By all accounts, and there were not many, he was quite wealthy but lived modestly.

'Have you ever met him?' Lacy asked.

Myers scoffed at the question. 'Don't be silly. No one meets this guy, okay? He lives in the shadows, sort of like me, I guess. You can't find three people in the Pensacola area who'll admit to knowing Vonn Dubose. I lived there for forty years and never heard of him until a few years ago. He comes and goes.'

'But he has no passport,' Hugo said.

'Valid passport. If they ever nail him, they'll find half a dozen fake ones.'

In 1936, the Bureau of Indian Affairs granted a charter to the Tappacola Nation, a small tribe of about four hundred scattered along the Panhandle, with most living in small homes in the swampy outback of Brunswick County. The tribe maintained a headquarters of sorts there, on a three-hundred-acre reservation ceded by the federal government eighty years earlier. By 1990, the mighty Seminole Nation of south Florida was discovering the bright lights of the casino trade, as were tribes across the country. Coincidentally, Vonn and his gang began buying cheap land adjacent to the Tappacola reservation. At some point in the early 1990s – no one would ever know for sure because the conversations had long since been buried – Dubose approached the Tappacola with a deal too good to be true.

'Treasure Key,' Hugo mumbled.

'You got it. The only casino in north Florida, conveniently located just ten miles south of Interstate 10 and ten miles north of the beaches. Full-service casino, open twenty-four/seven, Disney-style amusement fun for the entire family, largest water park in the state, condos for sale, lease, or time-share, take your pick. A veritable mecca for those who want to gamble and those who want to play in the sun, and it's perfectly situated within two hundred miles of five million people. Don't know the numbers, because the Indians who run the casinos report to no one, but it's believed Treasure Key is easily in the half-billion-dollar-a-year range.'

'We were there last summer,' Hugo admitted, as if he'd done something wrong. 'One of those last-minute weekend junkets for a buck-fifty. It wasn't bad.'

'Bad? It's fabulous. That's why the place is packed and the Tappacola are printing money.'

'And sharing it with Vonn and his boys?' Hugo asked.

'Among others, but let's not get ahead of ourselves.'

Lacy said, 'That's in Brunswick County, which is in the Twenty-Fourth Judicial District. There are two circuit judges in the Twenty-Fourth, one male, one female. Am I getting warm?'

Myers smiled and tapped a closed file in the center of the table. 'This is the complaint. I'll give it to you later. The judge is the Honorable Claudia McDover, on the bench now for seventeen years. We'll talk about her later. For now, please allow me to give you the backstory. It's crucial.'

Back to the Tappacola. The tribe was violently split over the issue of casino gambling. The opponents were led by an agitator named Son Razko, who was a Christian and opposed gambling on moral grounds. He organized his followers and they seemed to be in the majority. The proponents of the casino promised riches for all – new homes, lifetime pensions, better schools, free college tuition, health care, the list went on and on. Vonn Dubose was secretly funding the drive to approve the casino, but, as usual, his fingerprints could never be found. In 1993, the issue was put to a vote. Excluding those under eighteen, there were about three hundred eligible voters. All but fourteen made it to the polls, which were being watched by federal marshals, just in case things turned violent. Son Razko and his traditionalists won with 54 percent of the vote. A nasty lawsuit alleged

39

voter fraud and intimidation, but the circuit court judge threw it out. The casino was dead.

Soon thereafter, so was Son.

They found his body in another man's bedroom, along with the other man's wife, both shot twice in the head. They were naked and appeared to have been caught in the act. Her husband, a man named Junior Mace, was arrested and charged with both murders. He had been a close ally of Razko's during the gambling debate. Mace steadfastly maintained his innocence, but nonetheless found himself staring at the death penalty. Because of the notoriety, the newly elected Claudia McDover moved the trial to another county but insisted on maintaining jurisdiction. She presided over the trial and favored the prosecution at every turn.

The casino faced two significant obstacles. One was Son Razko. The second obstacle was its location. Much of the Tappacola land was low-lying swamps and bayous and almost uninhabitable, but there was enough high ground to build a large casino with the necessary acreage around it. Getting there was the problem. The road into the reservation was old, was badly maintained, and would never handle the traffic. With the prospect of tax revenue, good-paying jobs, and bright lights, the leaders of Brunswick County agreed to build a new four-lane road from State Route 288 to the reservation's border, which was a stone's throw from the spot where the casino was to be built.

But building the road would require the taking of private land by eminent domain, or condemnation, and the majority of the landowners of the proposed right-of-way were opposed to the casino.

The county filed eleven lawsuits at the same time, all seeking condemnation of eleven parcels of land along the proposed route. Judge McDover took charge of the litigation, ran roughshod over the lawyers, placed the cases on what amounted to her 'rocket docket,' and within months had the first one teed up for a trial. By then there was little doubt, at least among the lawyers, that she was squarely in the county's corner and wanted the road built as soon as possible. As the first trial approached, she organized a settlement meeting in her courtroom and required all lawyers to attend. In a marathon session, she hammered out an agreement in which the county would pay each landowner twice the appraised value of his property. Under Florida law, there was little doubt the county could take the land. The issue was compensation. And time. By ramrodding the litigation, Judge McDover saved the casino years of delays.

While the eminent domain cases were proceeding as planned, and with Son Razko out of the way, the gambling proponents petitioned for another referendum. They won the second time by thirty votes. Another lawsuit was filed claiming fraud, and Judge McDover dismissed it. The path was now clear to begin construction of Treasure Key, which opened in 2000.

Junior Mace's appeals crawled through the system, and though several reviewers were critical of the trial judge and her rulings, no one found serious errors. The conviction survived as the years passed.

'We studied that case in law school,' Hugo said.

'The murder was sixteen years ago, so you were what, twenty years old?' Myers asked.

'Something like that. I don't remember the murder, nor the trial, but it was mentioned in law school. Criminal procedure, I think. Something about the use of jailhouse snitches in capital murder trials.'

'I don't suppose you've heard of it?' Myers asked Lacy, who replied, 'No. I didn't grow up in Florida.'

Myers said, 'I have a thick file on the murder case, complete with the habeas filings. I've kept up with it over the years and know as much as anyone, just in case you need a resource.'

'So did Mace catch his wife in bed with Son and take offense?' Lacy asked.

'I doubt it. He claims he was somewhere else but his alibi witness was shaky. His court-appointed lawyer was a rookie with little experience and no match for the prosecutor, who was a real slick operator. Judge McDover allowed him to call two jailhouse snitches who said Mace bragged about the killings in jail.'

'Should we talk to Mace?' Hugo asked.

'That's where I'd start.'

'But why?' Lacy asked.

'Because Junior Mace may know something and there's a chance he'll talk to you. The Tappacola are a tight, closemouthed bunch, very suspicious of outsiders, especially those with authority or wearing uniforms. Plus, they are terrified of Dubose and his gang. They have been easily intimidated. And why not keep quiet? They're reaping a windfall. They have homes and cars, schools and health care, money for college. Why rock the boat? If the casino is doing a little dirty business with some gangsters, who cares? Speaking up might get you shot.'

'Can we talk about the judge?' Lacy asked.

'Sure. Claudia McDover, age fifty-six, first elected in 1994 and reelected every six years since then. By all accounts, a hardworking judge who's very serious about her job and her courtroom. She wins her reelections by landslides. Very bright, very driven. Her ex-husband was a big doctor in Pensacola and he was fond of young nurses. Bad divorce in which she, Claudia, got royally screwed by hubby and his gang of lawyers. Wounded and angry, she went to law school to get revenge, but at some point said to hell with the old boy. She settled in the town of Sterling, the seat of Brunswick County, where she joined a little real estate firm. She struggled and soon got bored with the small-town practice, and at some point her path crossed with that of Vonn Dubose. I don't know that part of the story. I've heard a rumor that they might have dated off and on, but, again, this has not and probably cannot be verified. In 1993, after the Tappacola had voted against the casino, Claudia McDover suddenly had an interest in politics and ran for circuit court judge. I knew none of this. At that time I was a busy lawyer in Pensacola and wasn't sure where Sterling was on the map. I had heard of the Tappacola and read about the casino fight, but I had no interest. From all accounts, her campaign was extremely well funded and well organized and she beat the incumbent by a thousand votes. A month after she took office, Son Razko was murdered, and, as I've said, she presided over the trial of Junior Mace. This was 1996, and during this time Vonn Dubose and his confederates and limited partners and offshore companies were buying large tracts of land in Brunswick County near the reservation. A few other speculators had jumped in when it looked like the Tappacola wanted a casino, but after the first vote these guys fled the market. Vonn was more than happy to take the property off their hands. He knew what was coming and soon had the Indian land surrounded. With Son Razko out of the way, and removed in such a dramatic fashion, the proponents won the second election. The rest is history.'

Lacy pecked on her laptop and soon had a large, official photo of Judge Claudia McDover, complete with a black robe and a gavel in hand. She had short dark hair cut in a bob, very stylish, with

44

designer eyeglasses that dominated her face and made it difficult to read her eyes. No smile, not a trace of warmth or humor, all business. Could she really be a party to the wrongful conviction of a man who'd been on death row fifteen years? It was hard to believe.

'Where's the corruption?' Lacy asked.

'Everywhere. Once the Tappacola started building the casino, Dubose started too. His first development was a golf community called Rabbit Run, which is adjacent to the casino property.'

Hugo said, 'We drove by it. I thought it was part of Treasure Key.'

'No, but from the driving range at the golf course you can walk to the casino in five minutes. Part of the conspiracy with the Tappacola is that they stay away from golf. They handle the gambling and amusement stuff; Dubose gets the golf and everything else. He started with eighteen holes at Rabbit Run, all the fairways lined with handsome condos.'

Myers slid a file onto the table and said, 'Here's the complaint, sworn to under oath by Greg Myers. In it I allege that the Honorable Claudia McDover owns at least four condos in the Rabbit Run development, courtesy of a faceless corporation called CFFX and domiciled in Belize.'

'Dubose?' Lacy asked.

'I'm sure but I can't prove it, yet.'

'What about the property records?' Hugo asked.

Myers tapped the file. 'They're here. They will

tell you that CFFX deeded at least twenty units to offshore companies. I have reason to believe Judge McDover has an interest in four, all showing ownership by foreign entities. We are dealing with sophisticated crooks who have excellent lawyers.'

'What's the value of the condos?' Lacy asked.

'Today, about a million each. Rabbit Run has been very successful, even managed to weather the Great Recession. Thanks to the casino, Dubose has plenty of cash and he likes gated communities with cookie-cutter houses and condos along the fairways. He went from eighteen holes to thirty-six to fifty-four, and has enough land for even more.'

'And why did he give the condos to Judge McDover?'

'Maybe because he's just a nice guy. It was part of the original deal, I suppose. Claudia McDover sold her soul to the devil to get elected and she's been getting paid ever since. The construction of the casino and the development of Brunswick County have created a ton of litigation. Zoning disputes, environmental claims, eminent domain, landowner lawsuits, and she has managed to keep herself smack in the middle of it. Those on the side of Dubose always seem to win. His enemies lose. She's smart as hell and can back up any decision with a thick, well-reasoned legal brief. She is rarely reversed on appeal. In 2001, she and Dubose had a disagreement, not sure what it was about, but it got ugly. It is believed that she wanted more of the skim from the casino cash. Dubose

46

thought she was being adequately compensated. So Judge McDover closed down the casino.'

'How, exactly, did she pull that off?' Lacy asked.

'Another good story. Once the casino was up and running, and it was printing money from day one, the county realized it would not be getting much in the way of tax revenue. In America, Indians don't pay taxes on casino profits. The Tappacola didn't want to share. The county felt jilted, especially after going to all the trouble of building a spanking-new four-lane highway that runs for over seven miles. So the county pulled a fast one and convinced the state legislature to allow it to collect tolls on the new road.'

Hugo laughed and said, 'Right, you gotta stop at a tollbooth about a mile from the casino and pay five bucks to keep going.'

'It's actually worked out fine. The Indians are happy now and the county gets a few bucks. So when Dubose and Judge McDover had their little spat, she got a lawyer buddy to ask for an injunction on the grounds that the tollbooths were crowded and unsafe. There might have been a couple of fender benders but nothing serious. It was completely bogus crap, but she immediately issued an injunction closing the toll road. The casino stayed open because a few folks managed to trickle in from the back roads and such, but it was effectively shut down. This went on for six days as Vonn and Claudia waited for the other to blink. Finally, they got on the same page, the bogus injunction was lifted, and everybody was happy. It was a pivotal moment in the history of the casino and the corruption it has created. Judge McDover let everybody know that she's in charge.'

Hugo said, 'You talk about Dubose as if everyone knows him.'

'No one knows him. I thought I made that clear. He runs an organization, a small one in which the big boys are related and everybody is getting plenty of money. He tells a cousin to charter an LLC out of Bermuda and buy some acreage. Another cousin incorporates in Barbados and trades some condos. Dubose is protected by layers of offshore shell companies. He has no profile, leaves no trail.'

'Who does his legal work?' Lacy asked.

'A small firm in Biloxi, a couple of tax lawyers who are skilled at dirty work. They've represented the Dubose gang for years.'

Lacy said, 'It sounds as though Judge McDover is not afraid of Dubose.'

'Dubose is too smart to take out a judge, though I'm sure he's thought about it. He needs her. She needs him. Think about it. You're an ambitious and crooked real estate developer in Florida, plus you practically own a casino, which is illegal of course, so you need a lot of protection. What could be more valuable than having a well-respected judge in your back pocket?'

'This has RICO stamped all over it,' Hugo said.

'Yes, but we're not going RICO, are we, Mr Hatch? RICO is federal; federal is FBI. I don't

48

care what happens to Dubose. I want to bust Judge McDover so my client can collect a small fortune for blowing the whistle.'

'How small?' Lacy asked.

Myers finished a beer and wiped his mouth with the back of his hand. 'I don't know. I guess your job is to find out.' Carlita stepped up from the cabin and said, 'Lunch is ready.'

Myers stood and said, 'Please join me.'

Lacy and Hugo exchanged quick glances. They had been there for two hours, were starving and not sure where they would find lunch, but suddenly uncertain as to whether it was a good idea to eat on the boat. Myers, though, was already stepping below. 'Come on, come on,' he said, and they followed him down into the cabin. Three places were set at a glass-top table in the cramped galley. An air conditioner somewhere was hard at work and the air was refreshingly cool. The smell of grilled fish hung heavy. Carlita scurried about, obviously delighted to have someone to cook for. She served a platter of fish tacos, poured sparkling water from a bottle, and asked if anyone wanted wine. No one did, and she disappeared deeper into the cabin.

Myers did not touch his food, but instead resumed his narrative. 'This complaint is not the one I want to file. In this one I allege corruption only to the extent of the condos owned by Judge McDover in Rabbit Run. The real money in this little conspiracy is her portion of the monthly skim

49

from the casino. That's what I'm really after because it's a gold mine for my client. If I can nail that down, I'll amend the complaint. If not, there are sufficient allegations to get her removed from the bench, and probably indicted.'

'Do you mention the name of Vonn Dubose in the complaint?' Lacy asked.

'No. I refer to his corporations as "criminal entities."'

'That's original,' Lacy said.

'You got a better idea, Ms Stoltz?' Myers shot back.

'Can we drop the Mister and Missus stuff?' Hugo asked. 'She's Lacy. You're Greg. I'm Hugo.'

'Fair enough.' All three took a bite, and as he chewed rapidly Myers kept talking, with his mouth barely closed. 'A question. The statute says you have forty-five days from today to serve a copy of the complaint on Judge McDover. From now until then, you do your investigation, the, uh, what's it called?'

'Assessment.'

'Right. Well, that worries me. I'm convinced these people have no idea that anyone is onto their enterprise, their dealings, and when Judge McDover gets a copy of this complaint she'll be shocked. Her first phone call will be to Dubose, and at that point a lot of crazy stuff could start happening. She'll lawyer up immediately, deny everything vehemently, and probably start moving assets around. Dubose will panic, circle the wagons, maybe even start looking for someone to intimidate.'

'Your question?'

'Okay, how long can you really wait before you lay this on her? How long can you stall? It seems to me it's crucial to do as much investigating as possible before she knows you're doing it.'

Lacy and Hugo studied each other. She shrugged and said, 'We're bureaucrats so we know how to stall. However, if she attacks the way you predict, her lawyers will nitpick everything. If we don't follow the statute to the letter, they'll push hard to dismiss the complaint.'

Hugo added, 'Let's play it safe and say we'll have forty-five days to do our assessment.'

'That's not enough time,' Myers said.

'That's all we have,' Lacy said.

'What can you tell us about your mysterious client?' Hugo asked. 'How does he know what he knows?'

Myers sipped some water and smiled. 'Once again, you assume the person is a "he."'

'Okay, what do you want to call him, or her?'

'There are only three links in our little chain. Me, the middleman who referred the client to me, and the client himself or herself. The middleman and I refer to the client as the mole. The mole could be male or female, old or young, black or white or brown, doesn't really matter right now.'

Lacy said, 'The mole? That's not very original.'

'What difference does it make? You got a more descriptive name?'

'I guess it will have to do. How does the mole know so much?'

51

Myers crammed half a soft taco into his mouth and chewed slowly. The boat rocked in the wake of something larger out there. Finally, he said, 'The mole is very close to Judge McDover, and is trusted implicitly by Her Honor. Trusted too much, it appears. That's all I can say right now.'

After a gap in the conversation, Lacy said, 'I have another question. You said these people, meaning Dubose and his gang, are very smart and use good lawyers. Obviously, McDover also needs a good lawyer to clean her share of the dirty money. Who does she hire?'

'Phyllis Turban, a trust and estate lawyer in Mobile.'

'Wow, the girls are getting a black eye in this story,' Lacy said.

'She and McDover were in law school together, both divorced with no children, and very close. So close that they might be more than just friends.'

They swallowed hard and digested this. Lacy said, 'So to summarize the case so far, our target, Judge Claudia McDover, takes bribes from thugs, skims casino cash from the Indians, and somehow launders the money with the help of a very close friend who happens to be an estate lawyer.'

Myers smiled and said, 'I'd say you're on the right track. I need a beer. Anybody want a beer? Carlita!'

They left him on the pier, waving good-bye and promising to keep in touch. He had dropped hints about disappearing into even deeper cover, now that the complaint was filed and would soon cause trouble. Lacy and Hugo had detected nothing that would indicate how or why Vonn Dubose and Claudia McDover would suspect Greg Myers, formerly known as Ramsey Mix and a man they had supposedly never met. It was another gap in his story, of which there were far too many.

CHAPTER 5

They spent the next day in the office, brainstorming with Geismar and putting together a plan. With the complaint on file, the clock was ticking. If things stayed on schedule, Lacy and Hugo would soon drive to the small town of Sterling and serve a copy of it upon the Honorable Claudia McDover. By then it would be imperative to know as much as possible.

First, though, they needed to visit death row. Hugo had been there once, on a field trip in law school. Lacy had heard about Starke her entire career, but had never found the excuse to see it. They left early enough to beat the morning rush around Tallahassee, and by the time the traffic thinned on I-10 Hugo was nodding off. The prison was two and a half hours away. Lacy had not been forced to walk the floors with a crying baby all night, but she had not slept much either. She and Hugo, as well as Geismar, felt as though they were probably sticking their noses into a mess that someone else should clean up. If Greg Myers could be believed, serious criminal activity had been rampant in Brunswick County for a long time.

Investigators with far more resources and experience should get the nod on this one. They were lawyers, after all, not cops. They didn't *want* to carry guns. They were trained to go after corrupt judges, not organized crime syndicates.

These thoughts had kept her from sleeping most of the night. When she caught herself yawning, she whipped into a fast-food drive-thru and ordered coffee. 'Wake up,' she scolded her partner. 'We have an hour and a half to go and I can't stay awake either.'

'Sorry,' Hugo said, rubbing his eyes.

They slugged coffee, and as she drove Hugo summarized one of Sadelle's memos. 'According to our colleague, from 2000 through 2009, there were ten lawsuits in Brunswick County involving a company called Nylan Title, a Bahamian outfit whose registered agent is a lawyer over in Biloxi. In each case, the opposing party tried to compel the identities of the real owners of Nylan Title, and each time the judge, our friend Claudia McDover, said no. Off-limits. A company domiciled in the Bahamas is governed by its laws, and they have a way of protecting their companies. It's all a shell game but it's legal. Anyway, Nylan Title must have some great lawyers because it is undefeated, at least in Judge McDover's courtroom. Ten to zero.'

'What kinds of cases?' Lacy asked.

'Zoning, breach of contract, diminution of property value, even an aborted class action by a bunch of condo owners claiming defective workmanship. The county sued Nylan in a dispute over property valuations and taxes.'

'Who shows up on behalf of Nylan?'

'The same lawyer out of Biloxi. He's the corporate mouthpiece and seems to know what's going on. If Nylan is indeed Vonn Dubose, then he's well hidden, just like Myers says. Layers of lawyers, as he put it. Nice phrase.'

'Sounds charming.'

Hugo took a sip of coffee and put down the memo. He said, 'Look, Lacy, I don't trust Greg Myers.'

'He doesn't really inspire trust.'

'But you have to admit that, so far, everything he has said has checked out. If he's using us, what's his endgame?'

'I was asking the same question at three thirty this morning. We have to catch Judge McDover with a pile of cash. Period. If it's recovered, the mole gets his or her share as a reward, and Myers takes a cut. If Vonn Dubose and his boys get busted, fine, but how does that help Myers?'

'It doesn't, unless of course McDover goes up in flames with Dubose.'

'He *is* using us, Hugo. He's filed a complaint alleging corrupt judicial practices, or outright thievery. It's our job to investigate. Anyone who files a complaint against a judge is using us to find the truth. That's the nature of our jobs.'

'Sure it is, but something is not right with this guy.'

'I have the same gut feeling. I like Geismar's strategy. We'll poke around a bit, nibble at the edges, develop some history, try to find out who owns those four condos, do our job but do it cautiously, and if we find real evidence of wrongdoing we'll go to the FBI. Myers can't stop us from doing that.'

'Agreed, but he can disappear and never talk to us again. If he has proof of corruption at the casino, we'll never get it if the FBI comes storming in.'

'What else did Sadelle pack for our pleasant drive to Starke?'

Hugo picked up another memo. 'Just some background on Judge McDover. Her elections, campaigns, opponents, stuff like that. Since elections are nonpartisan, we're not sure about her politics. No record of contributions to other candidates in other races. No previous complaints filed with BJC. No complaints filed with the State Bar. No felonies or misdemeanors. Since 1998, she has received the highest rating by the State Bar Association. She writes a lot and there's a long list of papers she's published in legal magazines and such. She also likes to speak at seminars and law schools. She even taught a course in trial practice at FSU three years ago. Quite the résumé, really. More so than our average circuit court judge. Not much in the way of assets. A home in downtown Sterling assessed at $230,000, built seventy years ago, with a mortgage of $110,000. Title issued in her name, McDover, which happens to be her maiden name. She reacquired it right after the divorce and has used it since. Single since 1988, no children, no other marriages. No record of memberships in churches, civic clubs, alumni associations, political parties, nothing. Law school was at Stetson, where she was a top student. Undergraduate degree from North Florida in Jacksonville. Some stuff about her divorce from her doctor husband but not worth the time.'

Lacy listened intently and sipped more coffee. 'If Myers is correct, she's skimming cash from an Indian casino. That's rather hard to believe, don't you think? I mean, one of our circuit judges elected by the people and so highly regarded.'

'It is indeed. We've seen judges do some bizarre things, but nothing as bold as this.'

'How do you explain it? What's her motive?'

'You're a single woman with a career. You answer the question.'

'I can't. What's the other memo?'

Hugo fished through his briefcase and pulled out some papers.

As they entered rural Bradford County, they began to see signs indicating there were prisons and correctional facilities just ahead. Near the small town of Starke, population five thousand, they turned and followed signs to the Florida State Prison, home to fifteen hundred inmates, including four hundred condemned men.

Only California had more men on death row than Florida. Texas was a close third, but since it was more focused on keeping its numbers down its population was around 330, give or take. California, with little interest in executing people, had 650. Florida longed to be another Texas, but its appellate courts kept getting in the way. Last year, 2010, only one man was lethally injected at Starke.

They parked in a crowded lot and hiked to an administration building. As lawyers working for the state, their visit had been facilitated. They were cleared through the checkpoints and escorted by a guard with enough clout to get all doors opened quickly. At Q Wing, Florida's notorious death row, they were cleared past another checkpoint and led to a long room. A sign on the door read 'Attorney Conferences.' The guard opened another door to a small enclosed area with a sheet of Plexiglas dividing it.

'First trip to death row?' the guard asked.

Lacy said, 'Yes.' Hugo said, 'I came here once when I was in law school.'

'That's nice. You got the consent form?'

'I do,' Hugo replied as he put his briefcase on the table and unzipped it. Junior Mace was represented pro bono by a large Washington firm. Before Lacy and Hugo could talk to him, they had to assure the law firm they would not discuss any of the issues pending in his current habeas corpus filing. Hugo pulled out a sheet of paper and the guard took his time reading it. When it met his approval, he handed it back and said, 'Mace is a strange one, I'll tell you that.'

Lacy looked away and didn't want to respond. While she wasn't sleeping the night before, worrying about all the crap that was cluttering her brain, she read a few online articles about Florida's death row. Each prisoner was kept in solitary confinement for twenty-three hours a day. The other hour was for 'recreation,' a chance to walk around a small, grassy area and look at the sun. Each cell was six feet by nine, with a nine-foot ceiling. Each bed was smaller than a twin-size and just inches away from a stainless steel toilet. There was no air-conditioning, no cellmate, almost no human contact except for the usual chatter from the guards at feeding time.

If Junior Mace had not been a 'strange one' before arriving fifteen years earlier, he could certainly be excused for being a bit odd now. Total isolation leads to sensory deprivation and all sorts of mental problems. Corrections experts were beginning to realize this, and a movement to reform the practice of solitary confinement was struggling to gain momentum. Said movement had not made it to Florida.

A door on the other side opened and a guard walked through it. He was followed by Junior Mace, handcuffed and wearing the standard blue prison pants and orange T-shirt reserved for death row inmates. Another guard followed him. They removed the handcuffs and left the room.

Junior Mace took two steps and sat down at the table on his side. The Plexiglas separated them.

Hugo and Lacy took their seats and for a few seconds things were awkward.

He was fifty-two years old. His hair was long, thick, and gray, swept back into a ponytail. His skin was dark and had not been bleached by the isolation. His eyes were dark too, large and brown and sad. He was tall and lean with well-formed biceps. Probably does a lot of push-ups, Hugo thought. According to the file, his wife, Eileen, was thirty-two when she died. They had three children, all raised by relatives after Junior was arrested and sent away.

Lacy took one of two phones on her side of the partition and said, 'Thanks for meeting with us.'

He was holding his phone. He shrugged, said nothing.

'I'm not sure you got our letter, but we work for the State Board on Judicial Conduct and we're investigating Judge Claudia McDover.'

'I got it,' he said. 'I'm here. I agreed to the meeting.' He spoke slowly, as if every word had to be considered first.

Hugo said, 'So, uh, we're not here to talk about your case. We can't help you there, and besides you have some good lawyers in Washington.'

'I'm still alive. I guess they're doing their job. What do you want from me?'

Lacy said, 'Information. We need the names of people we can talk to. Tappacola, the ones on the good side, your side. That is another world for us, and we can't just show up one day and start asking questions.'

61

His eyes narrowed and his mouth turned down, like an inverted smile. He nodded as he glared at them, and finally said, 'Look, my wife and Son Razko were murdered in 1995. I was convicted in 1996 and taken away, shackled in the back of a van. That was before the casino was built, so I'm not sure I can really help you. They had to get me out of the way, me and Son, before they could build it. They murdered Son, along with my wife, and they got me convicted for it.'

'Do you know who did it?' Hugo asked.

He actually smiled, though the humor did not make it to his eyes. Slowly, he said, 'Mr Hatch, for sixteen years I have said over and over that I do not know who killed my wife and Son Razko. There were some people in the background, some outsiders who eased their way into the picture. Our Chief at the time was a good man who got corrupted. These outside folks got to him, I'm not sure how but I'm sure it involved money, and he became convinced the casino was the answer. Son and I fought back and we won the first vote in 1993. They thought they were going to win and they were laying the groundwork to make a lot of money with the casino and the land around it. When our people turned it down the first time, these folks decided to get rid of Son. And me too, I guess. They figured out a way to do it. Son's gone. I'm here. The casino has been printing cash for a decade now.'

Lacy asked, 'Ever heard the name of Vonn Dubose?'

He paused and seemed to flinch slightly. It was obvious his answer would be yes, so when he said no, they both made a note. That would be an interesting conversation on the ride home. 'Remember,' he said, 'I've been gone for a long time. Fifteen years here in solitary eats away at your soul, your spirit, and your brain. I've lost a lot, and I can't always remember what I should.'

'But you wouldn't forget Vonn Dubose if you knew him,' Lacy said, pushing.

Junior clenched his jaws and shook his head. No. 'Don't know him.'

Hugo said, 'I'm assuming you have a low opinion of Judge McDover.'

'That's an understatement. She presided over a joke of a trial and made sure an innocent man was convicted. She's covering up, too. I've always suspected she knew more than she should have. It was all a nightmare, Mr Hatch. From the moment they told me my wife was dead, along with Son, and then the shock of being accused, and getting arrested and slammed into jail. By then the system was clicking right along and everybody I looked at was a bad guy. From the cops, the prosecutors, the judge, the witnesses, the jurors – I got chewed up by a system that was hitting on all cylinders. In no time flat I got framed, convicted, sentenced, and here I am.'

'What's the judge covering up?' Lacy asked.

'The truth. I suspect she knows I didn't kill Son and Eileen.'

'How many people know the truth?' Hugo asked.

Junior placed the phone on the table and rubbed his eyes as if he hadn't slept in days. With his right hand he raked his fingers through his thick hair, all the way to the ponytail. Slowly, he picked up the phone and said, 'Not many. Most people consider me a killer. They believe the story, and why not? I was convicted in a court of law and here I am, rotting away and waiting for the needle. I'll get it one day, and they'll haul me back to Brunswick County and bury me somewhere. The story will live on and on. Junior Mace caught his wife with another man and killed them both in an act of rage. That's a pretty good story, right?'

Nothing was said for a moment. Lacy and Hugo scribbled away as they tried to think of their next question. Junior broke the silence with 'Just so you'll know, this is an attorney visit so there's no time limit. If you're not in a hurry, believe me I'm not either. It's about a hundred degrees in my cell right now. There's no ventilation, so my little fan just pushes the hot air around. This is a nice break for me, and I welcome you back anytime you're in the neighborhood.'

'Thanks,' Hugo replied. 'Do you get many visitors?'

'Not as many as I would like. My kids stop by occasionally but those are hard visits. For years I wouldn't allow them to see me here and they really grew up fast. Now they're married. I'm even a grandfather, but I've never seen my grandkids. Got pictures, though, all over my wall. How would you like that? Four grandchildren and I've never been able to touch them.'

'Who raised your kids?' Lacy asked.

'My mother helped until she died. My brother Wilton and his wife did most of it, and they did the best they could. Just a bad situation. Imagine being a kid and your mother gets murdered. Everybody says your father did it and they send him to death row.'

'Do your kids think you're guilty?'

'No. They got the truth from Wilton and my mother.'

'Would Wilton talk to us?' Hugo asked.

'I don't know. You can try. I'm not sure he'll want to get involved. You gotta understand that life is pretty good these days for our people, much better than before. Looking back, I'm not sure Son and I were on the right side when we fought the casino. It's brought jobs, schools, roads, a hospital, a level of prosperity our people had never dreamed of. When a Tappacola turns eighteen, he or she qualifies for a lifetime pension of $5,000 a month, and that might go up. It's called the dividend. Even me, sitting here on death row, I'm collecting the dividends. I would save it for my kids but they don't need it. So, I send it to my lawyers in Washington, figure that's the least I could do. When they took my case, there was no dividend system and they certainly didn't expect any money. Every Tappacola gets free health care, free education, and college expenses if he or she wants it. We have our own bank and make low interest loans for houses and cars. As I said, life there is pretty good, much better than before. That's the good part. On the downside, there are pretty serious motivational problems, especially among the young. Why go to college and pursue a career when your income is guaranteed for life? Why try and find a job? The casino employs about half of the adults in the tribe, and that's a constant source of friction. Who gets an easy job and who doesn't? There's a lot of infighting and politics involved. But on the whole, the tribe realizes that it has a good thing going. Why rock the boat? Why should anyone worry about me? Why should Wilton help you bring down a crooked judge when everyone might get hurt in the process?'

'Are you aware of corruption at the casino?' Lacy asked.

Mace put the phone down and rummaged through his hair again, as if painfully pondering the question. His hesitancy suggested he was struggling not with the truth but with which version of it. He picked up the phone and said, 'Again, the casino opened a few years after I came here. I've never laid eyes on it.'

Hugo said, 'Come on, Mr Mace. You said yourself it's a tiny tribe. A big casino for a small group of people. It must be impossible to keep secrets. Surely you've heard the rumors.'

'Tell me about them.'

'Rumors of cash being skimmed and taken out

66

the back door. According to estimates, Treasure Key is now a half-billion-dollar casino, and 90 percent of the gross is in cash. Our source tells us there is a gang of organized criminals in bed with the Indian leaders and they're skimming like crazy. You've never heard this?'

'I may have heard that rumor but that doesn't mean I know anything.'

'Then who does? Who can we talk to?' Lacy asked.

'You must have a good source or you wouldn't be here. Go back to your source.'

Lacy and Hugo glanced at each other, both with the same image of Greg Myers puttering around the Bahamas on his boat, cold beer in hand, Jimmy Buffett on the stereo. 'Maybe later,' Hugo said. 'But for now, we need someone on the ground, someone who knows the casino.'

Mace was shaking his head. 'Wilton is my only source and he doesn't say much. I'm not sure how much he knows, but very little of it trickles all the way down here to Starke.'

Lacy asked, 'Would you call Wilton and say it's okay to talk to us?'

'And what do I gain from that? I don't know you. I don't know if you can be trusted. I'm sure your intentions are good, but you might be walking into a situation where things could get out of control. I don't know. I need to think about it.'

'Where does Wilton live?' Hugo asked.

'On the reservation, not far from the casino. He tried to get a job there but they turned him down.

No one in my family works at the casino. They won't hire them. It's very political.'

'So there's resentment?'

'Oh yes. Lots of it. Those who fought the casino are basically blacklisted and can't work there. They still get their checks, but they don't get the jobs.'

'And how do they feel about you?' Lacy asked.

'As I said, most of them believe I killed Son, their leader, so there's not much sympathy. Those who supported the casino hated me from the beginning. Needless to say, I don't have a lot of fans among my people. And my family pays the price.'

Hugo asked, 'If Judge McDover is exposed and the corruption is proven, is there a chance it could help your case?'

Mace stood slowly and stretched as if in pain, then took a few steps to the door, then back to the table. He stretched some more, cracked his knuckles, sat down, and picked up the phone. 'I don't see it. My trial was over a long time ago. All of her rulings have been picked apart on appeal, and by some very good lawyers. We think she was wrong on several of them. We think a new trial should have been granted a decade ago, and so on, but the appellate courts have all agreed with her. Not unanimously; indeed, all of the decisions in my case have been split, with very strong dissents in my favor. But the majority rules and here I am. The two jailhouse snitches who effectively nailed my conviction and sent me away disappeared years ago. Did you know that?'

Lacy said, 'I saw it in a memo.'

'Both vanished at about the same time.'

'Any ideas?'

'Two theories. One, and the best, is that both were rubbed out not long after my conviction was affirmed. Both were career criminals, real lizards who cleaned up nicely at trial and convinced the jury that I had bragged about the killings in jail. Well, the problem with snitches is that they often recant, so the first theory is that the real killers took out the snitches before they had the chance to change their stories. This I believe.'

'And the second theory?' Hugo asked.

'That they were taken out by my people in revenge. I doubt this, but it's not completely far-fetched. Emotions were high and I guess anything was possible. Regardless, the two snitches vanished and have not been seen in years. I hope they're dead. They put me here.'

Lacy said, 'We're not supposed to be talking about your case.'

'It's all I have to talk about, and who really cares? This is all a matter of public record now.'

'So that's at least four dead bodies,' Hugo said.

'At least.'

'Are there more?' Lacy asked.

He was nodding steadily, but they couldn't tell if it was just a nervous tic or an answer in the affirmative. Finally, he said, 'Depends on how hard you dig.'

CHAPTER 6

The first courthouse built by the taxpayers of Brunswick County burned to the ground. The second one was blown away. After the hurricane in 1970, the county leaders approved a design that included a lot of brick, concrete, and steel. The result was a hideous, Soviet-style hangar with three levels, few windows, and sweeping metal roofs that leaked from day one. At the time, the county, halfway between Pensacola and Tallahassee, was sparsely populated, its beaches free of sprawl and clutter. According to the 1970 census, there were 8,100 whites, 1,570 blacks, and 411 Native Americans. A few years after the 'new courthouse,' as it was known, opened for business, the coast along the Florida Panhandle sprang to life as developers rushed to build condos and hotels. With miles of wide and untouched beaches, the 'Emerald Coast' became an even more popular destination. The population increased, and in 1984 Brunswick County was forced to expand its courthouse. Holding true to the postmodern motif, it built a perplexing phallic-shaped annex that reminded many of a cancerous growth. Indeed, the locals referred to it as the Tumor, as opposed to its official designation of the Annex. Twelve years later, as the population continued to grow, the county added a matching tumor at the opposite end of the 'new courthouse' and declared itself ready for any and all business.

The county seat was the town of Sterling. Brunswick and two adjoining counties comprised Florida's Twenty-Fourth Judicial District. Of the two circuit court judges, Claudia McDover was the only one headquartered in Sterling; thus, she pretty much ruled the courthouse. She had seniority and clout and all county employees walked softly around her. Her spacious office was on the third floor, where she enjoyed a pleasant view and some sunlight from one of the few windows. She despised the building and often dreamed of ways to acquire enough power to tear it down and start over. But that was just a dream.

After a quiet day at her desk, she informed her secretary that she would be leaving at four, an early exit for her. Her timid and well-trained secretary absorbed this information but asked no questions. No one asked Claudia McDover why she did anything.

She left Sterling in her late-model Lexus and took a county road south. Twenty minutes later she turned in to the grand entryway of Treasure Key, a place she privately considered 'her casino.' She was convinced that it would not exist but for her efforts. She had the power to shut it down tomorrow if she wanted. That, though, would not be happening.

She took the periphery road along the edge of the property and smiled, as always, at the crowded parking lots, the busy shuttles running gamblers to and from their hotels, the gaudy neon billboards advertising shows by washed-up country crooners and cheap circus acts. All of it made her smile because it meant the Indians were prospering. People had jobs. People were having fun. Families were on vacation. Treasure Key was a wonderful place, and the fact that she was siphoning only a small piece of the action bothered her not in the least.

Nothing bothered Claudia McDover these days. After seventeen years on the bench her reputation was sound, her job secure, her ratings high. After eleven years of 'sharing' in the casino's profits, she was an incredibly rich woman, with assets hidden around the world and more piling up by the month. And though she was in business with people she didn't like, their swindling conspiracy was impervious to the outside world. There was no trail, no evidence. It had, after all, clicked right along for eleven years, since the day the casino opened.

She passed through a gate and entered the swanky golf course and residential development of Rabbit Run. She owned four condos there, or at least she owned the offshore companies that owned them. One she kept for herself. The other

72

three she leased through her attorney. Her unit on the fourth fairway was a two-story fortress with reinforced doors and windows. 'Hurricane protection' had been her reasoning years earlier when she beefed up the place. Inside a small bedroom she had built a ten-by-ten vault with concrete walls and security against fire and theft. Inside the vault she kept some portable assets – cash, gold, jewelry. There were also a few items that didn't move so easily – two Picasso lithographs, an Egyptian urn that was four thousand years old, a porcelain tea set from another dynasty, and a collection of rare first-edition novels from the nineteenth century. The bedroom door was hidden behind a swinging bookcase so that a person walking through the condo would not know the room, and the vault, existed. But no one walked through the condo. An occasional guest might be invited to sit on the patio for a drink, but the condo was not about drinking, or visiting, or living.

She opened the curtains and looked at the golf course. It was the dog days of August, the air hot and sticky and the course was deserted. She filled a teapot with water and placed it on a burner. While it warmed, she made two phone calls, both to lawyers with cases pending in her court.

At five, on time, her guest arrived. They met on the first Wednesday of each month at 5:00 p.m. Occasionally, when she was out of the country, they changed the meeting dates, but that was rare. Their communication was always face-to-face, in her condo, where there was no threat of hidden wires or bugs or surveillance of any type. They used phones only once or twice a year. They kept things simple and never left a trail. They were safe, and had been from the beginning, but they still took no chances.

Claudia sipped tea and Vonn enjoyed his vodka on ice. He had arrived with a brown satchel, which he had placed on the sofa, same as always. Inside the satchel were twenty-five stacks of $100 bills, each bound tightly by rubber bands, each of $10,000. The monthly skim was half a million dollars and they split it equally, as far as she knew. For years Claudia had wondered how much he really took from the Indians, and since he did the dirty work himself, she had no idea. Over time, though, she had become quite content with her haul. And why not?

She did not know the details. How, exactly, was the cash set aside? How was it kept off the books and away from security and surveillance? Who cooked the books to hide the skim? Who inside the depths of the casino actually took the loot and secured it for Vonn? Where did he go to get it? And who delivered it to him? How many on the inside were being bribed? She knew none of this. Nor did she know what he did with his share of the cash once it left the casino. They had never had such discussions.

She did not know anything about his gang, nor did she want to know. She dealt only with Vonn

Dubose and occasionally Hank, his faithful assistant. Vonn had found her eighteen years earlier, when she was a bored, small-town lawyer struggling to make a decent living and still plotting revenge against her ex-husband. He had a grand plan for massive development that would be fueled by a casino on Indian land, but there was an old judge in the way. Get rid of the judge, and perhaps an obstructionist or two, and Vonn would be free to start bulldozing. He offered to finance her campaign and do whatever was needed to get her elected.

He was around seventy, but could pass for sixty. With his perpetual tan and colorful golf shirts he could have been just another wealthy retiree living the good life in the Florida sun. He'd been through two divorces and had been single for years. After Claudia became a judge, he made a move but she had no interest. He was about fifteen years older, which was not that much really, but there were simply no sparks. Then, at the age of thirty-nine, she had also been coming to grips with the reality that she preferred women over men. And she found him boring, to be truthful. He was uneducated, interested in nothing but fishing, golf, and building the next strip mall or golf course, and his dark side still frightened her.

Over the years, as rumors circulated and details emerged and the appellate courts raised questions, Claudia had begun to doubt that Junior Mace had in fact killed his wife and Son Razko. Before and during the trial, she had been convinced of his guilt and wanted to deliver the right verdict for the voters who had just elected her. But with time and experience, she had developed serious doubts about his guilt. As the trial judge, though, her job had long been finished and there was little she could do to right a wrong. And why should she? Son and Junior were gone. The casino was built. Her life was good.

But the reality was that if Junior didn't do it, then someone in Vonn's gang had pumped two bullets into the heads of Son Razko and Eileen Mace, and someone had arranged the disappearances of the two jailhouse snitches who had nailed Junior. Though Claudia maintained a facade of ball-squeezing bravado, she was deathly afraid of Dubose and his boys. In their one and only shouting match, now some ten years in the past, she had convinced him that he would be immediately exposed if anything happened to her.

Over the years they had settled into a civilized relationship of mutual distrust, with each playing a well-defined role. She had the power to close the casino with an injunction for any half-baked reason, and had proven that she was unafraid to do so. He was in charge of the dirty work and kept the Tappacola in line. They prospered together, each getting richer by the month. It was amazing how much cordiality could be created, and how much suspicion could be overlooked, by truckloads of cash.

They were sitting inside, in the cool air, sipping their drinks, watching the deserted fairway, smug in their schemes and incredible wealth. 'How is North Dunes coming along?' she asked.

'It's on track,' he replied. 'Zoning board meets next week and is expected to green-light it. We should be moving dirt in two months.'

North Dunes was the latest addition to his golfing empire, with thirty-six holes, lakes and ponds, fancy condos and even fancier mansions, all wrapped around a contrived business center with a town square and amphitheater, and only a mile from the beach.

'The supervisors are in line?' she asked. A stupid question. The cash Dubose delivered to her was not the only bribe he spread around the county.

'Four to one,' he said. 'Poley dissenting of course.'

'Why don't you get rid of him?'

'No, no, he's necessary. We can't make it look too easy. Four to one works just fine.'

Bribes really weren't necessary in their part of the country. Take any form of growth, from high-end gated communities to low-end shopping centers, fix up a slick brochure filled with half-truths, label it 'economic development' with the promise of tax revenue and jobs, and elected officials reached for their rubber stamps. If anyone mentioned environmental issues, or traffic or crowded schools, they were dismissed as liberals or tree huggers or, much worse, 'northerners.' Vonn had mastered the game years ago.

'And the EC?' she asked. Extra condo.

'Of course, Your Honor. Golf course or high-rise?'

'How tall is the high-rise?'

'How tall would you like it?'

'I'd like to see the ocean. Is that possible?'

'No problem. It's a ten-story building as of now, and from halfway up the Gulf will soon be visible on a clear day.'

'I like that. Ocean view. Not the penthouse but something close.'

The idea of an extra unit had been perfected by a legendary Florida developer nicknamed Condo Conroy. In the rush and fury of throwing up an ocean-side tower, plans were modified on the fly, walls moved here and there, and the result was an extra condo the zoning board knew nothing about. It could be used for a dozen purposes, none of which were exactly legal. Vonn had learned the trick, and his favorite judge had accumulated an impressive portfolio of ECs over the years. Her balance sheet also included slices of legitimate businesses: a shopping mall, a water park, two restaurants, some small hotels, and a lot of raw land just waiting to be bulldozed.

'Another drink?' she asked. 'There are two things we need to discuss.'

'I'll get it.' He stood and walked to the kitchen counter where she kept the hard booze, stuff she never touched. He poured a shot, added two cubes of ice, and returned to his seat. 'I'm listening.'

She took a deep breath because this would not be easy. 'Wilson Vango.'

'What about him?' Dubose snapped.

'Just listen. He's served fourteen years and his health is very poor. He has emphysema, hepatitis, and some mental problems. He's survived a number of beatings and other assaults and there appears to be some brain damage.'

'Good.'

'He'll be eligible for parole in three years. Now his wife is dying of ovarian cancer, the family is destitute, and so on. A horrible situation. Anyway, someone got to the Governor and he wants to commute the rest of Vango's sentence, but only if I agree.'

Vonn's eyes flashed hot and he set his drink down. He pointed an angry finger at her and said, 'That sonofabitch stole $40,000 from one of my companies. I want him to die in prison, preferably after another assault. You understand, Claudia?'

'Come on, Vonn. I gave him the max because of you. He's served long enough. Poor guy is dying, so is his wife. Ease up.'

'Never, Claudia. I never ease up. He's lucky he got prison and not a hole in the head. Hell no, Claudia, Vango does not get out.'

'Okay, okay. Fix another drink. Settle down. Relax.'

'I'm fine. What else is on your mind?'

She took a sip of tea and let a minute pass. When the air was somewhat lighter, she said,

'Look, Vonn, I'm fifty-six years old. I've been wearing the robe for seventeen years, and I'm getting tired of the job. This is my third term, and with no opposition next year I'm guaranteed twenty-four years on the bench. That's enough. Phyllis is planning to retire too, and we want to travel the world. I'm tired of Sterling, Florida, and she's tired of Mobile. We have no kids to keep us grounded, so why not take off somewhere? Spend some of our Indian money.'

She paused and watched him. 'Your reaction?'

'I like things the way they are, obviously. The great thing about you, Claudia, is that you were so easy to corrupt, and, once corrupted, you fell hopelessly in love with the money. Same as me. The difference is that I was born into corruption, it's in my DNA. I'd rather steal money than earn it. You, on the other hand, were pure, but the ease of your conversion to the dark side was astonishing.'

'I wasn't pure. I was driven by hatred and a burning desire to humiliate my ex-husband. I wanted revenge and there's nothing pure about that.'

'My point is that I'm not sure I can find another judge so eager to be purchased.'

'Do you really need one at this point? If I leave, the casino loot is all yours, not a bad little safety net. You own the politicians. You've bull-dozed half the county and there's plenty of sprawl in your pipeline. It's pretty obvious, at least to me, that you'll do just fine without a judge on the payroll. I'm just tired of work, and, to be honest – which is not the right word to use in a conversation between us – I want to go straight for a while.'

'With money or sex?'

'Money, you ass,' she said with a chuckle.

Vonn smiled and sipped his vodka as the wheels turned. He was quietly thrilled at the idea. One less mouth to feed, and a big one. 'We'll survive,' he said.

'Of course you will. My decision has not been made, but I wanted you to know what I'm thinking. I'm really tired of refereeing divorces and sending kids to prison for life. And I haven't told anyone but Phyllis.'

'You can trust me with your darkest secrets, Your Honor.'

'Thick as thieves.'

Vonn stood and said, 'I need to go. Same time next month?'

'Yes.'

On the way out, he picked up an empty leather satchel, an identical match to the one he'd brought in, though somewhat lighter.

CHAPTER 7

The intermediary's name was Cooley, a former lawyer himself, though his exit from the profession was far less spectacular than that of his pal Greg Myers. Cooley had managed to avoid headlines by quickly pleading to an indictment in Georgia and surrendering his license. He had no plans to try and get it back.

They met in a quiet courtyard at the Pelican Hotel in South Beach, and over drinks on the small patio looked at the latest paperwork.

The first few sheets summarized Claudia McDover's travel for the past seven years, complete with dates, destinations, lengths of stay, and so on. The woman liked to travel and did so in style, usually by private jet, though none of the charters were booked in her name. Phyllis Turban, her lawyer, handled the details and generally used one of two flight companies based in Mobile. At least once a month, Claudia drove to Pensacola or Panama City, boarded a small jet, with Phyllis waiting, and took off to either New York or New Orleans for the weekend. There was no evidence of what they did on these trips, but the mole would have some ideas. Every summer Claudia spent two weeks in Singapore and was believed to own a home there. For those longer trips, she traveled on American Airlines and flew first-class. She went to Barbados at least three times a year by private jet. It was not clear whether Phyllis Turban accompanied her on the trips to Singapore and Barbados, but the mole, using prepaid and untraceable cell phones, repeatedly called Turban's office in Mobile and determined that she was not there when McDover was abroad. And the lawyer always returned to work when the judge did.

In a memo, the mole wrote, 'On the first Wednesday of each month, CM leaves the office a bit earlier than usual and drives to a condo in Rabbit Run. For some time it was impossible to determine where she went, but once a GPS tracking device was attached to the inside of her rear bumper, her exact movements became known. The address of the condo is 1614D Fairway Drive. According to the Brunswick County land records, the condo had changed hands twice and was now owned by a company registered in Belize. It is easy to speculate that she drives to the condo, receives a quantity of cash from the casino, then flies off with some or all of the money. Still speculating, the cash can be converted to gold, silver, diamonds, and collectibles. Certain dealers in New York and New Orleans are known to trade for cash, but for a stiff premium. Diamonds and jewelry are especially easy to smuggle out of the country. Cash can also be shipped by regular over-night parcel delivery to anywhere in the world, especially the Caribbean.'

Greg said, 'I don't like all this speculating. How much does he really know?'

Cooley replied, 'Are you kidding? Look at the travel summary. Precise movements over a seven-year period. Plus, it sounds like this guy knows something about money laundering.'

'Guy? As in male?'

'As in nothing. Neither male nor female as far as you're concerned.'

'But he or she is my client.'

'Knock it off, Greg. We have an understanding.'

'To know this much, he must have daily contact with the judge. A secretary maybe?'

'He or she told me once that McDover crushes secretaries, fires them after a year or two. Stop guessing, okay? The mole is living in fear. Have you filed the complaint?'

'Yes. They are investigating now and will slap it on the old gal in due course. Talk about shit hitting the fan. Can you imagine the horror show when McDover realizes her party is over?'

'She won't panic, because she's too cold and too smart,' Cooley said. 'She'll call in her lawyers and they'll get to work. She'll call Dubose and he'll start his mischief. What about you, Greg? Your name is on the complaint. You're making the allegations.'

'My name will be hard to trace. Remember, I've

never met McDover or Vonn Dubose. They don't know me from Adam. There are at least eighteen hundred Greg Myerses in this country and all have addresses, phone numbers, families, and jobs. Dubose won't know where to start looking. Besides, if I see a shadow I can haul ass in my little boat and become a speck in the ocean. He'll never find me. Why is the mole living in fear? His name will never be revealed.'

'Gee, Greg, I don't know. Maybe he or she is unsophisticated in the world of organized criminal violence. Maybe he or she is worried that divulging too much dirt on McDover might lead back to him or her.'

'Well, it's too late now,' Greg said. 'The complaint has been filed and the wheels are turning.'

'You gonna use this stuff anytime soon?' Cooley asked, waving some papers.

'I don't know. I need some time to think. Let's say they can prove the judge likes to travel on private jets with her partner. Big deal. McDover's lawyers will just say there's no foul as long as Phyllis is footing the bill, and since Phyllis has no cases pending in McDover's court, where's the damage?'

'Phyllis Turban runs a small shop in Mobile and her specialty is drawing up thick wills. I'll bet she nets a hundred and fifty a year max. The jets they're using cost $3,000 an hour and they're averaging eighty hours a year. Do the math. That's a quarter of a million bucks just in air charter fees, and that's just what we know about. As a circuit court judge McDover's salary this year is $146,000. Together they couldn't afford the jet fuel.'

'Phyllis Turban is not under investigation. Maybe she should be, I really don't care. If we're going to make any money off this case we have to nail a sitting judge.'

'Got it.'

'How often do you meet with the mole?' Myers asked.

'Not very often. He or she is quite timid these days, and scared to death.'

'Then why is he or she doing this?'

'Hatred of McDover. And money. I convinced our mole that this could lead to riches. I just hope I don't get anyone killed.'

Lacy lived in a two-bedroom apartment in a converted warehouse near the Florida State campus and a five-minute drive from her office. The architect who'd converted the building had done a fabulous job, and the twenty units had sold out quickly. Thanks to a loaded life insurance policy her father had maintained, and her mother's generosity, Lacy had been able to make a sizable down payment on her place. She suspected it would be the only nice gift from her parents. Her father had been dead for five years, and her mother, Ann Stoltz, seemed to grow stingier as she grew older. She was pushing seventy and not aging as well as Lacy would have liked. Ann no longer drove more than five miles from her home, so their visits had become less frequent.

Lacy's only companion was Frankie, her French bulldog. Since leaving for college at the age of eighteen, she had never lived with a man. Indeed, she had never been seriously tempted. A decade earlier, her one true love had begun hinting at cohabitation, but, as she soon learned, he was already plotting to run away with a married woman. Which he did, in scandalous fashion. The truth was that, at the age of thirty-six, Lacy was content to live alone, to sleep in the center of the bed, to clean up only after herself, to make and spend her own money, to come and go as she pleased, to pursue her career without worrying about his, to plan her evenings with input from no one else, to cook or not to cook, and to have sole possession of the remote control. About a third of her girlfriends were young divorcées, all scarred and wounded and wanting no part of another man, not for the moment anyway. Another third were stuck in bad marriages with little hope of getting out. And the rest of her girlfriends were content with their relationships and either pursuing careers or having children.

She didn't like the math. Nor did she like society's way of presuming she was unhappy because she had not found the right guy. Why should her life be determined by when and whom she married? She hated the assumption that she was lonely. If she'd never lived with a man, how could she miss one? And she was really tired of nosy inquiries from her family, especially her mother and her mother's sister, Aunt Trudy, neither of whom was capable of getting through a long conversation without asking if she was seeing anyone 'serious.'

'Who says I'm looking for anyone serious?' was her standard reply. She hated to admit it, but for the most part she preferred to avoid her mother and Trudy because of those conversations. Because she was happy and single and not prowling for Mr Right, they viewed her as a misfit, someone to be pitied because she was drifting through life all alone. Her mother was a perpetually grieving widow and Trudy had a dreadful husband, yet they somehow considered their lives better.

Oh well. Part of being single was dealing with the misconceptions of others.

She fixed another cup of green tea, caffeine free, and thought about watching an old movie. But it was almost ten, and a weeknight, and she needed sleep. Sadelle had e-mailed two of her latest memos, and Lacy decided to glance at one before she changed into her pajamas. For many years now she had known that Sadelle's memos were more effective than sleeping pills.

The thinner memo was titled 'Tappacola: Facts, Figures, Gossip.' And it read,

Population: Not sure of the exact number of Tappacola Native Americans (by the way, the term 'Native American' is a politically correct creation of clueless white people who feel better using it, when in reality the Native Americans refer to themselves as Indians and snicker at those of us who don't, but I digress). According to the Bureau of Indian Affairs, the 2010 population was 441, up from 402 in 2000. But the bonanza reaped by the casino has put new pressure on the population because, for the first time in history, so many more people seem desperate to become Tappacola. This is because of a distribution of wealth scheme commonly called 'dividends.' According to statements made by Junior Mace, every Tappacola eighteen or older gets a check for $5,000 a month. There is no way to verify this because, as in all matters, the tribe reports to no one. Once a woman marries, her monthly dividend is mysteriously cut in half.

Dividends vary greatly from tribe to tribe, from state to state. Years ago a tribe in Minnesota gained notoriety because its casino, which was grossing almost a billion a year, was owned by only 85 members. The annual dividend to each member topped $1 million. This is believed to still be the record.

There are 562 recognized tribes in the U.S., but only about 200 operate casinos. There are approximately 150 additional tribes seeking recognition, but the Feds have grown suspicious. New tribes face an uphill battle getting recognized. Many critics claim their sudden pride in their heritage is driven solely by the desire to get into the casino business. Most Indians do not share in these riches and many still live in poverty.

At any rate, like most tribes, the Tappacola have been inundated with folks claiming to be relatives. The dream of dividends has prompted this. The tribe has a committee that investigates and determines bloodlines. Anything less than being one-eighth Tappacola disqualifies the applicant. This has led to a lot of friction.

It appears as though friction is not unusual with the tribe. According to a story seven years ago in the *Pensacola News Journal,* the tribe holds an election every four years to elect a new Chief and council. There are ten council seats. Evidently the Chief has considerable power over all tribal matters, especially the casino. It must be an important position because the salary, at that time, was $350,000 a year. Also, the Chief is given wide latitude in employment matters and usually loads up the administration with family members, all of whom earn nice salaries. Therefore, the elections are hotly contested, bitter, and full of accusations of ballot stuffing and intimidation (must've learned this from us non-natives). It's sort of a winner-take-all scenario.

The current Chief is Elias Cappel (by the way, very few modern-day Indians use the colorful names from the old days; at some point in history most of them adopted Western names). Chief Cappel was elected in 2005 and reelected handily four years later. His son, Billy, sits on the council.

The tribe has used its money wisely, having built state-of-the-art schools, a free medical facility that appears to be more like a clinic than a hospital, recreational facilities, day care centers, roads, and most things good government provides. If a high school graduate wants to go to college, there is a fund to cover tuition to an in-state school, along with room and board. The tribe is also pouring more money into alcohol and drug prevention and treatment.

As a sovereign nation, the Tappacola make and enforce their own laws, with no real regard for outside interference. The tribe has a constable who operates much like a county sheriff, and a full force of cops, all apparently well trained and equipped. It has a beefed-up drug enforcement unit. (Tight-lipped as they are, the Chief and a few council members apparently don't mind divulging facts that tend to favor them, strong law enforcement being one of their favorite topics.) They have a tribal court consisting of three judges to deal with disputes and wrongdoing. The judges are appointed by the Chief and approved by the council. There is, of course, a jail, and a correctional facility for long-term offenders.

The Tappacola do an effective job of keeping their disputes and controversies contained. For years the *Pensacola News Journal,* and to a lesser extent the *Tallahassee Democrat,* have been snooping around looking for dirt, really just trying to find out how much money the tribe was making and which faction had the upper hand. Both newspapers have learned little. Evidently, the Tappacola are a closemouthed bunch of folks.

Though somewhat interesting, the memo worked its magic and Lacy began yawning. She changed into pajamas and went through her nightly rituals in the bathroom, with the door open, once again thankful that she was alone with no one to bother her. Just before 11:00 p.m., she was almost asleep when the phone rang. It was Hugo, sounding as tired as ever.

'This can't be good,' she said.

'No. Look, we need some help tonight. Verna's dead on her feet. I'm not much better. Pippin is at full throttle and the whole house is wired. We gotta get some sleep. Verna doesn't want my mother over here and I don't want hers. How about a big favor?'

'Sure. I'm on the way.'

It was the third time since the newborn's arrival that Lacy had been called in for midnight duty. She had kept the four kids on several occasions so Hugo and Verna could enjoy a quiet dinner, but only twice had she slept over. She dressed quickly in jeans and a T-shirt and left Frankie at the door, obviously confused. She hurried through the empty streets to the Meadows and arrived at the Hatch home twenty minutes after the phone call. Verna met her at the door, with Pippin, who was quiet for the moment. 'It's got to be a stomachache,' she whispered. 'She's been to the doctor three times this week. Kid just can't seem to sleep.'

'Where are the bottles?' Lacy asked, gingerly taking the baby from her mother.

'On the coffee table. The house is a wreck. I'm so sorry.' Her lip quivered and her eyes watered.

'Come on, Verna, it's me. Go to bed and get some sleep. Things will be better in the morning.'

Verna pecked her on the cheek and said, 'Thank you.' She disappeared into the hallway. Lacy heard a door close quietly. She squeezed Pippin and began walking back and forth across the cluttered den, humming gently and patting her on the rear. Everything was quiet but the lull didn't last. When she erupted again, Lacy stuck a bottle in her mouth

93

and settled into a rocking chair, cooing at her nonstop until she finally drifted away. Half an hour later, with the baby in a deep sleep, Lacy placed her in a portable rocking crib and turned on the switch for a quiet lullaby. Pippin frowned and fidgeted a bit, and for a moment seemed ready for another round of noise, but then relaxed and continued her nap.

After some time, Lacy left the baby and tiptoed into the kitchen, where she turned on the overhead light and was startled at the chaos. The sink was filled with dirty dishes. The counters were covered with pots and pans and food that needed to be put away. The table was strewn with empty snack boxes, backpacks, and even unfolded laundry. The kitchen needed a good scrubbing, but a proper job would be too noisy. She decided to wait until daybreak when the family was stirring. She turned off the kitchen light and, in one of those delightful moments that she could share with no one, smiled and thanked her good fortune at being single and so wonderfully unburdened.

She made a nest on the sofa near the baby and eventually fell asleep. Pippin awoke hungry and angry at 3:15, but a bottle thrust firmly into her mouth did the trick. Lacy changed her diaper, cooed and cajoled her into another nap, and slept until almost 6:00.

CHAPTER 8

Wilton Mace lived in a redbrick split-level on a gravel road two miles from the casino. On the phone he'd been reluctant to talk and said he would have to check with his brother. He called Hugo back the following day and agreed to a meeting. He was waiting in a lawn chair under a tree by the carport, swatting flies and drinking iced tea. The day was cloudy and not as hot. He offered Lacy and Hugo sweet tea to drink and they declined. He pointed to two other folding chairs and they sat down. A toddler in a diaper was playing in a plastic wading pool in the backyard, under the watchful eye of its grandmother.

Wilton was three years younger than Junior and could almost pass for his identical twin. Dark skin, even darker eyes, long gray hair, almost to his shoulders. He spoke with a deep voice and, like Junior, seemed to weigh every syllable.

'Is that your grandson?' Lacy asked, trying to break the ice because Wilton showed no interest in doing so.

'Granddaughter, the first one. That's my wife, Nell.'

95

'We met with Junior last week at Starke,' Hugo said.

'Thank you for going to see him. I make the trip twice a month and I know it's not the best way to spend the day. Junior has been forgotten by his people, and that's tough on a man, especially one as proud as Junior.'

'He said that most Tappacola believe he killed his wife and Son Razko,' Lacy said.

He nodded for a long time, then said, 'That's true. It's a good story, easy to repeat, easy to believe. He caught 'em in bed and shot 'em.'

'Can we assume you've talked to him since we were there?' Hugo asked.

'I called him yesterday. He gets twenty minutes a day on the phone. He told me what you're up to.'

'He said you tried to get a job at the casino but it didn't happen. Can you explain that?' Lacy asked.

'It's simple. The tribe is split down the middle with both sides entrenched. Goes back to the vote on gambling. The winners built the casino and their Chief runs everything, including the hiring and firing. Me, I was on the wrong side so I couldn't get a job. It takes two thousand people to run the casino and most of them are from the outside. The Tappacola who want to work must have their politics right to get a job there.'

'So feelings are still pretty raw?' Hugo asked.

Wilton grunted and smiled. 'We may as well be

two tribes, and blood enemies at that. There's been no effort at reconciliation. No one wants it, really.'

Lacy said, 'Junior says he and Son were wrong to fight the casino because it's been good for the tribe. You agree?'

Another long pause as he arranged his thoughts. His granddaughter began crying and was taken inside. He took a sip of tea and finally said, 'It's always hard to admit you're wrong, but I suppose we were. The casino has lifted us out of poverty and given us nice things, so that's a positive, a big one. We are healthier, happier, secure. There's a certain satisfaction in watching outsiders flock in here and hand us their cash. We feel like we're finally getting something back, perhaps a bit of revenge. Some of us worry, though, about living a life that's so grounded on handouts. Idleness leads to trouble. We're seeing more alcohol. Our kids are using more drugs.'

Hugo asked, 'If life is more prosperous, why aren't there more children?'

'Stupidity. The council is dominated by idiots and they make bad rules. When a woman turns eighteen, she is entitled to the monthly check, which has been $5,000 for many years now. But if she marries, then it's cut in half. I get $5,000; my wife gets $2,500. So, more and more of our young women frown on marriage. The men are drinking and causing trouble, so why bother with a husband when you get more money without one? There's also the theory that a reduction in our population means larger checks for those who survive. Another bad plan. You have to invest in children for a healthy society.'

Lacy glanced at Hugo and said, 'We should talk about McDover.'

'I know little about the judge,' Wilton said. 'I sat through the trial and thought she was too young and too inexperienced. She did nothing to protect the rights of my brother. She has been attacked on appeal, but her rulings have been upheld, often by the thinnest of margins.'

'You've read the appeals?' Hugo asked.

'I've read everything, Mr Hatch. Many times. My brother is facing death for crimes he did not commit. The least I can do is sweat the details and support him. And, obviously, I do have plenty of time.'

'Was Son Razko having an affair with Junior's wife?' Hugo asked.

'Highly unlikely, though, as you know, when it comes to that type of behavior anything can happen. Son was a man of principle and morals and he was happily married. I have never believed he was carrying on with my sister-in-law.'

'So who killed them?'

'I do not know. Not long after the casino opened, we began receiving our slice of the pie, though in smaller amounts. At the time I was a truck driver, non-union of course, and with my salary, my wife's wages as a cook, plus our dividend checks, we were able to save $25,000. I gave the money to a private investigator in Pensacola. He was supposed to be one of the best. He dug for the better part of a year and found nothing. My brother had a terrible lawyer at trial, a clueless kid who didn't know his way around the courtroom, but he's had some fine lawyers on appeal. They've been digging too, for many years, and they've found nothing. I cannot give you the name of a likely suspect, Mr Hatch. I wish I could. My brother was framed in a perfect setup, and it looks like the State of Florida will eventually kill him.'

'Do you know a man named Vonn Dubose?' Lacy asked.

'I've heard the name but never met the man.'

'What's the reputation?'

Wilton rattled the ice cubes in his glass and suddenly looked tired. Lacy felt sorry for him, and tried to imagine the weight of having a sibling on death row, especially one believed to be innocent. He finally said, 'There was once a legend around here that a big-time crook named Dubose masterminded all of this – the casino, the developments around it, the rapid sprawl from here to the coast. The legend extended to the murders of Son and Eileen. But it's all faded now, washed away in a tide of fun and games and cash and jackpots and waterslides and happy hours, not to mention the welfare state. It doesn't matter now, because life is good. If the man really exists and has his finger in the pie, no one cares, no one wants to cause him any trouble. If he walked through the front door of the casino and told the truth, he would be worshipped like a hero. He made it happen.'

'What do you believe?'

'What I believe doesn't matter, Mr Hatch.'

'Okay, it doesn't matter, but I'm still curious.'

'All right. Yes, there was an organized criminal element involved with the construction of the casino, and these guys, nameless and faceless, are still taking a cut. They use guns and they have thoroughly intimidated our Chief and his cronies.'

Lacy asked, 'What are our chances of finding someone from inside the casino who'll talk to us?'

He actually laughed, and when the moment passed he mumbled, 'You just don't understand.' He rattled his ice again and seemed to fixate on something across the road. Lacy and Hugo glanced at each other and waited. After a long gap, he said, 'As a tribe, a people, a race, we don't trust outsiders. We don't talk. Sure, I'm sitting here talking to you, but the subjects are general in nature. We don't tell secrets, not to anyone, not under any circumstances. It's just not in our blood. I despise my people who are on the other side, but I would never tell you anything about them.'

Lacy said, 'Perhaps a disgruntled employee, someone without your discretion. With all of this division and distrust, there must be a few people who are unhappy with the Chief and his cronies.'

'There are some people who hate the Chief, but bear in mind he got 70 percent of the vote in the last election. His inner circle is tight. They all have fingers in the pie and everyone is happy. It would be virtually impossible to find a snitch from within.' He paused and went silent. They endured another long gap, one that seemed not to bother him at all. Finally, he said, 'And I would advise you to stay away from it. If Judge McDover is in with the crooks, then she's well protected by some boys who like violence and intimidation. This is Indian land, Ms Stoltz, and all the rules that govern an orderly society, all the things you believe in, simply don't apply here. We govern ourselves. We make the laws. Neither the State of Florida nor the federal government has much say in what we do, especially when it comes to running the casino.'

They left him after an hour, after learning nothing that might help them, other than the warning, and returned to the Tappacola Tollway, the busy four-lane the county had built to rake off a few bucks. Near the entrance to the reservation, they stopped at a booth and paid five bucks for the privilege of proceeding. Hugo said, 'I suppose this is the spot where Judge McDover decided to stop the traffic with her injunction.'

'Have you read that case?' Lacy asked as she accelerated.

'I read Sadelle's summary. The judge claimed the traffic was a threat to public health and blocked the road with deputies for six days. Two thousand and one, ten years ago.'

'Can you imagine the conversations between her and Vonn Dubose?'

'She's lucky she didn't catch a bullet.'

'No, she's too smart for that. So is Dubose. They managed to find common ground and the injunction was lifted.'

Immediately past the booth they were greeted with gaudy signs telling them that they were now on Tappacola land. Other signs pointed the way to Rabbit Run, and in the distance there were waves of condos and homes lining fairways. Its property line was adjacent to the reservation, and, as Greg Myers had said, a person could walk from the golf shop to the casino in five minutes. On a map, the Tappacola property had more bends and jags than a carefully gerrymandered congressional district. Dubose and company had gobbled up most of the property around it. And someone, probably Dubose himself, had picked the casino site as close to his land as possible. It was brilliant.

They rounded a sweeping curve and the massive casino was before them, its soaring entrance in the center awash with neon and swirling spotlights. It was anchored on each end with matching high-rise hotels. They parked in a crowded lot and caught a shuttle to the front, where they split and roamed the gaming floors for an hour. They met at 4:00 p.m. for coffee in a bar overlooking the craps and blackjack tables and watched the action. With the piped-in music, the constant jangle of slot machines dumping coins onto the winners, the roar of voices at a hot craps table, and the boisterous sounds of people drinking too much, it was obvious that some serious cash was changing hands.

CHAPTER 9

The director of the Florida Gaming Commission was Eddie Naylor, a former state senator who had happily surrendered his seat for the fat salary the new agency offered when casino gambling arrived in the early 1990s and the state felt compelled to try and regulate it. His office was three blocks from Lacy's, and the meeting had been easy to arrange. Far from the grungy digs of the Board on Judicial Conduct, his suite was in a modern building with fine furnishings, a bustling staff, and apparently no budget constraints. Florida was happily in the gambling business and its pliant taxing schemes were working smoothly.

One look at Lacy and Naylor decided he should leave his large desk and chat around the coffee table. At least twice before the coffee arrived, she caught him glancing at her legs, which were on full display courtesy of a skirt that was almost too short. After some preliminaries she said, 'Obviously, our office investigates complaints against nonfederal judges in the state. There are a lot of them, and they keep us busy. Our investigations are

104

confidential, so I ask for your cooperation in that regard.'

'Certainly,' Naylor said. Nothing about the guy inspired trust, from his shifty eyes and greasy smile to his ill-fitting suit and dress shirt straining at the buttons. Probably has a generous expense account, she thought. He could easily pass for another lobbyist working the streets of Tallahassee.

To impress her, he went through a windy summary of duties of 'his commission.' All gambling in the state had been herded into one oversight agency, and he was the man in charge. Horse racing, dog racing, lottery, slots, casinos, cruise ships, even jai alai, were now under his jurisdiction. It seemed to be a mammoth undertaking, but he was up to the task.

'How much oversight do you have over the Indian casinos?' she asked.

'All casinos in Florida are run by the Indians, the Seminoles being by far the largest tribe and biggest operators. Frankly, though, and to be perfectly candid, when it comes to the Indian casinos we have very little oversight and control. A tribe that has federal recognition is its own nation and makes its own laws. In Florida, we have entered into treaties with all casino operators, and this allows us to collect a small tax on their profits. Very small, but it adds up. There are now nine casinos and they are all doing quite well.'

'Can you go into a casino and inspect its operations?'

He shook his head gravely and admitted, 'No, nor can we check the books. Each casino files a quarterly report showing its gross revenues and net profits, and we tax from there. But, frankly, we have to take their word for it.'

'So a casino can submit whatever it wants?'

'Yes, that's the current state of the law, and it's not likely to change.'

'And a casino pays no federal tax of any kind?'

'That's correct. By entering into treaties, we sort of cajole them into paying a little to the state. We do this by building a road here or there, and by providing a few services like emergency medical treatment and some educational support. On occasion they'll ask for the state's help for this and for that. But, truthfully, it's completely voluntary. If a tribe says no to any form of taxation, there's nothing we can do. Fortunately, none of them have taken that position.'

'How much do they pay?'

'One half of 1 percent of net. Last year that was about $40 million. It funds the bulk of our commission and the rest goes into the Florida rainy-day fund. May I ask where this is going?'

'Sure. A formal complaint has been filed alleging some bad behavior by a circuit court judge. It involves a developer who's apparently in bed with a tribe and its casino and a judge who's sharing in the profits.'

Naylor set down his coffee cup and shook his head. 'Quite frankly, Ms Stoltz, I'm not that surprised. If a casino wants to fudge on its financials and skim cash off the top, or under the table, doesn't really matter, there's little to stop it from doing so. It's a perfect storm for corruption. You start with people who are not that sophisticated, and suddenly they're raking in more profits than are imaginable. They attract all manner of crooks and con men who want to help. Add the fact that most of the business is in cash that's absolutely untraceable, and it's just a bad mix. We here at the commission are often frustrated by our lack of oversight.'

'So corruption does happen?'

'I didn't say it happens. I said the potential is there.'

'But nobody's watching?'

He recrossed his thick legs and thought about this. 'Well, the FBI has the authority to investigate wrongdoing on Indian land, any kind of bad behavior. That's pretty intimidating, I suppose. And again, these folks are not that sophisticated, so the idea of the Feds poking around keeps them in line. I should add that most of our casinos contract with reputable companies who know how to run casinos.'

'Could the FBI go in with warrants and grab the books?'

'I'm not sure. It's never been done, as far as I know. And over the past twenty years the FBI has shown little interest in Indian affairs.'

'Why is that?'

'Don't know exactly, but I suspect it's a question of manpower. The FBI is focused on fighting terror and cybercrime. A bit of swindling in an Indian casino is of little interest. Why bother? The Indians have never had it so good, at least not in the past two hundred years.' He dropped another cube of sugar into his coffee and stirred it with a finger. 'This wouldn't be the Tappacola, would it?'

'It is.'

'I'm not that surprised.'

'And why not?'

'There have been rumors over the years.' He took a sip and waited for the follow-up.

'Okay. What kinds of rumors?'

'Outside influence. Some shady guys got involved from the beginning and are making a killing on developments around the casino. Just suspicions, that's all. Our job does not include investigating crimes so we don't go near it. If we learn of wrongdoing, we're supposed to notify the FBI.'

'Rumors about skimming cash?'

He was shaking his head. 'No, haven't heard that one.'

'Rumors about a judge?'

Still shaking, he said, 'No. I'd be surprised if that were true.'

'It is surprising, but we have a source.'

'Well, there is a lot of cash, and it does strange things to people. I'd be very careful, Ms Stoltz. Very careful.'

'You seem to know more than you're willing to tell.'

'Not at all.'

'Okay. But please remember that our investigations are confidential.'

'You have my word.'

While Lacy was making her first and only call to the Florida Gaming Commission, her partner was making his first and only visit to a golf course. At the suggestion of Michael Geismar, and borrowing his seldom-used clubs, Hugo cajoled a BJC colleague named Justin Barrow into faking a round of golf. Justin had leaned on a friend who knew someone else, and after a fair amount of discreet manipulation and outright lying, a guest tee time at Rabbit Run had been arranged. Justin was a weekend player; thus, he knew the basic rules and enough etiquette not to arouse suspicions. Hugo had neither a clue nor a shred of interest. In the world he grew up in, golf was a white man's game played at white country clubs.

The first tee box at Rabbit Run East was around the corner from the driving range and clubhouse, so no one noticed when Justin teed off and Hugo did not. It was 10:30 on an August morning, the temperature was already above ninety, and the course was deserted. Though Hugo, the driver of the golf cart, knew nothing about the game, he chose not to withhold his comments about Justin's lack of skill. When Justin failed on three consecutive sand shots to get the ball out of a green-side bunker, Hugo was amused to the point of laughing out loud. On the third green, Hugo grabbed his borrowed putter and a ball and figured anybody could tap it into the cup. When it repeatedly failed to drop in from only ten feet away, Justin unleashed an avalanche of trash talk.

Using satellite photos, they had located the four condos allegedly owned, in one way or another, by Judge Claudia McDover. Geismar wanted site visits and photos. Standing at the fourth tee box, Hugo and Justin gazed at the long par 5, dogleg left, and studied a row of handsome condos 250 yards away and out-of-bounds to the right.

Hugo said, 'By now I know most of your shots go out-of-bounds, so try and place your tee shot over there by those condos. A hard slice, one of your specialties.'

Justin replied, 'Why don't you take a shot, big guy, and see how easy it is?'

'Game on.' Hugo stuck a tee in the grass, placed a ball on it, addressed the ball, tried to relax, and took a long easy swing. The ball went a mile in the air and slowly began to hook left. The hook gained momentum, and by the time the ball disappeared into the woods it was out of sight. Without a word, he yanked another ball out of his pocket, placed it on the tee, and with even more determination took a hack. The drive shot forward, low and hard, and slowly gained altitude. It appeared to be headed straight for the condos to the right but soon rose high enough to sail over them.

Justin said, 'Well, at least you're using the entire course. Those two shots are a mile apart and way out-of-bounds.'

'It's my first time out.'

'So I've heard.' Justin teed it up and looked at the fairway. 'I gotta be careful here because good contact could send the ball into the condos. Don't want to break any glass.'

'Just give it a ride and I'll spend some time looking for it.'

The shot went just as planned, a hard slice that rolled out-of-bounds and into some shrubbery bordering the condos. 'Perfect,' Hugo said.

'Gee, thanks.'

They hopped in the golf cart and sped down the middle of the fairway, then eased right, toward the condos. Justin dropped a ball onto the grass as if it were his tee shot, and he pulled out a small device that appeared to be a laser range finder, one used to measure the distance from his ball to the flag. It was really a video camera, and while Hugo nonchalantly strolled over to the edge of the patio of unit 1614D as if hunting a lost ball, Justin shot close-up footage of the condo. Hugo had on his belt a small digital camera that snapped stills as he poked through some shrubs with his seven iron.

Just a couple of bad golfers hunting lost balls. Happened every day, whether someone was watching or not.

Three hours later, after searching for many lost

balls, Hugo and Justin called it quits. As they drove away from the pro shop, Hugo silently vowed to never again set foot on a golf course.

On the way back to Tallahassee, they detoured to the small town of Eckman for a quick chat with a lawyer named Al Bennett. He had a nice office on Main Street and seemed to welcome Hugo to break the monotony of drafting deeds. Justin found a coffee shop to kill the hour.

Five years earlier, Bennett had entered politics for the first and last time when he challenged the reelection of Claudia McDover. He campaigned hard and spent too much money, and when only 31 percent of the voters favored him he hustled back home to Eckman with a diminished desire to serve the public. On the phone, Hugo had revealed nothing and promised just a few quick questions about a local judge.

In person, Hugo explained that the BJC was investigating a complaint against Judge McDover, that the investigation was confidential, and that the complaint could well be frivolous. It was a sensitive matter and Hugo needed Bennett's word that all would be kept quiet.

'Of course,' Bennett said, eager to be involved and a little excited. As they talked, Hugo wondered how the guy managed to get even 31 percent of the vote. He spoke rapidly, nervously, with a high-pitched voice that was obnoxious to the ears. Hugo could not imagine him on the stump or in front of a jury.

Hugo was wary of the meeting. Lawyers could usually be trusted to keep secrets that involved their own clients, but were often horrible gossips when it came to everyone else. The more witnesses they interviewed the more leaks there would be, and before long Judge McDover and her confederates would know they were being shadowed. Lacy agreed, but Geismar wanted to put a check in Bennett's box.

Hugo asked, 'Was it a rough campaign?'

Bennett replied, 'Well, you could say the outcome was rough. Hell, I got clobbered in a landslide. It hurt, but I'm almost over it.'

'Was it dirty?'

He thought for a moment and seemed to resist the temptation to trash his former opponent. 'It never got too personal. She made much of the fact that I have no experience on the bench. I couldn't argue with that, so I tried to take the high road and say, well, she didn't have any experience either until she got elected. But it took too long to explain this, and, as you know, voters have short attention spans. Plus, Mr Hatch, you gotta keep in mind that Judge McDover has a good reputation.'

'Did you attack her?'

'Not really. Couldn't find much.'

'Did anyone allege ethical violations on her part?'

He shook his head. 'No.' Then he asked, 'What kinds of ethical violations are you investigating?'

Hugo made the quick decision to avoid anything of substance. If Bennett went through a tough campaign against McDover and heard no rumors of misconduct, Hugo was not about to reveal the allegations. 'You heard nothing?' Hugo asked.

Bennett shrugged as if he had nothing. 'Not really. A long time ago she had a bad divorce. She's still single, lives alone, no kids, no real community involvement. We weren't looking for dirt and none came to the surface. Sorry.'

'That's okay. Thanks for your time.'

Leaving Eckman, with another check in the box, Hugo was certain he had wasted an entire day in the pursuit of Claudia McDover.

Lacy found the widow of Son Razko living in a small subdivision near Fort Walton Beach, about an hour from the Tappacola reservation. Since she'd remarried she was not technically a widow. Her name was Louise, and she was at first reluctant to talk. Halfway through the second phone call she agreed to meet at a waffle house and speak briefly. Since she had a job she was not available until after work. Lacy drove three hours and met her at 6:00 p.m. on the same day that Hugo buzzed around Rabbit Run in a golf cart.

According to the file and the records, Louise Razko had been thirty-one years old when her husband was found murdered, and naked, and in the same bedroom with the wife of Junior Mace. She and Son had two children, now young adults, and both had left Florida. Louise had remarried a few years earlier and moved away from the reservation.

She was pushing fifty, with gray hair and a squat figure. The years were not being good to her.

Lacy explained what she was up to, but Louise showed little interest. 'I am not going to talk about the murders and all that,' she said initially.

'Fine. Off-limits. Do you remember Judge McDover?'

She sipped iced tea through a straw and gave the impression of wanting desperately to be somewhere else. Finally, she shrugged and said, 'Only from the trial.'

'So you watched the trial?' Lacy asked, a throwaway, anything to ramp up the conversation.

'Of course I watched the trial. All of it.'

'What did you think of the judge?'

'Why does it matter now? The trial was many years ago. Are you investigating the judge for something she did back then?'

'No, not at all. The complaint we are investigating centers on allegations that the judge is involved in a conspiracy to take bribes and such. It all revolves around the casino.'

'I prefer not to talk about the casino. It is a blight on my people.'

Great, Louise! If we can't talk about the casino and we can't talk about your husband's murder, then why exactly did I drive all the way over here? Lacy scribbled on a notepad, as if deep in thought.

'Have any of your family members ever worked in the casino?'

'Why do you ask?'

'Because we need information about the casino and it's proving rather hard to find. Someone on the inside could be of great assistance.'

'You can forget that. No one will talk to you. The people who work there are happy to have jobs and to get the checks. The people who cannot work there are envious, maybe even bitter, but also content with their checks. No one is going to upset the casino.'

'Have you ever heard the name of Vonn Dubose?'

'No. Who is he?'

'What if I told you he is probably the man who killed your husband to get him out of the way so he could build a casino? Would you believe that?' Lacy did in fact believe it; the problem was that she had so little proof. She made the rather bold suggestion in an effort to jolt Louise into a conversation.

Louise took another sip and stared through a window. Lacy was learning a few things about the Tappacola. First, and not surprisingly, they did not trust outsiders. Couldn't blame them for that. Second, they were in no hurry when discussing matters. They were prone to slow, thoughtful speech, and long gaps in the conversation never seemed to bother them.

Finally, Louise looked at Lacy and said, 'Junior Mace killed my husband. It was proven in court. I was humiliated.'

116

As firmly as possible, Lacy said, 'What if Junior did not kill your husband? What if he and Eileen Mace were killed by the same criminals who convinced the Tappacola to build the casino, the same people who've made a fortune from the developments around the casino, the same people who are in all likelihood skimming large amounts of cash from the business? And these same people are in business with Judge McDover. Does this shock you, Louise?'

Her eyes watered and a tear spilled onto her right cheek. 'How do you know this?' she asked. After having believed one version for so many years, it would be difficult to suddenly believe something else.

'Because we're investigators. That's what we do.'

'But the crime was investigated by the police many years ago.'

'It was a bogus trial that produced a wrongful conviction. The two star witnesses were both jail-house snitches who were coerced by the cops and prosecutors to lie to the jury.'

'I said I didn't want to talk about the murders.'

'Right. So let's talk about the casino. I don't expect you to cooperate until you've thought about it carefully. But we need names of people, your people, who know what's happening. If you give us a name or two no one will ever know. I promise. It's our job to protect the identity of our witnesses.'

'I know nothing, Ms Stoltz. I have never set foot in the casino; never will. My family too. Most of us have moved away. Sure, we take the checks because it's our land, but the casino has destroyed the soul of our people. I know nothing about it. I despise the place and the people who run it.'

She was convincing and Lacy knew the conversation was over.

Another check in the box.

CHAPTER 10

Michael Geismar paced along one wall of his office, tie loosened, sleeves rolled up, with the harried look of an investigator who'd bumped into too many dead ends. Lacy was holding a photo of one of McDover's condos and wondering how it could be of any value. Hugo, as usual, was sipping another caffeine-laced energy drink and trying to stay awake. Sadelle was pecking on her laptop, chasing another elusive fact.

Michael said, 'We got nothing. Four condos owned by offshore companies owned by somebody deep in the shadows, somebody we can't identify. When confronted, Judge McDover, through her legal team no doubt, will simply deny ownership or claim she bought the condos as investments. Such investing might give the impression of impropriety, given her salary, but it's hardly a breach of judicial ethics. I don't have to remind you that she will lawyer up with enough legal talent to stall for the next decade. We need a lot more dirt.'

Hugo said, 'I'm not playing any more golf. What a waste of time, in more ways than one.'

Michael replied, 'Okay, bad call on my part. You have any better ideas?'

Lacy said, 'We're not giving up, Michael. We've uncovered enough to believe that Greg Myers is telling the truth, or at least something very close to it. We can't walk away.'

'I'm not suggesting that, not now. In three weeks, we have to either serve the complaint on McDover or inform Greg Myers that our initial assessment leads us to believe that his complaint has no merit. I think we all agree that it has merit. So, we serve the complaint, then subpoenas for all of her files and records. At that point, she'll be hiding behind a wall of lawyers, so every request we make will be contested. Let's say we eventually get her files. Court files, legal files, files relating to the cases she has heard or is currently handling. We still subpoena her personal financial records unless we have probable cause to believe that she has committed theft, bribery, or embezzlement.'

'We know the statute,' Hugo said.

'Of course we do, Hugo, but just humor me, okay? I'm trying to assess where we are, and since I'm the boss I'm allowed to do so. You want to go back to the golf course?'

'Please, no.'

'Anyone sophisticated enough to operate behind such elaborate shell companies is probably not going to keep her personal financial records in any place where we might find them, right?'

Lacy and Hugo nodded, pleasantly humoring the boss.

And then there was silence. Michael kept pacing and scratching his head. Hugo sipped his caffeine and tried to activate his brain. Lacy doodled on her legal pad, thinking. The only sound was the pecking from Sadelle's keyboard.

Michael finally said, 'Sadelle, you've been quiet.'

'I'm just a paralegal,' she reminded them. Then she coughed, almost gagged, and continued, 'I've gone back eleven years and tracked thirty-three construction projects in Brunswick County, everything from golf courses, shopping centers, subdivisions, the mini-mall at Sea Stall, even a movie theater with fourteen screens. Nylan Title from the Bahamas is involved in many of them, but there are dozens of other offshore companies that own other offshore companies, and LLCs that are owned by foreign corporations. Personally, I think it's a clear sign of somebody trying real hard to keep things secret. It smells bad. It's also unprecedented, really, to see so many offshore companies paying so much attention to a backward place like Brunswick County. I've dug some in the records of the other Panhandle counties – Okaloosa, Walton, even Escambia, where Pensacola sits – and while all of them have had far more development than Brunswick, they have far fewer offshore companies involved.'

'No luck with Nylan Title?' Hugo asked.

'None. The laws and procedures in the Bahamas

121

are impossible to penetrate. Impossible, unless of course the FBI gets involved.'

'That will have to wait.' Michael looked at Lacy and asked, 'Have you talked to Myers lately?'

'Oh no. I talk to Myers only when he decides he wants to talk.'

'Well, it's time for a conversation. It's time to inform Mr Myers that his complaint is in jeopardy. If he can't come through with more information, and quickly, then we might have to dismiss it.'

'Are you serious?' Lacy asked.

'Not really, not yet. But let's keep the pressure on him. He's the one with the inside source.'

It took two days and a dozen calls to three different cell phone numbers to get a response from Myers. When he finally called her back, he seemed excited to hear her voice and said he'd been thinking about another meeting. He had more information to pass along. Lacy asked if he might be able to meet at a more convenient place. St Augustine was lovely and all, but it was a three-and-a-half-hour drive for them. They had busy schedules; evidently he did not. For obvious reasons, he preferred to stay away from the Panhandle. 'Lots of old enemies there,' he sort of bragged. They agreed on Mexico Beach, a small Gulf-side town about two hours southeast of Tallahassee. They met at a local dive near the beach and ordered grilled shrimp for lunch.

Myers rambled on about his bonefishing exploits

near Belize and his scuba-diving adventures in the British Virgins. His tan was even darker and he looked a bit thinner. Not for the first time, Hugo caught himself envying the carefree lifestyle of this guy who lived on a nice boat and apparently had no financial worries. He drank beer from a cold, frosty mug, something else Hugo envied. Lacy was far from envious and found Myers even more irritating. She couldn't have cared less about his various adventures. She wanted facts, details, proof that his story was valid.

With a mouthful of shrimp, Myers asked, 'So how is the investigation going?'

'Pretty slow,' Lacy said. 'Our boss is pressuring us to find more dirt or we may have to dismiss your complaint. And, the clock is ticking.'

He stopped chomping, wiped his mouth with the back of his wrist, and removed his sunglasses. 'You can't dismiss the complaint. I swore to it, on my oath. McDover owns the four condos and they were given to her as bribes.'

Hugo asked, 'And how do we prove this when everything is buried offshore? We've hit brick walls there. All the records are tucked away in Barbados, Grand Cayman, Belize. Throw a dart at the offshore map and we've chased leads there, with no evidence. It's one thing to swear under oath she owns the companies that owns the condos, but we need proof, Greg.'

He smiled, took a chug of beer, and said, 'I got it. Just wait.'

Lacy and Hugo looked at each other. Greg stabbed another shrimp with his fork, drowned it in cocktail sauce, and shoved it in. 'You guys gonna eat?'

They poked around their shrimp baskets with their plastic forks, neither with much of an appetite. Evidently, Myers had not eaten in a while, and was thirsty, but he was also stalling. An odd-looking couple had the table next to them, too close for a serious conversation. They left as the waitress brought Myers his second beer.

'We're waiting,' Lacy said.

'Okay, okay,' he said as he took a sip and again wiped his mouth with the back of his hand. 'On the first Wednesday of every month, the judge leaves her office in Sterling an hour or so early and drives about twenty minutes to one of her condos in Rabbit Run. She parks her Lexus in the driveway, gets out, and walks to the front door. Two weeks ago she was wearing a navy sleeveless dress and pumps from Jimmy Choo, and she was carrying a small Chanel handbag, the same one she left the office with. She walked to the front door and unlocked it with her key. Proof of ownership, exhibit one. I have photographs. About an hour later, a Mercedes SUV parked next to the Lexus and a guy got out on the front passenger's side. The driver stayed behind the wheel, never moved. The passenger walked to the front door. I have photographs, and, yes, ladies and gentlemen, I think we finally have a glimpse of the elusive

Vonn Dubose. He was carrying a brown leather satchel that appeared to be filled with something. As he pressed the doorbell, he glanced around, and did not appear to be the least bit nervous. She let him in. He stayed thirty-six minutes, and when he reappeared he was carrying what looked like the same bag, though by the way he carried it, he might have left something behind. Can't really tell. He got in his vehicle and left. Fifteen minutes later, she did the same. This meeting takes place, as I said, on the first Wednesday of every month, and we are led to believe it is prearranged without the benefit of phones or e-mail.'

Myers shoved his empty shrimp basket aside, took another swallow, and from his ever-present olive-colored leather courier bag removed two unmarked files. He glanced around and handed one file to Lacy and one to Hugo. All the photos were eight by ten and in color, and apparently taken from across the street. Number one was the rear of the Lexus with the license plate clearly identifiable.

Greg said, 'Of course I checked the tags; car's registered to our gal Claudia McDover, evidently one of the few assets in her name. Purchased new last year from a dealer in Pensacola.'

Number two was full length of Claudia, her face partially hidden behind large sunglasses. Lacy studied her four-inch heels and asked, 'How do you know who designed the shoes?'

'The mole knows,' Myers said, and left it at that.

Number three was Claudia with her back to the camera as she opened the front door, presumably with a key, though one was not visible. Number four was the black Mercedes SUV parked beside the Lexus, its license plate also clearly visible. Myers said, 'It's registered to a man whose address is a high-rise condo near Destin, and not surprisingly his name is not Vonn Dubose. We're still digging. Take a look at number five.'

Number five was the man himself, a nice-looking, well-tanned Florida retiree in a golf shirt and golf slacks, thin and balding with a gold watch on his left wrist. Myers said, 'To my knowledge, and I have no idea what's in the FBI files, but I suspect they have nothing, this is the only photo of Vonn Dubose.'

'Who took it?' Lacy asked.

'Guy with a camera. It's also on video. Let's just say the mole is resourceful.'

'Not good enough, Greg,' Lacy shot back with a flash of anger. 'It's obvious someone is watching McDover's movements. Who is it? You're still playing cat and mouse and I'd like to know why.'

Hugo said, 'Look, Greg, we need to trust you, but we have to know what you know. Someone is following McDover. Who the hell is it?'

Out of habit, and an irritating one, Myers glanced around again, saw things were still clear, removed his aviator shades, and said in a low voice, 'I get my information from the middleman, still unnamed as far as you're concerned. He deals with the mole, whose name I still don't know and I'm still not sure I want to know. When the mole has something important to pass along, the middleman tracks me down, hands it over, I give it to you. I'm sorry if you don't like this arrangement, but please keep in mind that the mole and the middleman and me and you and everyone involved in this little story could easily wake up dead one day, with a bullet between the eyes. I don't care if you trust me or not. My job is to pass along enough information to help you nail Judge Claudia McDover. What else do you need?' A quick sip from his sweaty mug, and, 'Now, please return to photo number five. We don't know if this guy is Vonn Dubose, but let's assume he is. Check out his bag. Brown leather, large, more of a satchel than a briefcase, well worn, or maybe just the distressed look that's currently popular, and not small. This is no thin attaché containing a couple of files. No, this bag is being used to carry something. What? Well, our guy speculates that McDover and Dubose meet on the first Wednesday of each month for an exchange. Why would Dubose, who's dressed like a golfer, need a rather significant bag this late in the day? He's obviously delivering something. Check out photo number six. It was taken thirty-six minutes after number five. Same guy, same bag. If you study the video, you can argue that the bag possibly weighs less just by the way he moves with it. Frankly, I can't tell.'

'So he takes her the cash once a month,' Lacy said.

'He takes something to the condo.'

'How recent are these photos?' Hugo asked.

'Twelve days ago, August 3.'

'But there's no way to verify if this is really Vonn Dubose?' Lacy asked.

'Not to my knowledge. Again, Dubose has never been arrested. He has no criminal record, no identity. He uses only cash for living expenses. He hides behind underlings and associates and leaves no trail. We've done some digging, and I'm sure you have too, and there's no driver's license, Social Security number, or passport issued to a Vonn Dubose, anywhere in this country. He has a driver, as we can see. He could be living as Joe Blow for all we know, with perfect papers.'

Myers reached into his trick bag and pulled out two more files. He handed one to Hugo and one to Lacy, who asked, 'What's this?'

'A detailed summary of McDover's travel over the past seven years. Dates, places, chartered jets, and so on. She almost always goes with her buddy Phyllis Turban, who hires the jets and pays the bills. Turban also books the rooms when they use hotels. She handles all the details. Nothing, so far, is in McDover's name.'

'And why is this valuable?' Lacy asked.

'By itself, it's not that useful, but it does lend credence to the theory that these high-flying gals spend a shit pot full of money jetting around the country, presumably buying valuable things with dirty cash. Their combined earnings would not cover the cost of the jet fuel. We know the judge's salary. I can guess what Turban nets, and I'll bet it's less than McDover's take-home. There might come a time when it's necessary to build a case based on net worth and consumption and assets, so I'm gathering all the dirt I can find.'

Hugo said, 'Please keep digging. We need plenty of help.'

'You're not serious about dismissing my complaint. I mean, hell, look at the photos. How can you argue she doesn't own this condo when she's been going there for at least seven years and she has the key? It's registered to a shell in Belize and it's worth, on today's market, at least a million.'

'Does she ever spend the night there, or entertain?' Lacy asked.

'Don't think so.'

'I checked it out last week,' Hugo said. 'Played golf and took photos from the fairway.'

Myers shot him a quizzical look. 'What did you learn?'

'Absolutely nothing. A complete waste of time, like most rounds of golf.'

'Try bonefishing. It's much more fun.'

As Lacy was painting her toenails near the end of a Cary Grant movie, her phone buzzed with an unknown caller. A voice told her it might be Myers, and the voice was right.

'Breaking news,' he said. 'Tomorrow is Friday.'

'How'd you guess?'

'Hang on. Looks like the girls are headed to New York. Claudia will catch a jet at the airport at Panama City around noon, exact time doesn't matter because when you lease a jet you leave when you want. Lear 60, tail number N38WW, owned and operated by a charter company based in Mobile. Presumably, her lawyer pal will be on board and they're off to New York for fun and games, probably with a sackful of cash to do some serious shopping. In case you don't know, there's virtually no security with private jet travel. No scanners for bags or body searches. I guess the smart guys at Homeland Security figure rich people have little interest in blowing up their own jets en route. Anyway, you could literally pack a hundred pounds of pure heroin and fly anywhere domestically.'

'Interesting, but where's the payoff?'

'If I were you, and if I had nothing better to do, I'd be hanging around the general aviation terminal, it's called Gulf Aviation, and have a look. I'd keep Hugo in the car because you don't see too many black folks in the charter business so he might stand out. I'd also keep him in the car with a camera to take a few photos. Maybe Phyllis will get off the plane for a pit stop in the girls' room. Who knows? You might learn a lot and you can certainly see who you're dealing with.'

'Would I be conspicuous?'

'Lacy, dear, you're always conspicuous. You're too pretty not to be. Wear some jeans, pull your hair back, try different glasses. You'll be okay. There's a lounge area with magazines and newspapers and people sit there all the time. If anybody asks, just say you're waiting on a passenger. The place is open to the public so you won't be trespassing. I'd take a good look at Claudia. See what she's wearing, but also what she's taking with her. I wouldn't expect to see pockets stuffed with cash, but there might be an extra bag or two. Sort of a lark but not a bad way to spend some time. Personally, I'd like the chance to bump into a Florida gal who just happens to be the most corrupt judge in the history of America. And one who will soon be all over the front page, though she hasn't a clue. Go for it.'

'We'll give it a try.'

CHAPTER 11

Judge McDover parked close to the space where Hugo sat rather awkwardly in Lacy's Prius, his face hidden behind a newspaper, his camera by his side. To go with his collection of thoroughly useless photos of the east nine at Rabbit Run, he could now add a few shots of a Lear 60 out there on the tarmac. As Claudia rolled her small suitcase across the parking lot and headed for the front door of Gulf Aviation, he snapped a few of her backside. At fifty-six, she was slender and, at least from the rear, could pass for a lady twenty years younger. Actually, he had to admit, from this angle she looked better than Verna, who, after child number four, was struggling to drop the weight. He simply couldn't stop the habit of staring at the backsides of all nicely shaped females.

After she disappeared inside, Hugo put away his camera and his newspaper and fell asleep.

After years in crime, Claudia McDover had gradually learned how to think like a suspect. She noticed everything, from the black guy sitting in the passenger's seat of the small Toyota reading a

132

newspaper, which seemed a bit odd at noon, to the cute redhead who worked the front desk and gave her a big smile, to the harried business guy in the dark suit whose flight was obviously late, to the pretty girl on the sofa flipping through a copy of *Vanity Fair*. She seemed a bit out of place. In a matter of seconds Claudia sized up the lobby, deemed it safe and clear, and filed away all the faces. In her world, every phone could be tapped, every stranger could be watching, every letter could be violated, every e-mail could be hacked. But she wasn't paranoid and did not live in fear. She was only cautious, and after years of practice her caution was second nature.

A young man in a crisp uniform stepped forward, introduced himself as one of the pilots, and took her suitcase. The cute redhead hit a button, the doors slid open, and Claudia left the terminal. Such exits, though short on drama and unwitnessed by the world, still gave her a thrill. While the masses queued up in endless lines and waited for flights that were crowded, delayed, or canceled, and finally, if lucky, were then herded like cattle onto dirty airplanes packed with seats far too narrow for modern American rumps, she, Judge Claudia McDover of Florida's Twenty-Fourth Judicial District, strolled like a queen to her private jet, where the champagne was on ice and the flight would be on time and nonstop.

Phyllis was waiting. Once the pilots were strapped in and busy with their routines, Claudia gave her a kiss and held her hand. After takeoff, and once the jet leveled off at thirty-eight thousand feet, Phyllis popped the cork on a bottle of Veuve Clicquot and they toasted, as always, the Tappacola tribe.

They had met during their second year of law school at Stetson, and the similarities had been remarkable. Both were reeling from terrible first marriages. Both had chosen law school for the wrong reasons. Claudia had been wiped out and humiliated by her husband and his nasty lawyers and was plotting revenge. Phyllis's divorce decree required her ex to cover the cost of her continued education. She chose med school to drag things out as long as possible, but bombed the MCAT. She turned to law school and clipped him for three more years of postgraduate study. She and Claudia began dating on the sly during their third year, then went their separate ways after graduation. They were women in a weak job market and grabbed what they could find. Claudia went to a small firm in a small town. Phyllis worked as a public defender in Mobile until she got tired of street criminals and found refuge in an office practice. Now that the Indians had made them rich, they traveled in style, lived in understated luxury, and were plotting their final getaway to a place yet to be determined.

When the champagne was gone, both fell asleep. For seventeen years, Claudia had worked diligently at her job because she was, after all, always up for reelection. Phyllis, too, put in long hours in her busy little firm. They never had enough sleep. Two and a half hours after leaving Florida, the jet touched down at Teterboro, New Jersey, home to more private aircraft than any other airport in the world. A black town car was waiting and whisked them away. Twenty minutes later they arrived at their building in Hoboken, a sleek new high-rise on the Hudson, directly across the river from the financial district. From their perch on the fourteenth floor, they had a spectacular view of downtown Manhattan. Lady Liberty was only a stone's throw away. The apartment was spacious and sparsely decorated. It was an investment, not a home, just a place to keep until they chose to flip it. It was, of course, owned by an offshore shell entity, this one domiciled in the Canary Islands.

Phyllis took great delight in playing the international shell game, and was constantly moving money and companies around to find the hottest new tax haven. With time and experience, she had become an expert at hiding their money.

After dark, they put on jeans and took a car into the city, to SoHo, where they dined at a tiny French bistro. Later, in a dimly lit bar, they sipped more champagne and giggled at how far they'd traveled, not just in distance, but in life.

The Armenian's name was Papazian and they'd never known whether it was his first or last name. Not that it mattered. Their dealings were shrouded in secrecy. Neither side asked questions because no one wanted answers. He rang their doorbell at ten Saturday morning and, after the required pleasantries, opened his briefcase. On a small breakfast table he spread his dark blue felt and arranged his goodies – diamonds, rubies, and sapphires. As always, Phyllis served him a double espresso, which he sipped as he described each gem. After four years of doing business, they knew Papazian dealt in only the finest stones. He had a shop in midtown, where they had first met him, but now he was quite happy to make a house call. He had no clue who they were or where they came from. His only concern was the transaction, and the cash. In less than thirty minutes, they selected a fistful of his best – 'portable wealth' as Phyllis liked to say – and handed over the money. He slowly counted $230,000 in $100 bills, mumbling all the while in his native tongue. When everyone was happy, he gulped down the last of his espresso, his second, and left their apartment.

With the bulk of the dirty work out of the way, the girls got dressed and took a car into the city. They bought shoes at Barneys, had a long lunch at Le Bernardin, and eventually drifted to the diamond district, where they dropped in on one of their favorite dealers. With cash they bought a selection of new, uncirculated gold coins – Krugerrands from South Africa, Maple Leafs from Canada, and, to help the local economy, American Eagles. All cash, no paperwork, no records, no trail. The tiny shop had at least four surveillance cameras, and these had once been a concern. Someone somewhere might be watching, but those concerns had been set aside. In their business there were always risks. The trick was choosing which ones to accept.

Saturday night they watched a musical on Broadway, dined afterward at Orso but saw no celebrities, and went to bed after midnight, content with another successful day of laundering. Late Sunday morning, they packed their loot along with their handsome collection of new and horribly expensive shoes, and took a car back to Teterboro, where the jet was waiting for the return trip south.

CHAPTER 12

Hugo was late for the meeting, and while they waited Geismar reviewed the new photos and the travel records as Lacy returned e-mails. 'Any idea why these go back only seven years?' he asked.

'None. Myers doesn't know but speculates that the mole arrived on the scene at about that time. Obviously, the mole is someone close to McDover, and perhaps that's when he or she got involved.'

'Well, he or she is certainly spending some money. It's hard to believe these photos could have been taken by someone sitting in a car on the street. It's more likely that the photographer was inside one of the condos.'

'There are four of them in a unit directly across the street,' Lacy said. 'Two are available for rent, at a thousand a week. We are assuming he or she rented one, set up the camera, and knew precisely when McDover and Dubose would arrive. That's some pretty serious intel.'

'Indeed it is. Myers knows what he's talking about, Lacy. These guys are doing some dirty business. Not sure we can prove it, but the evidence is looking stronger. What will McDover say when confronted with all this?'

'I guess we'll find out soon enough.'

The door swung open and Hugo appeared. He said, 'Sorry I'm late. Another rough night.' He tossed his briefcase on the table and took a sip from a tall coffee. 'I would have been here sooner but I've been on the phone with a guy who won't give me his name.'

Geismar nodded, waiting, still holding one of the photos. Lacy said, 'Okay?'

'He called first around five this morning, a bit early but I just happened to be awake. Said he worked at the casino and had some information that might be useful. Said he knew we were investigating the tribe and the judge and he could help. I pressed a little and he hung up. About an hour ago, he called again, from a different number, and said he wanted to meet and talk about a deal. I asked what kind of deal and he got pretty vague. He said there was a lot of shady stuff going on and it was just a matter of time before it blew up. He's a member of the tribe, knows the Chief and the folks who run the casino, and doesn't want to get caught in the storm when it all hits the fan.'

Hugo was pacing around the room, as was his habit of late. Sitting made him sleepy.

Lacy said, 'This could be interesting.'

Geismar fell into his swivel and locked his hands behind his head. 'Nothing else?'

'No, but he wants to meet tonight. Said he works a late shift and is not free until after 9:00 p.m.'

'You think he's for real?' Geismar asked.

'Who knows? He certainly sounded nervous and he used two different phones, probably disposable. He repeatedly asked me about secrecy and wanted to know how we can protect his identity. He said a lot of his people are fed up with the corruption but afraid to talk.'

'Where does he want to meet?' Lacy asked.

'He lives not far from the casino, on the reservation. He said he'll find a spot and call us when we get close.'

'We gotta be careful here,' Geismar said. 'This could be a setup.'

'I don't think so,' Hugo said. 'I got the impression I was talking to a guy who needs help and wants to help.'

'Which cell phone are you using?'

'BJC's. I know the rules, Boss.'

'Okay, how did he get your number?' Geismar asked. 'So far, in this investigation, who have you given your numbers to? Both of you.'

Hugo and Lacy looked at each other and tried to remember. She said, 'Myers, Junior Mace, the authorities at the prison, Wilton Mace, Razko's widow, Al Bennett, the lawyer who ran against McDover five years ago, Naylor at the Gaming Commission, and I think that's it.'

'That's all,' Hugo said. 'Driving in, I asked myself the same question.'

'Sounds like enough to spring a leak,' Geismar said.

'But none of those people are even remotely involved with Dubose and the corruption,' Lacy said.

'As far as we know,' Hugo said.

'So, you want to go?' Geismar asked.

'Of course we're going,' Lacy said.

Geismar stood and walked to his narrow window. He said, 'This could be the break. Someone on the inside.'

'We're going,' Lacy said.

'Okay, but please be careful.'

They sat in Lacy's car at the far end of the casino parking lot until almost 11:00 p.m., waiting for the informant to check in. It was a Monday night, a slow evening at the tables and slots. Hugo, of course, catnapped while Lacy was online with her iPad. At 10:56, he called with directions. They left the casino, drove two miles along a dark, narrow, winding road, and stopped at an abandoned metal building. An ancient portable sign informed them that it had once been a bingo hall. One home was visible in the distance. The bright lights of Treasure Key were far away. The night was hot and sticky and thick with mosquitoes. Hugo got out of the car and stretched his legs. At six feet two and two hundred pounds, and still with the all-American's cockiness, he did not scare easily. Lacy was comforted by his presence. She would not have made the trip alone. Hugo redialed the most recent number but there was no answer.

Something moved in the shadows along the side of the building. 'Hello,' Hugo called into the darkness. Lacy got out of the car.

A voice said, 'Take a few steps this way.' A silhouette was partially visible and not moving. The man was wearing a cap and the red ember of a cigarette moved back and forth from his mouth. Together they inched forward until he said, 'That's far enough. You're not going to see my face.'

'Well, I guess you can see ours, right?' Hugo said.

'That's far enough. You are Mr Hatch, right?'

'That's right.'

'Who's the girl?'

'My name is Lacy Stoltz. We're colleagues.'

'You didn't tell me you were bringing a woman out here.'

'You didn't ask,' Hugo shot back. 'She's my partner and we're working together.'

'I don't like this.'

'Too bad.'

A pause as he took a puff and sized them up. He cleared his throat, spat, and said, 'I understand you're hot on the trail of Judge McDover.'

'We work for the Florida Board on Judicial Conduct,' Lacy said. 'We're lawyers, not cops. Our job is to investigate complaints against judges.'

'That judge needs to be in prison, along with a bunch of others.' His voice was quick and nervous.

He blew a lungful of smoke and the cloud drifted into the thick air.

'You said you work in the casino,' Hugo said.

A long pause, then, 'That's right. What do you know about the judge?'

Lacy said, 'A complaint has been filed alleging some bad behavior. We're not at liberty to go into details.'

'Bad behavior, huh?' he said and offered a nervous laugh. He flicked the cigarette to the ground, where it glowed for a second. 'Can you guys arrest people or are you just, you know, like, sticking your noses into this business?'

Hugo said, 'No, we don't arrest people.'

Another nervous laugh from the shadows. 'Then I'm wasting my time. I need to talk to somebody with some clout.'

Lacy said, 'We have the authority to investigate and remove a judge if necessary.'

'The judge is not the biggest problem here.'

They waited for more but got nothing but silence. They strained to see the silhouette but it had apparently vanished. The man had eased away. Hugo took a few steps closer and said, 'Are you there?' No response.

'That's far enough,' Lacy whispered. 'I think he's gone.'

A few seconds passed in the uneasy stillness, and Hugo said, 'I think you're right.'

'I don't like this. Let's get out of here.'

They quickly opened their doors and got in the

car. As she backed away, Lacy swept the side of the building with her headlights. No sign of anyone. She turned onto the road and headed in the direction of the casino. 'Pretty strange,' Hugo said. 'We could have had that conversation on the phone.'

Headlights approached in the distance.

'You think I scared him away?' she asked.

'Who knows? If he's legit, then he's thinking about passing on information that could ruin some people. Naturally, he's reluctant. I guess he got cold feet and ran.'

Hugo tapped his waist and said, 'This seat belt has come unlatched again. That's the third time tonight. Why don't you get it fixed?'

Lacy glanced over and was about to say something when Hugo screamed. Blinding lights were in their lane. A pickup truck had crossed the center line. The collision was head-on, bumper to bumper, with a force so violent that her Prius went airborne and spun 180 degrees. At six thousand pounds and twice the weight of the Prius, the truck, a Dodge Ram 2500, got the better end of the collision. It came to rest on the shoulder of the narrow road, its mangled front end almost in a shallow ditch.

The air bag in the steering wheel exploded onto Lacy's chest and into her face, and knocked her dizzy. The crown of her head struck the ceiling of the Prius as it caved in, cutting a nasty gash across her skull. The air bag on the passenger's side failed to open. With no seat belt and no air bag, Hugo smashed into the windshield, shattering it with his head and shoulders. The glass ripped his face to shreds and opened a long cut on his neck.

Glass and metal and wreckage sprayed the scene. The right front tire of the truck was spinning. Its driver slowly got out, removed his black motorcycle helmet and pads, and checked behind him. Another pickup was slowing down. He stretched his legs, rubbed his left knee, and walked with a limp to the front of the smashed Prius for a quick look. He saw the lady, her face covered with blood, her air bag draped before her, and he saw the black guy bleeding from his many injuries. He loitered for a moment, then stumbled away and climbed into the second pickup, where he waited and rubbed his leg. He noticed his nose was bleeding. Its driver got behind the wheel and they drove away, slowly, all lights off. The pickup turned into a field, and disappeared. No 911 call was made.

The nearest house was half a mile down the road. It was owned by the Beale family, and Iris Beale, the wife and mother, heard the collision, though initially she had no idea what had happened. But she was convinced it was unusual and needed looking into. She woke up her husband, Sam, and forced him to throw on some clothes and check things out. By the time Sam arrived on the scene, another car had stopped. Within minutes, sirens were heard and flashing lights came into view as two cars from the Tappacola Police Department arrived. They were followed by two units from the Tappacola Fire and Rescue. Almost immediately, a medevac helicopter was called from the nearest regional hospital in Panama City.

Hugo was extracted by removing what was left of the windshield and easing him through the opening. He was still alive but unconscious and with hardly a pulse. Hydraulic jacks were used to rip off the driver's door and remove Lacy, who was trying to speak but uttering only unintelligible grunts. She was placed in an ambulance and sent off to the tribe's clinic near the casino. There, she would wait on the helicopter. She lost consciousness en route to the center, so did not hear the news that Hugo had died. She would make the short flight to the hospital without her colleague.

At the scene, the police went about their business of taking photographs, videos, and measurements, and looking for witnesses. Evidently, there were none. Nor was there a driver for the pickup truck. The driver's side air bag had been fully deployed. There was no sign of blood or injuries, but a broken bottle of whiskey was found on the passenger's side floorboard. The driver had simply vanished. Even before the truck was towed away, the police knew it had been stolen six hours earlier from a shopping center in Foley, Alabama. Lacy's Prius was loaded onto a flatbed tow truck and taken to a holding yard near the tribe's administration complex.

Hugo's body was taken to the tribe's medical facility and placed in a frigid room in the basement where an occasional body was held. Across the street, the constable, Lyman Gritt, sat at his desk and stared at a small collection of Hugo's things – keys on a ring, folded dollar bills, some change, and a wallet. A sergeant sat on the other side of the desk, equally as mum. Neither volunteered to make the phone call.

The constable finally opened the wallet and removed one of Hugo's business cards. He went online and found BJC's website and tracked down Michael Geismar. 'He should make the phone call, right?' asked the constable. 'After all, he knows Mr Hatch, and probably knows his family.'

'Good idea,' said the sergeant.

At 2:20, Michael answered the phone and was met with 'I'm so sorry to call, but I believe you work with Mr Hugo Hatch. I'm the constable for the Tappacola tribe, over in Brunswick County.'

Michael stumbled to his feet as his wife turned on a light. 'Yes! What's happened?'

'There's been an accident, a bad car wreck, and Mr Hatch has been killed. Someone needs to notify his family.'

'What? Are you serious? No, you can't be serious. Who is this?'

'My name is Constable Lyman Gritt, sir, the chief law enforcement officer for the tribe. I assure you I'm serious. The accident happened on our reservation about two hours ago. The young lady,

Lacy Stoltz, has been taken to the hospital in Panama City.'

'I don't believe this.'

'I'm sorry, sir. Does he have a family?'

'Does he have a family? Yes, Mr Gritt, he has a family, a pretty young wife and four small children. Yes, a family. This is unreal.'

'I'm sorry, sir. Can you notify them?'

'Me? Why me? This can't be happening. How do I know this is not some prank or something?'

'Sir, you can go to our website and check me out. You can call the hospital in Panama City. The lady should be there by now. But I promise you this terrible news is real, and it won't be long before some news reporter finds out and calls the family.'

'Okay, okay. Just let me think for a second.'

'Take your time, sir.'

'And Lacy is okay?'

'I don't know, sir. She's injured but she's alive.'

'Okay. Sure, I'll drive over now. Give me your phone number just in case.'

'Certainly, sir, and if we can help in any way, please call.'

'Sure. And thanks. I know this can't be easy.'

'No, sir. It is not. A question, sir. Were they working on our reservation last night?'

'Yes, they were. They certainly were.'

'May I ask why? I am the constable.'

'I'm sorry, maybe later.'

*   *   *

148

Geismar stayed with Verna Hatch and the children until her mother arrived, then fled the house as quickly as possible. He would forever live with the horror, the shock, the agony, the sheer madness of the family hearing the news that Hugo would not be coming home, and then trying to convince each other that it simply could not be true. At times he was the villain, the hated messenger unduly burdened with the task of convincing them that Hugo was in fact dead.

He had never experienced such raw, emotional devastation, nor would he ever again endure such a nightmare. He caught himself weeping as he left Tallahassee in the predawn hours. He arrived in Panama City just after 6:00 a.m.

CHAPTER 13

Lacy was stable but still unconscious. The initial diagnosis included a gash to the left side of her head that required twenty-four stitches, a concussion that was causing swelling of the brain, abrasions on her face, the result of the violent sliding contact with the air bag, and small cuts on her neck, left shoulder, left elbow, hand, and knee. Her head was shaved and her doctors decided to keep her in an induced coma for at least twenty-four hours. One of them explained to Geismar that it would be a day or two before they could assess further damage, but he saw nothing, so far, that could be considered life threatening.

Her mother, Ann Stoltz, arrived from Clearwater at 8:00 a.m., along with Ann's sister, Trudy, and her husband, Ronald. They huddled with Michael, who passed along all the information he had, which wasn't much.

Once they were settled, Michael left and drove to the reservation. He waited half an hour at the police station until Lyman Gritt arrived for work. The constable explained that they were still investigating the accident but this much was known: The collision obviously happened when the truck crossed the center line and struck the Prius. The truck was stolen and was registered to a man in Alabama. No sign of the driver, but it appeared as though he had been drinking. No one saw him leave the scene and they had found no trace of him. The passenger's side air bag did not deploy and Mr Hatch was not wearing a seat belt. His injuries were substantial, he had an obvious head injury, and he appeared to have bled to death. 'Would you like to see the photographs?'

'Maybe later.'

'Would you like to see the vehicles?'

'Yes, I would,' Michael replied.

'Okay, we'll do that and I'll take you to the scene.'

'There seem to be quite a few unanswered questions.'

'We're still investigating, sir,' Gritt said. 'Perhaps you could shed some light on their activities here last night.'

'Perhaps, but not yet. We'll get to that later.'

'An investigation will require full cooperation, sir. I need to know everything. What were they doing here?'

'I can't give you those details right now,' Geismar said, fully aware that he was only adding to the suspicion. At that moment, though, he couldn't afford to trust anyone. 'Look, a man has been killed in a very suspicious car wreck. I need your word that the vehicles will be impounded and preserved until someone can examine them.'

'Someone? Who do you have in mind, sir?'

'I'm not sure.'

'Need I remind you that this happened on Tappacola land and we do the investigating around here? No one looks over our shoulder.'

'Sure, I understand that. I'm just a bit rattled, okay? Give me some time to think this through.'

Gritt stood and walked to a table in the corner of his office. 'Take a look at this stuff,' he said. In the center of the table there was a large, stylish lady's handbag and next to it was a set of keys. Two feet away was a wallet and keys. Michael stepped closer and stared at them. Gritt said, 'When there is a fatality, we normally go through the personal effects and make an inventory. I haven't done that yet. I opened the wallet only to retrieve a business card. That's how I found you. I have not looked inside the purse.'

'Where are their cell phones?' Michael asked.

Gritt was already shaking his head. 'No cell phones. We checked all of his pockets and searched the car and found none.'

'That's impossible,' Michael said, stunned. 'Someone took their cell phones.'

'Are you sure they had them?'

'Of course. Who doesn't carry a cell phone? And their phones would have their most recent calls, including the ones to the guy they were supposed to meet.'

'And who was this guy?'

'I don't know. I swear.' Michael was rubbing his eyes. He suddenly gasped and asked, 'What about their briefcases?'

Gritt shook his head again. 'No sign of briefcases.'

'I need to sit down.' Michael fell into a chair at the table and stared in shock at the personal effects.

'Would you like some water?' Gritt asked.

'Please.' The briefcases would have the files, and the files would have everything. A wave of nausea rolled through Michael as he thought of Vonn Dubose and Claudia McDover sifting through the paperwork. Photos of the four condos, photos of Vonn himself and Claudia going to and from their meeting, photos of the judge catching her flight to New York, all the detailed travel records, a copy of Greg Myers's complaint, memos from Sadelle, everything. Everything.

Michael sipped water from a bottle and wiped sweat from his forehead. When he had gathered enough strength to stand he did so, and said, 'Look, I'll be back tomorrow to retrieve this stuff and look at the vehicles. Right now I need to get to the office. Please keep everything secure.'

'That's our job, sir.'

'And I need to take her keys, if that's okay.'

'I see no problem.'

Michael took the keys, thanked the constable, and walked outside. He called Justin Barrow at BJC and instructed him to go immediately to Lacy's apartment and find the manager. Explain what had happened and that Lacy's boss had the key and was on the way. Since they did not know the code to her security system they needed the manager to disarm it. He said, 'Watch the apartment until I get there. Make sure no one comes and goes.'

Racing back to Tallahassee, Michael tried to convince himself that Lacy and Hugo, in all likelihood, would not have taken their briefcases with them. They would not have needed them, right? They were making a late-night rendezvous with an unknown witness. What good would the files have been? But then he knew they, like every other investigator, indeed every other lawyer, rarely went anywhere on business without the old trusty briefcase. He kicked himself for BJC's rather lax policy on file security. Did they really have a policy? Since all of their cases were handled with utmost confidentiality, it was a matter of practice to keep the files secure. It went with the territory, and he'd never felt the need to remind his staff to guard things.

He stopped twice for coffee and to stretch his legs. He battled fatigue by staying on the phone. He called Justin, who was at Lacy's apartment. The manager would not allow him inside until her boss arrived with her key. As he drove and gulped coffee, Geismar talked to two reporters who had called the office. He called Verna and spoke to a sister. Not surprisingly, she had little to say. Verna was in the bedroom with her two oldest children. He wanted

154

to ask if someone could look for Hugo's briefcase and cell phone, but the moment didn't seem right. They had enough to worry about. His secretary put together a conference call with his staff and he answered as many questions as possible. Understandably, they were too shocked to work.

The manager insisted on being present when they entered Lacy's apartment. Michael found the right key to the front door and opened it, and the manager quickly disarmed the security. Frankie, her French bulldog, was yelping for food and water and had made a mess in the kitchen. The manager said, 'Okay, I'll feed the damned thing while you guys hurry up.' As he looked for dog food, Michael and Justin went from room to room. Justin found Lacy's briefcase on a chair in her bedroom. Michael carefully opened it and removed a legal pad and two files. They were the official BJC work files, each with the case number, and between the two they contained all the valuable paperwork. They found her iPhone recharging on a bathroom counter. They thanked the manager, who was wiping the floor and mumbling just loud enough to be heard, and left with the briefcase and the iPhone.

Next to his car, Michael said, 'Look, Justin, I can't go back over there. They associate me with the horrible news. You have to ask Verna for his briefcase and cell phone, okay? Tell her it's crucial.'

Michael Geismar was the boss and Justin had little choice.

★   ★   ★

155

The Hatch home was easy to find because of the crowd. Cars lined both sides of the street and several men were loitering in the front yard, as if things were too crowded inside. Justin approached reluctantly and nodded to the men. They were polite but said little. One, a white guy in a shirt and tie, looked vaguely familiar. Justin explained to him that he worked with Hugo at BJC. The guy gave his name as Thomas and said he worked for the Attorney General's Office. He and Hugo had studied together in law school and had remained close. Almost in a whisper, Justin explained the nature of his visit. It was imperative to locate and secure Hugo's briefcase. It contained sensitive BJC files, and so on, and Thomas understood. And the cell phone issued by the office was missing. Was there a chance he left it at home? Thomas said, 'Not likely,' and eased into the house.

Two women came out of the front door in tears and were comforted by their men. Judging by the number of cars lining the street, Justin knew the house was packed with stunned family and friends.

After an eternity, Thomas came through the front door, empty-handed. He and Justin walked to the edge of the street for a little privacy. Thomas said, 'His briefcase is in there. I explained things to Verna and she allowed me to look through it. It appears to be in order, but she would not let me leave with it. I told her to make sure it was secure. I think she understands.'

'I'm not going to ask how she's doing.'

156

'It's awful. She's in the bedroom with the two oldest kids, and she can barely talk. Hugo's mother is laid out on a sofa. Aunts and uncles everywhere. There's a doctor with them. It's just awful.'

'No sign of a cell phone?'

'No, he had it with him. He called her last night around ten to check on things. I asked her if he had a personal cell phone and she said no. He used the BJC phone for everything.'

Justin took a deep breath and said, 'Thanks. I'll see you around.'

Driving away, Justin called Michael with the update.

Early in the afternoon, Hugo's body was transported by hearse to a funeral home in Tallahassee, where it was prepared for burial, though Verna had not yet been able to finalize the details.

Lacy remained in intensive care throughout the day. Her vitals were strong and her doctors were pleased with her progress. Another scan revealed a slight improvement in the swelling, and if all went well, the doctors planned to ease her out of the coma in thirty-six to forty-eight hours. Lyman Gritt wanted to talk to her but was told to wait.

After a restless night in bed, Michael went to the office at dawn Wednesday and waited on Justin. Still sleepwalking through the nightmare, he read about Hugo on the front page of the morning newspaper. There were two photos – one a publicity shot of Hugo when he played for Florida State, and one in a coat and tie taken for the BJC website. Michael read the names of his four children and felt like crying again. The funeral would be Saturday, three days away. He could not imagine what a nightmare it would be.

He and Justin left at seven and drove to the reservation. Lyman Gritt had inventoried the contents of Hugo's wallet, counted the money, and photographed everything. He asked Michael to sign an inventory sheet, then turned it all over to him. Michael also left with Lacy's handbag. They walked down the street to a small salvage yard with a dozen wrecked cars, a locked gate, and chain-link fencing all around. Without touching anything, they examined the two vehicles. The pickup still smelled like whiskey. The Prius was far more damaged, and there was so much blood that neither Michael nor Justin wanted to probe too much. Their friend's blood, and it was still fresh.

'There will probably be litigation,' Michael said gravely, though he had no real knowledge of this. 'So it's imperative to preserve these vehicles just as they are. Is that a problem?'

'Of course not,' Gritt said.

'Plus the insurance companies will be involved and they'll send out their adjusters.'

'We've been through this before, Mr Geismar.'

'And you've searched everywhere for the cell phones?'

'As I said, we've looked everywhere and found nothing.'

Michael and Justin exchanged glances as if they were skeptical. They asked if they could take photographs and Gritt said he didn't care. When they finished, they followed the constable to the county road where it happened. They looked around, tentatively at first, and were struck by the remoteness of the place. The perfect spot for an unwitnessed accident. They saw the Beale home in the distance, the old bingo shack not far away, and no other buildings.

Michael stared at the pavement and said, 'No skid marks.'

'Not a one,' Gritt said. 'She never had time to react. It looks to me like the truck crossed the center line and they hit right about here.' Gritt was standing in the center of the eastbound lane. 'Her car was spun around and was facing that way. It did not leave this lane. The truck, which was of course much heavier, bounced over here and almost went into the ditch. Evidently, it veered quickly into her lane, before she could do anything.'

'Any estimate of the speed at impact?' Michael asked.

'No, but a reconstruction expert could get pretty close.'

Michael and Justin took in the scene and noticed the oil stains, the specks of shattered glass, the bits of aluminum and metal. At the edge of the asphalt, almost on the shoulder, they noticed what could only be dried blood. In the grass, there was a piece of cloth, also stained. One of their colleagues had been killed there and another had been grievously injured. It seemed like such an unfitting place to die.

They took some more photos and suddenly wanted to leave.

Frog Freeman ran a country store and filling station two miles north of Sterling. He lived next door in an old house his grandfather had built, and because he was always around, and because the store was his life, he kept it open until ten each night. For all the business he drummed up in rural Brunswick County after dark, he could have easily closed at six, but he had nothing else to do. On Monday night, he had not closed at ten because of a water leak somewhere in the beer cooler. Frog sold a lot of beer, most of it ice-cold. A malfunctioning cooler was not acceptable, and since he handled all repairs himself, he was hard at work wrestling with the cooler when a customer walked in looking for ice, rubbing alcohol, and two cans of beer.

An odd combination, thought Frog, as he wiped off his hands and went to the cash register. He had owned the store for over fifty years and was an expert in predicting what his customers were up to based simply on what they bought. He'd seen everything, but ice, rubbing alcohol, and beer was unusual.

Frog had been robbed three times, twice at gunpoint, and years earlier began fighting back. He had six surveillance cameras around the store. Four visible, so potential thieves might realize the perils of their planned robbery, and two hidden, including one above the front porch.

Frog stepped inside his tiny office behind the cash register and checked the monitor. White pickup truck, Florida license plates. A young man sitting in the passenger's seat. Something was wrong with his nose. He was holding a cloth against it, and the cloth appeared to be stained. The driver stepped into view with the bag of ice and a small brown sack with the rubbing alcohol and beer. He crawled behind the wheel, said something to his passenger, then backed away.

'Boy's been in a fight,' Frog said, and went back to his repairs.

Auto fatalities were rare in Brunswick County. The following morning, Frog's coffee group was wild with rumors. Some black guy and a white girl from Tallahassee got lost on the reservation and a drunk hit 'em head-on. Stolen truck, and the drunk ran off. Just walked away. No sign of him yet. The notion of a drunk driver staggering away from the wreck, disappearing into the depths of the reservation, and emerging safely beyond its borders was a rich source of humor, speculation, and disbelief.

'He wouldn't last an hour out there,' one coffee drinker said.

'Probably still going around in circles,' said another.

'Don't worry. The Indians will screw it up,' said a third.

Later in the day, as the details accumulated, Frog began tying things together. He knew the sheriff well, and knew the sheriff had trouble with the Tappacola police. Because of their wealth, the tribe had built a police force twice the size of the county's, and with far nicer equipment. Resentment was inevitable.

He called Clive Pickett, the sheriff of Brunswick County, and said he might have something of interest. Pickett stopped by after work and they watched the video. His first words were 'That's weird.' He said the county had been quiet Monday night, same as virtually every other night, said as usual the only signs of life had been at the casino. No one had called in about a fight, assault, Peeping Tom, or suspicious characters. Indeed, nothing was stirring until the two vehicles collided.

'That's about ten miles from here, don't you think?' the sheriff said.

'As the crow flies.'

'So the time frame fits?'

'Appears so.'

The sheriff scratched his chin, deep in thought. 'So, if the boy with the busted nose was driving the stolen truck, how would he manage to get away and catch a ride with a stranger and get here within fifteen minutes?'

'Don't know. You're the sheriff.'

'Maybe the stranger ain't a stranger.'

'That's what I was thinking.'

Frog agreed to copy the video and e-mail it to the sheriff. They agreed to sit on it for a day or so before they informed the Indians.

CHAPTER 14

Late Wednesday afternoon, Michael assembled what was left of his Tallahassee staff. The two investigators in BJC's Fort Lauderdale office were not included. Justin Barrow, with six years of experience, was now the senior investigator. He had played bad golf with Hugo a week earlier, knew the basics of the complaint filed by Greg Myers, but was unaware of the vast conspiracy lurking in the background. He had his own cases to worry about. Maddy Reese, who'd been there less than a year, knew nothing of the story of Vonn Dubose, the corruption at the casino, and Judge Claudia McDover.

Michael started at the beginning, with Myers, and told them everything. They absorbed it with a combination of disbelief and fear. Surely, their boss was not about to hand over the case to them. He stressed that virtually none of the allegations in the Myers complaint had been proven, and he was quite certain BJC was in no position to prove them. However, he was convinced Lacy and Hugo had ventured into fatal territory. 'The accident reeks of suspicion,' he said. 'They were lured to a

164

remote place by a potential informant. We don't know if they actually met him, and we won't know until Lacy can talk. On a straight stretch of road, in clear weather, and with no other traffic, they were struck head-on by a stolen truck whose driver will likely never be found. The air bag on the passenger's side, along with the seat belt, were apparently tampered with and didn't work. And their BJC phones have disappeared. Presumably taken. We plan to push hard for an investigation, but we're dealing with the Tappacola tribe, not your typical law enforcement agency.'

'You're saying Hugo was murdered?' Maddy asked.

'Not yet. I'm only saying the circumstances surrounding his death are extremely suspicious.'

'What about the FBI? Doesn't it have jurisdiction?'

'It does, and we may ask for their help at some point, but not now.'

Maddy cleared her throat and asked, 'So what happens to this case in the meantime?'

'It's on my desk,' Michael said. 'Not sure what I'm going to do with it, but it's mine for the moment.'

'If you don't mind my saying so,' Justin said, 'I don't think we're really cut out for this. If this criminal activity is really happening, what the hell are we doing poking around it? This is for guys with guns and badges and all that crap.'

'Agreed. And I suppose your question is one I'll take to my grave. We thought there might be an element of danger, and our plan was to sort of sniff around the edges and see what we could find. Keep in mind, a formal complaint was filed, and once it was on our desk we had no choice but to investigate. I guess we should have been more careful. I should have told them not to go to the reservation Monday night.'

'True, but those two don't scare easily,' Maddy said.

There was a long, heavy pause as they thought of their colleagues. Finally, Maddy asked, 'When can we see Lacy?'

'They plan to ease her out of the coma soon. I'll be there in the morning. If all goes well, I'll have the chance to talk to her. Someone has to break the news about Hugo. Maybe in a couple of days you can visit. Remember, the funeral is Saturday and we'll all be there.'

'Can't wait,' Justin said.

The police in Foley, Alabama, were informed that the stolen Dodge Ram truck they were looking for had come to rest in a salvage yard on Indian land over in Florida. They notified the owner, who notified his insurance company. On Wednesday afternoon, a man appeared at the police station and said he knew something about the theft. He was a private investigator, known to some of the cops, and he was being paid to follow a young housewife because her husband suspected she was seeing someone else. The investigator had been hiding in his car in a shopping center lot when he saw a Honda pickup with Florida tags park near the Dodge Ram in question. Two men were in the Honda but they did not get out. They watched passing cars and pedestrians for about fifteen minutes and seemed out of place. The passenger eased out and approached the Dodge. At that point, the investigator, because he was bored and really had nothing else to do, pulled out his cell phone and started a video recording.

The thief deftly opened the driver's door with a flat blade – it was obvious he had experience – and within seconds cranked the engine and drove off, followed by his pal in the Honda. The video clearly showed the Honda's Florida license plates. Few auto thefts are so easily solved, and the Foley police kept the video and thanked the concerned citizen. They tracked the license plates to a man in DeFuniak Springs, Florida, in Walton County, about fifteen miles from the casino. The man, one Berl Munger, had a long and colorful record as a small-time felon and was currently on parole. Because it was only the theft of a truck and not a more serious crime, and because it would involve reaching into another state, the Foley police put the file in a basket for items to be done soon, but not tomorrow.

Greg Myers and his beloved boat were docked in Naples, Florida. He was having a late-afternoon drink on the *Conspirator* when he went through his daily routine of scanning the newspapers from Pensacola, Tallahassee, and Jacksonville. Living on a boat gave him a sense of rootlessness, of never being sure where he would be tomorrow. Keeping up with the news from his old haunts tied him to the past, the good days anyway, and had become important. Besides, he had a lot of enemies back there and they occasionally got their names in the papers.

He was shocked to read about Hugo, killed in an auto accident late at night on the Tappacola reservation, and his partner, Lacy Stoltz, badly injured. Terrible news, and for more than one reason. Investigations would follow, leads would be chased, fingers eventually pointed. As always, he suspected the worst – that Dubose was behind the accident, which wasn't at all what it seemed.

The more he read the worse he felt. Though he had met with Lacy and Hugo on only three occasions, he liked and admired them. They were smart and unpretentious, didn't make a lot of money, but were dedicated to their work. Because of him, they were on the trail of a crooked judge and her confederates. Because of him, Hugo was now dead.

Greg left the boat and walked along the pier. He found a bench overlooking the bay and sat there for a long time, cursing himself for what had happened. A dark little conspiracy had suddenly become far more dangerous.

CHAPTER 15

Geismar was at the hospital by 8:00 Thursday morning. He stopped by the waiting room to check on Ann Stoltz, who was alone. Lacy's vitals remained strong. The doctors had cut off the barbiturates the night before and she was slowly waking up. Thirty minutes later, a nurse came for Ann and said her daughter was alert. 'I'll break the news about Hugo,' Geismar said. 'You go ahead for a few minutes and I'll be right behind you.'

Because she was still in the ICU, Michael had not asked to see her. When he entered the room, he was stunned at the condition of her face. It was bruised, red and purple, with abrasions and small cuts, and swollen to the point of being unrecognizable. Through narrow, puffy slits he could barely see her pupils. The endotracheal tube was wedged into the corner of her mouth and taped into place. He gently touched her hand and said hello.

She nodded and tried to mumble something, but the tube was in the way. Ann Stoltz sat in a chair and wiped her eyes.

'How ya doing, Lacy?' Michael asked, himself on the verge of emotion. Such a beautiful face reduced to such a mess.

She nodded slightly.

Ann whispered, 'I told her nothing.' A nurse slipped into the room and stood next to Ann.

Michael eased closer and said, 'You guys were hit head-on. A terrible crash, Lacy.' He swallowed hard, glanced at Ann, and said, 'Lacy, Hugo didn't make it, okay? Hugo was killed.'

She groaned pitifully and closed the narrow slits. She squeezed his hand.

Michael's eyes watered and he pressed on. 'It wasn't your fault, Lacy, you gotta understand it. It wasn't your fault.'

She groaned again, and moved her head slightly from side to side.

A doctor eased to the side of the bed opposite Michael and stared at the patient. He said, 'Lacy, I'm Dr Hunt. You were unconscious for over forty-eight hours. Do you hear me?'

She nodded again, and took a deep breath. A small tear managed to find its way through the swelling and dropped onto her left cheek.

He proceeded with a quick exam of asking short questions, holding up fingers, and having her look at objects across the room. She responded well, though with some hesitation. 'Does your head hurt?' he asked.

She nodded. Yes.

Dr Hunt looked at the nurse and ordered a

170

painkiller. He looked at Michael and said, 'You can chat a few more minutes, but nothing about the accident. I understand the police want to talk to her, but that's not going to happen anytime soon. We'll see how she feels in a couple of days.' He backed away from the bed and left the room without another word.

Michael looked at Ann and said, 'We need to discuss something confidential. If you don't mind. Just take a second.' Ann nodded and slipped out of the room.

He said, 'Lacy, did you have your BJC phone with you Monday night?'

She nodded yes.

'It's missing; so is Hugo's. The police searched your car and the accident scene. They've looked everywhere, no cell phones. Don't ask me to explain, because I can't. But if the wrong people hacked into your phone, we have to assume they can find Myers.'

Her swollen eyes widened slightly and she kept nodding go on.

He said, 'Our tech guy says it's virtually impossible to hack the phones, but there's the chance. Do you have Myers's number?'

She nodded. Yes.

'In the file?'

She nodded. Yes.

'Great. I'll get to work on it.'

Another doctor popped in and wanted to poke around. Michael had had enough for one visit.

His dreaded mission was accomplished, and evidently he would not be asking any more questions about what happened Monday night. He leaned a bit closer and said, 'Lacy, I need to go. I'll tell Verna that you're okay and thinking about the family.'

She was crying again.

An hour later, the nurses took her off the ventilator and began pulling tubes. Her vitals were normal. She napped off and on throughout Thursday morning, but by noon was getting bored with so much sleep. Her voice was scratchy and weak but also getting stronger by the hour. She talked to Ann, Aunt Trudy, and Uncle Ronald, a man she had never been fond of but now appreciated.

ICU space was limited, and with Lacy stabilized and out of danger, the doctors decided that she could be moved to a private room. That move coincided with the arrival of Gunther, Lacy's older brother and only sibling. As usual, Gunther was heard before he was seen. He was in the hallway arguing with a nurse about the number of visitors the hospital allowed in each room at any given time. The rule was three. Gunther thought that was ludicrous, and besides he'd just driven nonstop from Atlanta to see his kid sister and if the nurse didn't like it, she could call security. And if she called security, Gunther might have to call his lawyers.

The sound of his voice was usually a sign of trouble, but to Lacy at that moment it was beautiful. She actually chuckled, and in doing so ached from her head to her knees. Ann Stoltz said, 'I guess he's here.' Trudy and Ronald snapped to attention as if bracing for something unpleasant.

The door swung open without being knocked on and Gunther rolled in, a nurse in pursuit. He pecked his mother on the forehead, ignored his aunt and uncle, and almost lunged at Lacy. 'Good God, girl, what have they done to you?' he asked as he kissed her on the forehead. She tried to smile.

He glanced over and said, 'Hello, Trudy. Hello, Ronald. Say good-bye, Ronald, because you need to wait in the hall. Nurse Ratched here is threatening to call security because of some arbitrary and unreasonable rule they have around this Podunk place.'

Trudy was reaching for her purse as Ronald said, 'We'll be going. Back in a few hours.' They hustled out of the room, obviously quite happy to get away from Gunther. He glared at Nurse Ratched, held up two fingers, and said, 'One visitor, two visitor. Me and Momma. Can you not count? Now that we're legal would you please leave us alone so I can talk to my sister in private?'

Nurse Ratched happily left too. Ann was shaking her head. Lacy wanted to laugh but knew it would be too painful.

Depending on the year, or even the month,

Gunther Stoltz was either one of the top ten commercial property developers in Atlanta or one of the five real estate swingers most likely headed for bankruptcy. At forty-one, he'd filed at least twice already, and seemed destined to live on that tightrope that some developers seem to thrive on. When times were good and money was cheap, he borrowed heavily, built like a maniac, and burned through cash like it would never end. When the market turned against him, he hid from the banks and unloaded assets at fire-sale prices. There was no middle ground, no thought of prudent planning, or, heaven forbid, the actual saving of some of the money. When he was down he never stopped betting on a brighter future, and when he was up he choked on the money and forgot about the bad times. Atlanta would never stop growing, and it was his calling in life to clutter it with even more strip malls, apartments, and office complexes.

During this brief invasion, Lacy had already picked up on an important clue. The fact that he'd driven from Atlanta, as opposed to using a private jet, was a clear sign that his developments were not going well.

Almost nose to nose, he said, 'I'm so sorry, Lacy, for not coming sooner. I was in Rome with Melanie and got back as fast as I could. How are you feeling, dear?'

'I've felt better,' she said with a scratchy voice. There was an excellent chance he hadn't been to

174

Rome in years. Part of his act was to drop names of fancy places. Melanie was wife number two, a woman Lacy loathed and, fortunately, rarely saw.

'She just woke up this morning,' Ann said from her chair. 'It would have been a waste to come earlier.'

'And how are you, Mother?' he asked without looking at Ann.

'Fine, thanks for asking. Did you have to be so rude to Trudy and Ronald?'

And just like that, family tension filled the air. Uncharacteristically, Gunther took a breath and let it pass. Still staring at his sister, he said, 'I've read the news stories. Just awful. And your friend was killed, Lacy? I can't believe this. What happened?'

Ann chimed in, 'The doctor said she is not to talk about the accident.'

Gunther glared at his mother and said, 'Well, I really don't care what the doctor said. I'm here and if I want to have a chat with my sister no one will tell me what to talk about.' He returned to Lacy and asked, 'What happened, Lacy? Who was driving the other vehicle?'

Ann said, 'She's not processing everything, Gunther. She's been in a coma since Monday night. Please back off, okay?'

But backing off was not in Gunther's playbook. He said, 'I know a great lawyer and we're going to sue that bastard for everything he has. It was all his fault, right, Lacy?'

Ann exhaled with as much noise as possible, then stood and walked out of the room.

Lacy shook her head slightly and said, 'I don't remember.' Then she closed her eyes and fell asleep.

By mid-afternoon, Gunther had laid claim to at least half of Lacy's private room. He had arranged two chairs, a cart on wheels, a night table that once held a lamp, and the small fold-out sofa into a configuration that allowed him to set up shop with his laptop, iPad, not one but two cell phones, and a stack of paperwork. Nurse Ratched had objected, but she had quickly learned that any comment from her would be met with a blistering and threatening response. Trudy and Ronald popped in a couple of times to check on Lacy, but got the impression they were now trespassers. Finally, Ann threw in the towel. Late in the day, she informed her two children that she was headed back to Clearwater for a day or two; that she would be back as soon as possible; and that if Lacy needed anything to please call.

When Lacy napped, Gunther either stayed off the phone or stepped into the hallway, and worked feverishly, but quietly, on his laptop. When she was awake, he was either in her face or growling on the phone as another deal teetered on the brink. He repeatedly badgered the nurses and orderlies to bring him more coffee, and when the coffee didn't materialize he stomped down to the cafeteria, where the food looked 'dreadful.' The doctors made their rounds, each glaring at him as he seemed ready for any confrontation. They were careful not to provoke.

For Lacy, though, his energy was infectious, even stimulating. He amused her, though she was still afraid to laugh. Once when she awoke, he was standing next to her bed, wiping tears from his cheeks.

At six, Nurse Ratched appeared and said her shift would be ending. She asked Gunther about his plans, and he replied, rather sternly, 'I'm not leaving. This sofa is here for a reason. And for what you folks charge, you could certainly provide something more comfortable than this flimsy fold-out. I mean, hell, an army cot would be more comfortable.'

'I'll pass that along,' she said. 'See you in the morning, Lacy.'

'What a bitch,' Gunther mumbled, just loud enough for her to hear as she closed the door.

For dinner, Gunther fed her ice cream and Jell-O while he ate nothing. They watched *Friends* reruns until she was exhausted. As she dozed off, he was back in his nest, hammering out e-mails with no sign of slowing down.

Throughout the night, the nurses eased in and out. At first Gunther bitched about the noise they made, but soon settled down when a cute one he fancied slipped him a Xanax. By midnight he was snoring, the flimsy fold-out sofa notwithstanding.

Around five Friday morning, Lacy began to fidget and moan. She was asleep and dreaming, and the dreams were not pleasant. Gunther patted her arm, whispered that everything was going to be fine, that she would be home in no time. She awoke with a jolt and breathed heavily.

'What is it?' he asked.

'Some water,' she said, and he lifted a straw to her mouth. She took a long sip and he wiped her mouth. 'I saw it, Gunther, I saw the truck just before we hit. Hugo screamed and I looked ahead, and there were bright lights right in front of us. Then everything went black.'

'Attagirl. Do you remember a sound? Maybe the collision, maybe the explosion of the air bag in your face?'

'Maybe, I'm not sure.'

'Did you see the other driver?'

'No, nothing but lights, really bright. It happened so fast, Gunther. I had no time to react.'

'Of course you didn't. It wasn't your fault. The truck crossed the center line.'

'It did, yes it did.' She closed her eyes again, and a few seconds passed before he realized she was crying.

'It's okay, Sis. It's okay.'

'Hugo's not really dead, is he, Gunther?'

'Yes, Lacy. You need to accept it and believe it and stop asking if it's really true. Hugo is dead.'

She cried and there was nothing he could do. He ached for her as she shivered and struggled and grieved for her friend. Finally, mercifully, she went back to sleep.

CHAPTER 16

After the early morning wave of doctors, nurses, and orderlies, things settled down somewhat and Gunther worked on his deals. Lacy was improving by the hour. The swelling in her face was easing, though her bruises were changing into various shades of blue. Around 9:00, Michael Geismar arrived and was startled to see such an elaborate makeshift office in Lacy's room. She was awake and sipping lukewarm coffee through a straw.

Gunther, unshaven, in his socks and with his shirttail to his knees, introduced himself as her brother and was immediately suspicious of this guy in a dark suit. Lacy said, 'Relax, he's my boss,' and Gunther stood down. He and Michael shook hands tentatively across the bed and all was peaceful.

Michael asked, 'Do you feel like talking?'

'I guess,' she said.

'Lyman Gritt is the constable for the reservation, and he wants to stop by and ask some questions. Probably a good idea if we cover things first.'

'Okay.'

Michael looked at Gunther, who showed no signs of even thinking about leaving the room. Michael said to him, 'This is quite confidential. It deals with one of our investigations.'

With no hesitation, Gunther said, 'I'm not budging. She's my sister and she needs my advice. I need to know everything and I get the concept of confidentiality. Right, Lacy?'

Lacy had no choice but to say 'He can stay.'

Michael was in no mood for a fight; plus, Gunther had a glow in his eyes that was clear evidence of a short fuse. What the hell. Michael said, 'No word from Myers. I called the three numbers in your file several times and got nothing but ringing on the other end. Guess he doesn't do voice mail.'

'I doubt if they could track him, Michael.'

'Who's Myers?' Gunther asked.

'I'll tell you later,' Lacy said.

'Or not,' Michael said. 'Back to Monday night, what can you tell me about the meeting with the informant?'

Lacy closed her eyes and took a deep breath, one that made her grimace. Slowly, she said, 'Not much, Michael, not much. We went to the casino. We waited in the parking lot. Then we drove down a dark road and stopped at a small building.' She paused for a long time and seemed to be napping.

Michael asked, 'Did you meet with the informant?'

She shook her head. 'Nothing, Michael. I don't remember.'

'Did Hugo talk to the guy on his cell phone?'

'I think so. Yes, he had to. The guy told us where to drive and meet him. Yes, I remember that.'

'What about the collision itself? Anything leading up to it? The other vehicle?'

She closed her eyes again as if her memory might work better in the dark. After a gap, Gunther said, 'Early this morning, she was having a nightmare. She woke up and said she could see the headlights, said she remembers Hugo screaming, and before she could react the truck was right there. She remembers it was a truck. She does not remember the impact or the noise or anything else. Nothing about the rescue, the ambulance, the medevac, the emergency room. Nothing.'

One of Gunther's muted cell phones erupted in vibration, a call so urgent that the device tried to bounce across the purloined feeding table in his half of the room. He glared at it and fought the temptation the way a drunk in recovery stares at a cold beer.

He let it pass.

Michael nodded toward the door, and the two stepped into the hallway. He asked, 'How much have you talked to her doctors?'

'Not much. I don't think they like me.'

What a surprise. 'Well, they tell me her memory will slowly come back. The best way to help is to stimulate her brain, primarily by talking. Make her talk, make her laugh, make her listen, as soon as possible get her some magazines and see if she'll read. She loves old movies so watch them with her. Less sleep and more noise is what she needs.'

Gunther hung on every word, thrilled to be taking charge of things. 'Got it.'

'Let's chat with her doctors and try to keep the constable away from her for as long as possible. He wants to know what she and Hugo were doing on his land, and, frankly, we don't want him to know. It's strictly confidential.'

'Got that, Michael, but I want to know the details of the wreck. Everything. Tell me what you know so far. I smell a rat.'

'With good reason. Find your shoes and let's get some coffee.'

After lunch on Friday, as Gunther stalked the halls with his phone and fought desperately to salvage one crumbling deal after another, Lacy typed an e-mail:

Dear Verna: Lacy here, on my brother's iPad. I'm still in the hospital and finally have enough strength and clarity to check in. I don't know where to start or what to say. I cannot believe this has happened. It is so surreal. I close my eyes and tell myself I'm not here, Hugo is fine, and when I wake up all will be well. But then I wake up and realize that this tragedy is real, that he has been taken, that you and the kids are suffering a loss that cannot be described.

I am so sorry, not only for the loss, but also for my role in it. I don't remember what happened, except that I was driving and Hugo was my passenger. That's not important now, though I'll carry it to my grave. I so wish I could see you right now, and hug you and the kids. I love you all and can't wait to see you. I'm so sorry I'll miss the service tomorrow. I'm crying just thinking about it. I'm crying a lot, but not nearly as much as you. My heart breaks for you and the kids, Verna. You are in my thoughts and prayers. Love, Lacy

Twenty-four hours later, the e-mail had not been answered.

The funeral service for Hugo Hatch began at 2:00 p.m. on Saturday, at a suburban megachurch with a soaring, modern sanctuary that seated almost two thousand. Hugo and Verna had joined Gateway Tabernacle years earlier and were semi-active members. The congregation was virtually all African-American, and many of their family members and most of their friends also attended. As 2:00 p.m. approached, the crowd settled in somberly as everyone braced for the waves of emotion to come. There were a few empty seats but not many.

First up was a slide show on a massive screen above the pulpit. As a mournful spiritual was piped in from the sound system, one photo after another of Hugo came across, each a painful reminder that he had indeed been taken much too soon. Cute little Hugo as a toddler; Hugo gap-toothed in grade school; Hugo in all manner of football shots; Hugo on his wedding day; Hugo playing with his kids. There were dozens of photos, and they provoked a lot of tears, and as the service continued there would be a lot of everything. Finally, after a gut-wrenching half hour, the screen disappeared as the choir loft filled with a hundred singers in beautiful burgundy robes. Their mini-concert swung haphazardly from low, mournful dirges to rowdy, foot-stomping old-time gospel favorites to which the entire congregation sang along.

There were a few white faces in the crowd. Michael and his wife had a front-row seat in the long, sweeping balcony. As he glanced around, he saw others from BJC. He noted that most white folks were in the balcony, as if trying to keep some distance from the rowdiness below. Michael, a child of the 1960s and Jim Crow, saw the irony of the blacks in the best seats while the whites seemed banished to the balcony.

After an hour of warm-ups, the reverend took charge and spoke for fifteen minutes, his opening. A gifted and seasoned orator with a powerful baritone, he offered comfort to the loved ones while making the crowd cry even harder. The first eulogy was from Hugo's older brother, who told funny stories from their childhood but broke down halfway through. The second eulogy was from his high school football coach, a tough, crusty old white guy who barely uttered three sentences before choking up and crying like a baby. The third eulogy was from a teammate at Florida State. The fourth was from a law school professor. Then a soprano gave a magnificent rendition of 'How Great Thou Art,' and when she finished there was not a dry eye to be found, including her own.

Verna, in the center of the front row, somehow managed to hold things together. She was surrounded by family and had the two older kids next to her. An aunt was keeping Pippin and the toddler. Even as others wailed and collapsed, Verna just stared at the casket, ten feet away, and wiped her eyes without making a sound.

Upon the advice of a doctor friend, and against tradition, she had decided to close the casket. A large handsome photo of her husband stood next to it on a tripod.

As the service ground on, Michael couldn't help but glance at his watch. He was a devout Presbyterian, and in his church sermons were strictly limited to twenty minutes, weddings to thirty, and if a funeral inched past forty-five minutes somebody would catch an earful.

But the clock did not matter on this day at the Gateway Tabernacle. This was the last song and dance for Hugo Hatch, and it would be a glorious send-off. The fifth eulogy was given by a cousin who'd served time for drugs and was now clean and working, thanks to Hugo.

It was all quite moving, but two hours in Michael was itching to leave. He was also relieved to be sitting comfortably in a padded chair and not worrying about standing down there behind the pulpit. The Hatch family had initially asked if he 'would consider' saying a few words at the funeral, but the offer was quickly withdrawn by Verna. Michael was aware of some initial grumblings on her part. Hugo's death, whether accident or something else, could probably have been prevented if his boss hadn't sent him into such a dangerous situation. Hugo's older brother had called twice, curious about the trip to the reservation that late at night. The family was getting over the shock and asking questions, and Michael smelled trouble.

The sixth and last eulogy was from Roderick, Hugo and Verna's oldest child. He wrote a three-page tribute to his father, and it was read by the reverend. Even Michael Geismar, a cold-blooded Presbyterian, finally succumbed to his emotions.

The reverend wrapped things up with a lengthy benediction, and as the choir hummed and swayed the pallbearers rolled Hugo down the aisle. Verna was close behind, holding a child with each hand, her jaw tight with determination, her head held high, her cheeks dripping with tears. She was followed by a pack of family members, few of whom were making any effort at restraint.

The mourners left the building and scattered into the parking lots. Most would reassemble in half an hour at the cemetery for another memorial that would be too long and too gut-wrenching. Through it all, not one harsh word was thrown at the person responsible for Hugo's death. Of course, no one knew his name. 'A drunk driver in a stolen truck who got away on foot' was the accepted version and so, with no one to blame, the reverend and the speakers took the high ground.

When Hugo Hatch was lowered into his grave, only Michael and a few others suspected his death had not been accidental. Not far away, on a slight incline at the rear of the cemetery, two men sat in a car and watched the crowd with binoculars.

CHAPTER 17

By noon Saturday, the nurses and doctors had concocted a perfect plan to get rid of Gunther. It was brilliant – just transfer his sister and he would have no reason to stay. On Friday, Lacy had asked a doctor when she might be stable enough to make the trip back to Tallahassee. There were plenty of hospitals there, and fine ones, and since she was simply recuperating and not awaiting surgery, why couldn't she return to her hometown? Not long after that conversation, a nurse made a noisy entrance into Lacy's room, waking from a nap not only the patient but her brother as well, and the situation unraveled quickly. Gunther, using strong language, demanded that the nurses and orderlies show some respect for privacy and 'simple human decency' and stop barging in at all hours of the day. A second nurse came to the rescue of the first, but succeeded only in doubling the level of abuse. The plot was hatched to get Gunther out of the hospital.

At about the time Hugo was being buried, Lacy left the hospital in Panama City in an ambulance for the two-hour drive to Tallahassee. Gunther left too, but not before leveling a few parting shots at the staff. He followed his sister in his Mercedes-Benz S600 sedan, pitch-black in color and gobbling up $3,100 a month on a four-year lease. Evidently, the folks in Panama City had called ahead and warned the folks in Tallahassee. As Lacy's gurney was being wheeled onto the elevator for the ride to a private room on the fourth floor, two large security guards joined her and glared at Gunther, who glared right back.

'Let it go,' Lacy hissed at her brother.

The new room was larger than the last one, and Gunther had a fine time rearranging the furniture into another cozy work space. After the doctors and nurses checked in, Gunther looked at his sister and announced, 'We're going for a walk. I can tell already these doctors are far better than the other ones, and they say it's important to move around. You're probably getting bedsores. Your legs are fine, so let's go.'

He gently wrestled her out of bed, put her feet into a pair of cheap cotton hospital slippers, and said, 'Grab my elbow.' They eased out of the room and into a wide hallway. He nodded to a large window at the far end and said, 'We're walking all the way down there and back. Okay?'

'Okay, but I'm very sore. Everything aches.'

'I know. Take your time, and if you feel faint, just say so.'

'Got it.'

They shuffled along, ignoring the casual glances

from the nurses, clutching each other as Lacy's feet and legs began to work. Her left knee was severely bruised and cut and painful to move. She gritted her teeth, determined to impress her brother. His grip was strong and comforting. He was not taking no for an answer. They touched the window and turned around. Her room seemed a mile away, and by the time they approached it her left knee was screaming. He helped her into bed and said, 'Okay, we're doing that once an hour until bedtime. Got it?'

'If you can do it, I can do it.'

'Attagirl.' He tucked in the sheets around her and sat on the edge of her bed. He patted her arm and said, 'Your face is looking better by the hour.'

'My face looks like hamburger meat.'

'Okay, but sirloin, maybe, grade A, organic, and pasture fed. Look, Lacy, we're going to talk and talk until you cannot talk anymore. Yesterday I spent some time with Michael, good guy, and he filled me in. I don't know everything about the investigation, and I shouldn't, but I know enough. I know you and Hugo went to the reservation Monday night to meet an informant. It was a trap, a setup, a situation too dangerous to walk into. Once they lured you there, they had you dead to rights, and on their property. The wreck was no accident. You were deliberately rammed head-on by a guy driving a stolen truck, and immediately after the collision he, or someone with him, went through your car and took both cell phones and your iPad. Then these assholes disappeared into the night and will probably never be found. Are you with me?'

'I think so.'

'So here's what we're going to do. We're going to start with you and Hugo driving to the reservation – time, route, what was on the radio, what did you talk about, everything. Same thing while you were sitting in your car waiting at the casino. Time, conversation, radio, e-mails, everything. And we're going to drive your car down the road to meet the informant. I'll do the questions, hundreds of them, and you come up with the answers. And after I grill you for thirty minutes, we'll take a time-out and you can nap if you want, then we're walking to the end of the hallway again. Sound like fun?'

'No.'

'Sorry, kid, you have no choice. We've got the legs working, now it's time for the brain. Okay? First question: What time did you leave Tallahassee Monday evening?'

She closed her eyes and licked her swollen lips. 'It was early evening but not dark. I guess around seven thirty or so.'

'Was there a reason you waited so late?'

She thought for a second, then began nodding, with a smile. 'Yes, the guy worked until nine, a later shift in the casino.'

'Perfect. What were you wearing?'

She opened her eyes. 'Seriously?'

'Dead serious, Lacy. Think hard and answer my questions. This is not a game.'

'Uh, jeans, I think, and a light shirt. It was hot and we were casual.'

'What route did you take?'

'Interstate 10, same as always. There's only one way to get there. Exit onto State 288, go south for ten miles, turn left onto the tollway.'

'Did you guys listen to the radio?'

'It's always on, but almost muted. I think Hugo was sleeping.' She groaned and immediately started crying. Her swollen lips quivered and tears ran down her cheeks. He wiped them for her with a tissue but said nothing. 'His funeral was today, right?' she asked.

'Yes.'

'I wish I could've gone.'

'Why? Hugo wouldn't know if you showed up or not. Funerals are such a waste of time. Nothing but a show for the living. The dead don't care. The trend now is not to have a funeral, but a "celebration." To celebrate what? The dead guy damned sure ain't celebrating.'

'Sorry I brought it up.'

'Back to Monday night.'

Word spread that Lacy was back in town, and by early evening visitors were bumping into one another. Since most were acquaintances, the mood grew festive and the nurses complained more than once. Gunther, always the flirt, took center stage, did most of the talking, hogged the attention, and fought with the nurses. Lacy was exhausted and content to let him do whatever.

At first, she was horrified at the thought of seeing anyone, or, rather, letting anyone see her. With her slick head, stitches, bruises, and puffy eyes and cheeks, she felt like an extra in a cheap monster flick. But Gunther put things in perspective with 'Chill. These people love you and they know you just survived a head-on collision. And in a month you'll be hot again and most of these poor folks will still be homely. We got the genes, baby.'

Visitation was over at 9:00 p.m., and the nurses happily cleared out Lacy's room. She was exhausted. Her afternoon torture session with Gunther had lasted for four hours and ended only with the arrival of friends. Four hours of constant grilling and long hikes down the hall, and he was promising more tomorrow. He closed the door, said he wished he could lock it and keep everyone out, then turned off the lights and made his nest on the sofa. With the aid of a mild sedative, Lacy soon fell into a deep sleep.

The scream. The sound of terror from a voice that never screamed, never showed emotion. Something was wrong with a seat belt. He was complaining. She glanced over, then the scream as his wide shoulders instinctively threw back. The lights, so bright, so close, so shockingly unavoidable. The impact, the sense of her body hurling forward for a split second before being caught and slammed backward. The noise, the explosion of a bomb in her lap as five tons of steel, metal, glass, aluminum, and rubber collided and tangled. The vicious blow to her face as the air bag a foot away detonated and shot forward at two hundred miles per hour, saving her life but doing its share of damage. The spinning, her car airborne for a second as it turned 180 degrees, slinging debris. Then nothing. How many times had she heard victims say, 'I must've been out of it for a few seconds'? No one ever knows how long. But there was movement. Hugo, stuck in the windshield, was moving his legs, trying to either get out or get back in. Hugo moaning. And to her left, a shadow, a figure, a man with a light crouching and looking at her. Did she see his face? No. And if she did she could not remember it. And then he was on the passenger's side, near Hugo, or was it another one? Were there two shadows moving around her car? Hugo was moaning. Her head was bleeding, pounding. Footsteps crunched on broken glass. The lights of a vehicle swept the wreckage and disappeared. Darkness. Blackness.

'There were two of them, Gunther. Two of them.'

'Okay, Sis. You're dreaming now, and you're sweating. You've been mumbling and shaking for half an hour. Let's wake up and talk, okay?'

'There were two of them.'

'I hear you. Wake up now, and look at me. It's okay, Sis, just another bad dream.' He turned on a small lamp on the table.

'What time is it?' she asked.

'What difference does it make? You're not catching a plane. It's two thirty in the morning and you've had quite a dream.'

'What did I say?'

'Nothing intelligible, lots of mumbling and groaning. You want some water?'

She took a sip from a straw and pushed a button to raise her bed. 'It's coming back,' she said. 'I'm seeing things now. I can remember some of it.'

'Attagirl. Now, these two figures you saw. Let's talk about them. One was obviously the driver of the truck. The other was probably driving the getaway vehicle. What did you see?'

'I don't know, not much. Both were men, I think. I'm pretty sure of that.'

'Okay. Can you see their faces?'

'No. Nothing. I'd just been hit, you know. Nothing is clear now.'

'Sure. Where did you keep your cell phone?'

'On the console, usually. I can't say for sure where it was at that moment, but probably on the console.'

'And where did Hugo keep his?'

'Always in his right rear pocket, unless he was wearing a jacket.'

'And he wasn't wearing one, right?'

'Right. As I said, it was hot and we were casual.'

'So someone had to reach inside the car to get the cell phones. Can you see that as it happened? Anyone touch you or Hugo?'

She closed her eyes and shook her head. 'No, I don't remember that.'

The door opened slowly and a nurse entered the room. She said, 'Everything okay? Your pulse spiked.'

Gunther said, 'She's dreaming. Everything's fine.'

The nurse ignored him and touched Lacy's arm. 'How do you feel, Lacy?'

'I'm good,' she said, her eyes still closed.

'You need to sleep, okay?'

To which Gunther responded, 'Well, it's kinda hard to sleep with you guys in here every other hour.'

'There's a motel across the street if you'd like it better over there,' the nurse responded coolly.

Gunther let it pass, and the nurse left.

CHAPTER 18

When Lyman Gritt arrived at the police station at five on Sunday afternoon, he had a suspicion that something unpleasant was under way. The Chief had never requested a meeting at such a time and he'd been vague about its purpose. He was waiting outside the station, along with his son, Billy Cappel, when Lyman parked his truck. Billy was one of the ten-member Tribal Council and had become a dominant force in the government. As they were exchanging greetings, the chairman of the council, Adam Horn, arrived on his motorcycle. There weren't many smiles, and as they entered the building Lyman was even more suspicious. The Chief had been calling daily since the accident, and he was obviously not pleased with Gritt's work. As an appointee, the constable served at the pleasure of the Chief, and the two had never been close. In fact, Lyman distrusted the Chief, as well as his son and Mr Horn, who was generally held in low regard by most Tappacola.

Elias Cappel had been the Chief for six years and was firmly in control of the tribe. If Billy was his right-hand man, then Horn was the left. The three had effectively outmaneuvered their political enemies and seemed intractable. They smothered dissension and ruled with a tight grip, and no one really objected as long as the casino was full and the dividend checks were flowing.

They gathered in Gritt's office and he took his spot behind his desk. As he faced the three of them, his chair suddenly felt like a hot seat. The Chief, a man of few words and limited social skills, began with 'We want to talk about the investigation into what happened Monday night.'

Horn added, 'There seem to be some unanswered questions.'

Lyman nodded along. 'Sure,' he said. 'What would you like to know?'

'Everything,' the Chief said.

Lyman opened a file, fiddled with some papers, and pulled out a report. He went through the basics of the accident, the vehicles involved, the injuries, the rescue, the death of Mr Hatch. The file was already two inches thick with reports and photos. The video from the police in Foley, however, was not in the file and not referenced. Gritt smelled trouble with the Chief and was maintaining two files; the official one on his desk, and a secret one outside his office. Because Frog's video had been handed over to the sheriff, there was an even chance that the Chief might be aware of it. Wisely, Gritt placed it in the official file but kept a copy at home.

'What were they doing here, on our land?' the Chief asked, and his tone left no doubt this was his most important question.

'That, I don't know yet. I'm supposed to meet with Mr Michael Geismar tomorrow and learn more. He's their boss. I've asked that question, but so far the answers have been vague.'

'These people investigate judges, right?' Horn asked.

'That's correct. They are not law enforcement, just investigators, with law degrees.'

'Then what the hell were they doing here?' the Chief demanded. 'They have no jurisdiction on our land. They were here, on business I presume, at midnight on a Monday night.'

'I'm digging, Chief, I'm digging, okay? There are a lot of questions and we're chasing leads.'

'Have you talked to the girl who was driving the car?'

'No. I tried to but her doctors said no. They moved her to Tallahassee yesterday, and I'll go there in a day or two and see what she has to say.'

Billy said, 'You should've already talked to her.'

Lyman bristled but kept his cool. 'As I said, her doctors would not allow it.' Tension was rising by the minute and it was becoming clearer, at least to Lyman, that the meeting would probably not end well.

'Have you talked to outsiders?' Horn asked.

'Of course. It's part of the investigation.'

'Who?'

'Well, let's see. I've had several conversations with a Mr Geismar. I've asked him twice what they were doing here and he was vague. I've spoken with her doctors, got nowhere. Both insurance companies have sent adjusters here to check on the vehicles, and I talked to them. And so on. I can't remember everyone I've talked to. Part of my job is dealing with outsiders.'

'Do you know any more about the stolen truck?' the Chief asked.

'Nothing new,' Gritt said, then repeated the basics without mentioning the video from Foley.

'And no idea who was driving it?' the Chief asked.

'Not until this morning.'

The three seemed to stiffen. 'Go on,' the Chief grunted.

'Sheriff Pickett stopped by late Friday for a coffee. You know Frog Freeman's store north of Sterling? Well, Frog was open late on Monday, not really open, but then not closed either, and a customer came in looking for ice. Frog's been robbed, so he's got cameras. Wanna see?'

The three nodded grimly. Lyman tapped some keys on his desktop and turned it around. The video appeared. The truck was parked in front of the store; the driver got out; the passenger held a bloody cloth to his nose; the driver disappeared into the store and returned a short time later; they drove off.

'And what does this prove?' the Chief asked.

200

'Nothing, but it's somewhat suspicious, given the time and location and the fact that there's virtually no one on the road at that hour.'

Horn asked, 'So, if you stretch things, we're supposed to believe that the guy with the busted nose was driving the stolen truck that caused the accident?'

Lyman shrugged and said, 'I'm not stretching anything. I didn't make the video; I'm just showing it to you.'

'Have you traced the license plates?' the Chief asked.

'Yes. Fake Florida tags. No such number in the records. Why would anyone bother with fake tags if they were not up to something bad? If you ask me, the fake tags point the finger directly at these two. The passenger got his face smacked with the air bag and it drew blood. They weren't smart enough to have some ice in the follow-up vehicle, the one with the fake tags and driven, of course, by the other guy in the video. So they make their escape and just happen to see Frog's store open late. They're trying to get away, not thinking too clearly, and probably not that smart to begin with, so they don't think about security cameras. Big mistake. They get their pictures taken and it's just a matter of time before we find 'em.'

The Chief said, 'Well, Lyman, that's not going to happen, at least not now, and not by you. I'm terminating you as of right now.'

Lyman absorbed this shot to the gut with more

composure than he knew he had. He stared at the three of them, all sitting over there with their arms folded across their thick bellies, and finally asked, 'On what grounds?'

The Chief offered a phony smile and said, 'I don't have to give a reason. It's called termination at will and it's clearly set out in our bylaws. As the Chief, I have the power to hire and fire all department heads. You know that.'

'Indeed I do.' Lyman stared at the three of them, realized it was over, and decided to have some fun. He said, 'So the big boys want the investigation quashed, right? This video will never see the light of day. And all the mysteries surrounding this car wreck will never be solved. A man gets killed, and the killers walk away. That sound about right, Chief?'

'I'm asking you to leave right now,' the Chief growled.

'This is my office and I have my stuff here.'

'It is no longer your office. Find a box and get it out of here. We'll wait.'

'You're kidding.'

'Dead serious. And hurry up, okay, it is Sunday afternoon.'

'I didn't call this meeting.'

'Shut up, Lyman, and start packing. Hand over your keys and your guns, don't touch those files, pack up your crap, and let's move. And, Lyman, it goes without saying that it's in your best interest to keep your mouth shut.'

'Of course. That's what we do around here, right? Bury our heads, keep our mouths shut, and cover up for the big boys.'

'You got it, and the part about shutting your mouth can begin right now,' the Chief said. Lyman began opening drawers.

Michael tapped on Lacy's door with some trepidation, and as he opened it his worst fears were confirmed. Gunther was still there! He was sitting on the edge of her bed, a small backgammon board between them. He reluctantly folded it and placed it on the sofa in his office. Michael and Lacy chatted for a few minutes, then Michael delicately inquired, 'Could we have a few moments in private?'

'For what?' Gunther demanded.

'Some sensitive matters.'

'If it's about her job, I think the conversation can wait until tomorrow. It is, after all, Sunday evening and she's in no condition to deal with issues related to work. If it's about the car wreck and the investigation and all that crap, then I'm not leaving the room. Lacy needs a second set of ears and she needs my advice.'

Lacy did not intervene. Michael raised his hands, surrendered, and said, 'Okay. I'll not discuss the office.' He eased into a chair beside her bed and looked at the side of her face. The swelling was almost gone and the bruises were changing colors.

Gunther asked, 'Have you had dinner? The

cafeteria has some frozen sandwiches that were made at least two years ago and taste like roofing shingles. They're hard to recommend but I've eaten three and I'm still alive.'

'Gee, I'll pass.'

'Some coffee perhaps. It's bad but drinkable.'

Michael said, 'A great idea. Thanks.' Anything to get him out of the room. Gunther found his shoes and took off. Michael wasted no time. 'I stopped by Verna's this afternoon, and, as you can expect, it's still a gloomy place.'

'I've e-mailed twice but got nothing. I've called twice and talked to whoever was answering her cell. I need to see her.'

'Well, that's what I want to talk about, and I'll shut up the moment he walks in the door. I'd rather keep this between us. Verna is still sleep-walking through this nightmare, as anyone would be, and she's still in shock. But she's coming around and I'm not sure I like what I'm hearing. There is a group of Hugo's friends, including a couple of pals from law school, and they are full of advice. They have big ideas about lawsuits, with the big target being the Tappacola. That's where the gold mine is located and they're dreaming of ways to get it. Frankly, and I'm no tort lawyer, I can't connect the liability. Just because the accident happened on the reservation doesn't mean the Indians are at fault. The accident is also subject to tribal law, which is not your average brand of tort law. Because he was a state employee, Verna will get half his salary for the rest of her life. As we know, that's not much. Hugo had a private life policy for $100,000 and it will be easy to collect. Next is the auto policy on the stolen truck. According to the guy who appears to be the main spokesman, and he's a real windbag, the truck was covered by Southern Mutual and had a liability limit of $250,000. Even though it was stolen, it was still covered. It might take a lawsuit, but he seems to like their chances. I'm not so sure. Now things might get complicated. There was a lot of talk about suing Toyota for the defective seat belt and air bag. That would necessarily involve you, and your insurance company, and that's what I didn't like about their tone.'

'You're kidding, Michael. Verna is blaming me?'

'Right now Verna is blaming everyone. She's broken, she's terrified, and she's not rational. And, I'm not sure she's getting good advice. I got the impression these guys are sitting around the table, her table, scheming ways to sue anyone who's remotely connected to Hugo's death. Your name got kicked around, and I heard no objection from Verna.'

'They discussed this in front of you?'

'Oh, they don't care. The house is packed with people, food is still arriving. Aunts, uncles, cousins, anybody with an opinion can grab a cupcake and pull up a chair. I left with a bad feeling.'

'I don't believe this, Michael. Verna and I have been close for years.'

'It will take time, Lacy. Time for you to heal, time for her to heal. Verna is a good person, and when she gets over the shock she'll come around. For now, though, I'd cool it.'

'I don't believe this,' she mumbled again.

Gunther barged in with a tray and three cups of steaming coffee. 'This stuff even smells bad,' he said. He passed out the coffee and excused himself while he stepped into the bathroom.

Michael leaned over and whispered, 'When is he leaving?'

'Tomorrow. I promise.'

'Not a moment too soon.'

CHAPTER 19

Ann Stoltz arrived late Monday morning to spend a day or two with her daughter. Fortunately, her son was not in the room, though it was apparent he had not yet closed down his office and moved out. Lacy explained that Gunther was running errands. The good news was that he would be leaving around noon, because, of course, Atlanta was collapsing in his absence and the city had to be saved. The even better news was that her doctor planned to release her on the following day. She had convinced him her hair would grow just as fast at home.

A nurse removed stitches as Ann prattled on about the gossip down in Clearwater. A physical therapist arrived for half an hour of stretching and he gave Lacy a chart of exercises to work on every day at home. When Gunther returned, he had a sackful of deli sandwiches and the urgent news that he must get home. After an hour with his mother, he couldn't wait to leave the hospital. After four days with him, Lacy needed a break.

He was wiping tears as he said good-bye. He begged Lacy to call him for anything, especially if slimeballs like insurance adjusters and ambulance-chasing lawyers came slithering around. He knew exactly how to handle such people. On the way out, he gave his mother a perfunctory peck on the cheek, and he was gone. Lacy closed her eyes and enjoyed the silence for a long time.

The following day, Tuesday, an orderly rolled her out of the hospital and helped her into Ann's car. She was perfectly capable of making the walk herself, but the hospital had its rules. Fifteen minutes later, Ann parked in the lot beside Lacy's building. Lacy looked at it and said, 'Only eight days ago, but it seems like a month.'

Ann said, 'I'll get the crutches.'

'I don't need crutches, Mom, and I'm not using them.'

'But the physical therapist said—'

'Please. He's not here, and I know what I can do.'

She walked without a limp into her apartment. Simon, her British neighbor, was waiting. He had been caring for Frankie, the Frenchie, and when Lacy saw her dog she slowly bent to her knees and grabbed him.

'How do I look?' Lacy asked Simon.

'Well, pretty good, I'd say, in spite of it all. I suppose things could be worse.'

'You should've seen me a week ago.'

'It's good seeing you now, Lacy. We've been quite worried.'

'Let's have some tea.'

It was exhilarating to be out of the hospital, and Lacy chattered away as Simon and Ann listened and laughed. The conversation stayed clear of Hugo and the accident. There would be enough of that later. Lacy hit her stride telling Gunther stories, all of which seemed even funnier now that he was gone.

Ann kept saying, 'His father raised him, not me.'

Throughout the afternoon, Lacy called friends, napped off and on, stretched and exercised precisely as told, laid off the painkillers, nibbled on nuts and fruit bars, and looked at a few of her work files.

At 4:00 p.m., Michael arrived for a meeting and Ann went to the nearest mall. Claiming to have a stiff back, Michael said he needed to stay on his feet. So he paced, back and forth along the wide front window of her apartment, walking and talking, a man troubled by his thoughts. 'Are you sure you don't want to take a leave of absence?' he asked. 'We can cover your salary for thirty days.'

'And what would I do for thirty days around here, Michael? Pull my hair out just as it starts sprouting?'

'You need the rest. The doctors said so.'

'Forget it,' she said bluntly. 'I'm not calling time-out. I'll be at the office next week, scars and all.'

'That's what I figured. Have you talked to Verna?'

'No. You discouraged it, remember?'

'Right. Nothing has changed since Sunday.

She's out of money, of course, no surprise there, and eager to collect the life insurance.'

'You know his salary, Michael. They were living week to week. Can we help in some way?'

'I don't think so. None of us are exactly overpaid. Plus, it's a big family. She'll survive until the checks arrive. Long term, though, it's going to be rough with four kids and half a salary.'

'Unless the lawsuits work.'

'A big unknown.' He stopped for a sip of water. She was reclining on the sofa, exhausted after her first few hours of freedom. He said, 'We have two weeks, Lacy. Two weeks to either serve the complaint on McDover or let it lapse. Do you still want the case or should I give it to Justin?'

'It's mine, Michael, all mine, especially now.'

'Why am I not surprised? Frankly, I don't think Justin is quite ready for it, nor does he want it. Can't blame him for that.'

'I'm keeping it.'

'Fine, then do you have a plan? As it now stands, the complaint, signed by our pal Greg Myers, who is in hiding and had better remain so, alleges bribery in the form of the ownership of four condos in Rabbit Run, properties given to McDover by developers in return for favorable rulings. The complaint has very few specifics and no evidence. It gives the names of the foreign companies that are the official owners, but we have no way of proving that she is involved in the background. We can walk in with subpoenas and take her files and records and such, but I seriously doubt we'll learn much. If the criminal activity is as sophisticated as Myers says it is, then I find it difficult to believe McDover would leave any of her dirty records where they might be found. So, it's probably best to save the subpoenas for later. McDover will lawyer up and bring in more legal talent than I care to think about. It will become a slugfest where every move we make is hotly contested by the other side. And, in the end, there's an excellent chance McDover can prove that she purchased the condos as investments, something not unheard of in Florida.'

'You don't sound too enthused, Michael.'

'I'm never enthused by one of our cases, but we really have no choice. By now both of us believe Myers. We believe what's in the complaint and we believe his other stories of wholesale corruption, money laundering, bribery, not to mention murder.'

'Well, now that you mentioned murder, let's talk about it. There was a gang involved, Michael. First, the informant who lured us to a spot deep inside the reservation, then vanished in mid-sentence. Second, the guy driving the truck. Third, his partner who joined him at the scene, took our cell phones, then gave him a ride in the getaway car. Add the guy who stole the truck. Somebody tampered with the seat belts and air bags in my car. So if you have that many foot soldiers there must be a brain or two calling the shots. That adds up to a gang. If we assume it's Dubose, and I'm at a loss to give you the name of another suspect, then it sounds like the type of violence that's right down his alley. Hugo was murdered, Michael, and we can't solve it. I doubt seriously if the Tappacola can either.'

'Are you suggesting the FBI?'

'You and I both know that's where it's going, eventually. The question is when. If we invite them to the party now, then we run the risk of alienating Greg Myers, who's still the most important player here because of the mole. If Myers gets mad and disappears, we lose a source that cannot be replaced. A great source who might possibly one day break the case. So we wait. We serve the complaint and McDover will lawyer up as you say, but she will not know what we know. She and Dubose will assume that we believe poor Hugo was killed by a drunk driver and I got hit in the cross fire. They'll assume we know nothing about her fondness for private jets, expensive travel, trips to New York, Singapore, Barbados, you name it. They will not have a clue that we suspect Phyllis Turban even exists. All we have is this one rather lame little complaint signed by a guy they've never heard of and can't find.'

'So why do we bother with it?' Michael asked. She was definitely back, her mind clicking right along. Post-concussion, post-swelling, there obviously was no damage. As always, she raked in the facts quicker than anyone and looked around corners for the big picture.

'Two reasons, and both of equal importance,' she said. 'First, to keep Myers happy and busy digging. If we break this case, Michael, it will likely come down to the dirt provided by the mole, who knows a lot and has access to our judge. Second, we need to watch McDover's reaction to the complaint. Myers is probably right. She has no idea of what's coming. For the past eleven years she and Dubose have had their way bulldozing the county, skimming cash from the casino, bribing anyone who raised an eyebrow, breaking legs, or worse. The money has been too easy and it's probably deadened their senses. Think of it, Michael, the cash has been flowing for eleven years and no one with authority has ever come snooping around. We show up with the complaint and it rocks their world.'

Geismar stopped pacing and stared at a funky creation with four mismatched legs. 'A chair?' he asked.

'Indeed, a Philippe Starck knockoff.'

'He live around here?'

'No, he does not. It works. Have a seat.'

Slowly, Michael settled into the chair and seemed surprised when it did not collapse. He gazed out the window and saw the Capitol in the distance. 'Nice view.'

'That's my plan,' she said. 'Do you have a different one?'

'No, not now.'

CHAPTER 20

By Wednesday, Lacy was bored and contemplating a return to work. Her face looked much better but she was still reluctant to be seen by her colleagues. Ann shopped and ran errands and did whatever Lacy wanted, but she was getting bored too. She drove Lacy to the grocery store and to a doctor's appointment. She drove her to the office of an insurance adjuster who handed over a check for the Prius, a total loss. Ann was a terrible driver and poked along regardless of the traffic. Lacy was numb with fear of moving vehicles, and her mother's dangerous driving didn't help matters.

Lacy was sleeping well and without pain medication. Her physical therapy was progressing nicely and her appetite was returning. So it was no surprise when Ann announced over Wednesday dinner that she needed to go home. Very diplomatically, Lacy encouraged this. She appreciated her mother's care and concern, but she was clearly on the mend and tired of the babysitting. She wanted her space all to herself.

More important, she'd met someone, a physical

therapist who'd dropped by late Tuesday for a quick session, one carefully observed by Ann. His name was Rafe and he was in his mid-twenties, a good ten years younger, which didn't bother Lacy at all. There was a spark or two as he worked on her knee, and perhaps another as he said good-bye. He did not seem the least bit bothered by her cuts and bruises. She e-mailed him a short hey-howdy Wednesday night, and he responded within an hour. Back and forth a few times, and it was established that neither was in a relationship and both were interested in a drink.

At last, Lacy thought, maybe something good might come from this catastrophe.

In bed, flipping through a magazine, Lacy was startled by an e-mail from Verna. It read,

Lacy – Sorry not to have written or called sooner. I hope you're doing fine and recuperating. I'm so relieved your injuries were not as bad as they could have been. Me, I'm hanging on by a thread. Actually, I am completely overwhelmed with anything and everything. The kids are a mess and refuse to go to school. Pippin cries even more. At times they're all crying and I want to give up. But I refuse to break down in front of them. They need someone to be strong, so I just go hide in the shower and bawl my eyes out. I can barely survive each day and I hate the thought of tomorrow. Tomorrow without Hugo. Next week, next month, next year without Hugo. I cannot comprehend the future. The present is a nightmare. The past seems so long ago and so happy that it makes me sick. My mother is here, along with my sister, so I'm getting plenty of help with the kids. But nothing is real; everything seems artificial. They can't stay so they'll leave soon and I'll be here with four kids and no husband. I'd like to see you but not now. I need some time. When I think of you I think of Hugo and the way he died. Sorry. Please, just give me some time. Don't answer right now. Verna

Lacy read it twice and went back to her magazine. She would think about Verna tomorrow.

Ann finally got away late Thursday morning, several hours after Lacy had hoped. Wonderfully alone for the first time in ten days, she fell onto the sofa with Frankie and enjoyed the stillness. She closed her eyes and heard nothing, and it was lovely. Then she thought of Verna and of all the horrible sounds echoing through the Hatch home – crying kids and ringing phones and kinfolk shuffling in and out. She felt guilty for the contrast.

She closed her eyes and was about to catch a wink when Frankie growled softly. There was a man standing at her door.

Lacy went to the front window for a closer look. The door was locked. She felt safe. One quick push of a button on the security panel and all manner of alarms would erupt. The man was vaguely familiar – deep tan, lots of long gray hair.

Mr Greg Myers, she decided. On dry land.

She spoke through the intercom. 'Hello.'

His voice was familiar. 'Looking for Lacy Stoltz,' he said.

'And who are you?'

'Last name is Myers.'

She opened the door with a grin and said hello. As he stepped inside, she scanned the parking lot and noticed nothing unusual.

'Where's the Panama hat and gaudy shirt?' she asked.

'I save that for the boat. What happened to all that beautiful hair?'

She pointed to the ugly scar on her head. 'Twenty-four stitches and still pretty sore.'

'You look great, Lacy. I was so afraid you were badly injured. The newspapers have not said much about your condition, only that you had a head injury.'

'Have a seat. I assume you want a beer.'

'No, I'm driving. Just some water.'

She pulled two bottles of fizzy water out of the fridge and they sat at a small table in the breakfast nook. 'So you've kept up through the papers?' she asked.

'Yes, an old habit, I suppose. Since I live on a boat I need some contact with reality.'

'I haven't looked at a newspaper since the wreck.'

'You haven't missed much. As for you and Hugo, they've already moved on.'

'I'm assuming I was easy to find here.'

'Quite. You're not trying to hide, are you?'

'No. I'm not living like that, Greg. I'm not afraid.'

'Must be nice. Look, Lacy, I've just driven five hours from Palm Harbor. I want to know what happened. You gotta tell me. It wasn't an accident, was it?'

'No, it wasn't.'

'Okay. I'm listening.'

'We'll talk, but first a question. Do you still use the same phones you were using a month ago?'

He thought for a second and said, 'One of them.'

'And where is it right now?'

'On the boat. Palm Harbor.'

'Is Carlita on the boat?'

'Yes. Why?'

'Can you call Carlita right now, tell her to get the phone and toss it overboard? Now! You have no choice.'

'Sure.' Myers whipped out a burner and did as instructed. When he ended the call, he said, 'Okay, what was that all about?'

'It's part of the story.'

'Let's hear it.'

Throughout the narrative, Myers at times showed remorse, and at times seemed indifferent to the tragedy. 'What a mistake,' he mumbled more than once as Lacy described taking the bait from the informant.

'Was there an autopsy?' he asked. As far as Lacy knew, an autopsy had never been mentioned.

'No. Why would they do an autopsy?'

'I don't know. Just curious.'

Lacy closed her eyes and began tapping her forehead as if in a trance.

'What is it?' Myers asked.

'He had a light, a light on his head, like a miner or something.'

'A headlamp.'

'I guess. I can see it now. He looked at me through my window, which was shattered.'

'Did you see his face?'

'No, the light was too bright.' She covered her face with both hands and gently massaged her forehead with her fingertips. A minute passed, then another. Gently, Myers asked, 'Did you see the other guy?'

She shook her head. 'No, it's gone now. I know there were two of them, two figures moving around. One with the headlamp thing, and I think the other had a regular flashlight. I heard their footsteps as they stepped on the broken glass.'

'Did they say anything?'

'Nothing I remember. I was stunned.'

'Sure you were, Lacy. You had a concussion. That'll screw up your memory.'

She smiled, stood, walked to the fridge, and took

out some orange juice. Myers said, 'What kinds of cell phones?'

'Older BlackBerry models, issued by BJC.' She poured two glasses and set them on the table. 'I have an iPhone but I left it here. Hugo used the state phone for everything. I'm not sure he had another. Our IT guy says it's impossible to hack into the state phones.'

'But it can be done. For the right money, they can hire the hackers.'

'Our guy says not to worry. He's also tried to track the phones but there's no signal, which means they're probably at the bottom of the ocean.'

'I worry about everything. That's why I'm still alive.'

Lacy walked to a tall kitchen window and looked at the clouds. With her back to Myers she posed the question, 'So, tell me, Greg, what did they gain by killing Hugo?'

Myers stood and stretched his legs. He took a sip of orange juice and said, 'Intimidation. Somehow they got wind you guys were snooping around, so they reacted. As far as the police are concerned, it looks like an accident. But taking the cell phones also sent the message to you and BJC.'

'Could I be next?'

'I doubt it. They had you on the ropes and could have easily finished you off. One dead guy is warning enough. If something happened to you now it would bring the full weight of the federal government.'

'And what about you?'

'Oh, I'll never be safe. Their first objective will be to find Greg Myers, whoever the hell he is, and take him, me, out quietly. But they'll never find me.'

'Can they find the mole?'

'No, I don't think so.'

'A lot of uncertainties, Greg.'

He walked to the window and stood beside her. The rain had started and drops were hitting the glass. 'You want to quit?' he asked. 'I can withdraw the complaint and get on with life. Same for you. You've shed enough blood. Life is too short.'

'I can't do that, Greg, not now. If we walk away, the bad guys win again. Hugo died for nothing. BJC would be a joke. No. I'm still in.'

'And what's the endgame?'

'The corruption is exposed. McDover and Dubose and company are indicted and prosecuted. The mole gets his rewards. Hugo's death is investigated and those responsible are brought to justice. Junior Mace walks after fifteen years on death row. And whoever killed Son Razko and Eileen Mace is put on trial.'

'Anything else?'

'No, that should keep me busy for the next month or so.'

'You can't do it by yourself, Lacy. You need a lot of help.'

'Yes, I do, and that's where the FBI comes in. They have the resources and expertise; we don't. If you want this case cracked and the bad guys rounded up, then you have to ease up on the FBI.'

'You're assuming they will investigate?'

'Yes, and that might be assuming too much.'

'When do you approach them?'

'It's unlikely the FBI will get involved if we're not involved first. As you know, the agency has shown an extreme reluctance to stick its nose into Indian matters. So, our plans are to serve your complaint on McDover. She'll have thirty days to respond. We'll take it one step at a time.'

'You must protect my identity at all times, Lacy. If you can't promise that, then I'm checking out now. And, I'm not working directly with the FBI. You can, and I'll feed you everything we get from the mole, but I will have no contact with the FBI. Understood?'

'Understood.'

'And you be careful, Lacy. These are dangerous people and they're desperate.'

'I get it, Greg. They killed Hugo, didn't they?'

'They did, and I'm sorry. I wish I'd never called you.'

'Too late for that.'

He pulled a thin burner from his pocket and handed it over. 'Use this for the next month. I have one too.'

She held it in the palm of her hand as if it were stolen, then finally nodded and said, 'Okay, I guess.'

'In thirty days, I'll send you another one. Keep it close at all times. If the wrong people get it, I'm a dead man, and I wouldn't like your chances either.'

She watched him drive away, in a rented car with Ohio plates, and gripped his cheap phone while wondering how in the world she had gotten herself into such a mess. During her first nine years at BJC, her most interesting case had been a Duval County circuit court judge who preyed on attractive women going through bad divorces on his docket. He'd also preyed on court reporters, clerks, and secretaries, any female, really, who had a nice figure and was unlucky enough to get near his courtroom. Lacy forced him to resign and he later went to jail.

But nothing like this.

The inevitable moment had arrived, and Lacy was not ready for it. Nor would she ever be; thus she had no choice. Simon, her neighbor, agreed to ride along and talk her through it. Tentatively, she approached the small Ford rental, a loaner provided by her insurance policy and delivered the day before. She opened the door and slowly eased herself behind the wheel. She gripped it hard and felt her pulse hammering through her hands. Simon got in, put on his seat belt, and suggested that she do the same. She inserted the key, started the engine, and sat paralyzed as the air-conditioning slowly came to life.

'Take a deep breath,' he said. 'This is going to be easy.'

'There is nothing easy about it.' She gently pulled the gear shift into reverse and released the brake. When the car actually moved she felt a wave of dizziness and hit the brake again.

'Come on, Lacy. Let's get this over with,' he said, a Brit with one of those stiff upper lips. 'You have no choice.'

'I know, I know.' She released the brake again and inched backward. She turned and left the space free, then stopped and moved the gear shift into drive. No other car was moving in the small lot next to her building, but she feared them anyway.

Too cheerily, Simon said, 'Now, Lacy, one must take pressure off the brake for the vehicle to move forward.'

'I know, I know,' she repeated, almost mumbling. The car began to ease forward, then turned and stopped at the street, which was lightly traveled on a busy day. 'Take a right here,' he said. 'I see nothing coming.'

'My hands are sweaty,' she said.

'So are mine. It's hot as hell in here. Now, move along, Lacy. You're doing fine. All is well.'

She turned onto the street and pressed the accelerator. It was impossible to ignore the memories of her last drive, but she tried her best. Mumbling helped, and she kept saying, 'This is working. This is working.'

'You're great, Lacy. A bit more speed if you will.'

She glanced at the speedometer as it topped twenty, then began to slow for a stop sign. She made the block, then another. Fifteen minutes later, she was back at the apartment, dry-mouthed and drenched with sweat.

'Shall we do it again?' Simon asked.

'Give me an hour,' she said. 'I need to lie down.'

'As you wish, dear. Just give me a ring.'

CHAPTER 21

None of the three had ever visited the town of Sterling, population thirty-five hundred, and after a quick loop around the hideous courthouse they were certain they would not want to drop in again. Michael parked his SUV near a war memorial and the three got out. Certain they were being watched, they walked purposefully along the front sidewalk and through the main door. For this somber occasion Michael and Justin wore dark suits, as if they were entering the courthouse for a major trial. Justin was just along for the ride, and to provide some muscle and give the impression that BJC had the manpower and meant business.

Lacy wore black slacks and flat shoes. She could walk without a limp but her left knee was still swollen. She also wore a beige blouse and a silk Hermès scarf on her head. She had debated whether to walk into the meeting with no hat, no scarf, nothing to hide her shaved scalp and jagged cut with the suture indentions still fresh. On the one hand, she wanted Claudia McDover to see the damage, to be forced to stare at a living, breathing casualty of her corruption. But on the other hand, Lacy's vanity said cover it up.

They climbed the stairs to the third floor and found the office of the Honorable Claudia F. McDover, Circuit Court Judge, Twenty-Fourth Judicial District. Inside, a receptionist greeted them without a smile. Michael said, 'I'm Mr Geismar and I believe I spoke with you on the phone. We have an appointment with the judge at 5:00 p.m.'

'I'll tell her.'

Five o'clock came and went. At 5:15, the receptionist opened the door and said, 'Judge McDover.' They walked into her office and she greeted them with a smile that was plainly forced. Lacy avoided shaking her hand. In a corner of the large room, two men rose from a conference table and introduced themselves as Judge McDover's lawyers. Their presence was not a surprise. Michael had called the day before to arrange the meeting; thus, Judge McDover had twenty-four hours to begin lawyering up.

The older guy was Edgar Killebrew, an infamous white-collar defense lawyer from Pensacola. He was tall and thick and sharply dressed in navy pinstripes, and his thinning gray hair was slicked back and fell beneath his collar. By reputation he was loud and flamboyant, and intimidating because he was always ready for a fight and seldom lost before juries. His associate was Ian Archer, an unsmiling sort who refused to shake hands with anyone and reeked of surliness.

Awkwardly, they settled around the conference table. Judge McDover sat on one side with a lawyer at each elbow. Michael faced her, with Lacy and Justin at his sides. Small talk was useless. Who cared about the weather?

Michael began, 'A formal complaint was filed against Judge McDover forty-five days ago. We've done the assessment, and as you know our initial threshold is not very high. If it appears that the complaint may have merit, then we pass it along to the judge. That's why we're here today.'

'We understand this,' Killebrew said sharply.

Lacy stared at McDover and wondered if it was all true. The years of payoffs in return for favorable decisions; the outright stealing from the Tappacola; the murder of Hugo Hatch; the private jets and unlimited cash and homes around the world; the wrongful conviction of Junior Mace. No, actually, at that moment it did not seem possible that this attractive woman, an elected judge from a small town, could be involved in such ugly and far-reaching crimes. And what did McDover see when she looked at Lacy? The scarf hiding the wounds? A lucky girl who could have died? A nuisance to be dealt with later? A threat? Whatever the judge was thinking, she revealed nothing. Her face was all business, as unpleasant as it was.

The beauty of Lacy's strategy was that at that moment McDover had no idea what the mole had already told them. No idea they had an inkling of the cash, jets, homes, all the goodies. She was about to realize that her four condos had raised suspicions, but that was all.

'Could we see the complaint?' Killebrew asked.

Michael slid across the original and three copies. McDover, Killebrew, and Archer grabbed them and began reading. But they were careful not to react. If the judge was shocked, she hid her surprise well. Nothing. No anger. No disbelief. Nothing but a cool, dispassionate reading of accusations. Her lawyers read the complaint and managed to convey a smug indifference. Archer made a few notes on a legal pad. The minutes ticked by. The tension was thick, palpable.

Finally, McDover said, without a trace of emotion, 'This is absurd.'

'Who is Greg Myers?' Killebrew said coolly.

'We're not going to reveal his identity at this time,' Michael replied.

'Well, we'll find out, won't we? I mean, this is defamatory as hell and we'll sue him immediately for a ton of cash. He can't hide.'

Michael shrugged and said, 'Sue who you gotta sue. That's none of our business.'

Archer asked, with an obnoxious nasal tone that indicated he was far more intelligent than anyone else in the room, 'During the assessment, what did you learn that indicated these allegations have merit?'

'We're not required to divulge that at this time. As I'm sure you know, from a careful review of the statutes, Judge McDover has thirty days to respond in writing. During that period, we will continue to investigate. Once we receive your response, we will respond to it.'

'I got a response for you right now,' Killebrew growled. 'This is defamatory, libelous, and a complete crock of shit. It's all lies. The Board on Judicial Conduct should be investigated for taking this rubbish seriously and defiling the name of one of the highest-rated judges in the State of Florida.'

'You gonna sue us too?' Lacy asked coolly and knocked him off stride. Killebrew glared at her but did not take the bait.

'I'm concerned about confidentiality,' Judge McDover said. 'I'm not worried about these allegations, because they are groundless and we'll prove that in short order. But I have a reputation to protect. This is the first complaint filed against me after seventeen years on the bench.'

'Which proves nothing,' Lacy said, itching for a little skirmish.

'Correct, Ms Stoltz, but I want assurances that this matter will be kept quiet.'

Michael replied, 'We are quite aware of the need for secrecy, that we are dealing with reputations, and for this we closely follow the statute that makes our investigations confidential.'

'But you'll be talking to potential witnesses,' Killebrew said. 'And word gets around. I know how these investigations go. They can become witch hunts where the gossip flies and people get hurt.'

'People have already been hurt,' Lacy said as she glared, unblinking, at Judge McDover, who returned the stare as if she could not have cared less.

For a moment there was no air to breathe. Michael finally moved on with 'We handle these investigations every day, Mr Killebrew. I assure you we know how to keep things quiet. Oftentimes, though, the chatter seems to come from the other side.'

'Nice try, sir, but there will be no chatter from us,' Killebrew said. 'We'll file a motion to dismiss as soon as practical and get this crap thrown out.'

Michael replied, 'I've been with the BJC for almost thirty years and I have yet to see a case in which the Board dismissed the complaint before the responses were filed. But go ahead and try.'

'That's great, Mr Geismar, and in your years of vast experience how often do you serve complaints in which the identity of the complaining party is not revealed?'

'His name is Greg Myers. Right there on the front page.'

'Thank you. But who is Mr Greg Myers, and where does he live? There is no address, no contact information, nothing.'

'It would be inappropriate for you to contact Mr Myers.'

'I didn't say I wanted to contact him. We just want to know who he is and why he is accusing my client of something that amounts to bribery. That's all.'

'To be discussed later,' Michael said.

'Anything else?' McDover asked. The judge was in charge and ready to adjourn.

'No, not from us,' Michael replied. 'We will await your response in thirty days, if not sooner.'

Without a handshake and with hardly a nod, they stood and left the room. Nothing was said as they walked to the car and drove away. As the town faded behind them, Michael finally said, 'Okay, let's hear it.'

Justin spoke first. 'The fact that she hired the most expensive lawyer around here before she knew what was coming raises suspicions. Would she hire him if she wasn't guilty of something? And how can she afford him on a judge's salary? Narco-traffickers and other big-time crooks have the cash for a guy like Killebrew, but not a circuit court judge.'

'I guess she's got the cash,' Lacy said.

Michael said, 'As cool as she was, I saw fear. And not the fear of a soiled reputation. That's the least of her worries. You agree, Lacy? Could you read her?'

'I didn't get the impression she's afraid. She's too cold-blooded for that.'

Justin said, 'Look, we know what she's going to do. She'll file a thick response in which she claims she purchased the condos years ago as investments. It's not against the law to do so with offshore companies. It may look suspicious, but it's not illegal or even unethical.'

232

Lacy said, 'Okay, but how can she prove she paid for them?'

Michael ventured a guess. 'She'll find some records. She has Vonn Dubose somewhere in the dark cooking the books, and now she has Edgar Killebrew blowing smoke. This will not be easy.'

'We've known that from the beginning,' Lacy said.

'We need more from Myers,' Michael said. 'We need the smoking gun.'

'Yes, we do, and Myers needs to lay as low as possible,' Justin added. 'You saw how eager they are to find him.'

'They're not going to find Myers,' Lacy said with authority, as if she knew more than her colleagues.

They had driven two hours for a fifteen-minute meeting, but that was the nature of their work. If there was time, Lacy wanted to at least see her wrecked car and check for forgotten odds and ends in its console and trunk. Michael had tried to persuade her otherwise. Whatever she left behind – old CDs, an umbrella, a few coins – would not be worth the horror of seeing the evidence of Hugo's fatal injuries.

But, since they were in the neighborhood and had a few minutes, Michael wanted to say hello to Constable Gritt and introduce him to Lacy. Gritt had been on the scene and had helped with her rescue, and Lacy wanted to at least say thanks. It was almost 6:00 p.m. when they arrived at the police station near the casino. A cop was loitering around the front desk, and when Michael asked for Constable Gritt he was informed that he no longer worked there. There was a new constable and he'd gone home for the day.

'What happened to Gritt?' Michael asked, immediately suspicious.

The cop shrugged as if he had no idea. 'You can ask the Chief but I doubt if you'll get an answer.'

They drove two blocks to the salvage yard, and through a locked chain-link gate looked at a dozen old wrecks. The sad collection did not include Lacy's Prius or the Dodge Ram that collided with it. They were gone.

'Oh, boy,' Michael mumbled. 'Gritt assured me the vehicles would be secured. I told him there might be an investigation. I thought we were on the same page.'

'How long was he the constable?' Lacy asked.

'I think he said four years.'

'I guess we need to talk to him.'

'We're going to be very careful, right, Lacy?'

CHAPTER 22

The new constable was Billy Cappel, the Chief's son and a council member. When the Chief announced Billy's appointment, he explained to the police force that it was only temporary. Billy would serve until a proper search could be completed and the right man hired for the job. Since the new guy would no doubt come from the tribe, a proper search wouldn't take long. Indeed, both the Chief and Billy knew that the interim position would soon evolve into a more permanent one. Billy earned $50,000 a year as a council member, in addition to his monthly dividends. As constable, his new salary was three times that, plus, thanks to a new rule, he could play head cop and stay on the council. It was a good deal, especially for the Cappel clan.

Billy's law enforcement résumé was rather thin, but then he really didn't need one. He had worked for a short time in casino security, before being elected, and he had volunteered for the rescue squad before it had been upgraded with full-time personnel.

During the second day of his new job, the police in Foley called with some interest in arresting Berl

Munger, the man in the video who helped steal the Dodge Ram. Since the Foley police could not cross the state line to make the arrest, and since the Tappacola police had no jurisdiction off their reservation, the situation was a bit complicated. Billy promised to contact the police in DeFuniak Springs and enlist their help. He did no such thing; rather, he called his father, who passed along the word. Berl Munger soon knew there was an Alabama warrant for his arrest.

Billy couldn't find the video the Foley police were talking about. He searched the police offices, all its files and computers, and found nothing. He suspected that Lyman Gritt had somehow hidden the video or taken it with him. He called his father again and said they might have a problem. He called Foley and asked for the video, but the police there were already skeptical and asking themselves 'what the hell those Indians were doing over there.' They said they would send the video but were in no hurry to do so.

Berl Munger vanished. Billy and the Chief paid a visit to the home of Lyman Gritt. In a tense meeting, Gritt swore he knew nothing about a video. He had no idea what the cops in Foley were talking about. The Chief offered the usual threats, but Gritt was not easily intimidated. He finally asked them to leave his property. As constable, he had found the Chief meddlesome and dishonest. Now that he was unemployed, he despised the man, along with the rest of his family.

The video was hidden in Gritt's attic, along with a copy of the one from Frog Freeman's store. Gritt considered himself an honest cop who'd been fired by politicians who had been compromised. If the day of reckoning ever arrived, he might need some leverage.

Honest, and also quite capable. Two days after the accident, as the questions were piling up and the answers were proving elusive, Gritt had driven, alone, to the scene of the accident. He was stumped by three obvious puzzles. The first: Why would a car thief steal a vehicle worth at least $30,000 and drive it three hours to a remote spot on an Indian reservation? The county road where it came to rest was in the middle of their tribal land and, literally, went nowhere. It began on the back side of the casino property, snaked its way deeper into the reservation, and was used by only a handful of Tappacola who lived in the boondocks. With bloated budgets, the tribe kept it paved and well maintained, but the same was now true for almost every pig trail and field road on the land. Judging by his actions on the video, the thief had experience, and veterans like him usually sold their stolen wheels to chop shops within hours. They did not roam around strange places at midnight sipping Jack Daniel's and driving recklessly. To Gritt's knowledge, there were no fencing operations in Brunswick County. He found it impossible to believe that the driver, drinking or even drunk, could survive a head-on collision, even with a small

Prius, absorb the blow from the air bag, and simply walk away. And where would he go? The reservation was half swamp and uninhabitable. The higher land was covered in thick woods. The only decent land had been taken by the casino. At midnight, an intruder wandering around the depths of the reservation would get hopelessly lost in five minutes. If the guy with the busted nose in Frog's video was indeed the driver of the stolen truck, then he had an accomplice, one driving another truck with fake Florida plates.

This was the first puzzle and none of the pieces fit.

The second one was even more confusing: What were two lawyers whose jobs were to investigate judicial misconduct doing on the reservation at midnight? They were not trespassing – try as they might, Native Americans had so far been unable to wall off outsiders – but the two had absolutely no jurisdiction. The Tribal Court had three members, well paid but thoroughly lacking in legal education. The Florida Board on Judicial Conduct couldn't touch them.

The third puzzle was just as obvious: How did the wreck happen? There was apparently no other traffic, just the two vehicles on a dark, flat stretch of road. The weather was clear. There was no posted speed limit, but with the twists and turns any driver would struggle to safely exceed fifty miles per hour. Even under the influence, the missing driver should have been able to stay in his lane.

Standing at the exact point of impact, and looking at the asphalt scarred with the stains of engine fluids and littered with debris, Gritt had admitted he was stumped. This was not an open-and-shut case of a deadly collision and a fleeing driver. There was obviously much more to it.

A dozen emergency vehicles had left a maze of tire marks on the shoulders and even in the ditches and the flat field to the east. If the second truck, the one with the fake Florida tags, scooped up the driver, then where would it go? Perhaps it would stay off the road and avoid being seen by a Tappacola leaving the casino after the late shift. So far, Gritt had spoken to every resident in the area and no one saw anything; most had been asleep. Only Mrs Beale had heard the sound of the impact.

In the dirt beyond a shallow roadside ditch, Gritt had noticed tracks that led away from the scene. Wide tires, wide body, heavy traction, probably a pickup truck. He followed them for fifty yards, and in a thicket of cockleburs found a wad of paper towels, four sheets crushed into a ball and held together by a dried substance that could only be blood. He didn't touch it, but returned to his patrol car and from the trunk removed a plastic ziplock bag. Using a stick, he gently placed the paper towels in the bag, then continued following the tracks. He lost them in some brush and grass and picked them up again a quarter of a mile from his car. They crossed an empty creek bed, continued on for about a hundred yards, and turned left onto a gravel road he'd never seen before. At that point, the tracks were impossible to follow. The road curved back and forth for half a mile, passed only one home in the distance, and ended at a paved road called Sandy Lane. Gritt had then slowly backtracked to the accident scene and got in his car. From Frog's video, he had a clear shot of the guy's face. Now, with some luck, he had a sample of his blood.

The driver of the truck knew the area better than the constable.

The meeting took place in an unfurnished condo on Seagrove Beach, one of many built and sold by another faceless entity lost in the maze of the Dubose organization. When Chief Cappel arrived in the parking lot, alone, he was escorted into the building by a man he knew only as Hank. After years of dealing with Dubose, the Chief was still amazed at how little he knew about the man and those around him. He figured Hank must have some clout because he stayed in the room for the meeting, saying nothing but hearing every word.

Dubose was at the end of a long day. Two hours earlier, he had met Claudia McDover at her condo in Rabbit Run and been briefed on the meeting with BJC. He had read the complaint, asked the usual questions about who the hell Greg Myers was, and tried to calm his somewhat frantic judge. Afterward, he was driven to the condo, where he waited on the Chief.

Cappel carried a briefcase, and from it he pulled out a laptop and placed it on the snack bar. There were no chairs or seats in the new condo; the place still smelled of fresh paint. Cappel said, 'There are two videos. The first is from the police in Foley, Alabama, and we finally got a copy of it this afternoon. We're almost certain they sent it over last week and Gritt managed to lose it, or hide it, or whatever. It's not in the file and there is no reference to it. Here it is.' The Chief tapped some keys and Dubose moved closer. They watched the video of the Dodge Ram being stolen from the parking lot in Foley. Dubose said nothing until it was over, then said, 'Play it again.' They watched it a second time.

'What do you know?' Dubose asked.

'The Honda pickup is owned by a man named Berl Munger, who got a call and has disappeared. What do you know about him?'

Dubose backed away and paced around the den. 'Nothing. It was a contract job. We needed a stolen truck, so we made a call. Munger is not part of the club, just an independent contractor. He knows nothing.'

'Well, he dealt with someone when he handed over the truck and took the cash. He's got something to say.'

'He does, yes. I'm assuming he was told to get lost and stay there.'

'He was. Who was the other guy, the one who stole the Dodge Ram?'

'I have no idea, someone working with Munger, I guess. Again, we don't know these people. We just paid cash for a stolen truck.' Dubose walked back to the counter and stared at the screen. 'Let me see the other video.'

The Chief tapped some keys and Frog's video appeared. Dubose watched it and began shaking his head in disgust. He watched again and began cursing. 'Dumbass, dumbass, dumbass,' he mumbled.

'So you know these guys, right?'

'Yes.'

'And the kid with the busted nose was driving the Dodge Ram when it wrecked, right?'

'Shit, shit, shit.'

'I guess that means yes, yes, yes. You know, Vonn, I really don't like all these secrets. You pull this job on our land and tell me nothing. I don't want to be your partner, but in many respects we are joined at the hip. If there's a leak in the dike, I need to know it.'

Dubose was pacing again, chewing on a nail, trying to stay cool but wanting to erupt. 'What do you want to know?' he snapped.

'Who is the guy with the busted nose? And how can you use people who are so blatantly stupid? They make a late-night stop at a country store, park not in the shadows but directly in front, just begging to get themselves on surveillance, and, presto, we've got photos of your men just after the big job.'

'They are stupid, okay? Who's seen this video, the second one?'

'Me, you, Billy, Frog, Sheriff Pickett, and Gritt.'

'So we can contain it, right?'

'Maybe. Gritt worries me. He lied about the first video, said he knew nothing about it, but the cops in Foley told Billy they sent it over a week ago. Gritt's up to something, and now that he's out of a job he's really pissed. I wouldn't be surprised if he's got copies of both videos hidden somewhere. I tried to talk to him but it didn't go well.'

'What the hell is he doing?'

'I had to fire him, remember? You were in on that decision. We had to get rid of him so we control the investigation. The BJC is sniffing around and they're suspicious as hell. Who knows? They might go to the Feds and convince them to take a closer look. Gritt was never much of a team player. He had to go.'

'All right, all right,' Dubose said as he looked through a sliding door and gazed into the darkness. 'Here's what we do. You arrange a meeting with Gritt and convince him he's playing with fire. He's wandering off the reservation, so rein him in.'

'I really don't like that metaphor.'

Dubose turned around and walked to the Chief as if he might throw a punch. His eyes were glowing, his temper about to explode. 'And I don't give a damn what you like. We're not going under because Gritt got his feelings hurt over losing a job. Explain to him who you're dealing with. He's got a wife and three kids and his life is pretty good, even without his cute little constable's uniform. There's too much at stake for him to find religion at this point. He shuts his mouth, turns over whatever he's hiding, and gets in line. Or else. Got it?'

'I'm not going to hurt a brother.'

'You won't have to. You don't understand intimidation, Chief. I wrote the book. It's all I've ever known. It's what I enjoy. And Gritt needs to understand this. If I go under, then so do you and so do a lot of other people. But it's not going to happen. Your job is to convince Gritt to shut up and get in line. Do that, and everything will be just fine.'

The Chief reached over and closed his laptop. 'What about Sheriff Pickett?' he asked.

'He has no jurisdiction over the accident. You do. It's one less wreck for him to worry about. Besides, I can take care of the sheriff. Get Gritt in line. Make sure Munger is gone. Stall the boys over in Foley. And we'll weather this little storm just fine.'

'And the guy with the busted nose?'

'He'll be a thousand miles away by noon tomorrow. Let me deal with him.'

CHAPTER 23

Lacy was back in the office full-time, and while her presence raised spirits somewhat, Hugo's absence was still a gaping hole. She and Geismar kept most of the details to themselves, but there was now an accepted belief that his death was more than a tragic accident. For a tiny agency, the mysterious death of one of its own was unsettling. No one at BJC had ever considered their jobs dangerous.

Though her movements were slow and her head was still covered with a growing collection of scarves, albeit fashionable ones, Lacy was a delight to be around and an inspiration to her colleagues. She was regaining her strength and working longer hours.

Two days after serving the complaint on Claudia McDover, Lacy was at her desk when she received a call from Edgar Killebrew. Pompous even on the phone, he began with a pleasant 'You know, Ms Stoltz, the more I study this complaint the more I find it appalling. It's groundless and I'm stunned that Conduct would even remotely consider pursuing it.'

'You've already said that,' Lacy replied calmly. 'Any objections to my recording this conversation?'

'I don't give a damn what you do.'

Lacy pressed the record button on her phone and asked, 'Now, what can I do for you?'

'You can dismiss this damned complaint, that's what you can do. And you can tell Mr Greg Myers that I'll keep his ass tied up in court for the next ten years fighting libel suits.'

'I'll pass that along, and I'm sure Mr Myers understands that there is nothing libelous or defamatory in his complaint because it has not been made public.'

'We'll see about that. I've decided not to file a motion to dismiss, simply because it will only draw attention to this matter. The Board has five members, five political hacks who sucked up to the Governor, and I don't trust any of them when it comes to keeping secrets, just like I don't trust anybody in your office. This has got to be kept as quiet as possible. Do you understand, Ms Stoltz?'

'We had this conversation in Judge McDover's office two days ago.'

'Well, we're having it again. And furthermore, I'd like to know more about your investigation. Doubtless it's going nowhere, so I'm afraid you'll get desperate and start cold-calling anybody who might possibly know my client. That's how rumors get started, vicious rumors, Ms Stoltz, and, well, I just don't trust you or anyone else to handle this matter with discretion.'

'You're worrying too much, Mr Killebrew. We do this every day and we understand confidentiality. And, I'm not at liberty to discuss our investigation.'

'Well, I'm warning you that if this case becomes a witch hunt and my client's reputation is damaged, I'll sue you and Mr Geismar and everybody else at Conduct for defamation.'

'Go ahead. And we'll countersue for filing a frivolous lawsuit.'

'Beautiful, just beautiful. I would relish the opportunity of seeing you guys in court. I live there, Ms Stoltz, and you do not.'

'Anything else, Mr Killebrew?'

'Nothing. Good day.'

As cool as she sounded on the phone, the call was nonetheless unsettling. Killebrew was a fearless litigator, infamous for his scorched-earth tactics. Such a lawsuit would ultimately be deemed frivolous, but the prospect of wrangling with him was intimidating. And he was right; he earned big money in front of juries, and Lacy had never seen one. She played the call for Michael, who managed a laugh. He had received such threats before; she had not. As long as BJC did its job and did not step out-of-bounds, the agency was basically immune from civil lawsuits. Otherwise, they would never serve a complaint.

She returned to her desk and tried to concentrate on other matters. For the second time, she called the constable's office and asked for Billy Cappel.

He was too busy at the moment. She called back an hour later and he was still in a meeting. She called her insurance company and eventually tracked down the adjuster who had her totaled Prius. He informed her that he had sold her wrecked car to a salvage yard near Panama City for $1,000, the usual price for a full loss. He claimed to know little about what happened to such vehicles after they landed at salvage yards, but he believed they were either crushed and sent to recycling plants or sold to scrap yards for parts. Two phone calls to the salvage yard netted no information. After lunch, she informed Michael she had a doctor's appointment and would not be back that afternoon.

Instead, she drove to Panama City, her first road trip alone. She stuck to the speed limit and tried not to flinch at every car that passed, but it was nerve-racking nonetheless. Her breathing was labored and a thick knot stayed in her stomach, but she was determined to get there and back. At the salvage yard, she parked in a gravel lot between a tow truck and a battered pickup and asked an old man with a greasy shirt and even dirtier beard about the office. He nodded toward a metal building with dented walls and an open front door. She walked through it and entered a room with a long counter where mechanics purchased used auto parts. The walls were covered with an impressive collection of hubcaps, though one corner was reserved for calendars of seminude women. The presence of a pretty

248

lady stopped all transactions. A man with the name Bo stenciled on his shirt smiled and said, 'Well, hello, miss, what can we do for you?'

She smiled, stepped forward, and said, 'I'm looking for my car. It was wrecked three weeks ago on the Tappacola reservation and brought here. I'd like to see it and retrieve some personal items.'

Bo stopped smiling and said, 'Well, if it was brought here, then it's not your car anymore. I'm assuming it was totaled.'

'Yes. I've talked to my insurance company and was told it was here.'

Bo stepped to a computer screen and asked, 'Do you have the VIN?' She handed over a photocopy of her title. He punched some keys as his pal Fred joined him. Two mechanics watched closely from the other end of the counter. Bo and Fred frowned and mumbled and seemed confused. Bo said, 'This way,' and left the counter. Lacy followed as they walked along a short hall and through a side entrance. Behind the building, and kept from view by a tall fence, was a field of mangled cars, trucks, and vans, hundreds of them. In the distance, a massive, clumsy machine was crushing a wrecked vehicle. Bo waved at another man and he eventually walked over. He wore a white shirt, one much cleaner than Bo's or Fred's, and without a name on it, and he seemed to be in charge. Bo handed him a sheet of paper and said, 'She's looking for that Prius that came from the Indian reservation. Says it was hers.'

The man frowned and shook his head. 'It's not here. Some guy showed up a few days ago and bought it for cash. Took it away on a flatbed hauler.'

Lacy, way out of her league, asked, 'Who bought it?'

'Can't say, ma'am, and really don't know. Don't think he ever gave a name, just wanted the car and had the cash. Happens all the time. These guys'll buy a wreck and sell off the parts. Never seen this dude before.'

'And there are no records?'

Bo laughed and his boss grinned at her ignorance. The boss said, 'No, ma'am. Once a car is totaled and the title is invalidated, no one cares what happens to it. Cash sales are not unusual in this business.'

She wasn't sure what to ask next. She assumed they were telling the truth. She looked at the acres of wrecked vehicles and realized that a search would be fruitless.

'Sorry, ma'am,' the boss said and walked away.

The text from Verna read 'You wanna talk?'

They exchanged a few more messages and agreed on a time.

Lacy arrived at the Hatch home after dinner. Verna was alone with the kids. The older two were doing homework at the kitchen table. Pippin and the toddler were asleep. Verna said the house had not been that quiet since before Hugo died. They sipped green tea on the patio and watched fireflies in the darkness. Verna was relieved that the relatives had finally cleared out, though her mother would be back tomorrow to help with Pippin. Verna was exhausted but sleeping more. She still awoke with the dream that Hugo was with her, but managed to work her way back to reality. With four kids she did not have the luxury of proper mourning. Life was not slowing down.

She said, 'I got the life insurance check today, so the pressure is off, for now anyway.'

'That's great, Verna.'

'We'll be okay for a year or so, but I'll have to find a job. Hugo made sixty thousand a year and we never saved a dime. I need to bury some of this money for the future, for the kids.'

She wanted to talk, and she wanted a listener who was not in the family. Her degree from FSU was in public health, and she'd been a social worker for a year or so before her first pregnancy. After the third, she put away any thoughts of a career. She said, 'I like the thought of a job. I've been a full-time mother for a long time now and I'm ready for a change. Hugo and I talked about this often and we had decided that as soon as Pippin was in preschool I would go back to work. Maybe with two salaries we could swing a bigger house, maybe start saving for the kids. Hugo was so supportive, Lacy. He had the big ego and all that, he couldn't help it, but he was not threatened by a working wife.'

Lacy listened and nodded. Verna had talked of a career a dozen times.

Verna took a sip of tea and closed her eyes for a moment. She snapped out of it with 'Can you believe I've already had folks asking me for money? So far two of Hugo's cousins hung around here long enough to ask for a loan. I said hell no and got rid of them, but they'll be back. What is it about people that makes them do horrible things like that, Lacy?'

The question couldn't be answered. Lacy responded with 'I don't know.'

Verna said, 'I got way too many people giving me advice these days. Even before the funeral everybody knew I was getting a hundred thousand in life insurance and some of these leeches were already trying to worm their way in. I'm sick of them, really. Not my mom or my sisters, but some of these cousins, some of these folks Hugo and I have barely seen in the past five years.'

'Geismar said there were some lawyers in the house, plotting lawsuits.'

'I got rid of them too. One big mouth said I could collect from the insurance policy that covered the stolen truck. Turns out that's not the case. When a vehicle is stolen like that, the policy becomes void, at least as far as liability. Lots of big lawsuits got kicked around. One was against Toyota for the faulty air bag and seat belt, but I'm not sure that's a good idea. Got a question, Lacy. When you and Hugo drove to the casino that night, was his seat belt working?'

'Not really. He complained because it wouldn't

252

stay latched. This had never happened before. He fiddled around with it and several times got it to click into place, but something was wrong with it.'

'You think someone tampered with it?'

'I do, Verna. I believe the air bag was disarmed and the seat belt was somehow compromised.'

'And the accident was not an accident?'

'No, it was not. We were deliberately hit by a truck that weighed twice as much as the Prius.'

'But why? You gotta tell me, Lacy. I deserve to know what's going on.'

'I'll tell you as much as I can, but you must promise to keep it quiet.'

'Come on, Lacy. You know me.'

'Do you have a lawyer?'

'Yes. One of Hugo's friends from law school is handling everything. I trust him.'

'Okay, but not even he needs to know the story, not now.'

'Tell me, please.'

It was almost ten when Roderick opened the door and said, 'Mom, Pippin's crying.'

Verna quickly wiped the tears from her cheeks and said, 'Well, what a surprise. That child.'

As the women stood and walked inside, Lacy said, 'I'll stay tonight, okay? I'll take care of Pippin and maybe we can talk some more.'

'Thank you, Lacy. I have some more questions.'

'I'm sure you do.'

CHAPTER 24

The meeting took place in the FBI's Tallahassee office, a ten-minute walk from BJC. The supervisor was an unsmiling career man named Luna, and from the moment they gathered around his wide conference table he seemed to doubt the importance of the meeting. To his right was a handsome and affable special agent named Pacheco, mid-thirties, no wedding band, and eyes that seemed to swallow Lacy the moment they said hello. At the far end of the table, as if needed but not really wanted, was the third agent, Hahn. Lacy faced Luna and Pacheco, with Geismar to her right.

She began with 'First, thanks for your time. We know you're busy and this will not be quick. Do we have time constraints here?'

Luna shook his head and said, 'No. We're listening.'

'Good. On the phone yesterday I asked you about a man named Vonn Dubose. We're curious as to whether you know anything about him.'

Pacheco picked up a sheet of paper and said, 'Yes, well, not much. Dubose has no criminal record, state or federal. The Catfish Mafia, or Coast Mafia as it came to be, has been known to us for a long time. I think you have its history. A small gang with a colorful past, but nothing of record here in Florida. About twenty years ago a man by the name of Duncan was caught with a truckload of marijuana near Winter Haven. DEA suspected he was working for an organized group, probably the same Coast Mafia, but they got nowhere because Duncan wouldn't talk or negotiate. He served a long sentence and was paroled three years ago. Never said a word. That's about it. As far as the man known as Vonn Dubose, we have yet to find anything.'

Luna added, 'So as far as we're concerned, there's really no outfit known as the Coast Mafia. We spend our time these days focusing on known entities – al-Qaeda, narco-traffickers, nice guys like that.'

Lacy said, 'Okay. We have an informant who we've grudgingly come to believe is telling the truth. He's a former lawyer, a convicted felon, and he seems to know where the bodies are buried. Not literally, of course, but he's convinced there is an organized gang with Dubose firmly in control. The informant contacted us about two months ago.'

Pacheco asked, 'This is Greg Myers?'

'Yes, that's the name in the complaint I sent over yesterday. But that's a new name, not his real one. According to Myers, Vonn Dubose and his brother got shot up in a bad drug deal many years ago in south Florida. The brother died. Vonn did not. No record of that?'

Pacheco was shaking his head. 'Nothing. How would Myers know this?'

'I have no idea. He is on the run and very secretive.'

'Who's he running from?' Luna asked.

'Not sure, but not you or any branch of law enforcement. When he pled guilty he squealed on a bunch of people and now he feels threatened.'

Pacheco said, 'Were his charges federal?'

'Yes, they were, and he served time in a federal facility. But please, for reasons I may be able to give you later, don't waste your time trying to find the real Greg Myers. He is not the reason we are here. You've read the formal complaint that's been filed against Judge McDover. We did our assessment and felt it had merit. The real story goes much deeper than what's in the complaint. According to Myers, Vonn Dubose and the Tappacola tribe struck a deal almost twenty years ago to build a casino and they've been skimming off the top since day one. Lots of cash, some of which is now shared with Judge McDover.'

'The judge is taking cash?' Luna asked.

'Yes, according to Myers.'

'And why would they give her the cash?'

'The formal complaint is our Exhibit A. You have a copy. Here is our Exhibit B.' Geismar slid copies across the table. Lacy continued, 'It's a concise summary of the Tappacola, their land, their federal recognition, and their efforts to build a casino. It involves at least two murders and a man named Junior Mace, who is now sitting on death row at Starke. I suggest you take a few minutes and read the exhibit.'

They were already reading, slowly. So far, the story had their attention. Methodically, they flipped pages, with Pacheco a bit quicker on the draw. At the far end, Hahn plowed through in silence. The air was heavy as they weighed every word. Lacy scribbled meaningless notes on a legal pad, while Michael read e-mails on his phone.

When they finished, Lacy said, 'Our Exhibit C is a rather detailed history of the construction of the casino, the building of a toll road, and all of the litigation that surrounded both. With a judge in his pocket, Dubose was able to fight off anyone who got in his way, and Treasure Key opened in 2000.' Geismar slid across copies of Exhibit C.

'And you want us to read this now?' Luna asked.

'Yes.'

'Okay. Would you like some coffee while we read?'

'That would be nice, thanks.' Hahn snapped to attention and hustled off to find a receptionist. The coffee arrived in real mugs – no paper – but neither Luna nor Pacheco seemed to notice. They were lost in Exhibit C.

Pacheco finished first, and rather than interrupt his boss, he made notes in the margins and waited. Luna lowered his copy and said, 'A question. This

Junior Mace on death row, are we to suspect that maybe he did not commit the two murders referenced in the earlier exhibit?'

Michael replied, 'Frankly, we don't know, but Greg Myers believes Mr Mace was framed and is innocent.'

Lacy added, 'I've met with Mace on death row, and he certainly claims to be innocent.'

Pacheco quipped, 'Doubt if he's the only one there who says he didn't do it.'

Smiles but no laughs. Luna glanced at his watch, stared at the paperwork in front of Geismar, and asked, 'How many of these exhibits do you have?'

'Not many.'

Lacy said, 'Well, in Exhibit D, you meet the judge.' Geismar slid them over. 'First you'll see photos of her at one of her condos at Rabbit Run.'

Pacheco looked at the photos and said, 'She's not exactly posing for the camera. Who took these?'

'We don't know,' Lacy said. 'Greg Myers has an informant whose name we do not know because Myers doesn't know. They correspond through an intermediary.'

From the far end Hahn exhaled as if in disbelief.

'It's a complicated story and it only gets better,' Lacy said, glancing at Hahn. 'Back to the exhibit. There's some background on McDover, not much, though, because she keeps a low profile. Her partner in crime, or one of her partners, is an estate lawyer in Mobile named Phyllis Turban. Her

258

photo was taken from the local bar directory. These women go way back, are very close, like to travel in style and always together. They spend far more than they earn. The exhibit summarizes their travel over the past seven years.'

Obviously intrigued, the three agents were already zipping through D. The room was silent again as they flipped the pages.

Lacy's coffee cup was empty. They had been at the table for an hour, and she was delighted at the reception so far. She and Michael did not know what to expect coming in. They assumed the story they were about to tell would be captivating, but they had no idea how it would be received. Now they had the FBI's attention. Though the agents were conscious of time, they seemed to be in no hurry.

Luna was looking at her. 'Next.'

'Next is Exhibit E, the thinnest one so far, and it's a timeline of our involvement in the case,' she said as Geismar spread more paperwork. They read it thoroughly.

Pacheco asked, 'How did McDover react when she was served with the complaint?'

'She was pretty cool,' Lacy said. 'Denied everything, of course.'

Michael said, 'I thought she looked scared, but my two colleagues disagreed. Not sure that it matters that much.'

Pacheco said, 'Well, she must be guilty of something if she hired Edgar Killebrew.'

Hahn surprised them with 'That's my first reaction. What a shyster.'

Luna raised a hand slightly to cut him off, and asked, 'One more exhibit?'

Lacy replied, 'Yes, the last one. I'm sure you saw that our colleague Hugo Hatch died in a car wreck on the reservation.'

They nodded sadly.

'Well, I was driving the car when it happened. I'm wearing a scarf because my head was shaved in the hospital. I had cuts and abrasions, a bunch of stitches, a concussion, but I was lucky. I don't remember much about it but things are coming back. Anyway, my friend and colleague died at the scene and his death was not an accident. We believe he was murdered.' Geismar slid over copies of F, which they grabbed with a bit more eagerness.

Photos of the Prius and the Dodge Ram; photos of the scene; summaries of conversations with the constable; a description of the air bag and seat belt that didn't work; the missing phones and iPad; and the conclusion that someone was behind the accident, thus the murder, and that someone was Vonn Dubose and his gang. She and Hugo allowed themselves to be lured to the back side of the reservation with the promise of information, and got ambushed. The motive was to frighten them, to intimidate them, to show them that they were in way over their heads, and that Dubose would resort to any measure to protect his empire. According to Myers, and they had no reason to doubt him, no one with authority had ever snooped around the casino and asked questions. BJC was the first, and Dubose moved decisively to send a message. He knew the limits of BJC's investigative authority, and assumed, correctly, that the agency had almost no crime-fighting capability. He assumed a good scare would scatter them.

'Wow,' Pacheco said as he put down the exhibit. 'You're not pulling any punches.'

'We have a dead friend,' she said. 'And we're not going away.'

Michael said, 'But at the same time, we do not have the resources or the authority to fully investigate this corruption. That's where you come in.'

For the first time, Luna showed a hint of either fatigue or frustration. He said, 'I don't know. This could be an awfully big case.'

If Luna showed reluctance, Pacheco seemed ready to sign on. 'It's a massive case,' he said with another smile in Lacy's direction.

'It is,' she said. 'And far too big for us. We simply cannot investigate organized crime. Our world revolves around judges who've cracked up and done stupid things. They violate ethics, but rarely break laws. We've never seen a case like this.'

Luna shoved his pile of paperwork away and locked his hands behind his head. 'Okay, you're not a cop, but you are an investigator. You've lived through this for the past several weeks. If you were us, Ms Stoltz, how would you proceed?'

'I'd start with the murder of Hugo Hatch. Sure,

261

I'm emotionally involved with it, but solving it might be easier than trying to penetrate a hundred offshore entities and chasing the money. Someone stole the truck. Perhaps another person was driving it. They were working for an organization, for a boss who ordered the hit. Oddly enough, I think the murder was a gift. Dubose overplayed his hand, overreacted, and did something that could come back to bite him. He's lived his entire life in a world of violence and intimidation. Sometimes those guys go too far. He felt threatened and his instinct was to hit hard.'

Pacheco asked, 'And there's no doubt the two cell phones and your iPad were taken?'

'No doubt at all. They obviously wanted the devices for information, but the theft was also a warning. Perhaps Dubose wanted to drop a not-so-subtle hint that they were there, at the scene.'

'And you know they were at the scene?' Pacheco asked gently.

'Yes. I don't recall much, but I remember someone moving around, someone with a light of some sort attached to his head. The light hit my face for an instant. I can remember the sound of footsteps on broken glass. I think there were two men moving around, but again I was barely conscious.'

'Of course you were,' Pacheco said.

Lacy continued, 'The wreck will not be thoroughly investigated by the Tappacola. The constable has already been replaced, and the new guy happens to be the son of the Chief. We can assume they are compromised and eager to close the book on just another tragic car accident.'

'You're assuming the Chief is in bed with Dubose?' Luna asked.

'Definitely. The Chief rules like a king and knows everything. It's impossible to believe they're skimming cash without his involvement.'

'Back to these phones,' Pacheco said. 'You're certain they got no intel from them?'

Michael replied, 'Yes. The phones are issued by the state. They have, or had, the usual five-digit pass code, but after that there was an encryption barrier. Our tech guys are sure they are secure.'

'But anything can be hacked,' Luna said. 'And if they were somehow able to do so, what would they find?'

'It would be extremely damaging,' Michael said. 'They would have the phone records, a trail of all the phone calls. And they would probably be able to find Greg Myers.'

'And Mr Myers is still alive and well, I presume?' asked Luna.

'Oh yes,' Lacy said. 'They're not going to find him. He was here in Tallahassee two weeks ago, stopped by my apartment to see how I was doing. All of his old phones are at the bottom of the ocean and he has a supply of new burners.'

'And your iPad?' Pacheco asked.

'There's nothing on it that would help them. All personal stuff.'

263

Luna pushed his chair back and stood. He stretched his legs and said, 'Hahn.'

At the far end, Hahn was shaking his head and eager to contribute. Perhaps he's the secret weapon, Lacy thought. He said, 'I don't know. So we swoop in with half a dozen agents. What happens then? The cash vanishes into their network of foreign accounts. The skimming stops. The Indians are terrified of Dubose and everyone clams up.'

Pacheco mumbled, 'I love it.'

Lacy said, 'I wouldn't do that. I would quietly go about the task of finding the driver of the truck. Say you get lucky and grab the guy. He's looking at spending the rest of his life in prison so he might want to talk, to deal.'

'Witness protection?' Pacheco asked.

'That's your game and I'm sure you guys know how to play it.'

Luna returned to his seat, shoved the paperwork even farther away, rubbed his eyes as if suddenly fatigued, and said, 'Look, here's our problem. Our boss is in the Jacksonville office. We make a recommendation to him and he makes the decision. Part of our job is to estimate the manpower and number of hours this case might ultimately consume. Frankly, it's always a waste of time because the target is steadily moving and it's impossible to know where an investigation might go. But rules are rules, and this is, after all, the federal government. So our boss looks at our recommendation. Right now he's not thinking about a little graft at

264

an Indian casino. He's probably not going to be too impressed with a car wreck that could've been something else. No, these days we're fighting terror. We spend our time tracking sleeper cells and American teenagers who are chatting with jihadists and homegrown idiots who are trying to assemble the ingredients to make bombs. And, I gotta tell you, there's a lot of bad stuff going on. We're understaffed and often feel as though we're getting further behind. We never forget that we were twenty-four hours late at 9/11. This is our world. This is the pressure we're under. Sorry for the speech.'

For a moment no one said a word. Michael broke the silence with 'I think we understand, but organized crime does go on.'

Luna actually smiled and said, 'Sure it does. And I think this is a perfect case for the FBI, but I'm not so sure our boss will agree.'

'Is it fair to ask what your recommendation will be?' Lacy asked.

'It's fair to ask but I can't give you an answer right now. We'll kick it around here for a couple of days, then send it to Jacksonville with a report.' His body language suggested he didn't want to get involved. Pacheco's suggested he was ready to whip out his badge and start grabbing witnesses. Hahn revealed nothing.

Lacy collected her papers and placed them into a neat stack. The meeting was over. She said, 'Well, thank you for listening. You've been very generous with your time. We will proceed with our investigation and wait to hear from you.'

Pacheco walked with them out of the office and rode with them on the elevator, eager to spend as much time with them as possible. Michael watched him carefully. When he and Lacy were alone in his car, he said, 'He'll call you within twenty-four hours and it will have nothing to do with a casino.'

'You're right,' Lacy said.

'Nice job in there.'

CHAPTER 25

L ike clockwork, the receptionist tapped on the door at 9:00 a.m. and without waiting for a reply laid the morning mail on Lacy's desk. She smiled and said thanks. All the junk had been culled and set aside for 'Florida Recycles!' That left six envelopes addressed to Lacy, five with proper return addresses. The sixth looked somewhat suspicious so she opened it first. In a handwritten scrawl it read,

> *To Lacy Stoltz: This is Wilton Mace. I tried to call but your phone isn't working. We need to talk, and soon. My number is 555-996-7702. I'm in town, waiting. Wilton*

Using her desk phone, she immediately called the number. Wilton answered and they had a brief conversation. He was in the DoubleTree hotel, three blocks from the Capitol, had been there since the day before waiting for her call, and wanted to meet face-to-face. He had important information. Lacy said she was on her way, and promptly relayed the conversation to Geismar, who was being overly protective and irritating her. He agreed, though, that a meeting in a busy downtown hotel held little danger. He was insisting that she advise him of any travel or interviews related to the McDover case. She agreed but doubted seriously if she would comply, even though her appetite for risk had been severely diminished.

As agreed, Wilton met her near the front entrance and they found a quiet table in a coffee bar at the edge of the lobby. For his trip to the big city he was dressed exactly as he had been when they met him under his shade tree a few weeks ago. It seemed like a year. Denim from head to toe, beads around his neck and wrists, long hair pulled back into a ponytail. She was reminded of how much he favored his brother. As they waited for their coffee he passed along his sincere sorrow about Hugo, a man he had liked. He asked about her injuries and said she looked great.

'How much do you know about the accident?' she asked. 'What's the buzz on the street?'

His words were just as slow in town as they had been on the reservation. The man was perpetually calm. 'Lots of suspicions,' he said.

A waitress placed the cups before them – dark roast for Wilton, a latte for Lacy. After a long pause, she said, 'Okay, I'm listening.'

'The name Todd Short ring a bell?' he asked.

'Maybe, I guess, somewhere. Help me out.'

'He was one of the two jailhouse snitches who testified against my brother. At different times before the trial, the cops placed each snitch in Junior's cell, then pulled them out after a day or two. Both lied to the jury and said Junior bragged about killing the sonofabitch he caught with his wife. And for good measure he killed her too. It was very effective testimony and it nailed Junior.'

Lacy sipped her latte and nodded. She had nothing to add and she refused to drag it out of him. He had arranged this meeting.

'Anyway, not long after the trial, Todd Short disappeared. So did the other snitch, a punk named Robles. Years passed and everybody assumed the two had been rubbed out, probably by the same people who killed Son and Eileen. Now, fifteen years later, Short has resurfaced and we have spoken.'

A pause as more coffee was consumed. Lacy was about to ask, 'Are you going to tell me what he said?' Wilton glanced around casually, cleared his throat, and said, 'I met him three days ago, off the reservation. When I saw him I remembered how much I hated him. I wanted to smash his face with a rock, but we were in a public place, some kind of fried chicken joint. He starts off by saying he's sorry and all that crap. He was a drifter with a drug habit and a criminal record and his life was going nowhere. He didn't know Robles very well but he got word not long after the trial that the punk had probably been killed, so he took off. Went to California, where he's been living under a rock ever since. Actually, he cleaned up his act

269

and has had a decent life. Now he's dying of cancer and wants to make nice, wants to bare his soul and confess his sins.'

'Which are?'

'Back then he was in jail in Sterling facing another drug charge, one that would get him locked up for years. He'd seen prison, didn't want to go back, so he was easy bait for the cops. They offered the deal. The prosecutor agreed to let him plead to something ridiculous, and after a few weeks in the county jail he'd be a free man. All he had to do was spend a couple of days in the cell with Junior, then testify at trial. I was in the courtroom and saw it all. Short was a great witness, very believable, and the jury ate up every word of his testimony. It was irresistible. Who doesn't like a good story about illicit sex? According to him, Junior enjoyed telling how he came home early, heard noises from the bedroom, realized what was happening, got his handgun, kicked open the bedroom door, and there was his wife and Son Razko going at it on the bed. In a rage, he shot Son twice in the head, and when Eileen wouldn't stop screaming he shot her too. Then, and this has never made sense, he took Son's wallet and fled the scene. All bullshit, of course, but Short sold the story to the jury. To claim it was an act of passion, an irresistible impulse, would have been to admit to the killings. Since Junior had nothing to do with it, he couldn't use the obvious defense. As I've said, he had a bad lawyer.'

'Did Short get cash?'

'Two thousand dollars, handed to him by a cop after he testified. He hung around the area for a few weeks, until he heard the rumors about Robles. Then he fled.'

Lacy's phone was on the table, muted. It vibrated and she glanced at it.

'Why did you change phone numbers?' Wilton asked.

'These are state-issued phones. My old one was stolen from my car just after the accident. My new one has a different number.'

'Who took it?'

'Probably the same people who caused the wreck. So what does Short want to do now?'

'He wants to tell his story to someone who'll listen. He lied, and the cops and prosecutor knew he was lying, and he feels terrible about it.'

'A real hero,' Lacy said as she took another sip of her latte and looked across the busy lobby. No one was watching or listening, but these days she couldn't help but notice people. 'Look, Wilton, this could be a big break, but this is not my case, okay? Junior's appeals have been handled by those guys in D.C. and he's lucky to have such fine lawyers. You need to sit down with them and let them decide what to do with Todd Short.'

'I've called them a couple of times but they're too busy. Not a word. Junior's last habeas appeal was turned down eight days ago. We expect he'll get an execution date pretty soon. His lawyers have put up a good fight, but we're at the end of the road.'

'Have you told Junior?'

'I'll see him tomorrow. He'll want to know what will happen now that one of the snitches is recanting. He trusts you, Lacy, and I do too.'

'Thanks, but I'm not a criminal defense lawyer and I have no idea if any of this is relevant after fifteen years. There are limitations on bringing up new evidence, but I don't know the law. If you're looking for advice, I'm the wrong person, the wrong lawyer. I would help if I could, but this is way out of my league.'

'Could you talk to his lawyers in D.C.? I can't get through.'

'Why can't Junior talk to them?'

'He says somebody is always listening in prison. He thinks the phones are tapped. And he hasn't seen the D.C. lawyers in a long time. He thinks they might be forgetting about him now that the end is in sight.'

'I disagree. If a snitch appears with a different story and swears under oath that the cops and prosecutor knew he was lying, and he got paid cash, believe me the D.C. lawyers will be excited.'

'So you think there's hope?'

'I don't know what to think, Wilton. Again, this is not my field.'

He smiled and went silent. A rodeo team in matching boots and Stetsons paraded through the lobby, their identical roller bags whining in a dull chorus. When they were finally gone and the racket was over, he asked, 'Have you met Lyman Gritt, the ex-constable?'

'No. I hear he's been replaced. Why?'

'He's a good man.'

'I'm sure he is. And why bring up his name?'

'He might know something.'

'Do you know what he might know, Wilton? Don't play games with me.'

'No, I don't. He got fired by the Chief. They are at odds. His firing came just days after your accident. There are a lot of rumors, Lacy. The tribe is uneasy. A black guy and a white girl were on the reservation at midnight, digging around for something. He ends up dead under suspicious circumstances.'

'Is his being black suspicious?'

'Not really. We're not hung up on skin color. But you have to admit it was unusual. It has been the general belief for a long time that bad people were behind the casino, in bed with our so-called leaders. Now, finally, it might be unraveling. Someone, you and Hugo, dared to show up and start asking questions. He met a tragic end. You came close. The investigation is getting buried by our new constable, who's not trustworthy. Lots of rumors and speculation, Lacy. And now, from nowhere, Todd Short sneaks into the picture again with a different story. It's unsettling, to say the least.'

Wait till the FBI rolls in, she thought. 'Promise to keep me posted?'

'It depends on what I hear.'

'I'll call the lawyers in D.C.,' she said. 'It's the least I can do.'

'Thanks.'

'And say hello to Junior.'

'Why don't you go see him? He doesn't get many visitors and it looks like he might be nearing the end.'

'I'll do that. Does he know about Hugo?'

'Yes. I told him.'

'Tell him I'll try and stop by as soon as I can get away.'

'He'll like that, Lacy.'

Lacy reported the meeting to Michael, then did a quick review of Junior's file. She called the law firm in D.C., and eventually managed to pull a lawyer named Salzman out of a meeting. His mega firm had a thousand lawyers and an excellent reputation for pro bono work. It had spent countless hours representing Junior since his conviction fifteen years earlier. She told him Todd Short was back from the dead and now facing a more certain demise. Salzman was at first incredulous. Short and Robles had been out of the picture for so long it was almost impossible to believe the news. Lacy confessed her ignorance in this field and asked if it was too late.

'Oh, it's late,' Salzman said. 'Very late, but in this business we never quit, not until the final moment. I'll be down as soon as I can get there.'

* * *

It was no real surprise when Special Agent Allie Pacheco stopped by the office for a visit. It was late in the day, and on the phone he said he was just around the corner, needed only a few minutes. Four days had passed since the meeting in Luna's office. To their surprise, Pacheco had not called or e-mailed Lacy.

They met in Michael's office, at one end of his cluttered worktable, and it was immediately obvious that Pacheco's mood was quite different. His quick smile was missing. He began with 'Luna and I spent yesterday in Jacksonville presenting the case to our boss. Our recommendation was to open an investigation, immediately. We agreed with your strategy that the first step should be to try and solve the murder of Hugo Hatch. At the same time, we would begin the rather formidable task of penetrating the syndicate's maze of offshore companies and tracking the money. We would place Judge McDover, Phyllis Turban, Chief Cappel, and Billy Cappel under surveillance and perhaps even obtain warrants to tap their phones and wire their offices. Our recommendation projected the need for five agents initially, with me in charge of the investigation. This morning the boss said no, said we simply cannot spare the manpower at this time. I pressed a little, but this guy is decisive and sticks to his guns. I asked if I could be allowed to investigate with perhaps one or two agents over the next month or so. Again, he said no. Our official answer is no. I'm sorry.

We did our best and pushed as hard as we could, under the circumstances, though "pushing" is perhaps not the right word.'

Michael seemed unfazed. Lacy wanted to curse. Instead, she asked, 'Is there a chance things can change if we learn more?'

'Who knows?' Pacheco replied, clearly exasperated. 'Things can change in the other direction too. Florida is a favorite point of entry, always has been. We're getting flooded with tips about illegals sneaking into the country, and they're not coming here to wash dishes and lay concrete. They're organizing homegrown talent to wage jihad. Finding, monitoring, and stopping them has a far greater priority than the corruption that once got us excited. But let's keep an open dialogue. I'm in the loop. If something happens, I want to know.'

If something happens. After he left, Michael and Lacy sat at the worktable for a long time and compared thoughts. Their disappointment was admitted, then set aside. Without much in the way of resources, they would be forced to become resourceful. At this stage, their primary weapon was the subpoena. Using one of Sadelle's many memos, they decided to prepare a list of the twenty or so cases McDover had decided in favor of the mysterious entities pushing to develop various parts of Brunswick County. Eleven of the lawsuits involved the condemnation proceedings that led to the building of the Tappacola Tollway.

Since they had great latitude in drafting the

subpoena, they decided to request McDover's files for only half of the lawsuits. Requesting her records for all of them would tip their hand and let her know what they suspected. Ask for some of the records now, see what she and her ace legal team were willing to hand over, then go back for more later if necessary. Complying with the subpoena would require hours of time by Killebrew and company, with their expensive meters ticking away.

Each lawsuit was on file in the clerk's office in the Brunswick County Courthouse, and Sadelle had long since retrieved copies of the voluminous records. They were now perfectly indexed and cross-referenced, and there was little doubt BJC's summaries would be far more organized than anything Killebrew sent over. But all judges kept their own office files that did not become part of the public record. It would be fascinating to see how closely McDover complied.

Lacy worked on the subpoena until dark. It kept her mind off the FBI.

CHAPTER 26

Gunther was back. He disrupted a lazy Saturday morning with the news that he was flying down and would be there by mid-afternoon. Though Lacy had nothing planned, she made a feeble attempt to sound busy. He would have none of it. He missed his little sister, was worried sick about her, and repeatedly apologized for not having returned sooner. He knew she needed him.

She stood in a window of the general aviation terminal and watched the private planes take off and land. At 3:00 p.m., his expected arrival time, she observed a small twin taxi near the terminal and shut down. Gunther got out, alone. His checkered flying career had spanned the past two decades and had been interrupted on at least two occasions when the FAA jerked his license. He had trouble with authority and had argued with air traffic controllers, in flight. Such arguments are never won by pilots, and Gunther found himself grounded. Evidently, he had now finagled some way to retrieve his license.

He carried a small overnight bag, which she took

as a good sign, as well as a thick briefcase undoubtedly bristling with the workings of important deals. He hugged her fiercely in the lobby, told her she looked great, and seemed on the verge of tears as he went on about how much he missed her. She did a passable job of conveying the same sentiments.

As they walked out of the terminal she said, 'So you're back in the air.'

'Yeah, those fools at FAA can't keep a good man on the ground. Got my license back two weeks ago.'

'Cute plane.'

'Borrowed it from a buddy.'

They walked to her car, the compact Ford she was still driving, and he commented on its lack of size.

'It's just a loaner,' she said. 'I haven't decided on a new one.'

Gunther knew everything about cars and immediately began a dissertation on the various models she should consider. He said, 'If we have time, we should go car shopping.'

'That's an idea,' she replied. His current ride was an expensive Mercedes. Lacy could recall a Maserati, a Hummer, a Porsche, a black Range Rover SUV, and there had once been talk of a Rolls-Royce. Regardless of the bumps in the real estate business, Gunther had always buzzed around Atlanta in style. He was the last person she knew who'd be helpful in selecting a new car on her budget.

They were on the street, in traffic, and her defensive driving was obvious. He asked, 'You okay behind the wheel?'

'Not really, but I'm getting there.'

'I've never had a bad wreck. Guess it takes time to get back in the saddle.'

'A long time.'

'You look great, Lacy,' he said for the third time. 'I like your hair. Have you thought about keeping it short?'

'No, not for a second,' she said with a laugh. A month after leaving the hospital, her scalp was now covered with a thin layer of fine hair that seemed a bit darker than what they'd shaved, but she wasn't worried. At least it was growing. She had retired the scarves and hats and didn't care if anyone stared.

He wanted to know the latest developments in her investigation of the crooked judge and the casino, and Lacy filled in some of the backstory. Gunther could keep a secret and obviously had no one to tell back in Atlanta, but Lacy could not completely ignore the rules of confidentiality. She admitted they had hit a wall when the FBI declined to get involved.

This gave Gunther a soapbox, one he didn't yield until they arrived at her apartment. He railed against the federal government, its bloated size and countless agencies and useless bureaucrats and senseless policies. He mentioned his own run-ins with the EPA, EEOC, IRS, even the

Department of Justice, though he didn't give details of any scrape with the law and Lacy didn't ask. How could the FBI, with a million agents and a billion dollars, decline to pursue such blatant corruption? A man has been killed, yet the 'Fibbies' refused to investigate. He was flabbergasted, even angry.

Inside, he tossed his bag and briefcase in the guest room and Lacy offered tea or water. Gunther asked for a diet soda. He had been in recovery for almost ten years and was well beyond the fragility of early sobriety. His drinking days had been the lore of family legend before turning dark and frightening. At their insistence, he had rehabbed twice and without success. A DUI, a divorce, and a bankruptcy all hit at once, and at the age of thirty-two Gunther gave up booze and drugs and surrendered to a higher power. He had been radically sober for years, to the point of volunteering in a rehab clinic for teenagers. When asked, he spoke freely of his addictions.

Gunther, as she well knew, spoke freely of anything and everything. To keep the conversation away from more sensitive matters, she told the story of her meeting with Wilton Mace at a downtown hotel. This led to a lengthy narrative about the murders of Son Razko and Eileen Mace, and Junior's trials and so on. That was not her case. Its record was public. Confidentiality was not important.

Gunther, like most white people, thought the

idea of an innocent man on death row was absurd. Surely Junior was guilty of something or he wouldn't be there. This led to a long and often heated and frustrating conversation about the criminal justice system. The law was Lacy's life and she understood its flaws. Gunther lived and breathed real estate and making money and had little interest in anything else. He admitted he seldom read a newspaper, unless he glanced at the business section. He hadn't heard a word about two recent, extremely high-profile DNA exonerations in Georgia, one involving a man who'd served twenty-nine years for a rape and murder committed by someone else. In Gunther's opinion, the prisons were full because of rampant crime.

Speaking of business, he had a few phone calls to make, finally. Lacy was exhausted and needed a break herself. She showed him to a small terrace off the kitchen. A wrought-iron table was the perfect spot for him to set up shop.

For dinner, they chose a Thai place near the FSU campus. After they settled into their seats, Gunther suddenly reached for a pocket and whipped out a cell phone. 'Gotta do this e-mail, Sis,' he said, already tapping away.

She watched with a frown, and when he finished she said, 'Here's the deal. All phones on the table, on mute, and the first one that vibrates gets the check.'

'I was going to treat anyway.'

'I'm sure you will.' From her purse she removed her iPhone and the new BlackBerry issued by BJC. He matched her two with two of his own. 'What's that?' he asked, pointing to the BlackBerry.

'State issue. Its predecessor was the one stolen from the car.'

'And no trace?'

'Nothing. Our tech guys said there's no way to hack in. I guess we're safe.' She reached for a front pocket of her slacks and said, 'Oh, almost forgot.' She pulled out the prepaid burner Myers had given her.

'You have three phones?' Gunther asked.

'This doesn't really count,' she said, placing the burner in a neat row with the others. 'It's what Myers uses. I think he goes through several each month.'

'Smart guy. When's the last time you talked to him?'

'A few weeks back. The day he gave me this phone.'

An exotic Asian girl appeared to take their orders. Gunther ordered tea and encouraged Lacy to order a glass of wine. This was a ritual they had gone through a hundred times. She would do nothing to tempt him, but he took pride in being beyond temptation. Besides, he had never been a wine drinker. Too mild, too civilized. Lacy asked for a glass of Chablis. They decided on a plate of crispy spring rolls to start with. When the drinks arrived, and they were comparing their latest conversations with their mother, Ann, one of the phones made a soft noise. Of the impressive collection in the center of the table, it was the least expected.

Myers was checking in. Lacy sighed, hesitated, then said, 'I guess I'd better take this.'

'Of course. And you can take the check too.'

She slowly opened the phone, glancing around as she did so, and quietly said, 'This better be good.'

A strange voice replied, 'I'm trying to find Lacy Stoltz.'

She hesitated again, certain that it was not Greg Myers. 'I'm Lacy. Who is this?'

'We've never met but we both know Greg. I'm the intermediary, the middleman, the guy who handles the mole. We need to talk.'

This was so wrong that Lacy's lungs froze and she felt faint. Her face must have registered horror because Gunther reached over and gently touched her arm. 'Where's Greg?' she asked. Gunther's eyes narrowed with concern.

'I don't know. That's what we need to talk about. I'm in town, not far from you. How soon can we meet?'

'I'm having dinner. I—'

'Two hours then. Let's say straight-up ten o'clock. Between the Capitol and the Old Capitol Building there is a courtyard. I'll meet you at the front steps there at ten.'

'What is the danger level right now, if I might ask?'

'Right now, between the two of us, I'd say there's no immediate danger.'

'Okay, but I'm bringing my brother, and he likes to play with guns. Should he bring one just in case?'

'No, Lacy, we are on the same side.'

'Has something happened to Greg?'

'We'll talk about it later.'

'I've lost my appetite. I'll be there in half an hour.'

The Capitol Grounds were well lit and a few other pedestrians were milling about. It was, after all, Saturday night and all state workers were enjoying the weekend. The lone figure near the steps of the Old Capitol was dressed in shorts, sneakers, and a baseball cap, and would not have attracted attention anywhere in town. He took one last drag of his cigarette, stepped on the butt, and walked to them. 'You must be Lacy,' he said with an outstretched hand.

'I am. This is my brother, Gunther.'

'My name's Cooley,' he said as everyone quickly shook hands. He nodded and said, 'Let's walk.' They strolled without purpose across the courtyard in the direction of the House Office Building. Cooley said, 'Don't know how much you know about me, probably very little.'

'I've never known your name,' she said. 'What's going on?' By then she knew something had happened to Greg; otherwise, Cooley would not be in the picture and they would not be meeting.

Cooley spoke softly as they walked. 'Four days ago, Myers and his girl, Carlita, were in Key Largo scuba diving.'

'I met Carlita.'

'They docked and he said he was going to a bar to meet someone. He walked down the pier and she stayed on the boat. He didn't come back. After a few hours she began to worry. Around dark, she noticed a couple of strangers looking at his boat from a distance, or so she thought. The harbor was busy, lots of boats and folks partying on the decks, and the two men didn't stay long. She called me that night, as was our contingency plan. Needless to say, she's distraught and frantic and has no idea what to do next. Greg rarely went ashore, and when he did she knew exactly when he would return. They bought supplies here and there, but Carlita usually did the shopping. They would venture off to a movie or a restaurant, but always together. Greg was careful and planned his movements.'

They were on Duval Street, drifting away from the Capitol, just three friends out for a stroll on a hot night.

Lacy asked, 'What about his phones, laptop, files, records?'

'There's some stuff on the boat, still being watched by her. Frankly, I don't know what's there. He doesn't know the identity of the mole. He and I talked either face-to-face or on disposable phones, careful not to leave a trail. But he's a lawyer, right?

So there's the chance that he's got notes and records. For now, Carlita's staying put and waiting. Waiting for him to return, waiting for me to tell her what to do. I can't run the risk of going there.'

'Could they identify you?' Lacy asked.

'Wanna take a crack at who *they* might be? No, I don't think I could be recognized in person, but who knows? I can't go get her.'

'And she can't move the boat?' Gunther asked.

'No way. She can't even start the engines and put it in reverse. And where would she go?'

Lacy noticed a bench and said, 'I'd like to sit down.' She and Gunther took a seat – he held her hand – as Cooley lit another cigarette and watched the traffic. No other pedestrians were close.

Lacy said, 'Greg's story was that he'd been living on the run for several years, that he'd made a lot of enemies when he got in trouble. Could that part of his past have caught up with him?'

Cooley blew a cloud of smoke. 'I doubt it. We met in prison. I was once a lawyer too until they asked me to leave the profession. So we were just a couple disbarred boys doing time in a federal joint in Texas. From another con I'd heard the story of Vonn Dubose and the Indian casino, so when I got out I came back to Florida and started sniffing around. It's a long story, but I knew the mole and got that ball rolling. Now it looks pretty foolish. You've been hurt. Your buddy is dead. Myers is probably drifting with the currents, a hundred feet down with a brick around his neck.'

'You think it's Dubose?' Gunther asked.

'He gets my vote. Sure Greg had enemies, but that story goes back a long way. And I know some of the people he squealed on. They were not organized crooks. Sure they screwed up, but they're not the type of people who'd spend years looking for Greg so they could put a bullet in his head and further complicate their lives. Kubiak, the ringleader, is still serving time. Now Greg signs his name on the complaint and threatens the Dubose clan, and, lo and behold, within a matter of days he's vanished. A procedural question?'

Lacy shrugged. Whatever.

'Can the formal complaint Myers filed against Judge McDover go forward if the complaining party disappears?'

Lacy thought about it for a moment. 'I'm not sure. To my knowledge, it's never happened before.'

'Are you sure you want it to go forward?' Gunther asked.

Neither Cooley nor Lacy responded. Cooley slowly finished his cigarette and casually flipped the butt onto the sidewalk, a thoughtless act of littering that she might have said something about. Now, though, it was unimportant.

'What's our priority?' she asked.

Cooley said, 'Carlita can't stay on the boat much longer. She's low on food and water and the harbormaster is pestering her for docking fees. I'd like to rescue her some way and secure his stuff – phones, files, anything that needs protecting.

But, again, it's just too risky. There's a good chance someone is watching and waiting.'

'I can do it,' Gunther said.

'No way,' Lacy said, surprised. 'You're not getting near this.'

'Listen, I have a small plane at the airport. I can be in Key Largo in two hours. They, if they are really there, have no idea who I am. Carlita will know I'm coming so she'll be ready. She'll tell us exactly where the boat is located. I'll be in and out before anybody knows what's happening. If they wake up and somehow manage to follow us to the airport, there's no way they can scramble a plane fast enough to chase us. I'll drop her off somewhere along the way and she can catch a bus to wherever she wants to go.'

'What if someone tries to confront you?' Cooley asked.

'You heard my sister, sir. I like guns and I'll have one in my pocket. I don't frighten too easily anyway.'

'I don't know, Gunther,' Lacy said. Cooley was quickly warming up to the idea. Lacy was not.

'We're going to do it, okay, Sis? It's low risk, high reward. I'm doing it to help the team and to protect you.'

CHAPTER 27

Geismar nixed the plan late Saturday night. He was furious that Gunther had once again managed to stick his nose into the McDover affair, and he scolded Lacy over her breach of professional discretion. She pushed back as much as possible by explaining that Cooley had called during their dinner and there was no way to hide it from her brother, who, as they well knew by now, had big ears and was quite pushy. She reminded her boss that he himself had told Gunther far too much over coffee in the hospital while she was still in a coma. This was not their typical investigation, and it required different rules.

The much larger issue was Myers's disappearance and all the sticky issues it created. Lacy insisted that they meet early Sunday morning at BJC. Geismar eventually relented, but insisted that Gunther not be present. So her brother waited in the car, barking nonstop on the phone at a banker he'd pulled out of bed.

Geismar had slept off his anger and was willing to listen. Lacy relayed the latest news from Cooley. He had spoken to Carlita early that morning and there had been no change. Certainly no sign of Myers. She was bustling around the boat as if all was well, cleaning the deck, washing windows, trying to make things appear normal, and really doing nothing but watching the movements of everyone in sight. She was heartbroken, terrified, stranded, and ready to go home, to Tampa, but had almost no money and no plan. She had gone through Myers's papers but was not sure what was relevant. There was a box of 'his legal stuff' under the bed, but he kept most of 'his papers' somewhere in Myrtle Beach. There were also two phones and a laptop. Cooley promised that help was on the way, but said so only to keep her calm.

Lacy argued that they had an obligation to rescue her, if it could be done without too much risk. Obviously, her situation was a direct result of their investigation. At the moment, there was no one else in a position to help her. She had possession of records, phones, and a laptop that could be damaging. Gunther was admittedly a loose cannon, but he was willing to fly down and back at his own expense. Otherwise, the drive was at least ten hours one way. Time was crucial.

More than once, Lacy said, 'Michael, I'm not taking no for an answer.'

'Why can't she call the police and report him missing?' he argued. 'Let them handle it. She can leave the boat with whatever she wants to take and go home. If a crime has been committed down there, then the police need to know about it.'

'Cooley mentioned that and it frightened her. Not sure why, but then we don't know everything about Myers and his boat. Maybe she doesn't want the cops poking around. Maybe she's undocumented.'

'Tell her to destroy the files, anything that looks suspicious, keep the phone she's using, and toss the other one, along with the laptop, overboard.'

'That sounds nice and efficient sitting here in your office, Michael, but we don't know what she knows. And you could be asking her to destroy evidence. Anyway, she's not going to do that. She's terrified and she doesn't know what to do. We need to help.'

'If she leaves, what happens to the boat?'

'Who cares? The cops will eventually be called, I guess. At some point they'll decide there is a missing person involved and they'll do whatever they need to do. We have enough problems of our own.'

'You're not going, Lacy. I'm not running the risk of you getting hurt again.'

'Okay, then Gunther can handle it by himself. He can fetch Carlita and get her off the boat.'

'Do you really trust him?'

'Yes. In certain situations he can be quite reliable.'

Michael was clearly troubled. Another casualty. Perhaps Myers left something crucial behind. BJC had no experience in matters such as these. Where were the real cops? He took a sip of coffee from a paper cup and said, 'You know, Lacy, if Dubose is behind this, then they know that the complaint against McDover was signed by a guy who has been neutralized. Game over, Lacy. We cannot proceed without the complaining party.'

'Let's worry about that tomorrow, please. Right now we need to get Carlita and whatever Myers might have left behind.'

'It's over, Lacy.'

'No, it's not, and I'm not taking no for an answer.'

'So I've heard.'

'Here's an idea, Michael. You and Gunther buzz down to Key Largo together and get her. The weather is perfect. He says the airplane holds four passengers. An easy trip.'

'I don't like small airplanes.'

'You don't like big ones either. Man up, Michael. You'll be back before you know it. We're not breaking any laws here. Just a quick flight down there, get her, drop her off somewhere, and you're back home.'

'And I'm stuck with Gunther for four hours in a small airplane?'

'I know, I know, but you know it's important.'

'Why bother, Lacy? This file is about to be closed.'

'Not if the FBI gets involved. When they find out a key witness has vanished, they might change their minds.'

'Sounds pretty desperate.'

'That's because we are desperate.'

Michael took a deep breath and shook his head in frustration. 'I can't go. We're having a small party for my mother-in-law this afternoon. It's her ninetieth birthday.'

'Then I'm going. I swear we'll be safe. Look, it's just a nice little flight on a beautiful Sunday. It's my day off. If I want to go flying, who can stop me?'

'I'll authorize you to go on one condition: You cannot get near the boat. If someone is watching, then that someone might recognize you. No one knows Gunther, but that's not the case for you. Make sure you get possession of Myers's papers, phones, and laptop. She knows you and she'll trust you more than your brother. Who wouldn't? Anyway, drop her off along the way, give her some money for a cab or a bus, and make sure she understands that she talks to no one.'

Lacy was already headed for the door. 'Got it, Michael.'

An hour later, they lifted off from the Tallahassee airport in the Beech Baron. Gunther, seizing the moment and thrilled with the adventure, sat in the left seat and flew the airplane. Lacy, with headphones, sat beside him and was captivated by the chatter between the controllers and the traffic. They headed almost due south and were soon over the Gulf. At nine thousand feet they leveled off and hit their maximum speed of 230 miles per hour. The din of the piston engines eased somewhat, though the cabin was far noisier than Lacy had ever experienced.

After two hours, they began to descend, and Lacy took in the view of the ocean and the islands. They touched down at 11:40. Gunther had called ahead for a courtesy car at general aviation. He drove and Lacy navigated from a tourist map. Cooley was still somewhere around Tallahassee and talking to Carlita. As they approached the Key Largo Harbor Marina, Cooley gave Gunther her number to facilitate the pickup. The harbor was busy with sailors heading out to sea and fishing boats arriving with their morning catches. A dive boat had just docked and a dozen divers were unloading their gear. Lacy stayed in the car and watched everything as Gunther strolled along the dock, just killing time and admiring boats. Carlita stepped off the *Conspirator* and managed to smile as if all was well. She had three bags: a backpack, a nylon sack stuffed with what appeared to be clothing, and Myers's olive courier bag. Gunther grabbed two of them and they casually walked back to the parking lot. In the car, Lacy scanned the entire marina and saw no one who appeared to be watching them. Carlita was thrilled to see her, a familiar face.

Gunther, always quick with an opinion, believed that after five days with no contact whatsoever, the people responsible for Myers's disappearance were long gone. If they had wanted to chat with Carlita or rummage through the boat, they would have made a move before now. An hour after leaving the airport, they returned to general aviation, quickly loaded the Baron, and took off at 1:15. Lacy called Geismar but he did not answer. Must be partying with his mother-in-law. She sent a text saying the mission was accomplished.

Lacy and Carlita sat in the rear of the cabin, close together. Once airborne, Carlita began crying. Lacy held her hand and assured her she was now safe. Carlita wanted to know if Lacy had heard anything about Myers. No, there had been no word. Nothing at all. What would happen to the boat? Lacy said she wasn't sure. The plan was to notify the authorities that Greg Myers was missing and let them go about their business. She quizzed Carlita about the boat: How long had she been living on it? Where did Myers buy it, or lease it? Did he own it outright or was a bank involved? Did anyone else ever visit them on the boat?

She knew very little. She had been living on it for about a year, but knew nothing of where it came from. Myers, she said, did not talk about his business. Occasionally, he would go ashore to meet someone but always returned within an hour. He was extremely careful, and fearful. He did not make mistakes. When he disappeared he was just going to the marina for a drink, nothing more. He was not supposed to be meeting anyone. He simply vanished.

When they leveled off and Key Largo was far behind, Carlita stopped the tears and grew quiet.

Lacy asked if they could keep the courier bag and the backpack. Carlita said sure, she wanted no part of his paperwork. She said Myers had been careful about what he left on the boat because it could be searched, either by the bad guys or by the authorities. Using the postal service, never the overnight delivery services, he'd sent a lot of paperwork to his brother in Myrtle Beach. She was not sure what he'd left behind on the boat but was pretty sure it was not important.

An hour later, they landed in Sarasota. Gunther had called ahead for a cab, and Lacy handed Carlita enough money to get to her place in Tampa. Lacy thanked her and hugged her and said good-bye, knowing she would never see her again.

Back in the air, with Gunther occupied with flying, Lacy opened the courier bag. She pulled out Myers's thin laptop and turned it on, but was stopped at the pass code. She found a prepaid cell phone and some files. One contained the boat's registration, to a company in the Bahamas, along with warranties, operating procedures, and a thick stack of fine print about insurance. Another file was filled with old cases involving corrupt judges. Lacy found not a single word about McDover, the Tappacola, Cooley, the mole, or herself. The backpack was just as clean; nothing but old research and newspaper clippings about Ramsey Mix, a.k.a. Greg Myers. Evidently, he kept the current materials somewhere onshore, at least the written ones. She suspected his laptop was loaded with evidence that could have been devastating in the wrong hands.

When they landed in Tallahassee, Lacy was hoping Gunther might simply stay on the plane and continue back to Atlanta. Apparently, that never crossed his mind. As they drove to her apartment, it became clear that Gunther now considered himself an active member of the BJC investigative team. He planned to stay a few more days, to keep an eye on his sister.

Lacy called Geismar again with a full update. They agreed to meet early Monday morning. Late in the afternoon, as Gunther paced around her terrace calling one partner or lawyer or accountant or banker after another, Lacy was returning e-mails when she got a surprise from Allie Pacheco. His text was simply 'Got time for a drink?'

She responded, 'Unofficial, after hours, no business?'

He replied, 'Of course.'

But business was exactly what she had in mind. She invited him to her apartment, warned him that her brother was there and that things would not be that private.

Pacheco arrived in shorts and a polo at 7:30. Lacy poured him a beer and introduced him to Gunther, who wanted to grill him. The unofficial status of the little rendezvous lasted for about five minutes, until Gunther blurted, 'We gotta talk about Myers.'

Pacheco put down his glass, looked at Lacy, and asked, 'Okay, what's up with Myers?'

'He's been missing for five days,' she said. 'That's his laptop on the counter. We got it off his boat this morning in Key Largo.'

'It's a long story,' Gunther said.

Pacheco stared at both of them. He raised both hands, showed them his palms, said, 'This is way off-limits, okay? Tell me all you can tell me, then I'll decide what to do with it.'

Gunther was remarkably quiet as Lacy told the story.

Sipping his second beer, Pacheco finally said, 'The boat needs to be secured, and to do that the police need to be notified. There's no federal issue here, not yet anyway, so we can't do it.'

'But you can notify the police, right?' Lacy asked. 'I'd rather not make the call, because then I would have to answer a lot of questions. I'd rather not have my name attached to a missing person case.'

'You're already attached to it because you have his laptop and files.'

'But they have nothing to do with his disappearance.'

'You don't know that. You don't know what's in the laptop. There may be a trail there, some reference to a meeting the day he disappeared.'

'Great,' Gunther said. 'We'll give it to you, everything, and you give it to the police. They'll take things far more seriously if they're notified by the FBI.'

'That might work,' Pacheco said. 'Is there a chance Myers simply walked away? Given his past, and his present, that's not completely far-fetched.'

Lacy said, 'Sure, I've thought about it. Maybe something frightened him. Maybe he got tired of the boat, or the woman, or both, and decided to vanish. He was at least thinking about dropping the complaint. When he came here to my apartment, he offered to drop it and walk away. He was sorry about Hugo, blamed himself, and said he wished he'd never started all this. He could have ditched the records, scrubbed his computer, and hit the road.'

'You don't believe that,' Gunther said.

'No, I don't. I've had this conversation with Cooley, and he'll never be convinced that Myers would run and hide again. Myers needs the money. He's an ex-con who's sixty years old and without much of a future. He was banking on a huge windfall from the whistle-blower statute. He knew that law inside and out and was already counting his money. He believed McDover and Dubose have stolen tens of millions and that a lot of the money can be recovered. I don't know how he paid for the boat but he was very proud of it. He loved island hopping and puttering around the Keys. He was a happy guy about to strike it rich. So, no, I don't think he walked away.'

Pacheco said, 'Well, the disappearance is now five days old and the investigation has not even started. That makes for an awfully cold trail.'

'And there's nothing the FBI can do?' Gunther asked.

'Not really. The locals have to go in first. If there's a kidnapping or something like that, they could call us. But I doubt it. Frankly, I'd say the chances of finding Myers alive are pretty slim.'

'All the more reason to go after Dubose,' Lacy said.

'I agree, but I'm not making that decision.'

'How many more dead folks do you need?' Gunther asked.

'Again, it's not my decision. Lacy can tell you that I would have jumped in a week ago.' Gunther stormed out of the room and returned to his terrace.

'Sorry,' Lacy said.

Pacheco had entered her apartment with thoughts of a pleasant drink with a pretty lady. He left with Myers's courier bag and backpack and no clear idea of what to do next.

CHAPTER 28

Lacy awoke early Monday morning with a new plan to get rid of her brother. It would take a trip to death row, a place he would not be welcome. And she would go by herself because the rules at BJC simply could not be bent enough to allow him to tag along. She rehearsed her story as the coffee brewed. She was pleasantly surprised when he appeared freshly showered and fully dressed. Not surprisingly, a deal was collapsing and he informed her he was needed at home. Indeed, he barely had enough time to devour a piece of toast before they hustled out the door and to her car. At the airport she thanked him again and made sure he promised to return. As the Beech lifted off, she smiled and took a deep breath and was thankful she was not on it.

At the office, she met with Michael and described in detail the trip to Key Largo. She detailed the contents of Myers's courier bag and backpack, and explained that they, along with his laptop, were in the possession of the FBI.

'You met with the FBI?' Michael asked, irritated.

'Pacheco has the hots for me and he stopped by

yesterday for a drink. One thing led to another, and, with Gunther's eager assistance, we got around to discussing Myers. Pacheco agreed to contact the police and report him missing. He thought it best if the FBI had possession of the stuff from the boat.'

'Please tell me your brother is leaving town.'

'Already gone, left this morning.'

'Thank heavens. Please tell me, Lacy, that he can keep his mouth shut.'

'Don't worry. No one in Atlanta cares, and, besides, he will always do what's best for me. Relax.'

'Relax? This is the biggest case in our history and it's collapsing on all fronts. I don't suppose you've heard from Killebrew.'

'No, and I don't expect to. They have eighteen days left to respond, and I'm sure they'll play it cool until the last minute. Any excitement on their part would be premature and might tip their hand. They're too smart to contact us now. The subpoena was served last Friday and I'm sure they're mulling it over.'

'All we can do is wait.'

'I can't sit around, Michael. I'm going to see Junior Mace on death row. Just want you to know my whereabouts.'

'Didn't realize you represented Junior Mace.'

'Of course I don't, but I promised to visit him. His D.C. lawyers will meet with him this afternoon. Salzman, the lead counsel, invited me to sit in. Junior doesn't mind. He likes me.'

'Don't get too close.'

'Salzman is confident that it will be delayed. If the snitch comes through and recants his testimony, Salzman thinks they stop the execution and maybe even get a new trial.'

'A new trial, after, what, fifteen years?'

'Something like that.'

'And where, exactly, do you fit in?'

'I didn't say I fit in. Let's just say I don't want to sit around the office all day. Besides, Junior Mace's wrongful conviction is part of the grand conspiracy. If it is set aside, new evidence might be discovered. If we assume the trail leads back to Dubose, then things could unravel. It's important for us to monitor his case.'

'Just be careful, please.'

'Death row is a pretty safe place, Michael.'

'If you say so.'

Lacy closed her office door and retrieved a thick file filled with Sadelle's memos. She removed one from the stack and read it again. Titled 'The Murders of Son Razko and Eileen Mace,' it read,

> Junior and Eileen Mace lived with their three children in a wood-framed house on Tinley Road, roughly two miles from the Tappacola reservation. (At the time about half of the Tappacola lived on tribal land, with many others scattered close by. About 80 percent lived in Brunswick County, but

some lived as far away as Jacksonville.) On the afternoon of January 17, 1995, while their three children were in school, Son Razko paid a visit to the Mace home. Razko and Junior Mace were friends and had led the opposition to the casino. Junior was driving a truck for a company out of Moreville, Florida, and was at work. If Son and Eileen were having an affair, then the purpose of his visit was obvious. If they were not, then it has never been known what prompted the visit. At any rate, they were found naked and dead in the bedroom by the oldest child when he got home from school, at about 4:00 in the afternoon. A pathologist testifying for the State estimated the time of death at somewhere between 2:00 p.m. and 3:00 p.m.

Junior was known to drink, and after making his deliveries he returned to the warehouse in Moreville, got in his truck, and stopped by a bar. He had a couple of beers and threw some darts with a man who has never been identified. At around 6:30 p.m. he was found in the parking lot, near his truck, unconscious and presumably drunk. The weapon used in the two murders was an unregistered Smith and Wesson .38 snub-nosed revolver. It was found under the seat of Junior's truck, along with a wallet belonging to Son. Mace was taken to the hospital in Moreville. The police, acting on an anonymous tip, went to the hospital and broke the news about his wife and Son. He spent the night in the hospital before being transported to jail. He was charged with both murders and was not allowed to attend the funeral of his wife. He maintained his innocence but no one listened.

At his trial, which was moved by Judge Claudia McDover from Brunswick County to Panama City, Mace presented two alibi witnesses who worked for businesses where he had made deliveries that afternoon. The first witness placed him about thirty miles from the scene of the crime between 2:00 p.m. and 3:00 p.m. The second witness placed him about fifteen miles away. Judging from the trial transcript, neither witness was particularly effective, and the prosecutor made much of the fact that Junior could have possibly made the two deliveries and still had time to stop by his house between 2:00 and 3:00. It was never clear how he could have parked his semi-rig, got into his pickup, drove home, killed two people, then switched trucks again.

The State relied heavily on the testimony of two jailhouse informants – Todd Short and Digger Robles. Both testified that they had shared a cell with Junior at various times, and that he openly bragged of catching his wife in bed with another man and shooting both of them. In testimony that was remarkably similar, they told the jury that Junior was proud of what he'd done, had no remorse, and couldn't understand why he was being prosecuted. (According to hearsay and local lore, both snitches disappeared from the area not long after the trial.)

The presence of Son's wallet in Junior's truck was crucial. Under Florida law, a capital case must include murder, obviously, but another crime as well – rape, burglary, kidnapping, and so on. Thus, the fact that Junior stole the wallet elevated the case from first-degree murder to capital murder.

The presence of the gun in Junior's truck was fatal to his defense. Ballistics experts from the State crime lab testified that there was no doubt the bullets removed from the bodies were fired by the .38-caliber revolver.

Against the advice of counsel (Junior's defense lawyer was a court-appointed rookie handling his first capital case) Junior took the stand in his own defense. He vehemently denied any involvement in the deaths of his wife and friend. He claimed he was being framed in retaliation for his opposition to the casino. He said someone spiked his beer at the bar, that he drank only three of them, then blacked out and did not remember leaving the bar. The bartender testified that he had at least three beers and that he, the bartender, helped Junior to his truck and left him there.

On the stand, it appears from the trial transcript that Junior handled himself with dignity, though the cross-examination was lengthy.

With the gun, the wallet, two informants, a defense that relied on two shaky alibi witnesses, and a defendant who was apparently drunk and didn't remember much, the jury had enough for a conviction. During the sentencing phase, Junior's lawyer called his brother Wilton and a cousin, both of whom testified that Junior was a devoted husband and father, was not a heavy drinker, did not own a gun, and had not fired one in years.

The jury returned two death verdicts.

Throughout the eight-day trial, Judge McDover, who was presiding over her first capital murder trial, favored the prosecution on virtually every issue. Only in agreeing to change venue did she show any concern for the rights of Mace. She gave the State's witnesses great latitude with their testimony and continually overruled objections by the defense. With the defense witnesses, she sustained almost every objection by the prosecution. Her handling of the trial has been repeatedly attacked on appeal, and some concerns have been noted in various appellate rulings. However, the courts have continually upheld the convictions.

Throughout the two-and-a-half-hour drive to the prison, Lacy's thoughts were on Hugo. Less than two months earlier, they had made this trip together, both sleep deprived and slugging coffee to stay awake. They had discussed their distrust of Greg Myers and their reluctance to indulge his theory of a grand conspiracy. They had admitted the sense of danger they felt.

They had been so naive.

She entered Bradford County and followed the signs to Starke, then to the prison. It took half an hour to make her way to Q Wing. It was noon Monday, and no other attorneys were there. She waited in a small conference room for fifteen minutes until Junior appeared in chains. His guards unshackled him and he took his seat on the other side of the plastic wall. He took his receiver, smiled, said, 'Thanks for coming.'

'Hello, Junior. It's good to see you again.'

'You look good, Lacy, in spite of what happened. I trust your injuries are healing.'

'Well, my hair is growing and that's all that matters.'

He chuckled at this. He was more animated, more eager to talk. Lacy assumed he was awaiting the arrival of his D.C. lawyers with great anticipation. For the first time in many years, there was hope.

'I'm sorry about your friend Hugo,' he said. 'I liked him.'

'Thanks.' She really didn't want to talk about Hugo, but with plenty of time to kill they could chat about anything. She said his family was coping and trying to get by, but the days were long and difficult. He wanted to know about the accident, how and when it happened and what had been learned since then. He doubted it was really an accident and she assured him it was not. He was curious as to why no one 'from the outside' had stepped in to investigate Hugo's death. Careful with her words, she explained that, hopefully, things were moving in that direction. They talked about Wilton, Todd Short, the D.C. lawyers, and a little of life on death row.

After a long pause, one of many, he said, 'I had a visitor yesterday, one that was not at all expected.'

'Who was it?'

'A man named Lyman Gritt. Heard of him?'

'Yes, we've actually met, though I don't remember. I'm told he was with the rescue team that worked the accident and got me to the hospital. I stopped by his office to say hello and thanks, but he seems to have been replaced. The timing looks suspicious.'

Junior smiled and leaned closer. 'It's all suspicious, Lacy. Wheels are turning and you'd best be careful.'

She shrugged. Keep talking.

He said, 'Gritt's a good man. He was in favor of the casino, so we were on opposite sides long ago. But we have a history. My father and his uncle were raised together in a shack just off the reservation. They were like brothers. I can't say the families are close now, because we fought over the casino. But Gritt has a conscience and he knows about the corruption. He never liked the Chief; now he really despises him and his family. The Chief's son is now the constable, so any investigation into your accident will go nowhere. It's all being covered up, as I'm sure you suspect. But Gritt knows the truth, and he thinks he has the evidence to prove it. That's why he wants to talk to you.'

'To me?'

'That's right. He thinks he can trust you. He doesn't trust the local boys in Brunswick County, not that they would get involved. As you've probably learned, our tribe is wary of outsiders, especially those with badges. But Gritt has some evidence.'

'What kind of evidence?'

'He didn't say, or wouldn't say. These walls have been known to hear too much, so we were cautious. You need to understand, Lacy, that Gritt is being threatened. He has a wife and three kids, and the Chief and his pals can be effectively intimidating. The entire tribe lives under a cloud of fear and people just don't talk. Plus, with the casino life is better these days, so why rock the boat?'

Lacy had serious doubts about the prison authorities eavesdropping on conversations between attorneys and their death row clients, but then she realized that the meeting with Gritt took place in another part of Q Wing. Gritt was not a lawyer.

'What makes him think he can trust me? We've never met.'

'Because you're not a cop and you're the first person to set foot on the reservation and ask questions. You and Mr Hatch.'

'Okay. How am I supposed to meet with Gritt?'

'Wilton will facilitate it.'

'So who makes the next move?'

'Gritt and I agreed that I'll contact Wilton and he'll arrange things. That is, if you're willing to talk to him.'

'Of course I'm willing to talk.'

'Then I'll get word to Wilton. Needless to say, Lacy, this has to be handled as delicately as possible. Everyone is scared. They're watching Gritt, and probably Wilton too.'

'Do they, whoever they might be, know that Todd Short is back in town?'

'I don't think so. My lawyers met with Short this morning, somewhere far away from the reservation. If he follows through with his promise to recant his testimony, it won't be long before everyone knows it. At that point, he'll be a marked man.'

'They can't keep killing people, Junior.'

'They killed your buddy Mr Hatch. And Son

312

and Eileen. And they probably took care of Digger Robles, the other snitch, may he rest in peace.'

And not to mention Greg Myers.

He continued, 'And they're perfectly willing to let the State of Florida kill me. They'll stop at nothing, Lacy. Don't ever forget that.'

'How can I?'

Salzman and an associate named Fuller arrived just after 1:00 p.m. They were dressed casually in khakis and loafers, a far cry from the dark, pin-striped world of D.C. law. Their firm had a thousand lawyers on all major continents. Its pro bono efforts on behalf of condemned killers were laudatory, even staggering. Lacy had read about the firm online and was astonished at the manpower it threw into the fight against the death penalty.

Their meeting with Todd Short had gone beautifully. The snitch had given a two-hour video deposition in which he admitted being recruited by the police and prosecutor to exchange bogus testimony for leniency and cash. They had found him to be believable and truly remorseful. Junior would always hate the guy who sent him to death row, but he was nonetheless thrilled at his change of heart.

Salzman explained that they would immediately file a petition for post-conviction relief in state court and seek a stay of execution. Once that was in hand, they would slug it out with the Florida Attorney General's Office, and go to federal court

313

if necessary. The flurry of potential litigation was bewildering, to Lacy at least, but Salzman had been through it many times. He was a seasoned expert in the world of habeas corpus, and exuded a confidence that was contagious. His goal was a new trial, one to be held far away from the meddlesome self-interest of Claudia McDover.

CHAPTER 29

The burner Lacy kept in her pocket vibrated early Tuesday morning. Cooley was checking in, if only to inform her that he had not heard from Greg Myers. No surprise there. He also said he had mailed her another prepaid phone and it should arrive later in the morning. When she had it, she was to destroy the one she was holding.

For lunch, she met Allie Pacheco at a sandwich shop near the Capitol. Over a bowl of soup, he relayed the information that the police in Key Largo had sequestered the *Conspirator* and it was now safely under lock and key. He would meet with them in a day or so and hand over the laptop, courier bag, and backpack. It was their investigation, not his, but the FBI was promising full cooperation. The police were interviewing regulars at the marina, but so far had found no one who had seen anything unusual. With no photo and only a general description of the missing person, and not to mention a cold trail to begin with, finding him seemed virtually impossible.

After a few minutes of business, Pacheco said, 'This soup is okay, but what about dinner?'

'Where are we professionally?' she asked.

'Oh, I think we're on solid ground,' he said with a smile. 'We're certainly on the same team. Ethically, I'm not supposed to hit on chicks who work for the bureau, so we're good to go.'

'Chicks?'

'Just a figure of speech. No harm intended. I'm thirty-four years old. I'm guessing you're somewhere in that range. We're both single, and, frankly, it's refreshing to meet a nice woman in real life and not on some dating site. You do the online stuff?'

'Twice, both disasters.'

'Oh, I could tell some stories, but I won't bore you. So how about dinner?'

If she said yes, she would do so only because he was nice looking and personable, though a bit cocky, but then she had never met a young FBI agent who wasn't brimming with confidence. She would not say yes because BJC was desperate for help.

'When?' she asked.

'I don't know. Tonight?'

'And what if at some point the bureau gets involved with my little conspiracy? Would that make your boss uncomfortable?'

'You met Luna. He's always uncomfortable; he prefers it. But, no, I see no conflict. Again, we would be working on the same side of the street.

Besides, you've already told us everything. There are no secrets, right?'

'There are a lot of secrets. I just don't know them yet.'

'And I won't ask. What about your boss?'

'He's a pushover.'

'Thought so. I got the impression that when you're in the room you're pretty much in charge. Dinner, nice bottle of wine, hell, maybe even some candles? I'll pick you up at seven, assuming of course your brother is not around.'

'He's not.'

'Good. What a piece of work.'

'Gunther is very protective of his little sister.'

'Can't say I blame him. Seven?'

'Seven thirty. And pick a nice place but not something too fancy. Forget the candles. We work for the government and we'll split the check.'

'Deal.'

He picked her up in a late-model SUV, one just washed and shined and vacuumed for the occasion. For the first five minutes they talked about cars. Lacy was tired of the rental she'd been driving and ready for a new set of wheels. She loved her old hybrid, but the crash had her thinking of something a bit sturdier. They were heading south, away from downtown.

'You like Cajun food?' he asked.

'Love it.'

'Ever been to Johnny Ray's?'

'No, but I've heard it's great.'

'Let's try it.'

She liked the SUV but found it a bit on the masculine side. She was curious about its cost. Through some quick research she had learned that the current starting salary for a special agent was $52,000. Allie had been with the bureau for five years, so she figured they were earning about the same. He had commented on how nice her apartment was, and said he was sharing one with another agent. Reassignment was a way of life in the bureau, and he was hesitant to buy a place.

They waded through the background pleasantries, though each knew the other had dug through the Internet. He grew up in Omaha; college and law school at Nebraska. Off duty, he had the relaxed easiness of a midwesterner, with a complete lack of pretension. Her undergraduate degree was from William & Mary; law school at Tulane. They found common ground in New Orleans, where he'd spent his first two years with the bureau. Neither really missed the place, too much humidity and crime, though the way they talked about it now they seemed downright homesick. By the time they parked and walked into the restaurant, Lacy was giving the guy high marks on every front. Be cool, she told herself, they always disappoint.

At a quiet corner table, they opened the menus. When the waiter stepped away, she said, 'Just a reminder. We're splitting the check.'

'Okay, but I would like to pay. After all, I invited you.'

'Thanks, but we'll split it.' And that was the end of that conversation.

They decided to start with a dozen raw oysters each and agreed on a bottle of Sancerre. When the menus were gone, he said, 'So what would you like to talk about?'

She chuckled at his bluntness. 'Anything but the case.'

'Fair enough. You pick a topic, then I'll pick one. And anything is fair game, anything but the casino and all that.'

'That's pretty broad. You go first and let's see how things unwind.'

'Okay, I have a great question. And if you don't want to talk about it, I understand. What's it like getting hit with an air bag?'

'I take it you've missed that experience so far.'

'Yes, so far.'

She took a sip of water and a deep breath. 'It's loud, sudden, jolting. One second it's just sitting there, invisible inside the steering wheel, never to be thought about, and a millisecond later it's exploding in your face at two hundred miles an hour. That, along with the impact, knocked me out. Not for very long, because I remember someone moving around the car. After that, I blacked out. The air bag saved my life, but it's a rough way to go. Once is enough.'

'I'm sure it is. Have you completely recovered?'

'For the most part. There's still some soreness here and there, but every day is better. I wish my hair would grow faster.'

'You're beautiful with short hair.'

The wine arrived. Lacy tasted it and approved. They touched glasses and had a drink. 'Your turn,' he said.

'What? You've had enough of air bags?'

'Just curious. I had a friend who was behind the wheel when he swerved to miss a pedestrian. Instead he hit a utility pole, going about twenty miles an hour. He would've been fine but the air bag banged him around pretty bad. He kept ice packs on his face for a week.'

'I prefer to have them. Why'd you go to law school?'

'My father is a lawyer in Omaha and it just seemed like the thing to do. I never thought about changing the world, like most first-year law students; I was just thinking of a nice job. My father has done pretty well, and I actually practiced with him for a year. Got bored real fast and decided it was time to leave Nebraska.'

'Why the FBI?'

'Excitement. No eight to five, behind-the-desk routine. When you're chasing crooks – big ones, small ones, smart ones, dumb ones – there aren't too many dull moments. And you? What made you want to investigate judges?'

'Well, it wasn't something I was dreaming about when I started law school. The job market was pretty soft when I graduated, plus I had no desire to do the big-firm routine. They're finally hiring a lot of women, half my class was female, but I didn't want to work a hundred hours a week. I have friends who went that route and they're all miserable. My parents had retired to Florida. I was here and I saw an ad for a job with the Board on Judicial Conduct.'

'You interviewed and got the job. What a surprise.'

The oysters arrived on platters of ice, and the conversation stopped as they went about the ritual, New Orleans style, of squeezing lemons and adding horseradish to the cocktail sauce. Pacheco gulped his from the shells while Lacy used saltines, both acceptable methods.

He said, 'So you visited Junior Mace yesterday.'

'I did, for the second time. Ever been to death row?'

'No, but I'm sure I will one day. Anything interesting?'

'Are you fishing for information?'

'Always. I can't help it. It's in my DNA.'

'Maybe a tip, a lead, or something. Junior may have information. Mainly, though, I think he just enjoys visitors.'

'So you're not going to tell me anything new?'

'No, well, maybe. You've no doubt studied our exhibit detailing his trial and conviction.'

'I've read every word.'

'So you remember the part of the story where the two jailhouse snitches disappeared shortly after the trial.'

'Todd Short and Digger Robles.'

She smiled. Impressive. 'Right. For years, the legend was that they were taken out before they could recant, which is often what snitches do. It appears as if one is really gone. The other, though, has made a miraculous comeback. Back from the dead, sort of, and he's talking. He's dying of cancer and wants to set the record straight.'

'That's great news, right?'

'Maybe. Junior's lawyers from D.C. were at Starke yesterday, and they asked me to sit in. They're pretty excited about his chances of, first, staying the execution and, second, getting a new trial.'

'A new trial? It's been, what, fifteen years?'

'Fifteen. Seems like a long shot to me, but these guys know their stuff.'

'But this is not your case, right? You're not involved with Junior's habeas appeals. So you went to see him for some other reason.'

'Right. Like I said, he thinks he might know something.'

Allie smiled and let it pass. It was obvious she was not sharing anything else. They finished the oysters and debated the entrées. He decided to settle for another dozen. She ordered a bowl of gumbo.

'Whose turn is it?' he asked.

'Yours, I think.'

'Okay, what other interesting cases are you working on?'

She smiled and sipped more wine. 'Well, within

the bounds of confidentiality, with no names being mentioned, we're trying to remove a judge who's hitting the bottle pretty hard. Two lawyers and two litigants have complained. Poor guy has been fighting alcoholism for a long time and now he's losing badly. He won't schedule hearings until after lunch. Sometimes he forgets them altogether. One of his court reporters says he keeps a flask under his robe and pours the stuff in his coffee cup. His docket has a backlog and no one's happy. Pretty sad, really.'

'Should be easy then.'

'It's never easy to remove a judge. They like their jobs and usually have no place to land when they hang up their robes. My turn. What are you working on?'

For an hour they traded war stories. Pacheco's world of tracking sleeper cells and narco-traffickers was far more exciting than hounding derelict judges, but he was not judgmental and seemed fascinated by her work. When the wine was gone, they ordered coffee and kept talking.

At her apartment, he walked her to the steps like a gentleman and stopped at the door. 'Can we talk business?' he asked.

'If you mean sex, the answer is no. I'm still too sore to get in the mood.'

'I wasn't thinking about sex.'

'Is that your first lie of the night?'

'Maybe the second.' He faced her and stepped closer. 'Luna is close, Lacy. The disappearance of

Myers has our attention. I spent most of the day trying to convince him that this case is potentially much bigger than we can imagine. We need something else, another smoking gun, and Luna might be ready.'

'What about your big boss in Jacksonville?'

'He's tough, but he's also ambitious. If he sees the potential the way we do, he'll reconsider. Just give us something else.'

'I'm trying.'

'I know you are. And I'm waiting by the phone.'

'Enjoyed the evening.'

'And so did I.' He pecked her on the cheek and said good night.

CHAPTER 30

Wilton Mace said he was calling from a pay phone, and he did indeed sound nervous, even jumpy, as if looking over his shoulder. Tomorrow, Lyman Gritt was taking his wife to see a doctor in Panama City, a specialist of some variety. He wanted to meet Lacy at the doctor's office, a place no one would suspect. Wilton gave her the details and asked if she could identify Gritt. She said no, she had never met him, but her boss could. And her boss would insist on being with her. Wilton wasn't sure how this would sit with Gritt, but they could figure things out at the doctor's office. Don't be surprised, though, if Gritt didn't like it.

Lacy and Michael arrived an hour early. While he stayed in the car, she entered the building, part of a busy medical arts complex with doctors and dentists on four levels. She loitered around the ground floor, read the directory, stopped by a café, then took the elevator to the third floor. The office belonged to a group of gynecologists, and its large, modern waiting room was filled with women, only two accompanied by men. Lacy returned to the car and waited while Michael went inside and covered the same territory. When he returned, they agreed the place was harmless. A perfect spot for a clandestine meeting. Dozens of patients were entering and leaving the building. At 1:45, Michael nodded to a couple leaving their car and said, 'That's Gritt.' About six feet tall, thin but with a potbelly. His wife had long dark hair that was braided, and she was much shorter and stockier.

'Got 'em?' Michael asked.

'Yep.' When they entered the building, Lacy eased out of the car and followed. Michael would sit and wait and hope there was no frantic call. He watched the foot traffic carefully, hoping to see nothing suspicious. Inside, Lacy read the directory again, killed a few minutes, and took the elevator to the third floor. She entered the waiting room and saw Gritt and his wife sitting against a far wall, looking as uncomfortable as everybody else. She picked up a magazine and found a chair on the other side of the room. Amy Gritt stared at the floor as if she might be expecting some awful news. Lyman casually flipped through a *People* magazine. Lacy had no idea if Wilton had described her looks to Gritt, but he seemed to have no interest in her. The receptionist was too busy to notice the young lady who had not bothered to check in. A name was called. The patient slowly walked to the desk, was greeted by a harried nurse, and disappeared around a corner. The languid pace continued for half an hour as more women arrived to replace those who were leaving. Lacy peered over her magazine and watched Gritt. After an hour, he glanced at his watch as if growing frustrated. Finally, the name of Amy Gritt was called, and she walked to the desk. As soon as she was out of sight, Lacy stood and stared at Lyman. When he made eye contact, she nodded slightly and left the waiting room. She walked to the end of the hallway and waited only a few seconds before Gritt closed the door behind him and walked to her.

She offered a hand and quietly said, 'I'm Lacy Stoltz.'

He shook it gently, smiled, and instinctively glanced over his shoulder. 'I'm Lyman Gritt, and you look much better than the last time I saw you.'

'I'm doing fine. Thanks for that night.'

'It's my job. It was a bad scene. Sorry about your friend.'

'Thank you.'

He walked to a window and leaned against it, facing the hallway and the foot traffic. Patients were coming and going to several offices, but no one noticed them.

'We don't have much time,' he said. 'I'm not involved in any of the shenanigans on our land. I'm a cop, an honest one, and I have a family to protect. My name can never be used in any investigation. I will not testify in any court. I will not point the fingers at any of my people or the crooks they're involved with. Understood?'

'Understood, but you know that I can't control everything that might happen. You have my word and that's all I can control.'

He reached into a front pocket of his jeans and pulled out a flash drive. 'There are two videos here. The first is the property of the police in Foley, Alabama. They got lucky when someone, and I don't know who, caught the theft of the truck on video. The second video was taken about fifteen minutes after the crash, at a country store just north of the town of Sterling. I think it clearly shows the guy who was driving the truck when it crashed into your car. I've included a memo with all the details I'm aware of.'

Lacy took the flash drive.

Gritt reached into another pocket and removed a plastic bag. 'This is what I believe to be a small piece of a paper towel covered with blood. I found this about a quarter of a mile from the scene two days after the accident. My theory is that the blood belongs to the passenger in the second video. If I were you I'd get DNA testing immediately, and pray for a hit. If you're lucky, you'll get a name, one you can then match to the guy in the video.'

Lacy took the plastic bag. 'And you have copies?'

'I do, and I have the rest of the paper towel, though no one could ever find it.'

'I don't know what to say.'

'Say nothing. Just do your job and nail these bastards, and keep my name out of it.'

'I promise.'

'Thank you, Ms Stoltz. This meeting never happened.' He began walking away, and she said, 'Thanks, and I hope your wife is okay.'

'She's fine. Just a routine checkup. She's afraid of doctors, so I tag along.'

Neither Michael nor Lacy had thought to stick a laptop in a briefcase; otherwise, they would have wheeled into an empty parking lot of a fast-food joint, bought coffees, found a table in the corner, and rolled the footage. Instead, they raced home, speculating nonstop as to what the videos might reveal.

'Why didn't you ask him?' Michael demanded, with some irritation.

'Because he was in a hurry,' she shot back. 'He handed it over, said what he wanted to say, and that was it.'

'I would've asked.'

'You don't know what you would have done. Stop bitching. Who's the head of the state Department of Law Enforcement?'

'Gus Lambert. He's new and I don't know him.'

'Well, who do you know?'

'An old friend.' Michael called the old friend twice and couldn't get him. Lacy called a girlfriend in the Attorney General's Office, and got the name of a supervisor with the Regional

Crime Lab in Tallahassee. The supervisor was busy and uncooperative and promised to call back tomorrow.

When they were both off the phone, Michael said, 'The crime lab won't do it unless DLE is involved.'

Lacy said, 'I'll call Gus Lambert. I'm sure I can charm his pants off.'

Commissioner Lambert's secretary was beyond charm, said the boss was in a meeting and was a very busy man. Michael's old friend called back and asked what was going on. Michael explained, as they blitzed down the passing lane of Interstate 10, that it was an urgent matter dealing with the suspicious death of a state employee. Abbott, the friend, said he recalled the story of the death of Hugo Hatch. Michael said, 'We have reason to believe it was more complicated than a bad car wreck. We have a source from within the tribe and we now have possession of a blood sample that could be important. How do we get access to the crime lab?'

As they talked, Lacy searched the web with her phone. Having never dealt with DNA testing, she knew almost nothing about it. According to an article on a science site, forensic technicians are now able to test a suspect's DNA in two hours, quick enough for the police to ram it through their crime databases and determine if the man in custody has committed the crime in question, as well as others. As recently as five years earlier, the testing took between twenty-four and seventy-two hours, enough time for the suspect to post bail and walk out of jail.

Michael was saying, 'No, there's no open investigation, not by the locals and not by DLE. It happened on tribal land and the Tappacola are in charge. That's part of the problem. I'm talking about a favor here, Abbott. And a quick one.'

Michael listened, said, 'Thanks,' and ended the call. 'He says he'll try and see the commissioner.'

It was almost 5:00 p.m. when Michael and Lacy arrived at the DLE's Regional Crime Lab on the outskirts of Tallahassee. Abbott was waiting at the front door, along with Dr Joe Vasquez, the head of the lab. Quick introductions were made, and they followed him to a small conference room. Lacy placed the plastic ziplock bag on the table in front of Dr Vasquez, who looked at it but didn't touch it.

He asked, 'What do we know about this?'

Lacy replied, 'Not much. We got it less than two hours ago from our confidential source. He thinks it's a piece of a paper towel with blood on it.'

'Who's handled it?'

'We have no idea, but our source considers himself a law enforcement professional. I'd bet it's been handled very little.'

'How long will it take?' Michael asked.

Vasquez smiled proudly and said, 'Give us two hours.'

'That's incredible.'

'Indeed it is. The technology is changing rapidly, and we think that within two years detectives at the crime scene will be able to check blood and semen with a handheld device. It's called DNA testing on a chip.'

Lacy asked, 'And how long to run the results through the state's database?'

Vasquez looked at Abbott, who shrugged and said, 'Half an hour.'

They stopped for Chinese takeout at a favorite spot near the Capitol. BJC was deserted, as they were hoping, when they arrived just after six. Ignoring their dinner, they went straight to Michael's desktop and plugged in the flash drive. They watched the two videos, printed Gritt's two-page memo, read it carefully, discussed it line by line, and watched the videos again and again. Lacy was almost numb with the realization that she was looking at the murder weapon, the truck, and perhaps even the murderer, the punk with the bloody nose.

There were two men in each video; all four were different. Could this be the first glimpse of others in the Dubose crime family? They had photos of Vonn entering the condo at Rabbit Run, but no one else. The driver in the second video, the one from Frog's store, was particularly fascinating. He was older than the other three, perhaps forty-five, and was better dressed, wearing a golf shirt and pressed khakis. He had planned things well enough to attach a set of perfectly faked Florida tags to his truck. He wasn't Vonn, but could he be a ranking member? Was he in charge of the operation? Could he have been at the scene, with a light, poking around Lacy's smashed Prius, looking for the cell phones while Hugo was bleeding and dying? Clever as he was, he had made the bone-headed mistake of parking directly in front of Frog's store and getting himself captured on video. Allie had said more than once that even the smartest criminals do stupid things.

They finally ate cold chicken chow mein, but neither was hungry. Michael's cell phone rattled at 7:50, and Abbott announced cheerfully, 'Got your boy.'

The blood belonged to one Zeke Foreman, a twenty-three-year-old parolee with two drug-related convictions under his belt. His DNA had been in the state's database for five years, since his first arrest. Abbott had three photos, two of the mug-shot variety and one from the prison archives. He was sending them over by e-mail.

Michael told Abbott he owed him one, and a big one at that, and said thanks.

Lacy was standing by the printer when the three photos rolled off. Michael stopped the second video with a clear shot of both faces. The passenger, even with a bloody nose, looked very similar to Zeke Foreman.

★   ★   ★

Allie Pacheco was more than happy to hustle over to Lacy's for a late-night drink, though her tone was clearly not romantic. She said it was urgent but offered nothing else. They watched the videos and studied the photos. They read Gritt's memo and talked about the case until midnight, finishing off a bottle of wine in the process.

CHAPTER 31

Zeke Foreman had been living with his mother near the small town of Milton, Florida, not far from Pensacola. The FBI watched his house for two days but saw no sign of him or his 1998 Nissan. His parole officer said he was due for their monthly checkup on October 4, and he had never missed a meeting. To do so could lead to a revocation and a return to prison. Foreman worked odd jobs and had managed to stay out of trouble for the past thirteen months.

Sure enough, on the fourth Foreman walked into the Probation Office in downtown Pensacola and said hello to his parole officer. When asked where he'd been, he offered a well-rehearsed story of driving a truck for a friend down to Miami. Sit tight, the parole officer said, there are a couple of guys who'd like to say hello. He opened the door, and Agents Allie Pacheco and Doug Hahn walked in and introduced themselves. The parole officer left the room.

'What's this all about?' asked Foreman, already flinching at the sudden appearance of the FBI.

Neither agent sat down. Pacheco said, 'Back on

August 22, a Monday, you were on the Tappacola Indian reservation around midnight. What were you doing there?'

Foreman tried his best to appear surprised, though he looked like he was about to faint. He shrugged, gave a dumb look, and said, 'Not sure what you're talking about.'

'You know exactly what we're talking about. You were driving a stolen truck and it was involved in an accident. You fled the scene. Recall any of this?'

'You got the wrong guy.'

'Is that the best you can do?' Pacheco nodded to Hahn, who whipped out a set of handcuffs. Pacheco said, 'Stand up. You're under arrest for capital murder.'

'You gotta be kidding.'

'Oh sure, this is just a comedy routine. Stand up and put your hands behind your back.' They handcuffed him, searched him, took his cell phone, and led him out of the office and through a side exit of the building. They put him in the rear seat of their car and drove four blocks to the offices of the FBI. No one said a word during the drive.

Inside their building, they walked him to an elevator that stopped on the sixth floor. They went through a maze of hallways and entered a small conference room. A young lawyer was waiting, and with a smile she said, 'Mr Foreman, I'm Rebecca Webb, Assistant U.S. Attorney. Please have a seat.'

Agent Hahn removed the handcuffs and said, 'You might be here for a while.' He gently pressed Foreman into a chair, and everyone sat down.

'What's going on?' Foreman asked. Though he was only twenty-three, he did not project the airs of a frightened kid. He'd had time to collect himself and was a tough guy again. He'd been around, had long hair, hard features, and a full collection of cheap prison tattoos.

Pacheco read him his *Miranda* rights and handed over a form with the same words in writing. Foreman read it slowly, then signed at the bottom acknowledging his understanding of what was happening. He had been through this before.

Pacheco said, 'You're facing federal capital murder charges, the death penalty, lethal injection, and all that jazz.'

'So who'd I kill?'

'Guy named Hugo Hatch, the passenger in the other car, but we're not going to argue about that. We know you were on the reservation that night, driving a stolen truck, a big Dodge Ram, and we know you deliberately crossed the center line and struck a Toyota Prius. You hung around awhile, you and the driver of your getaway truck, and the two of you removed two cell phones and an iPad from the Prius. We know that for a fact so it's not debatable.'

Foreman kept his composure and revealed nothing.

Pacheco continued, 'Fifteen minutes after you

fled the scene, you and your pal stopped at a country store and bought ice, beer, and rubbing alcohol. This ring a bell?'

'No.'

'Didn't think so.' From a file, Pacheco removed a photo from Frog's video and slid it over to Foreman. 'I guess that's not you, with the busted nose.'

Foreman looked at it and shook his head. 'I guess I need a lawyer.'

'We'll get you one, in a minute. First, though, let me explain that this is not what you might call one of our typical interrogations. We're not here to grill you about your involvement, because we know what happened. Deny all you want to, we don't care. We've got the proof and we'll be happy to see you at trial. I'll let Ms Webb enlighten you as to why we're really here.'

Foreman refused to look at her. She stared at him and said, 'We have a deal for you, Zeke. And a sweet one it is. We know you didn't steal the truck yourself, and for some reason drive to the back side of the reservation, and cause a wreck, and flee the scene, and leave a man dying, all for the sheer adventure of it. We know you were working for some other people, some serious and sophisticated criminals. They probably paid you with a nice wad of cash, then told you to leave town for a spell. Maybe you've done other dirty work for them. Whatever. We're only concerned with the murder, and the men who planned it.

We're after bigger crooks, here, Zeke, and you're just a bit player. A murderer, yes, but a small fish as far as we're concerned.'

'What kind of deal?' he asked, looking at her.

'The deal of, literally, a lifetime. You talk and you walk. You tell us everything you know, you name names, give us phone numbers, histories, everything, and we'll eventually dismiss the charges. We'll place you in witness protection, set you up in a nice apartment far away, some place like California, give you a new name, new papers, new job, new life. Your past will be forgotten and you'll be as free as a bird. Otherwise, you're headed for death row, where you'll rot away for ten, maybe fifteen years until your appeals run out and you get the needle.'

His shoulders finally sagged as his chin dropped.

Webb continued, 'And the deal is good for now, and now only. If you say no and leave this room, you'll never take another breath as a free man.'

'I think I need a lawyer.'

'Okay, for your last conviction you were represented by a court-appointed lawyer named Parker Logan. Remember him?'

'Yes.'

'Were you pleased with his services?'

'I guess so.'

'He's waiting downstairs. You want to talk to him?'

'Uh, sure.'

Hahn left the room and returned minutes later with Parker Logan, a veteran of the indigent grind in Pensacola. Quick introductions were made around the table, and Logan shook hands with his former client. He sat next to Foreman and said, 'Okay, what's up?'

Webb pulled some papers out of a file and said, 'The magistrate has appointed you to represent Mr Foreman. Here's the paperwork, along with the indictment.' Logan took the papers and began reading. He flipped a page and said, 'You guys seem to be in a hurry.'

Webb replied, 'We'll get to that in a minute.'

Logan kept reading, and when he finished he signed his name on one form and gave it to Foreman. 'Sign here.' Foreman signed his name.

Webb produced more paperwork and handed it to Logan. She said, 'Here's the agreement. The indictment will be sealed and held in abeyance until such time as Mr Foreman is no longer needed by the prosecution.'

'Witness protection?' Logan asked.

'That's right. Starting today.'

'Okay, okay. I need to talk to my client.'

Webb, Pacheco, and Hahn stood and walked to the door. Pacheco stopped and said, 'I need your cell phone. No calls.'

This irritated Logan and for a second he hesitated. Then he pulled out his cell phone and handed it over.

An hour later, Logan opened the door and said they were ready. Webb, Pacheco, and Hahn reentered the room and took their seats. Logan, now with his jacket off and his sleeves rolled up, said, 'First, as the defense lawyer, I feel compelled to at least inquire as to what proof the government has against my client.'

Pacheco said, 'We're not going to waste time arguing about the evidence, but let's just say that we have DNA proof taken from a blood sample found near the scene. Your client was there.'

Logan shrugged as if to say, 'Not bad.' Instead, he asked, 'Okay, so what happens when my client leaves this room, assuming he takes the deal?'

Webb replied, 'As you know, witness protection is handled by the U.S. Marshals. They will take him from here, get him out of town, out of Florida, and relocate him someplace far away. A nice place.'

'He's concerned about his mother and younger sister.'

'They'll have the option of joining him. It's not unusual for witness protection to move entire families.'

Pacheco said, 'And I might add that the U.S. Marshals have never lost a witness and they've protected over five thousand. They're usually dealing with large organized crime syndicates that operate on a national scale, not locals like the boys we're after.'

Logan nodded along, mulled things over, and finally looked at his client and said, 'As your lawyer, I recommend you take this deal.'

Foreman picked up a pen and said, 'Let's do it.'

Webb reached for a small video camera mounted on a tripod. She focused it on Foreman while Hahn placed a recorder on the table in front of him. When he and his lawyer had finished signing the agreement, Pacheco placed a photo in front of him. He pointed to the driver of the truck with fake tags and asked, 'Who is he?'

'Clyde Westbay.'

'All right, now tell us everything you know about Clyde Westbay. We're on the same team now, Zeke, so I want the whole story. Everything.'

'Westbay owns a couple of hotels in Fort Walton Beach. I—'

'Names, Zeke, names of the hotels?'

'The Blue Chateau and the Surfbreaker. I got a job there two years ago, sort of a part-time gig cleaning the pools, landscaping, crap like that, got paid in cash, off the books. I saw Westbay around occasionally and somebody told me he was the owner. One day he caught me in the parking lot of the Surfbreaker and asked me about my criminal record. He said they didn't normally hire felons so I'd better behave myself. He was pretty much of an ass at first, but he softened up some. He called me Jailbird, which I didn't like but I let it slide. He's not the kinda guy you talk back to. The hotels are nicer than some of the others and they stayed busy. I liked the work because there were always a lot of girls around the pools, nice scenery.'

'We're not here to talk about girls,' Pacheco said.

'Who else worked at the hotels, and I don't mean the grunts like you? Who was the manager, the assistant manager, guys like that?'

Foreman scratched his beard, gave them a few names, tried to think of more. Hahn was pecking away at his keyboard. At the FBI office in Tallahassee, two agents watched Foreman on a monitor and worked their laptops. Within minutes, they knew the Blue Chateau and the Surfbreaker were owned by a company called Starr S, domiciled in Belize. A quick cross-reference revealed the same company owned a strip mall in Brunswick County. A small piece of the Dubose empire puzzle fell into place.

'What do you know about Westbay?' Pacheco asked.

'Not much, really. After I'd worked there for a few months I heard rumors that he was involved with some guys who owned a bunch of land and golf courses and even bars and strip clubs, but it was all hush-hush. It was all rumors, nothing concrete. But then, I was just, as you say, a grunt.'

'Tell us about August 22, that Monday.'

'Well, the day before, Westbay cornered me and said he had a job for me, one that might be dangerous and require a great deal of secrecy, said it paid five thousand bucks in cash, and asked if I was interested. I said sure, why not? I mean, I really felt like I was in no position to say no. I guess I wanted to impress the guy, plus Westbay is the kinda guy who'd fire me if he got pissed off.

343

It's not easy finding work with a rap sheet, you know? So, Monday afternoon, I was at the Blue Chateau, and I waited and waited until about dark when he and I got into his truck and came here to Pensacola. We stopped at a bar east of town and he told me to wait in the truck. He was inside for half an hour, and when he came out he handed me the keys to a truck, the Dodge Ram, which was also parked outside the bar. I noticed it had Alabama tags but I had no idea it was stolen. I got in the truck and followed him to the casino. We parked behind it. He got in my truck and explained what we were going to do, said we were going to cause a wreck. We drove deeper into the reservation, along a zigzagging road, and he said that was where it would happen. I was to smash into a little Toyota, get out, and he would be there to drive me away. I gotta tell you, I really wanted out at that point, but there was nowhere to go. We went back to the casino and he got his truck. We drove back into the reservation, to the same stretch of the road, and we waited in some woods for a long time. He was pacing around my truck, pretty nervous, talking on the phone. Finally he said let's go. He gave me a black motorcycle helmet and some padded gloves and knee pads, the kind dirt bikers use. We saw some lights in the distance, coming our way, and he said that's the car. Build up as much speed as possible, then cross the center line. The truck was twice as heavy and he assured me I would be fine. It was pretty scary stuff, to be honest. I don't think the car was going very fast. I hit about fifty, then at the last second crossed the center line. The air bag knocked the hell out of me, sort of stunned me for a second or two, and by the time I got out of the truck Westbay was right there. I removed the helmet, gloves, and knee pads and gave them to him. He noticed my nose was bleeding and he checked the air bag in the truck for blood. Found nothing. My nose wasn't broken and it didn't bleed much at first, then it started gushing. We walked around the car. The girl, the driver, was trying to move and talk but she was in bad shape. The black guy was stuck in the windshield and really tore up. A lot of blood.'

His voice cracked just a little and he swallowed hard.

Pacheco asked, 'There was a broken bottle of whiskey in the truck. Were you drinking?'

'No, not a drop. That was just part of the act, I guess.'

'Did Westbay have a flashlight?'

'No, he had put on a small headlamp. He told me to get in the truck, his truck, and I guess I did. He spent a minute or two at the car. I was sort of dazed and I'm not sure I remember all that much. It was happening fast and I was pretty scared, to be honest. You ever walk away from a head-on collision?'

'Not that I recall. When Westbay returned to his truck did he have anything with him?'

'Like what?'

345

'Like two cell phones and an iPad.'

He shook his head. 'No, I don't remember seeing anything like that. He was in a hurry. He looked at me and said something about the blood. He had a roll of paper towels in the truck and tore off several. I wiped my nose.'

Pacheco looked at Logan and said, 'We have a sample of the paper towels, with blood.'

Logan said, 'He's talking, isn't he?'

'Did you have any other injuries?' Pacheco asked.

'I banged my knee and it was hurting like hell, but that's all.'

'And so you drove away?'

'I guess. Westbay cut through a field, which was tricky because his lights were off. I had no idea where we were going. I think I was still rattled after seeing that black guy covered in blood. I remember thinking that this was worth a helluva lot more than five thousand bucks. Anyway, we came out a gravel road and he turned on his lights. When we got to a paved road, he picked up speed and we left the reservation. At one point, I asked him, "Who were those people?" and he said, "What people?" So I didn't say anything else. He said we needed some ice to put on my nose, so he stopped at a store that was open late. I guess that's where you got that photo.'

'And after you left the store?'

'We drove back to the Blue Chateau in Fort Walton. He put me up in a room for the night, brought me a clean T-shirt, and told me to keep ice on my face. He said that if anybody asked, I was to say that I'd been in a fight. That's what I told my mother.'

'And he paid you?'

'Yep, the next day, he gave me the money and told me to keep my mouth shut. Said that if anyone ever found out, then I would be charged with leaving the scene of an accident and probably something worse. Gotta tell you, I was scared shitless, so I kept my mouth shut. Scared of the cops, but also scared of Westbay. A few weeks went by and I figured I was in the clear. Then Westbay grabbed me one day at the hotel and he told me to get in my car and leave Florida immediately. He gave me a thousand bucks and said stay away until he called.'

'Has he called?'

'Once, but I didn't answer. I thought about never coming back, but I was worried about my mother and I didn't want to miss a meeting with my parole officer. I sort of snuck back into town today and I was planning to see my mother tonight.'

With the general narrative in place, Pacheco returned to the beginning of the story and hammered out more details. He dissected every movement and pushed the witness to remember every name. After four hours, Foreman was exhausted and eager to leave town again. When Pacheco finally relented, two U.S. marshals entered the room and left with Zeke Foreman. They drove him to a hotel in Gulfport, Mississippi, where he spent the first night of his new life.

Clyde Westbay lived with his second wife in a nice home behind gates not far from the beach in Brunswick County. He was forty-seven years old and had no criminal record. He held a Florida driver's license and a current U.S. passport and had never registered to vote, at least not in Florida. According to state employment records, he was the manager of the Surfbreaker Hotel in Fort Walton Beach. He carried two cell phones and used two landlines, one at his office and one at home. Three hours after Zeke left Florida, FBI agents were listening to all four phones.

CHAPTER 32

The morning mail included three thick packages from the law offices of Edgar Killebrew. Lacy reluctantly opened them and found his cover letter. He explained, in typical terse and arrogant language, that the 'enclosed' was Judge McDover's response to Lacy's 'frivolous' subpoenas. Attached to the letter was his formal demand that all allegations against his client be dropped and the investigation terminated. In the alternative, he demanded 'an immediate and confidential hearing before the full Board on Judicial Conduct.'

Lacy had requested all of his client's records, both official and personal, for ten specific lawsuits. As she began plowing through the stack, it became apparent nothing new was being offered. Killebrew and his associates had simply copied the court filings and lumped them together in a haphazard manner. There was an occasional memo dictated by the judge and not filed, and even a few handwritten notes, but nothing that revealed her thoughts, intentions, or observations; nothing that would implicate her in favoring one side or the other. But in all ten cases she had ruled for the faceless offshore entities and against the local property owners and litigants.

Not surprisingly, the paperwork was far less organized than the material Sadelle had indexed long ago. Nonetheless, Lacy had no choice but to review every document and record. When she finished, she reported to Geismar.

On October 5, the first Wednesday of the month, Judge McDover left her office an hour earlier than usual and drove to the same condo at Rabbit Run, her second visit there since the filing of the complaint that accused her of receiving the unit in a bribery scheme. She parked her Lexus in the same spot, leaving room for another vehicle, and entered the condo. She gave no indication of being the least bit jumpy or nervous, never once looked over her shoulder or up and down the street.

Inside, she checked the patio door and all windows. She went to her vault and spent a few moments admiring her 'assets,' goodies she'd been collecting for so long that she now believed she deserved them. Cash and diamonds in small, portable, fireproof safes. Locked steel cabinets filled with jewelry, rare coins, vintage silver goblets and cups and flatware, limited signed first editions of famous novels, ancient crystal, and small paintings from contemporary artists. All of it had been acquired by casino cash, skillfully laundered

350

through the systematic purchasing from dozens of dealers who never suspected that she and Phyllis Turban were violating those pesky reporting laws. The genius of their scheme was patience. Buy fine and rare goods in small quantities and, with time, watch their collection grow. Find the right dealers, avoid those who asked questions or seemed hesitant, and, when possible, move the goods out of the country.

She adored her collection, but for the first time in eleven years she felt the beginnings of a panic. All of this stuff should have been shipped or smuggled to a safer place. Now she had been accused. Someone knew about her condos and the mysterious companies that owned them. Vonn Dubose may have ice water in his veins, but Claudia McDover did not. Her insatiable appetite for cash was finally fading. She had enough. She and Phyllis could travel the world in style and laugh about the Indians. Most important, she could cut all ties to Dubose.

He arrived and fixed a double vodka. She sipped green tea as they sat at a breakfast table and watched the golf course. The two satchels were on the sofa; one filled with loot, the other empty.

'Talk to me about Killebrew,' he said after the usual chitchat.

'He's loaded them down with paperwork, at five hundred bucks an hour, I might add. And he's demanded that everything be dropped, of course. He's blowing smoke about a prompt hearing but thinks he can delay it for at least six months. Where will we be in six months, Vonn?'

'Right here, counting our money. Nothing is changing, Claudia. Are you worried?'

'Of course I'm worried. These people aren't stupid. I can show them the canceled checks when I bought the condos, ten thousand down for each when the market value was a lot more. I can show them the promissory note for the balance, most of which I still owe to some shady bank down in the Caribbean.'

'You've made payments over the years. Your arrangement with the bank is none of their business.'

'Very small payments, Vonn, very small. And the payments got rerouted back to me through another offshore bank.'

'They can never trace that, Claudia. How many times have we discussed this?'

'I don't know, Vonn. What if I just resign?'

'Resign?'

'Think about it, Vonn. I can blame it on health issues, feed the press some bogus crap, and leave office. Killebrew would raise hell and claim that BJC would no longer have jurisdiction. There's a good chance the complaint would go away.'

'The complaint is dead anyway.'

She took a deep breath, then a sip of tea. 'Myers?'

'Myers has disappeared.'

She shoved the cup and saucer away and said, 'I can't take this anymore, Vonn. This is your world, not mine.'

'He's on the run, okay? We don't have him yet, but we're closing in.'

Nothing was said for a long time as she counted the dead bodies and he thought about the extra cash he could pocket with her in retirement. 'Who is the guy?' she asked.

'A disbarred lawyer from Pensacola named Ramsey Mix. Served some time in a federal joint, got out, found some money he buried when the Feds came in, changed his name to Greg Myers, and lived on a boat with his little Mexican sweetheart.'

'How'd you find him?'

'That's not important. What is important is that BJC cannot go forward without him. It's over, Claudia. It was a nice little scare, but it's over. You can relax now.'

'I wouldn't be so sure about that. I've studied BJC's rules inside and out, and there's no hard-and-fast procedure that dismisses the charges when the complaining party loses interest.'

She was a lawyer. He was not, and he wouldn't argue with her. 'Are you sure they'll go away if you retire?'

'Again, I can't predict what they'll do. Their procedures are not always clear-cut. But, if I'm not on the bench, why should they care?'

'Perhaps they won't.'

She did not know about the two videos and Vonn's frantic efforts to contain the damage they might have created. She did not know about

Lyman Gritt and his suspicious activities. There was a lot she didn't know because, in his world, knowledge could be dangerous. Trusted confidants can be convinced to talk. Secrets get exposed. She had enough to worry about anyway.

There was another long gap in the conversation. Neither seemed eager to talk, though both minds were spinning. He rattled his ice cubes and finally said, 'So the question remains, Judge, how did Myers find out about the condos? Any possible paper trail would take him nowhere. There are too many firewalls, too many foreign companies governed by laws that cannot be penetrated. Someone told Myers, which means, of course, that there was a leak. Look at the people around me, and look at the people around you. My guys are professionals who run an organization that's airtight, and we've been in business for a long time with no leaks. What about you, Judge?'

'We've had this conversation.'

'We're having it again. What about Phyllis? She knows everything. How secure is her office?'

'Phyllis is my partner in crime, Vonn. She's just as guilty as me.'

'I'm not suggesting she might talk. But who's around her these days? I know she has no partners, only flunkies, but who are they?'

'She's a fanatic about security. Nothing sensitive is kept in her office, nor in her home. For the important stuff, she works out of a small office no one knows about. It's all very secure.'

354

'What about your office?'

'I've told you, Vonn. I use one full-time secretary that I run off every eighteen months or so. Not a single one has ever lasted two years because I don't want them getting comfortable and nosing around. Occasionally, I'll have an intern for a year, but those poor kids can't take the pressure. And I have a court reporter who's been with me for years and I'd trust with my life.'

'JoHelen.'

'JoHelen Hooper. A very sweet girl who does her job beautifully but keeps her distance from anything else related to the courthouse.'

'And how long has she been your court reporter?'

'Seven or eight years. We get along because she says little, kisses my ass when it needs kissing, and otherwise stays out of my way.'

'And why do you trust her so completely?'

'Because I know her. Why do you trust your boys so much?'

He ignored her question and asked, 'Does she have access to your office?'

'Never. No one has access.'

'There's no such thing as complete trust, Judge. And it's often the one you trust the most who'll cut your throat for the right price.'

'You should know about these things.'

'Damned right I do. Keep an eye on her, okay? Trust no one.'

'I don't trust anyone, Vonn, especially you.'

'Attagirl. I wouldn't trust me either.'

They managed a forced chuckle at their own crook-edness. Vonn went for more vodka and she sipped cold tea. As he was sitting down he said, 'Let's do this. Let's take it one week at a time, meet here each Wednesday at five, and monitor things. And give me some time to think about your retirement.'

'Oh, I'm sure you'll warm up to the retirement plan. You're already counting the extra cash each month.'

'True, but, as I've learned, it's so handy to have a judge in my pocket. You've spoiled me, Claudia, and I'm not sure I'll ever be able to find another judge so easily corruptible.'

'Let's hope not.'

'Getting religion in later years?'

'No. I'm just tired of working. I had to take a child away from its mother today. She's a meth head and a complete wreck, and the child was in danger, but it's still not easy. It's the third time I've snatched a kid away from this woman, and after a six-hour hearing, with all manner of emotion and name-calling, I had to order social services to take the child. So, as she's leaving, the mother announces in open court, "Hey, no big deal, I'm already pregnant again."'

'What an awful way to make a buck.'

'I'm tired of it. Stealing from the Indians is much more enjoyable.'

Lacy was on a yoga mat, trying painfully to complete a seated forward fold, a basic yoga move that she had done for years but not since the crash. With both legs straight and together on the floor, she was almost touching her toes when Cooley's burner rattled on the coffee table. Since she couldn't live without it these days, she had learned to despise it. Nonetheless, she immediately forgot about yoga and grabbed the phone.

'Just checking in, Lacy,' he said. 'No sign of Myers. Not that I expected any, but troubling nonetheless. The cops in Key Largo are looking for him but it's a pretty cold trail. Some bank repossessed his boat a couple of days ago. Just talked to the mole. Nothing new there either, except that our gal met with Dubose today for their monthly cash party.'

'How does he know this?' Lacy asked, but by now it was an old question.

'Maybe you can ask him one day. I don't know. Look, Lacy, if the bad guys can find Myers then they can find me as well. I'm pretty spooked. I'm moving around these days, one cheap motel after another, and I'm worn out, to be honest. I'm sending you a package tomorrow with another burner, along with a phone number. It belongs to a phone in the possession of the mole. We change every month. If something happens to me, you call the number.'

'Nothing will happen to you.'

'Thanks, but you have no idea what you're talking about. Myers thought he was clever.'

'True, but he also signed his name on the

complaint. The bad guys have no idea who you are.'

'I'm not sure I believe that anymore. At any rate, gotta run. Be careful, Lacy.' The call ended and Lacy stared at the cheap phone, expecting more.

CHAPTER 33

With the autumn season approaching, the Surfbreaker readied itself for the annual invasion of Canadians. The lobby was quiet, the pool and parking lot practically empty. Clyde Westbay stepped onto an elevator for a quick ride to the third floor, to check on some room renovations. A guest in shorts and sandals entered the elevator just as the door was closing and punched the button for the sixth floor. When the elevator began to move, the guest said, 'Got a few minutes, Mr Westbay?'

Clyde looked him over and asked, 'Are you a guest here?'

'I am. The Dolphin Suite. Name is Allie Pacheco, FBI.'

Clyde's gaze dropped to the sandals as Allie pulled out his badge.

'What's the FBI doing in my hotel?'

'Paying a fat rate for an okay suite. We're here to talk to you.'

The elevator stopped on the third floor, but Clyde did not get off. No one got on. The door closed and they continued upward.

'Maybe I'm busy right now.'

'So are we. Just a few questions, that's all.'

Clyde shrugged and stepped off on the sixth floor. He followed Pacheco to the end and watched as he opened the door to the Dolphin Suite.

'How do you like my hotel?' Clyde asked.

'It's okay. Room service sucks. Found a cockroach in my shower this morning. Dead.'

Inside were three other gentlemen, all in shorts and sandals, along with a young lady who looked as though she was ready for tennis. The men were FBI. She was Rebecca Webb, Assistant U.S. Attorney.

Westbay looked around the spacious room and said, 'Well, I don't really like the looks of this party. I suppose I could order you out of my hotel.'

Pacheco said, 'Sure, we'll be happy to leave, but you're going with us, in handcuffs and ankle chains, right through the main lobby, a perp walk for the benefit of your guests and employees. We might even tip off the local reporters.'

'I'm under arrest?'

'You are, for capital murder.'

His face turned pale and his knees buckled. He reached for the back of a chair and fumbled his way into it. Agent Hahn handed him a bottle of water, which he gulped as it splashed down his chin. He breathed deeply and looked into the eyes of the agents, desperate for help. An innocent man might have already protested.

Finally, he managed to mumble, 'This can't be

happening.' But it was, and Westbay's life was over. He was now entering a nightmare.

Rebecca Webb placed some papers in his lap and said, 'Here's the indictment, sealed, handed down yesterday by a federal grand jury in Tallahassee. One count of capital murder, punishable by death. The killing of Hugo Hatch was a murder for hire; thus the aggravating circumstances make it a capital case. Plus the stolen truck you bought for cash crossed a state line. Not very smart.'

'I didn't do it,' he almost whimpered. 'I swear.'

'Swear all you want to, Clyde. It's not going to help,' Pacheco said in mock sympathy.

'I want a lawyer.'

'Great. We'll get one for you, but first some paperwork. Let's sit over here at the table and have a chat.' The table was small and round, with only two chairs. Westbay took one and Pacheco sat opposite. Hahn and the other two agents stood behind Pacheco, a show of force that was intimidating in spite of the golf shirts, shorts, and pale legs.

Pacheco said, 'As far as we can determine, you have no criminal record, right?'

'Right.'

'So, is this your first arrest?'

'I think so, yes.' Thinking was difficult. He was bewildered, his eyes darting from face to face.

Pacheco slowly and crisply read Clyde his *Miranda* rights, then handed him a sheet of paper with the language printed. He shook his head as he read, some of the color finally returning to his face. He signed his name at the bottom with a pen Pacheco helpfully handed over.

'Do I have the right to make a phone call?' Westbay asked.

'Sure, but you need to know that we've been listening to your phone calls for the past three days. You have at least two cell phones, and if you use one now we'll hear every word.'

'You what?' Westbay asked, incredulous.

Ms Webb produced another set of papers and placed them on the table. 'Here's the wiretapping warrant signed by a U.S. magistrate.'

Pacheco said, 'It appears as though you use the iPhone for most of your personal calls. Your Nokia is paid for by the hotel and seems to be used for business, and for calls to your girlfriend, Tammy James, a former waitress at Hooters. I'm assuming your wife does not know about Miss Tammy.'

Clyde's jaw dropped but he couldn't speak. Could the revelations about Tammy be more troubling than the murder charge? Perhaps, but his brain was scrambled and nothing made sense.

Pacheco, thoroughly enjoying the moment, continued, 'And by the way, we got a warrant for Tammy's phone too, and she's also sleeping with a guy named Burke and another named Walter, and there could be others. But you need to forget about Tammy because your chances of ever touching her warm body again are quite slim.'

From somewhere in Westbay's throat there was

362

a rumbling, burping noise that only one agent managed to read. He grabbed a plastic wastebasket and said, 'Here' just as the defendant turned and began retching loudly. His face turned blood red as he gagged and wheezed and finally managed to vomit properly. Everyone looked away for a few seconds, though the sounds were just as sickening. When all of his breakfast was finally at the bottom of the bin, Westbay wiped his mouth with the back of a hand. He kept his head down and made a strange whimpering noise. An agent handed him a wet hand towel and he wiped his mouth again. Eventually, he sat up straight and gritted his teeth, as if now fortified and ready for the firing squad.

A putrid odor began radiating from the wastebasket. An agent took it to the restroom.

Hahn took a step toward the table and said proudly, 'Plus, we have records of all calls on both phones for the past two years. We're tracking down those numbers as we speak. Somewhere in there is Vonn Dubose. We'll eventually find his number.'

Westbay appeared to stop breathing. He gawked wild-eyed at Pacheco across the table, and finally managed to say, 'I want a lawyer.'

'Who do you have in mind?'

His mind was paralyzed at the moment. He closed his eyes and tried to think of the name of a lawyer, any lawyer, or anyone who could possibly rescue him. There was a real estate lawyer he played golf with; a bankruptcy lawyer he drank with; a divorce lawyer who'd banished his first wife; and so on. Finally, 'Okay, Gary Bullington.'

Pacheco shrugged and said, 'Call him. Let's hope he makes house calls.'

'I don't have his number.'

'I got it,' said one of the other agents, looking at his laptop. He rattled off the number but Westbay's hands were shaking too badly. He succeeded on the third try and stuck the phone to his ear. Mr Bullington was in a meeting, but Westbay wouldn't take no for an answer. As he waited, he looked at Pacheco and asked, 'Can I have some privacy?'

Pacheco said, 'Why bother? We're listening anyway. Judge gave us permission.'

'Please.'

'Sure. It's your hotel. In the bedroom.' Pacheco led him into the bedroom, but remained there with him. It was amusing to hear Westbay introduce himself to Bullington when he finally got him on the other end. If the two had ever met, it was not apparent. Westbay tried to explain his predicament, but Bullington, the lawyer, kept peppering him with questions. With his back to Pacheco, Westbay struggled to complete a sentence. 'No, yes, look, they're here right now, the FBI, lots of them, in Fort Walton, at the hotel . . . Yes, the indictment . . . federal, but . . . Would you just listen to me? I need for you to come to the hotel immediately. Drop everything . . . Your fee? Sure, how much . . . You gotta be kidding . . . Yes, federal capital murder . . . An FBI agent is staring at me right now, hearing every word . . . Okay . . .'

Westbay turned to Pacheco and said, 'The lawyer says for you to leave the room.'

'Tell the lawyer to kiss my ass. I'm not leaving.'

Westbay turned around and said, 'He says to kiss his ass. Look, how much for just today, you know, for hustling over here and giving me some advice before they string me up? . . . Wow. Why so much? . . . I got it, I got it. Okay, but hurry up.'

Westbay ended the call and said, 'He says it'll take him an hour.'

'We're in no hurry, Clyde. In fact, we've got the suite for two days, at a rate that's supposed to be off season but is still too high.'

They returned to the front room, where Hahn and the other agents were tinkering with two cameras on tripods. Pacheco said, 'Now, Clyde, this is not an interrogation. We'll wait for your lawyer before we quiz you. But to play it safe, we're going to record everything that happens from this point forward. We don't want some gunslinger to later claim there was a *Miranda* violation, do we? While we wait on Mr Bullington, we have some video footage you might find interesting.'

Westbay was seated at the table, as was Pacheco. A laptop was placed between them and Hahn pressed a key. Pacheco said, 'This is actual footage of the Dodge Ram being stolen in Foley, Alabama, you know the one you paid cash for at that bar just east of Pensacola on the evening of August 22, while young Zeke Foreman waited in your truck, the one with the fake Florida tags. Take a look.'

Westbay's eyes narrowed to tiny slits as he stared at the screen. After seeing it the second time, he asked, 'Who shot the video?'

Pacheco held up his hands. 'Hold it! You don't interrogate. We don't interrogate. Not until your lawyer is here. This is simply for your own information. Perhaps these videos will help you make some good decisions later in the day.'

Hahn explained the second video, the one from Frog Freeman's store. When Clyde saw himself parking the truck and getting out, his shoulders sagged an inch or so. With the sagging, the vomiting, the near fainting, the face blanching, and the weak, unsteady voice, Westbay was turning into putty. Allie sensed a quick kill, though the lawyer could complicate things, as they so often did.

Twisting the knife, Pacheco said, 'Pretty stupid to park directly in front of the store and get your picture taken.' Westbay nodded in defeat.

Hahn ran the second video twice and asked, 'Seen enough?'

Westbay nodded and sat back in his seat. Allie said, 'Since we have some time to kill, there's a much longer video we think you'll find equally compelling. We had a chat with your pal Zeke Foreman a few days ago. Remember Zeke?'

'I'm not answering any questions.'

'Right. So we roughed him up a bit, scared the boy really, and he started singing. I mean, he really sang. Play the music, Hahn.'

Zeke's frightened face appeared on the laptop. He swore to tell the truth, then did so for fifty-six minutes. Clyde listened intently, as his life slipped away with each minute.

By the time Gary Bullington arrived, the FBI had his profile, which was not that impressive. He was forty years old, a basic ham-and-egg street hustler with two billboards to his name and a practice that yearned for lucrative car wrecks but survived on workers' comp and mid-level drug cases. His billboard image was that of a well-dressed young lawyer with a thin waist and plenty of hair, obviously Photoshopped for advertising and ego purposes. In the flesh, he wore a wrinkled suit that stretched around a belly, and wild hair that was both graying and thinning. After awkward introductions, he took his client into the bedroom, slammed the door, and kept him there for another hour.

Meanwhile, Pacheco ordered a platter of sandwiches from room service and gave a passing thought to charging the food to the hotel's owner. He did not; nothing to be gained by causing Westbay more embarrassment than what was coming.

When Westbay and Bullington returned to the

front room, they looked as though they'd just finished a heated argument. Pacheco offered sandwiches and bananas. Bullington grabbed one of each but his client had no appetite.

Pacheco asked, 'May we now proceed?'

Bullington, mouth full, said, 'I've advised my client to answer no questions.'

'Great. But we're not here for an interrogation.'

'Then what the hell?'

Rebecca Webb was sitting on a small sofa, scribbling on a legal pad. She said, 'We're prepared to offer a plea agreement. Guilty to one count of first-degree murder. The capital charge will be dropped later, as things progress. First degree carries life, but we'll recommend a lot less.'

'How much less?' Bullington asked.

'We'll start at twenty years and see how he does. It will be possible for your client to work off his prison time.'

'What kind of work?'

'Inside work. Informing. We doubt if infiltration will be necessary because your client is already a part of the gang. He'll have to wear a wire, create a few conversations, that sort of thing.'

Westbay shot her a look of pure terror.

Pacheco said, 'The short version, Mr Bullington, is that we want your client to deliver the Coast Mafia.'

'And what does he get in return?'

Webb said, 'Maybe as few as five years. That could be our recommendation, though, as you know, the final decision will be up to the judge.'

Pacheco said, 'Five years, then a soft life in witness protection. That, or the next ten years on death row before a date with the executioner.'

'Don't threaten my client,' Bullington said angrily.

'I'm not threatening. I'm promising. He's dead guilty right now of capital murder, and the U.S. Attorney will have an easy time proving it. We're offering a sweetheart deal that includes the possibility of Mr Westbay walking in five years.'

'All right, all right,' Bullington said, finishing the sandwich in one huge bite. 'Let me see these damned videos.'

It was almost 4:30 when lawyer and client reemerged from the bedroom after another tense meeting. Two agents were playing gin rummy at the table. Rebecca Webb was on the phone. Hahn was catnapping on the sofa. Pacheco was telling the housekeeper to go away. They had promised Mr Bullington that the meeting would last all night, if necessary. They had nowhere to go, at the moment, and if no deal could be reached, they would leave with Mr Westbay in chains and take him to Tallahassee, where he would be tossed into a jail cell, the first of many that would confine him for the rest of his life. If they left with no deal, there would not be another chance.

Bullington's jacket was hanging on a doorknob. He wore red suspenders that strained to keep his slacks in place. He stood in the center of the room and addressed the government. 'I think I've convinced my client that the case against him is rather strong and that the likelihood of a not-guilty verdict appears rather small. Not surprisingly, he wishes to avoid as much time in prison as possible, not to mention that business with the needle.'

Westbay was aging by the hour. He was pale, and, not a large man to begin with, he seemed to have shrunk into a near-lifeless state. He avoided eye contact with everyone in the room, his mind clearly elsewhere. The agents were observing him closely, and during the last lawyer-client meeting in the bedroom they agreed that they were worried about him. Wearing a wire into a room with Vonn Dubose would take guts and nerves and require a convincing performance. Westbay, now in his diminished state, was not inspiring confidence. The agents at first had enjoyed his tough-guy routine, which they expected, but were astonished at how quickly it melted.

Oh well, you don't always get to pick your snitches, and they had coached far shakier.

Bullington said, 'So what's the drill?'

Ms Webb replied, 'He'll be indicted for capital murder along with the rest of the gang. That indictment will be set aside while we see how hard he's willing to work. If he delivers, he'll eventually plead to first degree and we'll lobby hard for a light sentence. If he does something stupid like run away or blow his cover, we lower the boom and he goes away for life.'

'That's what I thought. Mr Westbay?'

Clyde gently threw up his hands in defeat and offered a goofy laugh. 'Do I really have a choice?'

CHAPTER 34

It had never been clear, at least not to Clyde, whether Vonn Dubose was a real name or an alias. Clyde was not one of the five 'Cousins,' the nickname of the gang's ruling membership. None of the other four used the surname Dubose. Vonn's younger brother had been shot and killed in a bad drug deal in Coral Gables in 1990, and his name was Nash Kinney. According to the FBI's research, Nash Kinney had been born in Louisiana in 1951 and had no brothers.

Clyde admitted that most of what he had learned about the gang's history had come along in snippets and was unreliable. The boys didn't sit around the poker table and talk about the glory days. He'd actually spent very little time with the Cousins. He wasn't even sure they were related by blood. Clyde had been on the payroll for two years before he met all five.

Vonn Dubose had no address, driver's license, Social Security number, taxpayer ID number, passport, bank accounts, or credit cards. This had been verified by the FBI, which had developed the theory the name was an alias that had been created and carefully protected over the years. There was no record of an income tax return ever being filed by such a person. According to Greg Myers, Dubose had been married and divorced more than once. However, the FBI had found no evidence of marriage licenses or divorce decrees.

Henry Skoley was the first Cousin they needed to figure out. He went by Hank and was supposed to be Vonn's nephew, the son of the brother who was shot and killed. But if there was no brother, then who the hell was Hank? The story was already breaking down.

Hank was about forty years old and worked as Vonn's driver, bodyguard, golfing companion, drinking buddy, you name it. Everything Vonn wanted or needed was in Hank's name. If Vonn wanted a new car, Hank was sent to buy one in his name. If Vonn wanted to go to Vegas for a weekend of fun, Hank arranged the airplane, the limo, the hotel rooms, the hookers, and of course went along to sweat the details. Most important, Hank passed along Vonn's commands to the others. Vonn did not use phones or e-mails, not for his dirty work anyway.

Clyde handed over both of his cell phones, gave the pass codes, and watched as two agents began downloading his data. There were two numbers for Hank Skoley, but the FBI already knew this.

Clyde did not know where Vonn lived at the present time. He moved around a lot, spending a few months here and there in new condos he'd built along the Florida Panhandle. Nor did he know if Dubose lived alone.

Two Cousins, Vance and Floyd Maton, were thought to be relatives of Dubose's. Counting Hank, that made four. The fifth was Ron Skinner, an alleged nephew of Vonn's. Skinner lived on the coast near Panama City and ran the gang's bars, liquor stores, convenience stores, and strip clubs, establishments that were essential in money laundering. The Maton brothers ran the gang's sprawling real estate developments. Hank oversaw the hotels, restaurants, and amusement parks. It was a tight and disciplined management team, with all big decisions made by Vonn and everything anchored by the cash skimmed from Treasure Key.

The next layer consisted of the managers, men like Clyde who ran many of the seemingly legitimate businesses. There were about a dozen in this group, though Clyde had not met all of them. Again, this was not one big happy corporate family with annual picnics and bring-the-kids-to-work days. It was as if Vonn did not want one division to know much about the others. Ten years earlier, Clyde had been working at a hotel in Orlando when he heard of a job opening in Fort Walton Beach. He made the move because he enjoyed living near the ocean. A year later he got an assistant manager's job at the Blue Chateau, and unwittingly entered the criminal world of the Coast Mafia, though he had never heard that term. He met Hank, liked him a lot, and was soon promoted to manager and given a huge pay increase. He was being paid well, far above the industry average, and he believed this was common throughout the Dubose empire. Buying loyalty. Once Clyde was in charge and doing a good job, Hank informed him that the company had just purchased the Surfbreaker half a mile down the beach. The company, an odd outfit headquartered in Belize, was being restructured, and Clyde would be running the two hotels in the Fort Walton Beach area. His salary was doubled again and he was given a 5 percent share of Starr S, the new company. He was led to believe that Hank and some associates owned the other 95 percent, but did not know for certain. Later, he would learn that it was all part of the same conspiracy.

His life in crime began when Hank arrived one day with $40,000 in cash, all in $100 bills. Hank explained that it's difficult to clean dirty money through hotels because almost all transactions are by credit card. However, each of the hotels had busy bars where a lot of patrons still paid by cash. Hank proceeded to outline in detail how the dirty cash would be systematically added to each bar's cash intakes. Hank never used the term 'money laundering,' opting instead for the old standby 'cooking the books.' From that day on, each bar's daily cash receipts would be handled by Clyde and no one else. Over time he learned how to adjust the numbers depending on the flow of traffic in the hotels. He even devised a method to run dirty cash through the gross receipts at the front desks. The cooked books appeared spotless. The accountants in Pensacola congratulated him on the increase in sales but never inquired about anything suspicious.

Clyde had kept records on a notepad, far away from the computers, and with a quick look he could tell the FBI exactly how much money he'd laundered through his hotels and bars over the past nine years. His best guess was about $300,000 a year. And this was just the small stuff. The serious laundering took place in their bars, liquor stores, and strip clubs.

The gang slowly sucked him in. After two years as a manager, he was invited to Vegas for a boys' trip. He flew on a private jet with Hank and the Maton brothers. A limo took them to a grand casino where Clyde had his own suite. All expenses were covered by Hank – steak dinners, fine wines, gorgeous hookers. On a Saturday night, Hank invited him to a penthouse suite for a drink with Vonn. Just Vonn Dubose and the Cousins, and Clyde Westbay, now a trusted member of the organization. The following day, he and Hank had coffee in a casino bar, and a few of the rules were laid out. They were basic and amounted to (1) do what you're told; (2) keep your mouth shut; (3) trust no one but us; (4) keep your eyes open and don't ever forget that you're breaking the law; and (5) never snitch because snitching can be fatal for you and your family. Loyalty was demanded, and in return Clyde would make a lot of money. He had no problem with the rules.

The managers were also expected to visit the casino at least twice a month. The laundering was simple. Clyde would be given between $5,000 and $10,000 in cash by Hank to gamble with – cash that had come from the casino, through Dubose, through Hank and Clyde, and now given back to the casino. In return, Clyde, the gambler, would be given a stack of $100 chips. His favorite game was blackjack and he could play it well enough to almost break even. After buying, say, $2,000 in chips, he would play for an hour and take a break. Instead of leaving with his chips, he would tell the pit boss to 'cash him out' and add the balance to his house account, one he held in a fictitious name. Once a year, he transferred the balance to a bank account controlled by Hank. Last year, 2010, Clyde moved $147,000 of clean money out of the casino.

He was almost certain that the Cousins and all managers washed money this way through casino chips.

Looking back, he did not remember the exact moment when he decided to cross the line and begin breaking the law. He did what his boss told him to do, and there seemed to be no harm in doing it. He knew the laundering was illegal, but it was so easy. There was no way to get caught. Hell, their own accountants had no clue. Besides, he was being paid a lot of money, and spending a lot, and life was good. Sure he was working for a criminal organization, but his bit part in the racketeering certainly could not amount to much. Over time it became his life, his security. He would drive along the coast in Brunswick County, notice a new high-rise going up or see signs for a new gated golf course community, and feel a bit of pride because Vonn was kicking ass. If the Feds ever came snooping around, surely they would go after the big boys, the Cousins, and not worry about the small fish like him.

No one was looking, though. No one seemed to care. After a few years it was simply business as usual.

That was why it was so startling when Hank called to say they could have a problem. Judge McDover, a person he'd never met, was receiving some unwelcome attention. Clyde lived in another judicial district and hardly knew her name. He did not understand her role in the Dubose organization, but assumed it was significant, given the level of alarm. Hank, who rarely mentioned his uncle, admitted that Vonn was worried. Something had to be done.

Hank paid a visit to Clyde's office at the Surfbreaker, and over coffee at a poolside table informed him that Vonn needed a favor. Vonn had chosen him, Clyde Westbay, for some dirty business because no one would ever suspect Clyde. Murder was never mentioned. It was to be intimidation only, though certainly of a most violent nature. A car crash, on tribal land, late at night. Obviously, Clyde didn't want to do it, but found it impossible to say no. Indeed, he managed to take it in stride as if it was all in a day's work – anything for the Cousins.

Hank agreed that Zeke Foreman would make a suitable stooge. Hank arranged the delivery of the stolen truck; Clyde had no knowledge of those arrangements. This was typical of the gang: keep information limited so leaks can be controlled. Hank provided the fake Florida tags for the truck driven by Clyde. The operation went smoothly, with Hank on the ground and on the phones directing traffic. Clyde did not know the identity of the man who pretended to be an informant and lured Lacy and Hugo to the reservation. Seconds after the collision, Clyde parked behind the Dodge Ram and told Zeke to get away from the Prius, to get in his truck. By then Zeke's nose was bleeding. Clyde checked the air bag in the Dodge and found no blood. Hugo was a mess, stuck in the shattered windshield, groaning and kicking about and bleeding like hell. His cell phone was in the right rear pocket of his jeans. Clyde noticed his seat belt had not been fastened but could not tell if the passenger's air bag deployed.

No, he had no knowledge of anyone tampering with the seat belt and air bag. No, he did not touch Hugo in any manner except to remove his cell phone. He wore rubber gloves and was horrified to be so close to a man who was struggling and bleeding profusely. Westbay admitted to feeling terrible about being there. But he had orders. Lacy's cell phone and iPad were on the left rear floorboard, but the rear door had been crimped shut by the collision. He managed to open the door behind Hugo and remove both of them. She was bleeding and mumbling and trying to move about.

Clyde got through this part of his narrative with no emotion. If he felt remorse, he refused to show it. He did, though, need a break for the bathroom. It was almost 6:00 p.m.

He and Zeke left on a dirt trail, one he and Hank had found the day before. No he did not remember Zeke tossing anything out of the window. Pacheco showed him a sample of the bloody paper towel. He could not explain why he parked in front of Frog's store. His only excuse was that he wasn't sure it was even open. Plus the place was such a dump – could it really have surveillance cameras? Pretty stupid, in retrospect. He and Zeke drank a beer as they left Brunswick County. They stopped at a rest area on Interstate 10 and waited for Hank. Clyde gave him a shopping bag containing the two cell phones and iPad. From there they returned to Fort Walton Beach and to the Blue Chateau, where the kid went to a room and spent the night. The next day Clyde took him to the doctor and an X-ray revealed no broken bones. He gave Zeke $5,000 in cash and thought the matter was behind them. Clyde watched the news all morning and was stunned when he heard that Hugo Hatch had died. A week or so later, Hank stopped by the office, furious and fuming about the video. He said Vonn was furious and scrambling to contain the damage. They ran Zeke out of town with instructions to stay far away until further notice.

No, he, Clyde, had not spoken to Vonn since long before the accident, and now he really didn't want to. Though Clyde had been looking over his shoulder and sleeping fitfully, things seemed to have settled down, until today anyway. Now the world was upside down.

Hahn ordered more sandwiches and fruit, and when they were delivered Westbay, and Bullington, stepped into the bedroom. It was almost 8:00 p.m., and Westbay said his wife might be getting worried. He called her and said he was taking care of some unexpected business.

As they ate, Allie Pacheco and Rebecca Webb tag teamed through another round of interrogation. When they finally finished, at almost 10:00 p.m., Clyde Westbay had been on video for over six hours and had given more than enough information to launch the assault against Dubose and his Cousins. Back in Tallahassee, another team of agents had watched and listened to it all, and were already weaving their web.

Clyde left the Surfbreaker a free man, free in the sense that he wore no handcuffs nor ankle chains. But he had left his soul up there in the

Dolphin Suite, all duly recorded on film and filed away to torment him later. He would have a few days, maybe weeks of freedom before being snatched in a high-profile raid. Panic from his wife and kids; photos on the front page; frantic calls from family and friends. Clyde, as a member of a criminal syndicate, indicted for capital murder.

As he drove aimlessly around Destin, he gave a passing thought to his ex-girlfriend Tammy. What a slut! Sleeping with half the town, including that worm Walter. Perhaps his wife would never know. And how much should he tell her now? Should he get it all over with or wait for the raid, for the horror of being led away in chains?

How the hell was he supposed to know what to do? His life was over.

The more he drove the more he liked the idea of a bullet to the brain, of checking out on his terms, as opposed to some nasty hit ordered by Dubose. Or perhaps a long dive off a tall bridge, or a bottle of pills. The FBI had him on tape.

CHAPTER 35

Vonn's dirtiest work was handled by a long-time gun thug known as Delgado. Whether this was an actual name or just another fiction in Vonn's world was not clear.

For his day job, Delgado ran a bar, one of the company's many cash cows and laundry sites, but his real value to the organization was his moonlighting. He possessed astonishing technical skills with weapons, mechanics, and electronics. Delgado had taken Son Razko to the Mace home and calmly shot him and Eileen in the bedroom, then disappeared without a trace. An hour later, he bumped into Junior in a bar and bought him a drink.

After Junior's trial, Delgado took the first snitch, Digger Robles, for a midnight boat ride and dropped him in the Gulf with chains around his ankles. The second snitch, Todd Short, came within five seconds of getting his head blown off by a deer rifle Delgado was aiming. The bullet would have hit his left ear before either ear could have heard the shot, but another head moved into view and Todd lived another day. He wisely fled the area. Delgado almost caught him in Oklahoma.

The ultimate mistake of Vonn's career was choosing Clyde Westbay to take out Hugo, rather than Delgado. He picked an amateur and not a pro. His rationale had been solid: no one would ever suspect Clyde; guns were not involved; it was a simple operation, in relative terms; and Vonn wanted Clyde to advance in the organization. He saw talent there, and he needed deeper loyalty. Involve Clyde in a more sinister crime, and Vonn would own him for life. The deciding factor, though, which surfaced only at the last minute, had been Delgado's sudden flare-up of kidney stones, a bout so severe he was hospitalized for three days. The debilitating pain hit just hours after he had broken into Lacy's car and tampered with the passenger's side air bag and seat belt. With Delgado temporarily disabled, and with the situation urgent, Vonn instructed Hank to visit Clyde and lay out the plan.

Delgado lived in a world of surveillance cameras and would never have gotten himself filmed at Frog's.

At any rate, his kidneys were now free and clear and he was back in business. He parked his little red 'Blann's Pest Control' truck in the driveway of a small home on a golf course five miles north of the Gulf. The entire development was a gated community, but then Delgado knew the gate code. A company from the Bahamas built the place. A company from Nevis owned the company from the Bahamas. Somewhere far up the chain of title sat Vonn Dubose. The owner of this particular home was in court, where she spent her working hours. She recorded important matters for Judge McDover, who'd made the original suggestion to buy the place.

Delgado wore a cute uniform, red shirt and matching cap, and he carried a bulky spray can as if he just might annihilate every insect along the Florida Panhandle. He rang the doorbell but knew no one was home. He deftly slipped a thin screwdriver between bolt and latch and turned the knob. With the proper key, he could not have opened the door any faster. He closed it behind him and listened for a warning from the alarm. After a few seconds it began beeping. In thirty seconds all hell would break loose. He stepped to the panel behind the door and calmly punched in the five-number pass code, which he had hacked from the security company. Delgado took a deep breath and appreciated the complete silence. If the code had not worked, he would have simply left and driven away.

He put on a pair of tight rubber gloves and checked to make sure both front and rear doors were locked. He could now take his time. There were two bedrooms. The large one was obviously used by the owner; the smaller had a set of cheap bunk beds. Delgado knew the woman lived alone. She was forty-three years old and divorced, no children. He went through two chests of drawers and found nothing but clothing. Same in the closets and in the two bathrooms. In her small, cluttered home office he found a desktop computer and a printer sitting on a set of low-slung file cabinets. Slowly, methodically, he went through every drawer, every file, every sheet of paper.

There was a man in her house! JoHelen Hooper tapped her iPhone. The home security app alerted her that her system had been disarmed at 9:44, two minutes earlier. She tapped again and found the footage. The camera hidden in the ceiling fan of the den caught him as he shuffled by, headed for the rear. White, male, age about forty, with a goofy red shirt and cap, pretending to be someone else. The camera hidden in the air vent above her bed caught him as he entered her room and began carefully going through her drawers. He touched everything.

She swallowed hard and tried to maintain her composure. She was sitting less than twenty feet from Judge McDover, in the main courtroom in Sterling, waiting as a group of harried lawyers huddled by the jury box and tried to make decisions. Thankfully, there was no jury; Her Honor was only hearing motions.

In front of JoHelen was her steno writer on its tripod stand. On her table was a notepad, some paperwork, and her iPhone, which she tried to look at casually without seeming alarmed. Alarmed! There was a man in her house slowly going through her underwear. Now he's closing that drawer and moving to the one below it.

386

A lawyer started speaking and JoHelen began recording. It was a worthless hearing in a meaningless case and if she missed a word here or there she could always check the audiotape. Her mind was spinning and she was terrified, but she stared at the lawyer, focused on his lips, and tried to concentrate. The app would record all footage from the four cameras hidden in her home, so she would miss nothing when she reviewed it during lunch.

Be calm, be cool, look bored as you capture their legal gibberish at two hundred words a minute. After eight years of flawless court reporting she could almost do it in her sleep. Sleep, though, would now be another issue.

Her big moment had finally arrived. For the past week, Her Honor had tipped her hand with her abrupt change of temperature. Never known to be warm and fuzzy, she had always been pleasant and professional with JoHelen, and they had enjoyed each other's company as they often gossiped and laughed about things that happened in court. They were not close friends, because Claudia was too aloof for ordinary relationships. She saved her attentions for Phyllis Turban, a person JoHelen knew well but by reputation only.

Since the day the officials from BJC arrived and handed over the complaint, Claudia had not been herself. She had been edgier, somewhat distant, as if distracted and worried. Normally, she kept her emotions on an even keel and was not given to moods. Lately, though, and especially in the past few days, she had been short and abrupt with JoHelen, and even tried to avoid her, while at the same time trying to gloss over her feelings with a phony smile and the occasional pandering comment. For eight years, the two women had spent almost every working day in the same room. JoHelen knew something had changed.

What about the alarm? It was a new system with monitors on every window and door, installed by Cooley two months earlier. To bypass it meant the guy in the red shirt and cap was a professional.

A brief pause as the lawyer looked for a piece of paper, and JoHelen glanced at her phone. Her intruder could barely be seen in her closet, rifling through her wardrobe. Should she call the police and bust the guy? Should she call Neighborhood Watch? No – calls leave trails, and these days it seemed as if most trails were leading back to JoHelen.

Two lawyers were suddenly talking at once, something that happened every day in her world, and she deftly separated the two on the official record without missing a word. Her only real pet peeve was when three lawyers were talking simultaneously. A simple glance from her to the bench and Judge McDover would restore order. They often communicated with slight movements of the face or hands, but today JoHelen was trying not to look at her boss.

The intruder would find nothing incriminating. She wasn't stupid enough to hide records in a place so easy to find. Her records were elsewhere, locked and secure. But what would *they* do next? They had killed a man to intimidate and impede the investigation by BJC. Evidently, they had tracked down Greg Myers and silenced him. Now Cooley, her friend, confidant, handler, and co-conspirator, was either leaving or already gone, freaking out and seemingly on the verge of a nervous breakdown. He assured her she was safe, that her identity would never be revealed, but those were hollow words from last week.

Her Honor called for a ten-minute recess, and JoHelen calmly walked down the hall to her small office, where she locked the door and watched, in real time, her intruder. The man was still in her house, now going through the kitchen drawers, carefully removing the pots and pans and then replacing them just as he found them. He was not a thief and would not leave a trail. He was wearing gloves. He finally made his way to her office, where he took a seat and looked around. He began removing files from her drawers as if he had all the time in the world.

He worked for Vonn Dubose. And *they* now suspected her.

Allie Pacheco stopped by at noon for an update. They met in Geismar's office, at the worktable cluttered with files of other pending cases. Allie wasn't smug when he talked about their success with Clyde Westbay, but he was obviously proud of their work. And, the best was yet to come.

All of their requests for wiretapping and surveillance had been approved by a federal judge, and their tech team was listening to dozens of phones. The FBI had located the homes of Vance and Floyd Maton, Ron Skinner, and Hank Skoley, four of the five Cousins. Their boss, Mr Dubose, was currently living in a cottage in Rosemary Beach. The night before, Hank had driven Vonn to a swanky restaurant near Panama City where they met a third man, a guy who just happened to be a Brunswick County supervisor. The purpose of the meeting was not clear and the FBI was not eavesdropping.

Dubose still had them baffled. They were now in agreement that the name had to be fictitious, and that he had done a marvelous job for the past thirty or forty years living as someone else. As to bloodlines, the past was murky. Given the moral vagaries of their ancestors, it was proving to be difficult ascertaining the degree to which the Cousins were actually related. But this mattered only in their search for Vonn's real identity.

Clyde gave them the names of seven other managers. So far, the FBI had identified almost thirty bars, restaurants, hotels, shopping centers, strip clubs, liquor stores, convenience stores, residential developments, gated communities, and golf courses believed to be managed by the eight men, including Clyde. Every single entity was owned by an offshore company, most registered in Belize, the Bahamas, or the Cayman Islands.

Their investigation was expanding by the hour. Their boss in Jacksonville was committing all the manpower and resources Tallahassee was asking for. Luna, Pacheco's supervisor, had dropped everything and was running the operation. The U.S. Attorney's Office had four lawyers tag teaming with the FBI.

Pacheco was wired and all business. They were pulling twenty hours a day; he seemed to have little interest in Lacy, at least outside the office. When he raced off, Geismar asked her, 'Are you seeing him?'

'Just saw him.'

'You know what I mean.'

'We've had a lunch, two dinners, and two late-night bottles of wine. I think I like him but we're going real slow.'

'Don't you always go slow?'

'I do. Does it bother you?'

'Sort of. It's in the gray area.'

'He and I have talked about it. We're on the same side of the street, but not in the same office. He couldn't date another agent in this town, but their rules do not include me. You want me to break it off?'

'What if I said yes?'

'You're the boss and I would do as instructed. He'll be around. He's not going anywhere.'

'I'm not asking. I think you're okay with him, but just be careful what you say. You can rest assured he's not telling us everything.'

'True, but he knows a lot more than we do.'

CHAPTER 36

During the slow drive home, JoHelen mulled her options and realized that none were attractive. She couldn't simply run away and disappear. She had to at least go inside and look around and see if anything was missing, though the footage clearly showed the intruder leaving with nothing of hers. He was inside for ninety-three minutes, far too long for the monthly service. He came and went without a key but with her alarm pass code. What would stop him from returning at two in the morning for another house call? Should she stay at home or leave? If she left, where would she go?

She cursed Cooley with a bitterness that surprised her. They had started this little conspiracy joined at the hip, partners in a scheme to do good and make a bundle along the way, but now he had cracked up. He was gone, running away before Dubose could get him too, and leaving her behind, unguarded, vulnerable, frightened, and directionless.

The gate was opened automatically by the magnetic sticker on her parking decal. Sandy

Gables, unit 58. She parked in her driveway, stared at her home, and knew it would never be the same. This was the moment, right? Stay? Run? Hide? How was she supposed to know? At this critical point, she was supposed to have a friend to protect her.

She grabbed her purse, got out, and walked to the front door. She unlocked it but did not open it. Across the street she saw Mr Armstrong puttering around his carport. She went over and explained that her door was unlocked and she was spooked. Could he come over? She hated to ask and she was probably overreacting anyway, but nowadays a girl can't be too careful, can she? Mr Armstrong was a kindly soul, retired and bored, and he said sure. They entered together and she turned off the alarm. He stood in the den and talked about his wife's latest flare-up of shingles as JoHelen scurried about, checking every room while asking every conceivable question about the affliction. She poked in the closets, looked under the beds, in the showers, the pantry, anywhere a person could possibly hide. She knew no one was there but it didn't matter. If she didn't at least search the place she couldn't think of staying.

She thanked Mr Armstrong and offered him a diet soda. He seized the opportunity for a chat and an hour later was still there. She was in no hurry to be alone. When he finally left, she sat in the den and tried to collect her thoughts. A plank popped in the attic and she jumped out of her skin. As her heart raced and her breathing intensified, she listened for another sound. Could it be a footstep? But there was nothing but silence. She made up her mind to leave and quickly changed into jeans. What to pack? If *they* were watching and she left with a piece of luggage, her plans would be obvious. She could wait until dark and sneak a bag to her car, maybe two, but she had no desire to be in the house after dark. She took her bulkiest purse and packed it with toiletries and underwear. She filled a paper grocery sack with an empty gym bag and two changes of clothing. There were stores in the area; she could always buy what she needed.

As she drove away, she waved at Mr Armstrong and wondered when she might return.

She drove south to the beaches, turned west on Highway 98, and drifted with the traffic along the coast, through seaside communities, and along the occasional stretch of untouched shoreline. As she drove she tried to watch everything behind her, but soon gave up. If *they* wanted to track her across the country, how was she supposed to stop them? She filled up with gas in Destin and kept going, soon skirting around Pensacola on smaller roads. When she realized she was in Alabama she turned east and made a long loop back to Interstate 10. At dark she stopped at a motel and paid cash for a room.

*　　*　　*

JoHelen had never spoken to Greg Myers. She knew his name, but he knew nothing about her. Through Cooley, she had received a copy of the complaint filed against her boss by Myers. He was willing to run the risk of exposing the corruption for a slice of the pie, though none of the three – Myers, Cooley, JoHelen – had any conceivable idea of when the whistle-blower claim would be filed. Myers, the lawyer and accuser, was to spearhead the legal efforts to claim the money. Cooley, the ex-lawyer, would handle Myers and JoHelen and facilitate matters for a healthy cut. Same for Myers. She would get the rest. The deal was nice and tidy and looked good in theory.

Now Myers was presumed dead. Cooley had cracked up and fled. And JoHelen Hooper was hiding in a cheap motel, staring at a disposable prepaid cell phone with only one number to call. There was no one else. It was almost 10:00 p.m. when she said, 'Ms Stoltz, my name is JoHelen Hooper. Cooley gave me your number. You remember him?'

'Yes.'

'And this is the phone he gave you?'

'Yes. You're the informant?'

'That's me. The mole, the source, the informant. Actually, Cooley said Myers liked to refer to me as the Whistler because I'm supposed to blow the whistle on Judge McDover. What do you know about me?'

'Nothing, didn't even know you were a woman. Why are you calling me?'

'Because Cooley gave me your number, said you had a burner, said to call you if things got bad and I got scared. Well, I'm scared.'

'Where's Cooley?'

'Don't know. He cracked up and ran away, said he was leaving the country before Dubose found him. He found Myers, you know. I have no one else to talk to.'

'Okay, let's talk. How do you know Judge McDover?'

'I've been her court reporter for the past eight years, but that's another story for another day. While we were in court today a man broke into my home and went through every inch of the place. I know this because I have hidden cameras in my home with an app that allows real-time surveillance on my phone. He took nothing because he wasn't a thief. He found nothing because I do not keep sensitive stuff at home, for obvious reasons. Cooley and I started planning this little adventure years ago, and we've been very cautious. So he added home security, the burners, the off-site storage of records, and a lot of other protective measures and habits.'

'Does anyone else live there?'

'Oh no. I'm single, divorced, no kids.'

'Any idea who your visitor was?'

'None, but I would recognize him, I think, though I doubt I'll get the chance. I'm sure he works for Dubose in some capacity, and I suspect they're closing in on me. The information I gave Cooley and Myers about Claudia could come from only a small number of people. I'm on the list. I'm sorry about your friend.'

'Thanks.'

'I'm serious. He would be alive if I hadn't decided to bring down the judge.'

'Why are you bringing down the judge?'

'It's another story. Let's save it for later. Right now I need advice, and I have no one else to turn to. I'm hiding in a motel because I could not stay at home tonight. I'm not sure about tomorrow. If I don't show up for work, warning bells go off. I haven't missed many days in eight years, and Claudia is already suspicious. If I go to work, I run the risk of walking back to her turf and that makes me nervous. What if they, whoever the hell they are, have made the decision that I need to go? I'm a sitting duck at work, or going or coming. You know how dangerous the roads can be.'

'Call in sick, a stomach virus that's highly contagious. Happens to everyone.'

JoHelen smiled. So simple, why hadn't she thought of it? Perhaps because her mind was spinning and nothing was clear. 'Maybe, but what do I do tomorrow?'

'Keep moving around.'

'Did you know that Cooley hid a tracking device on the inside of Claudia's car? He paid $300 for it and it took him about a minute to install. Said it was a piece of cake. Did you know about that?'

'We knew that she was being tracked, yes. Didn't know who or how.'

'My point is that it's easy to follow people, so moving around is not the answer. They can bug my car, hack my cell phone, who knows what else. Dubose has the money to buy what it takes. I'm feeling pretty vulnerable right now, Ms Stoltz.'

'Call me Lacy. Is there a bar in the motel?'

'I think so.'

'Go hang out in the bar until it closes. If an incredibly handsome young man with a flat stomach hits on you, take him back to your room for the night. If you don't get lucky, get in your car and find an all-night diner, maybe a truck stop. Kill a few hours. If the motel has a night clerk, hang out in the lobby until sunrise. Call me then.'

'I can do that.'

'Just stay around other people.'

'Thanks, Lacy.'

CHAPTER 37

As instructed, Clyde met Hank Skoley at a sprawling construction site two miles west of Panama City and a mile north of the Gulf. Huge signs announced the arrival of Honey Grove, a planned community with lovely homes, fantastic shopping, golf galore, all just minutes from the Emerald Coast. In the distance bull-dozers leveled a forest. Closer, crews were putting in curbs and gutters. And near the main road homes were going up.

Clyde parked his car and took a seat in Hank's black Mercedes SUV. They rode along one of the few paved streets, weaving around dozens of contractors' trucks and vans parked haphazardly on dirt lots. Hundreds of workers hustled about. Toward the end of the street the homes were almost finished, and at the very end were three spanking-new model homes being used to entice buyers. Hank parked in one of the driveways and they went inside. The carport door was unlocked. The house was empty of people and furniture. 'Follow me,' Hank said, and they climbed the stairs.

Vonn Dubose was waiting in the empty master

bedroom. He was looking out a front window, as if admiring the frenzy of yet another scorched-earth development. They spoke, shook hands, and Vonn actually smiled and seemed in good spirits. Clyde had not seen him in over a year and he had not changed at all. Slim, nice tan, golf shirt, and khakis, just another affluent retiree.

Vonn said, 'So, what's on your mind?'

The bug was built into the Timex watch on Clyde's left wrist, a watch identical to the one he'd been wearing for the past three years. Clyde had not noticed the watches worn by Hank or Vonn, and he was almost certain they had paid no attention to his. Men tend not to notice such things, but Pacheco and his technicians were taking no chances. The leather band was tight because of a tiny vibrator on the back facing of the watch. When the van was within range, the facing would vibrate and Clyde would know they were in business.

It was an exact replica of a FedEx delivery van, and it rolled to a stop in front of the house next door. The driver, dressed in official FedEx garb, got out and popped the hood; some mechanical failure. In the rear was the FBI – Allie Pacheco and three technicians with their gear. When they were within two hundred feet of the Timex, they pushed a button and it vibrated. Inside the bedroom, the mike in the watch would pick up a whisper from thirty feet away.

The day before, Clyde had spent four hours with

Allie Pacheco and two other agents rehearsing his role. Now it was time for his big moment. Deliver Vonn Dubose, and he, Clyde Westbay, would serve a few years and grow old a free man.

Clyde began, 'Two things, Vonn. I can't find Zeke Foreman. I told him to disappear two weeks ago and call me every other day. We spoke a few times, then his phone went silent. I think the kid probably just freaked out and ran away.'

Vonn looked at Hank, shrugged, looked at Clyde, and said, 'I know this already.'

Clyde, his stomach flipping fast enough to make sounds for the Timex, shuffled his feet and continued, 'Look, Vonn, this is all my fault and I'm taking responsibility. It was a stupid mistake on my part, and, well, who knows what might happen.'

Vonn looked at Hank again and said, 'I thought I told you to pass along my displeasure with what happened.' He looked at Clyde and said, 'Sure, it was stupid, but it's done and I'm over it. It looks like the damage is contained. You just do your job running the hotels and I'll get other folks for the dirty work.'

'Thanks, Vonn,' Clyde said. 'The other thing is that, I just want you to know, I'm willing to leave town for a year or so. I think it might be smart if I just, you know, took a trip and vanished until this blows over. You see, Vonn, my wife and I aren't doing so well these days, and, frankly, it's a good time for me to get away from her. We're not giving up, but she's cool if I hit the road for a while.'

'Maybe not a bad idea. I'll think about it.'

'I mean, that's my face in the video, and I'm not sure what I'll do if some cop shows up at the office asking questions. Makes me kind of nervous, Vonn. I'd rather just leave for now. I have good people under me and I'll check in every week. The hotels will be fine.'

'Like I said, I'll think about it.'

'Okay.' Clyde shrugged as if he had nothing else to say. He took a step toward the door, stopped, and turned toward Vonn. Time for the Oscar.

'Look, Vonn, I gotta tell you, I love my job and I'm proud to be part of your organization, but, well, you mentioned the "dirty work," and . . .' His voice began to break, his words were scratchy. 'Look, Vonn, I'm just not cut out for that stuff, you know what I mean? I didn't know that guy was going to die. I didn't know it was all, well, you know, planned. Somebody tampered with the seat belt and the air bag and the poor guy went flying through the windshield. You should've seen him, Vonn. His face was cut all to hell, blood pouring everywhere, and he was thrashing around. He looked at me, Vonn. He gave me this look that said, "Please! Please!" I have nightmares about it, Vonn. I just left him there. I didn't know what I was doing. Somebody should've told me what was going on, Vonn.'

'You were told to do a job,' Vonn growled and took a step closer.

'But I didn't know the job involved killing someone.'

'It's called intimidation, Clyde. That's the name of the game and that's how I run things. If not for intimidation, I wouldn't be here and you wouldn't be making a fat salary running my hotels. Sometimes, in this business, you gotta put folks in line, and sometimes these folks understand nothing but intimidation. If you don't want to do it, fine. I guess I misjudged you. Thought you had some balls.'

'I thought I had some too, but I lost them when I saw that guy bleeding to death.'

'That's part of it.'

'You ever watched someone bleed to death, Vonn?'

'Yes,' Vonn said proudly.

'Stupid question.'

'Anything else?' Vonn glared at Hank as if to say 'Get him outta here.'

Clyde raised his hands in surrender and backed away. 'Okay, okay, but I really want to leave for a year, to get away from all this. Please, Vonn.'

'I'll think about it.'

In the van, Allie Pacheco removed his earphones and smiled at the technicians. He mumbled to himself, 'Beautiful. "It's called intimidation, Clyde. That's the name of the game and that's how I run things."'

The FedEx man suddenly found a way to start his van. He drove away just as Clyde and Hank were leaving the model home. Clyde noticed it but had no idea it was loaded with FBI.

Hank said nothing as he weaved through the construction maze. Traffic was blocked by a truck loaded with brick. In front of them the FedEx van was also waiting. Hank tapped his fingers on the steering wheel and said, 'Wonder what FedEx is doing here. Nobody's moved in yet.'

Clyde said, 'I guess they're everywhere.'

The Timex vibrated again. Pacheco was close by and saying, 'Keep talking.'

Clyde said, 'So, Hank, do you think I was wrong to say what I said to Vonn, about me not wanting to do the dirty work?'

'It wasn't smart. Vonn despises weak people. You would have been better off saying nothing. You wanted to meet so you could offer to disappear. That was fine. But the chickenshit stuff doesn't sit well with Vonn.'

'I was trying to make the point that I didn't sign on to kill people.'

'No, you didn't. But Vonn thought he saw something in you. So did I. Guess we were wrong.'

'And what was that? What did you think you saw?'

'A guy who might enjoy getting his hands dirty.'

'Do you?'

'Why don't you shut up, Clyde? You've said enough for one day.'

And so have you, Allie thought as he smiled again.

Clyde drove away from Honey Grove and, as directed, returned to the Surfbreaker Hotel in Fort Walton Beach. He checked in with his secretary, made a phone call, and left. Using a rear door near a loading ramp, he walked out of the building and jumped into the rear seat of a gray SUV. Two FBI agents had the front. As they left the Surfbreaker, the driver said over his shoulder, 'Nice work. Pacheco says you were marvelous. Nailed him.'

Clyde said nothing. He didn't want to talk or be congratulated. He felt like a worm for ratting on his colleagues and he knew things would only get worse. He could not begin to contemplate one day walking into a crowded courtroom and narrating the story, for the benefit of a jury, of the killing of Hugo Hatch while Vonn Dubose looked on from the defense table.

He took off the watch and handed it to the agent in front of him. He said, 'I'm taking a nap. Wake me when we get to Tallahassee.'

By 9:00 a.m. on Friday, Lacy had not heard from JoHelen and she was not answering the phone she'd used the night before. Lacy briefed Geismar and they were concerned. Using an office landline, Lacy called the circuit clerk's office in Sterling and, after being passed around, was informed that Judge McDover was not in the courthouse that morning. She might possibly be presiding over in the town of Eckman. Since there was a chance JoHelen had gone to work, Lacy called the clerk's office in Eckman, where a girl on the phone said yes, Her Honor was in the building, but not presiding. There was nothing on the docket.

After a few more dead ends, Lacy had no choice but to sit and wait. She returned a call from Gunther and had a pleasant chat. He had nothing planned for the weekend, other than the usual 'pending deals,' and said he might pop down for dinner Saturday night. She promised to call back later.

JoHelen awoke to bright sunshine and a dead phone. The burner, the last one Cooley had given her, was out of juice and she'd left its charger at home. Using her cell phone, she called Claudia, and rather convincingly went through the upset-stomach routine. Claudia seemed somewhat convinced and mildly sympathetic. Fortunately, there was nothing on the docket that day that would require a court reporter. It was not a day off. JoHelen lived with a permanent backlog of trial transcripts to prepare.

She had to have that damned charger, which would necessitate a return home. She had closed the bar down at midnight. The only possible bedtime companion had been a forty-year-old truck driver with a scraggly beard that wiggled all the way down to his ample potbelly. She allowed him to buy her a drink but had not been remotely tempted to go further.

She checked out of the motel at nine and drove toward the beaches, an hour south and east. Along the way she repeatedly reminded herself to keep an eye on the rearview mirror, but she was not up to the cloak-and-dagger crap. She parked in her driveway with a knot in her stomach and told herself she would never be able to live in the house again. Every inch of her private space had been touched and examined by a man with bad intentions. Even if she changed the locks and doubled down on the security, she would never again relax there. Mr Armstrong was pulling weeds near his front porch and apparently wanted to flirt some more. She charmed him over with a big smile and said, 'Let's have something to drink.' He entered the house with her and stood in the door as she disarmed the security. She went to her bedroom, checking every room along the way and talking nonstop, curious about Mrs Armstrong's shingles and all. She found the charger where she'd left it, on the counter of her bathroom. She plugged it into the burner and returned to the den.

'Where'd you stay last night?' he asked. He and his wife were infamous for their curiosity and lack of discretion. They monitored things on the street and wanted to know everyone's business.

'My sister's,' JoHelen replied, knowing the question was coming.

'Where does she live?'

'Pensacola.'

With the house apparently safe, she said, 'On second thought, let's go have a soda with Gloria.'

'Oh, she'd love that.'

They sat in the shade of the Armstrongs' back porch and sipped beverages through straws. Fortunately, the shingles were on Gloria's lower back and a proper viewing would reveal a bit too much skin. JoHelen was spared the examination.

'You got a clogged drain?' Mr Armstrong asked.

'Don't think so. Why?'

'That plumber showed up around nine this morning.'

Plumber? JoHelen quickly decided not to worry them. She said, 'Got a leak, but he was supposed to come Monday.'

'Pushy guy, I'll tell you that. Wouldn't trust him if I were you.'

'Why not?'

'Well, I watched him go to the door and ring the bell. Then he started fiddling with the door, you know, even reached into his pocket and pulled out a blade of some sort like he was breaking in. Hope you don't mind, but I yelled at him and went over. Asked what the hell he was doing. He stuck the blade or whatever it was back in his pocket and tried to act like it was nothing. I said you were not home. He mumbled something about coming back later and couldn't wait to get out of here. Me, I'd find me another plumber. I swear he was suspicious.'

'You just can't trust anybody these days,' JoHelen said, and returned to the shingles, a subject Gloria was keen to discuss at length. As she talked about them, her third episode in twenty years, JoHelen's mind was racing.

Abruptly, Gloria asked her husband, 'Did you tell her about that pest control guy yesterday?'

'No, I forgot. I was on the golf course, and Gloria swears a pest control guy was in your house for at least an hour yesterday.'

Again, preferring not to alarm them and provoke a hundred other questions, JoHelen said, 'Oh, that's just the new guy, Freddie. He's got a key.'

'Sure takes his time,' Gloria said.

At the next opportunity, JoHelen wiggled out of the conversation and said she was going to call the plumbing company and lodge a complaint. She said good-bye and crossed the street. She went straight to the burner, called Lacy, and reported in.

CHAPTER 38

The current federal grand jury was convened at 1:00 p.m. on Friday, October 14. When organized four months earlier, it had twenty-three members, all registered voters and otherwise duly qualified residents from the six counties that constituted Florida's Northern District. Serving was a demanding job, especially for citizens who didn't exactly volunteer. The pay was low, $40 a day, and their expenses were barely covered. However, the job was important and at times exciting, especially when the FBI and the U.S. Attorney's Office were on the trail of organized criminals.

Seventeen were able to answer the bell on short notice, and since only sixteen were needed for a quorum they quickly got down to business. With the investigation growing by the hour, and with the rare possibility of indicting rich white men for capital murder, the U.S. Attorney had seized control of the case. Her name was Paula Galloway, an Obama appointee and a veteran prosecutor. Her top assistant was Rebecca Webb, who by then knew more about the case than anyone but Allie Pacheco, who was called as the first witness.

Since they had already indicted Zeke Foreman and Clyde Westbay, the grand jurors already knew the facts surrounding the death of Hugo Hatch. Allie recapped them quickly and answered a few questions from around the table. Ms Galloway surprised them by calling as her next witness the driver himself.

From the depths of the Feds' witness protection world, Zeke Foreman appeared and swore to tell the truth. Neither his plea agreement nor his whereabouts were to be discussed. He told his story, and the grand jurors were captivated by it. Since they had already indicted him, they seemed pleased with their decision and fascinated by his detailed account of the events of August 22. They asked a lot of questions and Zeke handled himself well. He was relaxed, remorseful, and completely believable. Galloway, Webb, Pacheco, and the other FBI agents in the room watched him carefully. He would one day testify in court against the Cousins, and their lawyers would attempt to annihilate him.

The next witness was Clyde Westbay, who seemed to be at ease in the presence of the same federal grand jury that had indicted him for murder less than a week earlier. Clyde had just survived his first big test, a face-to-face chat with the boss himself while wearing a wire and snagging incriminating statements. For the first hour, Clyde discussed his role in the car crash. For the next two hours he talked about the Dubose organization and his part in it. He knew nothing of the skimming at the casino, but enthralled the grand jurors with his descriptions of laundering money at its black-jack tables.

One juror, a Mr Craft from Apalachicola, confessed a fondness for blackjack and said he spent a lot of time at Treasure Key. He was fascinated by the laundering scheme and asked so many detailed questions that Ms Galloway suggested they move along to more testimony.

Late in the afternoon, Pacheco played the audio of Clyde's conversation eight hours earlier with Vonn Dubose.

When Clyde was finished, after almost five hours of testimony, Ms Galloway instructed the jurors on the applicable federal laws. The fact that the stolen truck crossed state lines meant the murder weapon was used in interstate commerce. The fact that Zeke was paid $5,000 for his role placed the crime squarely in the murder-for-hire category; thus a capital crime. And the fact that there was an organized criminal gang, and that one or more members of the gang did a crime that benefited the organization, meant all the gang members were subject to prosecution.

It was almost 8:00 p.m. when the grand jury voted unanimously to indict Vonn Dubose, Hank Skoley, Floyd Maton, Vance Maton, and Ron Skinner for the capital murder of Hugo Hatch, and for the aggravated assault of Lacy Stoltz. Clyde Westbay was added as a defendant, though he would be dropped later. His plea agreement for first-degree murder would supersede the capital one. It was crucial for Dubose and the others to consider Clyde a co-defendant and still part of the team. Much later they would learn of his agreement with the government.

Lacy was at the stove, stirring the final ingredient, fresh mussels, into her version of cioppino, an Italian fish stew that included scallops, clams, shrimp, and cod. The table was set, the candles lit, the Sancerre on ice. Allie called as soon as he left the federal building ten minutes away. She met him at the door with a proper but affectionate kiss. They were still kissing; but nothing more, at least in the physical sense. They were undoubtedly taking the full measure of one another and wondering what the future might hold. Lacy was neither physically nor emotionally ready for the next step, and there was no pressure from him. He seemed to adore her and was willing to wait.

She poured wine as he took off his jacket and tie. The eighteen- and twenty-hour days were adding up and he was exhausted. Though grand jury proceedings were deeply secretive, he knew he could trust her. They were, after all, on the same team and understood confidentiality.

The indictments were in place, sealed for now, but soon to be served as the FBI rounded up the gang. He didn't know exactly when, but arrests were imminent.

Paula Galloway and the FBI had adopted the

strategy of using two indictments. The first was the most urgent and important, and also the easiest. With the testimony of Zeke Foreman and Clyde Westbay, the case for murder was clear and the proof appeared to be beyond a reasonable doubt. Assuming Dubose and his boys had no idea what was coming, they would be arrested within days and locked away with no chance of bail. At the same time, the FBI would raid their homes and offices, along with those of Claudia McDover, Phyllis Turban, Chief Cappel, Billy Cappel, and the lawyers in Biloxi who had represented Dubose for twenty years. Every business that had been identified so far as being part of the organization would be raided, and many of them closed temporarily. The casino would be swarmed by agents with search warrants. The U.S. Attorney was trying to convince a federal judge to close it indefinitely. The second indictment, for racketeering, would include a wave of arrests that would be coordinated with the raids, with McDover getting top billing, and perhaps the Chief right behind her.

Lacy said, 'Myers liked to call it a RICO cluster bomb. That's what nailed him.'

'And a pretty good description. It will be two inches thick. So as Dubose is just finding his way around his jail cell and wondering how in the hell he got charged with murder, he'll be handed a little RICO gift.'

'He'll need ten lawyers.'

'True, but he can't hire them. All of his accounts will be frozen.'

'Myers, Myers. I wonder where he is. I really liked the guy.'

'Well, I doubt if you'll see him again.'

'Will we ever know what happened to him?'

'I doubt it. The police in Key Largo have found nothing. It's a cold trail and if Dubose was behind it, we'll probably never know, unless one of his hit men can be convinced to come clean.'

She poured more wine. The grand jury would work tomorrow, Saturday, and Sunday if necessary. The urgency was obvious: a protracted investigation with witnesses being hauled before the grand jury could cause a leak and tip their hand. Those who worked for the organization had the means and the expertise to disappear instantly. Once the Cousins were arrested for murder, their managers, errand boys, drivers, bodyguards, and couriers might feel the need to start running. After eight days of intensive, around-the-clock eavesdropping, the FBI had twenty-nine names on its list of likely gang members.

'So you shoot first and ask questions later,' Lacy said.

'Something like that. And keep in mind, we can always amend an indictment. We can always add or dismiss defendants. It's a massive investigation and it'll take a long time to sort through it, but we plan to hit hard and get everybody locked up before they can tamper with evidence. I'm starving.'

'Did you have lunch?'

'No. I had a greasy burger from a drive-thru.'

He tossed the salad as she scooped up the cioppino and filled two bowls. 'This is a tomato sauce so I'm thinking a red might be better. You have an opinion?'

'I'd go with red.'

'Good. Open that Barolo over there.'

She pulled a buttered baguette from the oven and served the salads. They sat across the table and sipped the wine. He said, 'Smells delicious. Thanks for waiting.'

'I didn't really want to eat alone.'

'You cook often?'

'No. There's no need. Gotta question for you.'

'Fire away.'

'At this point in the investigation, how does the informant figure into it?'

'Which informant?'

'The mole, the one close to McDover, the one feeding details to Cooley, who passed them on to Myers.'

Allie chewed on a mouthful of salad and studied her face. 'He's not important right now, but we'll need him later.'

'He's a she, and she called me yesterday, really frightened. Someone broke into her house and went through her things. She sees McDover daily and thinks the judge is suspicious.'

'Who is she?'

'I swore not to reveal her identity, at least not

now. Maybe later. As I said, she's frightened and confused and she doesn't know who to trust.'

'She'll eventually be an important witness.'

'I'm not sure she'll come forward.'

'She may have no choice.'

'But you can't make her testify.'

'No, we can't, but there are ways to convince her. This stew is delicious.' He dipped a piece of bread into the broth and ate it with his fingers.

'I'm glad you like it. So are you working tomorrow?'

'Oh yes. The grand jury convenes at nine. I have to be there at eight for what should be another long day. Sunday as well.'

'You guys always work like this?'

'No, but then we rarely get cases this big. The adrenaline kicks in. Like this morning when I was in the back of the van with three of our technicians, temperature about 120, and we listened to Westbay as he met with Dubose. That can really get your heart rate up there. It's a rush, and one of the reasons I love this job.'

'How much can you tell me?'

Allie glanced around the kitchen as if spies were at hand. 'What do you want to know?'

'Everything. What did Dubose say?'

'It's beautiful.'

CHAPTER 39

L acy slept until almost seven Saturday, a late hour for her, and even then wasn't ready to start the day. However, her dog, Frankie, was going through his usual early morning routine of sniffing and snorting and making sure she couldn't sleep because he needed to pee. She finally turned him out and went for the coffee beans. While it was brewing, her iPhone buzzed. Allie Pacheco, 7:02.

'Enjoyed dinner,' he said. 'Sleep well?'

'Great. You?'

'No, too much going on. Look, we picked up some chatter last night that is troublesome to say the least. I don't suppose the informant you mentioned last night would be a court reporter.'

'Why?'

'Because if she's McDover's court reporter, then she's in danger. We're listening to a lot of phones right now, and I can't give you the exact language, it was in some goofy semi-code, but it appears as though the boss has given the order.'

'She's the informant, Allie. Myers called her the Whistler.'

'Well, they're onto her. Do you know where she is?'

'No.'

'Can you contact her?'

'I'll try.'

'Do that and call me back.'

Lacy let the dog in and poured a cup of coffee. She picked up the burner and called JoHelen's number. After the fifth ring, a timid voice said, 'Is this Lacy?'

'It is. Where are you?'

A long pause, then, 'What if someone is listening?'

'No one is listening. No one knows about these phones. Where are you?'

'Panama City Beach, a cheap hotel, paid in cash. I'm looking at the ocean.'

'I just spoke with the FBI. One of their wiretaps caught a conversation early this morning. They think you're in danger.'

'I've been telling you that for two days.'

'Stay in your room. I'll call the FBI.'

'No! Don't do that, Lacy. Cooley told me to never trust the FBI. Don't call them.'

Lacy bit a nail and looked down at Frankie, who now wanted breakfast. 'You have to trust them, JoHelen. Your life is in danger.'

The phone went dead. Lacy called twice but with no answer. She quickly fed the dog, threw on some jeans, and left her apartment. Behind the wheel of her shiny new Mazda hatchback, which she'd bought four days earlier and was still trying to relax in, she called Allie and told him what was going on. He said that at the moment he was busy with the grand jury, but to keep him posted. JoHelen finally answered the fifth call. She sounded terrified and refused to give Lacy the name of the hotel. Lacy knew that Panama City Beach was a busy strip of Highway 98, with dozens of small hotels packed together on the ocean side and fast-food joints and T-shirt shops across the road.

'Why'd you hang up a while ago?' Lacy asked.

'I don't know. I'm scared and I'm afraid someone is listening.'

'The phones are safe. Keep the door locked and if you see anything suspicious, call the front desk or the police. I'm on the way.'

'You're what?'

'I'm coming to get you, JoHelen. Just hang on. I'll be there in an hour or so.'

Delgado had a room on the third floor next door at the West Bay Inn. She was at the Neptune. Both were low-end motels half-filled with tourists from up north looking for bargains after the summer season. Her door opened onto a narrow, concrete walkway on the second level. The stairs were nearby. Beach towels and swimsuits hung to dry over the railings. But she had not been swimming. That would make it too easy for him.

From a hundred feet away, he watched her door and window. She had pulled her curtains tight, which had saved her life. With his sniper rifle, all he needed was a sliver, but so far he had not had such an opening. So he waited patiently, and as the hours passed Saturday morning he thought of simply walking over and ringing her bell. 'Sorry, ma'am, wrong room,' then he would kick the door open and it would be over in seconds. The obvious problem there was the chance of a short scream or shriek or other panicked noise that might attract attention; just too risky. If she left the room he would follow and wait for an opportunity, though he wasn't optimistic. The motels and cafés along the strip were far from deserted. There were just too many people around and he didn't like the layout.

He waited and wondered why she was hiding. Why hide if you're not afraid, or guilty? What had happened to spook her enough to run away and pay cash for small rooms in cheap hotels? Her home was less than an hour away and was much nicer than these dumps. Perhaps the neighbors had seen him there as the pest control guy on Thursday. Perhaps that pesky man across the street told her how clumsy the plumber acted Friday morning. She knew she was guilty and now she was paranoid.

Delgado wondered if she was meeting a man, one she should not be meeting, but there was no sign of any hanky-panky. She was alone in there, just killing time, waiting for what? Sex was probably the last thing on her mind. A walk on the beach would be a sensible thing to do. Or a swim in the ocean.

Do what everyone else is doing and create some opportunities. But the door never opened, nor was she moving around, as far as he could tell.

Pacheco said, 'I don't like this, Lacy. You don't know what you're doing.'

'Relax.'

'Let the local cops handle it. Get the name of the hotel and call the cops.'

'She won't give me the name of the hotel and she won't talk to the police. She's terrified and she's not rational, Allie. She's hardly talking to me.'

'I can get two agents from our office in Panama City in a moment's notice.'

'No, she's afraid of the FBI.'

'That seems rather stupid, under the circumstances. How will you find her if you don't know where she is?'

'I'm hoping she'll tell me when I get there.'

'Okay, okay. I have to get back to the grand jury. Call me in an hour.'

'Will do.'

She thought of calling Geismar for an update but didn't want to disturb his Saturday. She was actually under orders to discuss any trips she might get the urge to take these days, but he was being overly protective. It was her day off and she didn't feel like checking in. And where was the danger anyway? If she found JoHelen she would drive her away and find a safe place.

★   ★   ★

423

JoHelen knew he was next door at the West Bay Inn, watching and waiting. He wasn't as clever as he thought. He had no idea she had seen him in her little home video, easing from one room to the next, getting his image stolen and recorded by her cameras as he admired her lingerie and picked through her files. A big man, at least six feet two inches, with a narrow waist and thick arms, and a slight limp to the left side. She had seen him just before sunrise walking across the motel parking lot with an odd-shaped bag. Even without his cute little pest control uniform she knew it was the same man.

She had called Cooley but he did not answer. What a coward, a creep, a gutless liar, who'd fled and left her all alone. She knew it was a waste of time to fixate on her former partner, but she was bitter. She had thought of calling Lacy but she was in Tallahassee. What could she do anyway? So JoHelen waited and tried to think clearly. Her speed dial was ready at 911 in case someone knocked on the door.

At 9:50 the burner rang and she grabbed it. 'Hello, Lacy,' she said as calmly as possible.

'I'm on the strip. Where are you?'

'At a place called the Neptune Motel, across the street from a McDonald's. What are you driving?'

'A red Mazda hatchback.'

'Okay, I'll go to the front lobby and wait. Hurry.'

JoHelen slipped through her door and closed it quietly. She walked with a purpose but not a panic and descended the steps to the first floor. She crossed a courtyard and walked by the pool, where an old couple was lathering on sunscreen. In the lobby she said hello to the clerk and stood near a window to watch the motel next door. Minutes passed. The clerk asked if she needed anything. Sure, how about an assault rifle. No thanks, she said. When she saw a shiny red hatchback turn from the highway into the motel parking lot, she left through a side door of the lobby and walked to meet it. As she opened the door she glanced over at the West Bay Inn. He was jogging along the third-level walkway, looking at her, but there was no way he could catch them.

'I assume you're JoHelen Hooper,' Lacy said as she closed the door.

'Yes. Nice to meet you. He's coming. Get the hell out of here.'

They turned onto Highway 98 and headed east. JoHelen turned and watched the traffic behind them. Lacy asked, 'Okay, who is he?'

'Don't know his name. We haven't met and I really don't want to. Let's lose him.'

Lacy turned left at a busy light, then right at the next one. There was no sign of anyone giving chase. JoHelen found a street map on her iPhone and navigated as they zigzagged out of Panama City Beach and headed north, away from the coast. The congestion thinned, as did the traffic. Lacy was flying, unafraid of any cops because at that moment they would be welcome. Still using the map, they turned either right or left on every county route and state highway.

Both watched the road behind them and said little. After an hour, they crossed under Interstate 10, and half an hour later saw a sign welcoming them to Georgia. 'Any idea where we're going?' JoHelen asked.

'Valdosta.'

'Who picked Valdosta?'

'I figured no one would expect us to go there. You been there?'

'Don't think so. You?'

'No.'

'You look a lot different than your photo on that website, the one for BJC.'

'I had hair back then,' Lacy said. She had slowed to a reasonable speed. In the town of Bainbridge, they stopped at a fast-food restaurant, used the restrooms, and decided to eat inside and watch the traffic. Both were convinced no one could have followed them, but they could not relax. They sat side by side near the front window, hunched over burgers and fries, and watched every car that passed on the highway.

Lacy said, 'I have a thousand questions.'

'I'm not sure I have that many answers, but give it a shot.'

'Name, rank, and serial number. The basics.'

'Forty-three years old, born in 1968 in Pensacola to a sixteen-year-old mother who was part Indian. Small part, not quite enough, it seems. Father was a tomcat who loved on the run, never met him. I've been married twice and don't think much of that arrangement now. You, Lacy?'

'Single, never married.'

Both were starving and ate quickly. Lacy asked, 'The Indian thing, is that a factor in this story?'

'Yes, indeed. I was raised by my grandmother, a fine woman, and she was one-half Indian. Her husband was a man with no blood, Indian or otherwise, so my mother was one-fourth. She claimed my father was one-half, but this couldn't be verified because he was long gone. I spent years trying to find him, not for any emotional or sentimental reason, but purely for money. If he is, or was, one-half, then I'm one-eighth.'

'Tappacola, right?'

'Of course, and one-eighth gets you "registered." A dreadful term, don't you think? We're supposed to register felons and sex offenders, but not real people with mixed blood. I fought with the tribe over my heritage but simply didn't have enough proof. And, because of someone back there in my gene pool I have these hazel eyes and lighter hair, so I don't look the part. Anyway, those in charge of racial classification eventually ruled against me, and I was denied entry to the tribe. Not that I was ever a real member.'

'No dividends.'

'No dividends. There are those with thinner bloodlines who've made the cut and live off the casino, but I got screwed.'

'I haven't met many Tappacola, but you certainly don't look the part.' JoHelen was an inch or two taller than Lacy, thin and fit in tight jeans and tight blouse. Her large hazel eyes twinkled even when she was worried. Her face was free from wrinkles or any hint of aging. She wore no makeup and didn't need it.

'Thanks, I guess. My looks have caused me nothing but trouble.'

Lacy stuffed the last bite of her cheeseburger in the bag and said, 'Let's get out of here.'

She drove east on Highway 84. With one eye on the road behind her, and with little traffic to worry about, she stayed within the speed limits. And she listened.

Not surprisingly, Cooley was not his real name, and JoHelen never revealed it. She had met him almost twenty years earlier when her first marriage broke up. He had a small office in Destin and a decent reputation as a divorce lawyer. Her first husband was a heavy drinker and physically abusive, and she became a big fan of Cooley's when he protected her during an altercation at his office. She was meeting him there to discuss matters when her husband barged in, drunk and looking for trouble. Cooley pulled out a gun and got rid of him. The divorce went off smoothly and her ex disappeared. Before long, Cooley, who was himself divorced, called to check on her. They dated off and on for several years, with neither willing to commit. He married someone else, another bad choice, and she made the same mistake. Cooley handled her second divorce and they resumed their dating games.

He was a good lawyer who could have been much better if he had stayed away from the dark side. He loved to handle sleazy divorces and criminal cases that involved drug dealers and bikers. He hung out with shadier men who ran strip clubs and bars along the Panhandle. It was inevitable that his path would cross with that of Vonn Dubose. They never did business and Cooley told her more than once that he'd never met Dubose, but he was envious of his organization. Fifteen years ago, Cooley heard the rumor that the Coast Mafia was involved with the Indians and their proposed casino. He wanted some of the action, but was sidetracked when the Feds nailed him for tax evasion. He lost his license and went to prison, and there he met one Ramsey Mix, another fallen lawyer and his future partner in crime.

She was unaware of the name of Greg Myers until she saw it on the complaint filed against Claudia McDover. Cooley and JoHelen were much too frightened to sign a complaint and accuse her boss of wrongdoing. It was his idea to find a third person to do so, someone who would run the risk for a nice piece of the action.

She was curious about Myers, so Lacy told her stories: their first meeting on his boat in the marina in St Augustine; his little Mexican friend Carlita;

their second meeting in the same place; their third meeting for lunch at Mexico Beach; his surprise visit to her apartment after she was injured; his disappearance in Key Largo; and their rescue of Carlita. According to her source at the FBI, the investigation into this disappearance was going nowhere.

Lacy wanted to know whom they were running from, who was back there at the motel watching her. JoHelen didn't know his name, but she had him on video. Lacy stopped at a country store near the town of Cairo, and on JoHelen's iPhone watched part of the video of a man combing through her apartment. JoHelen explained that Cooley was a whiz with electronics and gadgets and had installed the cameras. He was also the guy who stuck a GPS monitor on the inside of the rear bumper of Claudia's Lexus, and he also rented a condo across the street and took photos and videos of her and Vonn coming and going on the first Wednesday of each month.

What happened to Cooley? JoHelen wasn't sure, but she was angry. This entire operation was his idea. He knew enough about Vonn Dubose and the casino. He and JoHelen had been intimate, on and off, for many years, and he preyed on her resentment toward the tribe. He convinced her to apply for a job as McDover's court reporter when she fired her old one eight years earlier. Once she was in place, as a state employee, they had a clear path to recovery under the whistle-blower statute.

He knew the law and dug through the cases and filings and rulings and became convinced McDover was in Vonn's pocket. He studied the development in Brunswick County and tried to track the maze of offshore companies at work. He recruited Greg Myers to front the attack. He was smart enough to keep her identity away from Myers. He'd been scheming for years, methodically putting his grand plan in place, and there were times when it indeed looked brilliant.

Now Hugo Hatch was dead and Myers was missing, if not dead too. Cooley had jumped ship and left her all alone. As much as she hated Claudia McDover, she had wished a thousand times already that she had never agreed to help bring her down.

JoHelen speculated that if Dubose got his hands on Myers he could make him talk, and quickly. At that point, Cooley became a marked man. Sooner or later they would suspect her as the informant, and there was no one to protect her.

Before prison, Cooley had been a tough guy who carried guns and liked to hang out with small-time mobsters. But his three years behind bars changed him. He lost his cockiness, his nerve, and when he got out he desperately needed money. With no law license and a criminal record, his options were limited. A legal shakedown with a whistle-blower seemed the perfect operation for him.

CHAPTER 40

They had no trouble finding the general aviation terminal at the Valdosta Regional Airport. As Lacy locked her car, she glanced around one more time and saw nothing suspicious. Gunther was inside, chatting up the girl behind the desk, and he hugged his sister as if he hadn't seen her in years. She did not introduce him to JoHelen because she did not want to use names.

'No luggage,' he said.

'We're lucky to have our handbags,' Lacy said. 'Let's go.'

They hurried out of the terminal, passed several small planes on the tarmac, and stopped at the same Beech Baron Gunther had used to rescue Carlita. Again, he said it belonged to a friend. As the day wore on, they would learn that Gunther had some good friends. Just before she climbed through the small door, Lacy called Allie Pacheco for the latest. He answered immediately, said the grand jury was still in session and working hard, and where in the hell was she? She said they were safe and about to go flying. She'd call later.

Gunther strapped them in and climbed into the cockpit. The cabin felt like a sauna and they were instantly sweating. He started both engines and the airplane shook from its props to its tail. As he began to taxi, he cracked a window and a slight breeze broke the stifling heat. There was no other traffic and he was cleared for takeoff. As he released the brakes and they lurched forward, JoHelen closed her eyes and grabbed Lacy's arm. Thankfully, the weather was clear – still hot and sticky, though it was October. October 15 to be exact, almost two months since Hugo's death.

JoHelen managed to relax as they passed through five thousand feet. The air conditioner was on now, and the cabin was comfortable. The constant roar of the two engines made it difficult to talk, but JoHelen tried. 'Just curious. Where are we going?'

Lacy replied, 'Don't know. He wouldn't tell me.'

'Great.'

The Baron leveled off at a cruise altitude of eight thousand feet, and the engine noise quieted from a roar to a hum. JoHelen had spent the past two nights in cheap motels, on the run and expecting the worst, and fatigue hit her hard. Her chin dropped to her chest as she fell into a deep sleep. Lacy, with nothing to do, also took a nap.

When she awoke an hour later, Gunther passed back a set of headphones. She adjusted her mike and said, 'Hello.' He nodded and kept his eyes forward, on his instruments. He said, 'So, how you doing, Sis?'

'Fine, Gunther, and thanks.'

'She okay?'

'She appears to be in a coma. Been a rough two days. I'll fill you in on the ground.'

'Whenever. Just happy to help.'

'Where are we going?'

'Up in the mountains. I've got a friend with a cabin no one can find. You'll love it.'

An hour and a half later, he reduced the throttles slightly and the Baron began a slow descent. The terrain below was far different from the flatland they had covered fleeing from Florida to Valdosta just a few hours earlier. As far as Lacy could see there were ridges of dark, rolling mountains already in shades of red, yellow, and orange. They drew closer as Gunther positioned the plane for final approach. She shook JoHelen's arm and woke her. The runway was in a valley, beautiful hills all around, and Gunther touched it perfectly. They taxied to the small terminal, passing four other parked aircraft, all small Cessnas.

When he killed the engines, he said, 'Welcome to the Macon County Airport, Franklin, North Carolina.' He crawled out of the cockpit, opened the cabin door, and helped them onto the deck. As they walked to the terminal, he said, 'We'll meet a guy named Rusty, a local who'll take us in, about a thirty-minute drive, straight up. He watches some of the cabins around here.'

'Are you staying?' Lacy asked.

'Sure. I'm not leaving you, Sis. How about this weather? And we're only at two thousand feet.'

Rusty was a bear, with a thick beard and chest and a big smile that seemed to leer a bit at the two attractive ladies. He drove a Ford Explorer that gave every appearance of having spent its entire life on mountain trails. As they left the airport, he asked, 'Are we stopping in town?'

Lacy said, 'A toothbrush would be nice.'

He pulled into the parking lot of a small grocery store. 'Is the cabin stocked?' Gunther asked.

'Whiskey, beer, popcorn. You want anything else you'd better buy it.'

'How long might we be staying?' JoHelen asked. She had said little, as if in shock at the change of scenery.

'Couple of days,' Lacy said. 'Who knows?'

They bought toiletries, eggs, bread, and packaged deli meats and cheese. At the edge of town, Rusty turned onto a gravel road, leaving the asphalt far behind. He climbed a hill, the first of many, and Lacy realized her ears were popping. He talked nonstop and far too casually as he sped along the edges of cliffs and across wooden bridges with rushing creeks beneath them. As it turned out, Gunther had been there only a month earlier, with his wife, for a week of cool temperatures and early foliage. The men talked; the women in the rear seat just listened. The gravel road yielded to a narrow one of dirt. The final charge uphill was straight and terrifying, and when they topped a ridge a beautiful lake was before them. The cabin sat snug to its shoreline.

Rusty helped them unload their supplies and showed them around the cabin. By the time they arrived, Lacy was expecting some rustic lean-to with outdoor plumbing, but she was very wrong. The cabin was spectacular, an A-frame with three levels, decks and porches, a dock over the water with a boat moored at its end, and more modern conveniences than her apartment in Tallahassee. A shiny Jeep Wrangler was parked in a small carport. Gunther said its owner, a friend, had made a mint in hotels and built the place to escape Atlanta's muggy summers.

Rusty said good-bye and told them to call if they needed anything. Cell phone service was good, and all three had calls to make. Lacy called her apartment manager and asked him to ask her neighbor Simon to take care of Frankie. She called Pacheco and explained that they were hiding in the mountains and were as safe as they could possibly be. JoHelen called Mr Armstrong and asked him to watch her house, something he and Gloria did at least fifteen hours a day anyway. Gunther, of course, had some deals pending and was frantic on the phone.

Slowly, they relaxed. Fresh from the Florida heat, they marveled at the clear, light air. According to an old thermometer on the porch, it was sixty-four degrees. The cabin, at an altitude of forty-one hundred feet, had everything but air-conditioning.

Late in the afternoon, with the sun setting behind the mountains, and with Gunther on the phone and pacing along a porch far away, Lacy and JoHelen sat at the end of the dock, near the small fishing boat, and sipped cold beer from cans. Lacy said, 'Tell me about Claudia McDover.'

'Wow. Where to start?'

'Day one. Why did she hire you and keep you for eight years?'

'Well, let's say I'm very good at what I do. After my first divorce, I decided to become a court reporter, and I worked hard at it. I trained with the best, worked with the best, and kept up with the evolving technology. When Cooley found out that Claudia needed a new girl, he pushed me to apply for the job. When I got it, his master scheme fell into place because he suddenly had someone on the inside. Court reporters know everything, Lacy, and when I took the job I was already suspicious of Claudia. She had no idea and that made it easier. I noticed some things. Her wardrobe was expensive but she tried to conceal it. If she had a big day in court with a lot of people around, she would dress down. But, a slow day around the office and she would put on the fine things. She couldn't help it; she loved designer stuff. Her jewelry was always changing, lots of diamonds and rubies, but I'm not sure anyone else noticed, especially in a place like Sterling, Florida. She spent a fortune on clothes and jewelry, more than you would expect from a person with her salary. She got a new secretary every other year because she didn't want anyone to get too close. She was aloof, distant, always tough, but she never suspected me because I kept my distance. Or so she thought. One day we were in the middle of a trial and I snatched her key ring. Cooley ran by the courthouse and I gave it to him. He had a full replica made. After a frenzied search, she found the keys near a wastebasket and had no clue they'd been copied. Once Cooley had access to her office, he had a field day. He tapped her phones and paid a hacker to get into her computer. That's how we got so much information. She was careful, especially when she dealt with Phyllis Turban. She used her desktop for official business and one laptop for personal. Then she had another laptop she used for a lot of the secret stuff. He didn't tell Myers all of this, because, again, he was afraid that if something happened to Myers, then the entire operation would be compromised. He fed Myers just enough to convince him to convince you to start snooping around.' She took a long sip. They watched the water ripple where the fish were feeding.

'The clothing and jewelry caught my attention, but when we realized she and Phyllis were jetting here and there – New York, New Orleans, the Caribbean – we knew there was a lot of money

438

coming from somewhere. And all the jets were booked by Phyllis, nothing in Claudia's name. Then we discovered an apartment in New Jersey, a home in Singapore, a villa in Barbados, I can't remember everything. And it was all well hidden, or so they thought. But Cooley was watching.'

'Why didn't he go to the FBI and leave us out of it?'

'They talked about it, but neither really trusted the Feds, especially Myers. In fact, he said he would not be involved if the FBI was involved. I think they screwed him when he got busted and he was afraid of them. Since the state police have no jurisdiction over the Indians, they finally settled on the plan to involve BJC. They knew you had limited powers, but the investigation had to start somewhere. There was no way to predict how it would unfold, but no one expected dead bodies.'

Lacy's phone vibrated beside her. Pacheco. She said, 'I need to take this.'

'Sure.'

She walked back toward the cabin and softly said, 'Yes.'

'Where are you?'

'Somewhere deep in the mountains of North Carolina. Gunther flew us up here and he's standing guard, sort of.'

'So he's still involved?'

'Oh yes. He's been great.'

'Look, the grand jury adjourned for the day. It will reconvene tomorrow. We have arrest warrants.'

'When?'

'We're meeting now to decide. I'll keep you posted.'

'Be careful.'

'Careful? This is the fun part. I think we'll be up all night.'

At dusk, they built a fire in a stone pit by the lake and huddled under blankets in old wicker chairs. Gunther found a jug of red wine that Lacy deemed suitable for drinking. She drank a little, JoHelen even less. Gunther the teetotaler sipped decaf coffee and tended the fire.

JoHelen wanted to hear the story of the awful crash and Hugo's death, so Lacy gave her best version. Gunther wanted to know all about Cooley and his astonishing efforts at stalking McDover. JoHelen talked for an hour. Lacy wanted to know how her brother had survived three bankruptcies and was still in business, and Gunther's war stories carried the evening. They dined on ham and cheese sandwiches, white bread of course, by the fire, and talked and laughed until late in the night.

CHAPTER 41

The first arrests were gifts.

Of the seven golf courses Vonn owned, his favorite was Rolling Dunes, an exclusive club in southernmost Brunswick County, with picturesque views of the Gulf and all the privacy a serious golfer could want. For a man wary of rituals, he did allow himself a weekly indulgence. Each Sunday morning at 8:00, he and his cronies gathered in the men's grill in the Rolling Dunes clubhouse for breakfast and Bloody Marys. The mood was always lighthearted, free-spirited, even boisterous. For men in their sixties and seventies, it was playtime with no women around. They were about to spend five hours on a beautiful course, drinking beer, smoking fine cigars, gambling on every hole, cheating when possible, cursing at will, telling raunchy jokes, and doing it all without the interference of caddies or other golfers. Their tee time was always 9:00 a.m. and Vonn blocked out thirty minutes before and thirty minutes after. He hated a crowded course and once fired a starter on the spot when he had to wait five minutes for a sluggish foursome ahead of them.

The Maton brothers, Vance and Floyd, bickered constantly and thus had to be separated. Vonn always played with Floyd. Ron Skinner always played with Vance. On Sunday, October 16, four of the five Cousins teed off at 9:00, oblivious to what awaited them. They were just starting their final round of golf.

The fifth, Hank Skoley, dropped off his boss at the grill with plans to fetch him in five hours. Hank hated golf and usually spent his Sunday mornings by the pool with his wife and her small children. He was driving home, minding his business, driving sensibly and under the speed limit, when a Florida state trooper stopped him on Highway 98. He was less than courteous to the officer, and as he was claiming his innocence to any possible traffic offense he was informed that he was under arrest for murder. Minutes after being stopped, he was in the rear seat of a patrol car wearing tight handcuffs.

Hole number four at Rolling Dunes was a long par 5 with a dogleg to the right. From the tee box, the green was not visible, and it was near the edge of the property, next to a public street that was shielded by trees and thick vegetation. From there, Allie Pacheco and his team watched and waited. When the two golf carts rattled their way along the cart path and stopped near a green-side bunker, the agents waited until Vonn, Floyd, Vance, and Ron walked onto the green with their putters. They were smoking cigars and laughing when a dozen men in dark suits materialized from nowhere and informed them the game was over. They were handcuffed on the green, led through the trees and vegetation, and whisked away. Their cell phones and wallets were confiscated, but their clubs, keys, and cold beers were left behind in the carts. Their putters, balls, and cigars lay scattered on the green.

It would be half an hour before the next foursome arrived on the scene. The mystery of the missing golfers would baffle the club for twenty-four hours.

The Cousins were placed in separate vehicles. Allie Pacheco rode in the rear seat with Vonn Dubose, who, after a few minutes of confinement, said, 'This is a bitch. I was having a good round back there. One under after three holes.'

'Glad you enjoyed it,' Allie said.

'Mind telling me what this is all about?'

'Capital murder.'

'And who is the alleged victim?'

'Too many to remember, right, Vonn? Hugo Hatch.'

He took it calmly and did not say another word. True to their code, Hank Skoley, the Maton brothers, and Ron Skinner rode to jail in complete silence.

As soon as they were handcuffed and their cell phones taken, teams of FBI agents raided their homes and offices and began hauling away computers, phones, checkbooks, entire file cabinets, anything that might possibly yield evidence. The Matons and Ron Skinner ran seemingly legitimate offices with assistants and secretaries, but since it was Sunday there was no one around to witness the intrusions by the FBI. Hank Skoley kept his records in the basement of his home, and his terrified wife and kids watched as grim-faced agents loaded up a rental truck. Vonn Dubose kept nothing on his person or in his cottage that might implicate him in anything.

After being fingerprinted and photographed, the freshly indicted defendants were placed in separate cells. Indeed, it would be months before any one of the five caught a glimpse of another.

Vonn was offered a stale sandwich for lunch. He refused and was led to an interrogation room where Allie Pacheco and Doug Hahn were waiting. He said no to coffee and water and said he wanted a lawyer. Pacheco read him his *Miranda* rights, but he refused to sign the form acknowledging this. Again, he demanded a lawyer and the right to make a phone call.

'This is not an interrogation, Jack,' Allie said coolly. 'It's just a chat, sort of a meet-and-greet session now that we know your real name. Fingerprints. We rammed 'em through and got a hit from your 1972 arrest for aggravated assault with intent to kill. Then you were Jack Henderson, part of a gang of good ole boys who ran drugs and whores and played the numbers. After you were convicted in Slidell, Louisiana, you decided prison was not for you, so you pulled a pretty slick escape. Ditched the old name, became Vonn Dubose, and for the past forty years have done a rather remarkable job of being the invisible man. But the party's over, Jack.'

'I want a lawyer.'

'Sure, we'll get you one, Jack, but not some slick talker you have in mind. Those guys cost a bundle and, as of nine o'clock in the morning, you'll be as broke as your daddy was when he hanged himself in prison. All your bank accounts will be frozen, Jack. All that money tied up forever, untouchable.'

'Get me a lawyer.'

Clyde Westbay was given the courtesy of a semi-private arrest. Early Sunday morning he received a call from an FBI agent who informed him that the hour had arrived. Clyde told his wife there was a problem at the office and left the house. He drove to the empty parking lot of a shopping center and parked next to a black Chevy Tahoe. He put the car keys on the floorboard, got out, got hand-cuffed, and took a seat in the rear of the Tahoe. He had not told his wife what was about to happen to him. He simply did not have the guts.

Using his office keys, two teams of FBI agents raided the offices at the hotels he managed for Starr S, the offshore company. On Monday, all guests would be asked to leave, and all reservations would be canceled. The hotels would be closed indefinitely.

As the Cousins were finally allowed phone calls, word of the arrests soon leaked; then it spread like wildfire through the organization. To run or not to run – that was the panicked question the managers asked themselves. Before they could decide, most were under arrest while their offices were practically ransacked by the FBI.

In Biloxi, a lawyer named Stavish was walking with his wife into a Catholic church for Sunday Mass when two agents stopped and announced a detour. Once it was made clear that he and his partner had been indicted for RICO violations, and that he was under arrest, he was given the choice of handing over the keys to their offices or having the FBI kick in the doors. Stavish kissed his wife good-bye, ignored the stunned looks from his fellow parishioners, and left in tears with the agents for his office.

At Treasure Key, four agents found the manager on duty and informed him the casino was about to close. Make the announcement, get everybody out. Another agent phoned Chief Cappel and asked him to come to the casino. It was urgent. When he arrived twenty minutes later, he was urgently arrested. A squad of U.S. marshals helped herd the angry gamblers out of the building and into the parking lot. Those staying in the two hotels were told to immediately pack and leave. When Billy Cappel arrived in a rush, he too was arrested, along with Adam Horn and three casino managers. They left the marshals in charge of the chaos as gamblers, guests, and employees milled about, not wanting to leave but realizing that locks were being placed on all the doors.

Around 3:00 p.m. on Sunday, Phyllis Turban was having iced tea on her veranda and reading a book. Her cell phone buzzed with an unknown number. She said hello, and an anonymous caller said, 'You've been indicted along with your gal McDover and Vonn Dubose and about a hundred other crooks. The FBI is raiding offices all along the coast, and yours will be next.' Using a burner, but one known to the FBI, she immediately called Claudia, who had heard nothing. Claudia called her contact, Hank Skoley, but got no answer. Both ladies scanned the Internet for news, but saw nothing. Phyllis suggested they take a trip to be on the safe side, and called a charter company in Mobile. A jet was available and could be scrambled in two hours.

As instructed, the charter company called the FBI. Agents followed Phyllis as she hurried to her secret office in a high-end suburban strip mall near the airport. She entered with nothing but keys in her hands, but exited with two bulky Prada bags. They tracked her as she drove to the general aviation terminal at the Mobile Regional Airport.

The charter company informed the FBI that the client, a regular, wished to make a stop in Panama

City to pick up one passenger, the ultimate destination being Barbados. The FBI, in conjunction with the FAA, instructed the charter company to proceed. At 4:50, the Lear 60 took off from Mobile for the twenty-minute flight to Panama City.

Meanwhile, Judge McDover sprinted to her favorite condo in Rabbit Run, picked up a few items, stuffed them in a large handbag, and raced to the airport. She was there at 5:15 when the Lear taxied to a stop, and she hurriedly made her way to it. The captain greeted her, welcomed her aboard, then went inside the terminal for the required paperwork. After fifteen minutes, the co-captain informed Claudia and Phyllis that there was some weather over the Gulf and they would be delayed.

'You can't just go around it?' Phyllis barked.

'Sorry.'

Two black SUVs appeared from behind the jet and parked in front of its left wing. Claudia saw them first and mumbled, 'Oh shit.'

After the ladies were handcuffed and taken away, the agents searched the jet. The women had hardly bothered with clothing; instead, they had grabbed all the goodies they could carry. Diamonds, rubies, rare coins, and stacks of cash. Months later it would be inventoried and appraised at $4.2 million. When asked how they planned to get it by customs in Barbados, they did not reply.

Even more loot was seized in raids at McDover's Rabbit Run condo. When agents finally found her safe room, they were stunned at the cash, jewelry, art, rare books, rare watches, and antiquities. The raid on her home, on the other hand, yielded little in the way of valuable assets. In her office, the agents confiscated the usual list of computers, phones, and files. Phyllis Turban's office computers were apparently not used for the dirty work. However, the two laptops in her secret office were filled with records of bank accounts, wire transfers, corporate records, real estate records, and correspondence to lawyers in countries famous for being tax havens.

The sweep along the Panhandle was broad and swift. By dusk Sunday, twenty-one men and two women were under arrest and facing a battery of racketeering charges that would only increase in the coming weeks. Included in that number was Delgado, who was pumping serious iron in a gym when two agents spoiled his day. On paper, he worked for a bar owned by a company owned by others, and he was charged with the usual money-laundering crimes. Years would pass before his more serious crimes came to light.

CHAPTER 42

Cable news discovered the story around 6:00 Sunday evening and seemed unprepared for it. Since the crimes were unknown, as were the defendants, there was little coverage. That changed dramatically with two events: news of the closing of the casino, and the discovery by some unknown researcher of the term 'Coast Mafia.' The latter was simply too sensational to ignore, and there were soon live reports from the locked gates of Treasure Key.

Lacy and JoHelen stared at the television with a fascination that bordered on disbelief. The conspiracy was destroyed. The syndicate was busted. The corruption was exposed. The criminals were in jail. The notion of justice was alive. It was overwhelming to even think that they had unleashed these startling events. So much had been lost along the way that it was difficult to feel a sense of pride, at least at that moment. When a 'breaking story' interrupted another report, and the face of Judge Claudia McDover appeared on the screen, JoHelen put her hands over her mouth and started crying. The reporter gushed on about

Judge McDover and her lawyer getting arrested on a private jet as they tried to flee the country. About half the details were right, but what the reporter lacked in veracity she made up for with enthusiasm.

'Are those tears of joy?' Lacy asked.

'Maybe. I don't know right now. I'm certainly not sad. It's just hard to believe.'

'It really is. A few short months ago I'd never heard of those people and I don't recall thinking much about the casino.'

'When will it be okay to go home?'

'Not sure. Let's wait until I talk to the FBI.'

Gunther had taken the Jeep to town in search of red meat and charcoal. He was on the porch now, with rib eyes on the grill and potatoes baking in the embers. He popped in occasionally to catch the latest, but by dark the same stories were being recycled. More than once he said, 'Congratulations, girls, you've just brought down the most corrupt judge in American history. Cheers!'

But they were in no mood to celebrate. JoHelen was almost certain she would keep her job, though the judge who replaced McDover would be free to hire a new court reporter. If she was thinking about her claim under the whistle-blower statute, she never mentioned it. At that moment, such a plan seemed too complicated and time-consuming; that, plus she'd lost her lawyer, the guy who was supposed to know how to navigate the statute.

Before dinner, Lacy called Geismar and they

compared notes. She called Verna and they talked about the arrests of the men charged with killing Hugo. She called Allie Pacheco, but got no answer. They had not spoken the entire day, and that was fine with her. She suspected he might be rather busy.

At nine on Monday morning, U.S. Attorney Paula Galloway appeared before a federal judge in Tallahassee and requested a series of rulings that would immediately close thirty-seven businesses. Most were in Brunswick County, but the entire Panhandle was affected. These included bars, liquor stores, restaurants, strip clubs, hotels, convenience stores, shopping centers, amusement parks, public golf courses, and three residential developments under construction. The organization's tentacles stretched into several residential communities, such as Rabbit Run, but because the majority of the properties had been sold to individuals they would be left alone. Ms Galloway provided the judge with a list of eighty-four bank accounts and asked that they be frozen for the time being. Most were related to the businesses but some were for individuals. Hank Skoley, for example, kept $200,000 in a low-yielding CD and about $40,000 in a joint checking account. Both were iced by His Honor, a veteran who was very much a team player with Ms Galloway. Because of the nature of the proceedings, there was no one to oppose her requests. She asked that a certain lawyer with a big firm in Tallahassee be named as the receiver for all companies named so far.

The receiver's duties would be extensive. He would assume legal control over all of the businesses that had derived their funding, in whole or in part, from the criminal activities of what was now being properly referred to as the 'Dubose syndicate.' He would reach back to the beginning of each business and company and reconstruct accurate accounting records. With the aid of forensic accountants, he would attempt to weave together the money trails that tied the enterprises together and track them to the syndicate. Working with the FBI, he would attempt to penetrate the maze of offshore companies set up by Dubose and discover the assets of each. Most important, the receiver would handle the forfeiture, or sale, of all of the properties linked to the Dubose syndicate.

Two hours later, Ms Galloway held a well-choreographed press conference, something all U.S. Attorneys dream of. She faced a crowd of reporters and spoke into a nest of microphones. Behind her were her assistants, including Rebecca Webb, and several FBI agents. To her right, on a large screen, were the enlarged mug shots of the five Cousins and Clyde Westbay. She explained the murder charges against them, said they were already in custody, and, yes, she planned to seek the death penalty. Holding off questions until the end, she moved from the murder indictment to the RICO charges. The roundup was still under way, but twenty-six of the thirty-three defendants were under arrest. The FBI and her office were in the early stage of the investigation with a lot of ground yet to cover. The criminal activities of the Dubose syndicate were extensive and well organized.

When she asked for questions, she was bombarded.

By noon Monday, the mountain getaway was losing its appeal. They were tired of watching the news; tired of napping; tired of trying to read old books someone else had selected for them; tired of sitting on the deck and soaking up the colors of early autumn, as beautiful as they were. Gunther's buddy wanted his airplane back. Lacy had work to do. And JoHelen was eager to walk into the Brunswick County Courthouse knowing that she would never again see the face of Claudia McDover. She couldn't wait to hear the gossip.

Most important, in Allie's opinion the threat to JoHelen had passed. Dubose had matters far more important than a loose-lipped court reporter to worry about. With all the major players locked away and without phones, it would be difficult for him to get things done. Allie also said the FBI would keep an eye on JoHelen for a couple of weeks.

Rusty picked them up at 2:00, and the ride straight down the mountain was more terrifying than on the way up. Even Gunther felt nauseous by the time they arrived in Franklin. They thanked Rusty, went through the empty rituals of promising to see him again, and took off.

Lacy wanted to fly straight home, but that was not possible. She had left her new hatchback in Valdosta and had no choice but to stop there. The flight was rough, with Gunther dodging storms and trying in vain to find a smooth altitude. By the time they landed, Lacy and JoHelen were rattled and happy to be getting in a car. They hugged Gunther and said thanks and good-bye. They waited until he was airborne and quickly left town. Tallahassee was halfway between Valdosta and Panama City, where JoHelen had left her car in the Neptune Motel parking lot.

As the long drive stretched before them, Lacy had a better idea. They would spend the night in Tallahassee, at her place, and invite Allie for dinner. Over some pasta and good wine, they would listen to his stories from the past three days. They would pump him for the details they were eager to know. Who collared Dubose and what did he say? Tell us about Claudia and her attempted getaway. Who are the other defendants and where are they now? Who was threatening JoHelen? As the miles flew past, they thought of dozens of questions.

Lacy called Allie and asked about dinner. The

added bonus was that JoHelen Hooper would be there.

'So I get to meet the Whistler?' he asked.

'Live and in person.'

'I can't wait.'

EPILOGUE

In the days after the arrests and raids, the story was front-page news throughout Florida and the Southeast. Reporters from everywhere scurried about, digging here and there, chasing leads, and angling for the latest. The locked gates of Treasure Key became the favorite backdrop for their televised reports. They camped out in Verna's driveway until they were forced to leave, so they retreated to the street in front of her home and blocked traffic. After two were arrested, and after they realized Verna had nothing to say, they lost interest and drifted away. Paula Galloway, the U.S. Attorney, held daily briefings in which almost nothing new was revealed. Allie Pacheco, speaking officially for the FBI, refused to speak altogether. For a couple of days the reporters filmed outside McDover's home in Sterling, and in front of the Brunswick County Courthouse. They filmed outside Phyllis Turban's locked office, as well as the law firm in Biloxi. Slowly, the story went from page 1 to page 2.

With the focus on the FBI and the U.S. Attorney's Office, there was little interest in the Board on

Judicial Conduct. Indeed, the tiny agency survived the storm while attracting almost no attention. Lacy and Geismar got a few calls from reporters, none of which they returned. Like everyone else, they followed the story in the press, and marveled at the amount of misinformation being kicked around. As far as BJC was concerned, the case was closed. Their target was in jail and expected to soon resign.

Moving on, though, was difficult, at least for Lacy. She was too emotionally involved in the case to simply close it and open another file. The biggest case of her career was over, but it would consume her life for months to come. She and Pacheco were spending a lot of time together and found it impossible to talk about anything else.

Two weeks after the arrests of McDover and the Dubose gang, Lacy returned to her apartment late one afternoon. She was about to get out of her car when she noticed a man sitting casually on her doorstep, waiting. She phoned Simon, her neighbor, and asked him to take a look. He was already watching. As Lacy approached her apartment, Simon stepped outside to monitor the situation.

The man was wearing a white golf shirt and khaki shorts, with a baseball cap pulled low and almost covering his eyes. His hair was short and dyed jet-black. As she approached him, he smiled and said, 'Hello, Lacy.'

It was Greg Myers.

She waved Simon off, and they went inside.

As she closed the front door behind them, she said, 'I thought you were dead.'

Myers laughed and said, 'Almost. I really need a beer.'

'That makes two of us.'

She opened two bottles and they sat at the kitchen table. Lacy said, 'I don't suppose you've seen Carlita.'

He laughed again and said, 'Spent last night with her. She's fine. Thanks for rescuing her.'

'Thanks? Come on, Myers, start talking.'

'What do you want to know?'

'Everything. Why did you disappear?'

'It's a long story.'

'Figures. Start talking.'

Myers was ready to talk, ready to reinsert himself into the narrative that he had helped to create. He took a long pull on the bottle, wiped his mouth with the back of his hand, a clumsy swipe that Lacy had seen before, and began. 'Why did I disappear? Two reasons, as it turned out. First, it was a backup plan all along. I knew the FBI would be reluctant to get involved, and, as things evolved, I was right. If I vanished, then you and the FBI would believe that Dubose had found me. Another murder, mine, would prompt the FBI to take a second look. I didn't want the FBI in the picture, but we, all of us, soon realized the case would go nowhere without them. Was I right about that?'

'Maybe. Your disappearance certainly made it

more interesting, but it didn't exactly change the FBI's decision.'

'What did?'

'DNA. We had a blood sample from the scene and it led to the driver of the truck. Once he was identified, the FBI knew the case could be cracked. They smelled a huge win and came in with guns blazing, so to speak.'

'How did you obtain a blood sample?'

'I'll tell you about that later. You said there were two reasons you jumped ship.'

'Yes, well, the second one was far more important than the first. I was on the boat one morning in Key Largo, sort of minding my own business, fiddling with an engine, when the burner in my pocket vibrated. I popped it open, said hello or something like that, and a voice said, "Myers?" I figured it was Cooley, then something told me it wasn't. I hung up and called Cooley on another phone. He said, no, he had not just tried to call me. I knew someone had picked up my trail and that someone was Vonn Dubose. I went below, erased everything on my laptop, stuffed my pockets with cash, and told Carlita I was walking to the marina to buy some ice. I hung around the marina for half an hour, watching everything, and finally bribed a local to drive me to Homestead. From there, I drifted into Miami and went underground. It was a close call and scared the hell out of me.'

'Why did you leave Carlita alone like that?'

Another long pull on the bottle. 'I knew they

wouldn't hurt her. They might threaten her and frighten her, but I figured she would be safe. It was risky. And I had to convince her, Cooley, you, and maybe the FBI that I was just another casualty. People can be made to talk, even Carlita and Cooley. It was important that they knew nothing about my disappearance.'

'You ran away. Cooley ran away. And you left the girls behind to deal with the danger.'

'Okay, it looks that way, but it was far more complicated. I had to either run or catch a bullet. Cooley ran for different reasons. Once I was gone, he figured he had been compromised. He freaked out and hid under a rock.'

'And now you're back looking for the pot of gold.'

'Damned right we are. Keep in mind, Lacy, that none of this would have happened without us. Cooley was the brains who put it all together over a long period of time. He's the real genius behind it. He recruited JoHelen and handled her beautifully, until, of course, he got scared. As for me, I had the guts to sign the complaint, and came within an inch of paying dearly for it.'

'So did she.'

'And she'll get her rewards, believe me. There will be enough for all three of us.'

'Has Cooley kissed and made up with JoHelen?'

'Let's just say they're negotiating. They have been sleeping together for twenty years, off and on, and they understand each other.'

461

Lacy exhaled and shook her head. She had not taken a sip of beer but his bottle was empty. She got another from the fridge and walked to a window.

Myers said, 'Look at it like this, Lacy. Cooley, JoHelen, and I planned this entire assault on Dubose and McDover. Things went wrong. Your buddy got killed. You got hurt. We're lucky there were no other casualties. Looking back with perfect hindsight, I would not have done it. But it's done, and the bad guys are locked up, and the three of us are still standing. We're in the process of making peace, and we'll eventually have fun splitting the pie.'

'I'm sure you've been reading the newspapers.'

'Every word.'

'So you've seen the name of Allie Pacheco?'

'Oh yes. Seems to be a hotshot agent.'

'Well, we're dating, and I think he needs to hear this story.'

'Bring him on. I've done nothing wrong and I want to talk.'

The FBI's investigation into the Dubose syndicate lasted for another fourteen months and produced six more indictments. In all, thirty-nine people were arrested, and virtually all were deemed flight risks and held without bond. About half of them were lesser targets who worked for businesses owned by the syndicate but knew little about the money laundering and nothing about the skimming at Treasure Key. With their bank accounts tied up and their freedom curtailed, and with court-appointed lawyers, they began snagging plea bargains as fast as Paula Galloway could lay them on the table. Within six months of the arrest of Vonn Dubose, about a dozen of his co-defendants had agreed to plead guilty and point their fingers at their bosses. As the government chipped away at the fringes, the noose grew tighter around the necks of the real crooks. But they held firm. None of the eleven managers, except of course Clyde Westbay, and certainly none of the five Cousins, cracked.

A soft spot, though, was found outside the syndicate. Gavin Prince, a well-regarded Tappacola with a degree from FSU, decided he had no future in jail. He had been second-in-command at the casino and knew most of the dirty secrets. His lawyer convinced Paula Galloway that Prince was not a crook and could help their case immensely for the right deal. He agreed to plead to one count for probation.

According to Prince, each gambling table – blackjack, roulette, poker, and craps – has a cash box that cannot be accessed by the dealer. Ninety percent of the money arrives in the form of cash, which the dealer takes, counts for the benefit of the players and the cameras, stuffs into the cash box attached to the table, and converts to chips. Blackjack tables generate the most cash; roulette the least. The casino never closed, not even on

Christmas Day, and its slowest hour was 5:00 a.m. At that time every day, armed guards collected the cash boxes, put them on a cart, and replaced them with empty boxes. They were taken to a fortified room – the official 'count room' – where a team of four professional counters – the 'count team' – went through each box. Each counter had a security guard standing behind him or her, and a camera directly above. Each box was counted four times. There were usually around sixty cash boxes. Prince's mission each morning was to remove box number BJ-17 from the highest-grossing blackjack table. He did this by simply taking it off the cart before the cart was rolled into the count room. He never said a word. The guards looked the other way. It was business as usual. With BJ-17, Prince stepped into a small room, one without cameras, and placed the cash box in a locked drawer. To his knowledge there was only one other key and it belonged to the Chief, who visited the casino every day and removed the cash.

On average, the cash boxes from the blackjack tables collected $21,000 a day, though BJ-17 was known to do even more business. Prince estimated the box yielded at least $8 million a year, all of it gone and unaccounted for.

The surveillance tapes of that table were mysteriously erased every three days, just in case someone asked questions, though no one ever did. Who, exactly, might come poking around? They were on tribal land!

Prince was one of three supervisors who rerouted the cash to the Chief's little drawer. All three were in jail, indicted, and facing lengthy sentences. When he folded, the other two quickly fell in line. All three claimed they had no choice but to facilitate the skimming. They knew the Chief was not keeping all of the money, that it was being used to bribe other people, and so on. But they worked in a don't-ask-don't-tell environment where they made their own laws and truly believed they would never get caught. None of the three claimed to know anything about Vonn Dubose.

The casino was closed for three weeks. With two thousand people out of work and dividends in jeopardy, the Tappacola hired some expensive lawyers who finally convinced a judge that they could clean up their act. They agreed to engage a professional management team from Harrah's.

With Chief Cappel in jail and facing the likelihood of being there for decades, and with the tribe thoroughly humiliated, a recall effort began. Ninety percent of the Tappacola signed a petition calling for his resignation and for a new election. He stepped down, as did his son Billy and their sidekick Adam Horn. Two months later Lyman Gritt was elected Chief in a landslide. After his election, he made a promise to Wilton Mace to get his brother out of prison.

Lawyers for the Cousins sought unsuccessfully to loosen up some of their money. They wanted to retain some big-league lawyers who could dig for loopholes. The judge, however, was not keen on the idea of allowing tainted cash to be spent on legal fees. He said no, and emphatically, and appointed experienced criminal lawyers to defend them.

Though far more serious than the RICO indictment, the capital murder case was easier to prepare. Absent Clyde Westbay, there would be only five defendants at trial, as opposed to twenty or so in the RICO case. Paula Galloway had long since decided to push hard for the murder trial, hope for convictions, and, with the Cousins locked away for either life or death, negotiate aggressively with the remaining RICO defendants. Once everyone was caught and in jail, she and her team believed the murder trial could be set in about eighteen months. The RICO trial could take as long as two years to put together.

In April 2012, some six months after the arrests, the court-appointed receiver began selling assets. Using an infamous and controversial federal statute, he organized an auction for nine late-model automobiles, four boats, and two twin-engine airplanes. Lawyers for the Cousins objected, claiming such a forfeiture, while their clients were still, technically, considered innocent, was premature. It was the same argument defense attorneys had been screaming about for twenty years. Unfair as it seemed, the law was the law, and the auction netted $3.3 million. The first drop in what would become a very large bucket.

A week later, the receiver sold a shopping center for $2.1 million and the assumption of debt. The dismantling of the Dubose syndicate was under way.

Watching closely was a lawyer who represented Verna Hatch. After the auction, he filed a $10 million wrongful death lawsuit under the civil RICO statute, and notified the receiver that he intended to place a lien against the estate. The receiver really didn't care. It wasn't his money. Following Verna's lead, Lacy filed a lawsuit for her own injuries.

Tracking the assets of Claudia McDover and Phyllis Turban was not quite as complicated as chasing the dirty money used by the syndicate. Once the FBI had all of Turban's records, the trail became clear. Fronted by offshore companies, the ladies had purchased a villa in Barbados, the apartment in New Jersey, and a home in Singapore. The real estate was unloaded in an orderly fashion and netted $6.3 million. They controlled eleven corporate bank accounts hidden around the world, with an aggregate balance of just over $5 million. Under court order and pressure from the State Department, a bank in Singapore opened a lockbox owned by the two. It was filled with diamonds, rubies, sapphires, rare coins, and ten-ounce gold bars. The appraisal was $11 million. The same pressure was applied to a bank in Barbados, and it produced the same type of loot. Its appraisal was $8.8 million. The four condos in Rabbit Run were sold for about $1 million each.

Around the FBI offices in Tallahassee, the impressive loot acquired by the ladies was referred to as the Whistler Fund. Its assets were slowly sold off by the receiver, and a year after their arrests the Whistler Fund had a balance of $38 million. On paper, the figure was astonishing, though as it slowly increased over the months the shock wore off.

Attorney Greg Myers filed a claim for a reward from the Whistler Fund. Court-appointed attorneys for McDover and Turban filed the standard objections to the selling of the assets, with no luck at all. Once everything had been forfeited, and there was nothing but a pile of cash, the attorneys had no real argument. What could they say? The money was not stolen? So they retreated, then disappeared.

Attorneys for the Tappacola argued the money belonged to the tribe, and the judge agreed. However, the money would never have been found, and the entire web of corruption exposed, if not for the courage of JoHelen, Cooley, and Greg Myers. The Tappacola were not blameless. They had elected and reelected a crooked Chief. Of the $38 million, the judge awarded $10 million – half to JoHelen, and 25 percent each to Myers and Cooley. He also left no doubt they would be entitled to an even larger award one day in the distant future when all of the assets from the Dubose syndicate were finally found and sold.

On January 14, 2013, fifteen months after they were arrested, the five Cousins were put on trial in the federal courthouse in Pensacola. By then, they knew that Clyde Westbay and Zeke Foreman would testify against them. They knew that Clyde had pled guilty to first-degree murder the day he was arrested, and that he would serve a lesser sentence, yet to be decided. They had no idea where Zeke Foreman was hiding, and didn't really care. Their party was over. They were concentrating on their grim futures.

In a courtroom with a lot of spectators, Paula Galloway, a lawyer who still loved the arena, presented the government's case. Her first witness was Verna Hatch. Lacy was the second. There were photos and videos of the accident scene. She was on the stand for an entire day and found the experience exhausting. She hung around, though, and sat through the entire trial with Verna. Many of Hugo's friends and family came and went during the eight-day trial. They watched the video of the Dodge Ram being stolen, and the one from Frog's store. Zeke Foreman was an excellent witness. Clyde Westbay nailed the convictions, though he was nervous and refused to look at any of the defendants. None of them testified. Their defense remained unified throughout. All for one, one for all. If they went down, they would all flame out together.

The jury deliberated six hours and convicted all five. The following week, Paula Galloway pursued her quest for the death penalty, but came up short. The jurors had little trouble sentencing Vonn Dubose and Hank Skoley to death. Vonn had ordered the hit. Hank had arranged the details. But it was never made clear if the Maton brothers or Ron Skinner even knew about the plan. Under the law, a gang member is guilty for the crimes of his gang, whether involved in them or not, but the jury could not bring itself to sentence the other three to death. Instead, they were given life with no parole.

With the Cousins convicted and banished forever, Paula Galloway was more willing to cut deals with the other RICO defendants. Most agreed to plead to reduced charges and received, on average, sixty months in prison.

One, a longtime, trusted gofer named Willis Moran, wanted no part of prison. He had a brother who'd been raped and murdered in one, and he, Willis, was terrified of the possibility. During several interrogations, he hinted that he knew something about the murders of Son Razko and Eileen Mace, and even the disappearance of Digger Robles, the jailhouse snitch. The FBI had little interest in busting Moran with a long sentence, or a short one for that matter, and a plea deal was negotiated in which he would serve only the time he'd already spent in jail.

Over the years, Moran had at times worked with Delgado, who was Vonn's favorite hit man. It was known, at least among the veterans, that

Delgado was very accomplished at taking people out, and that he was the most likely killer of Son and Eileen.

Reluctantly, Allie Pacheco opened yet another chapter in the Dubose story.

Two months after the murder trial, Claudia McDover and Phyllis Turban were brought into a courtroom in the federal building in Tallahassee, surrounded by their lawyers. Both had already pled guilty to bribery and money laundering. Now they would be sentenced. The judge addressed Phyllis first and, after a good scolding, sent her away for ten years.

His attack on Claudia was one for the archives. In a prepared text, he lashed out at her 'astonishing greed,' her 'sickening dishonesty,' her 'cowardly betrayal' of the trust given to her by the voters. A stable society is built on notions of fairness and justice, and it's left to 'judges like you and me' to make sure all citizens are protected from the corrupt, the violent, and the forces of evil. At times scathing, at times caustic and sarcastic, and never for a moment the least bit sympathetic, the judge's sentencing tirade raged for thirty minutes and startled many in the courtroom. Claudia, frail and much thinner after seventeen months of jailhouse food, stood as straight as possible and absorbed the blows. Only once did she seem to waver, as if her knees were losing strength. Never did she shed a tear, nor did she take her eyes off the judge.

He gave her twenty-five years.

In the front row, Lacy, with Allie on one side and JoHelen on the other, almost felt sorry for her.